THE FORGOTTEN QUEEN

KORTNEY KEISEL

First edition September 2021

Cover design by Seventh Star Art

Map design by Foreign Worlds Cartography

www.kortneykeisel.com

To Mason, Sadie, Kenley, Nixon, and Tyce. As requested, a book has been dedicated to you and your name is "in print."

Thanks for being excited about my goals and aspirations. I love you and will always cheer you on with your own dreams.

NORTHLAND
Northwater
Cold Mountain
North Palace
Kenmare
ENDERLIN
Enderlin Castle
Dakotaland
Government Center
Camgrove
Axville
Portlake
NEW
HOPE
TOLSTEN
Tolsten House
Lakerlain
Oakefor
Ruler's Palace
Kearney
Vassel
Wellenbreck
Dacoma
ALBION
APPA
Ruler's Mansion
Calicristole
Southcove
CRISTOLE
Cristole Castle
Colonias
Post-Desolation
Distance in Miles
0
200
400
SB 2020

1

Sydria

The Kingdom of Cristole
Summer 2261

Faceless people stared with tilted heads, trying to get a better look. A long aisle stretched out in front of her. It seemed miles long, but at the same time, the shortness of it squeezed her stomach. She couldn't catch her breath. Each step she took weighed her down until she found herself in front of a faceless man.

The scenery changed.

The people and flowers were gone. Sand filled in, and her body slowly sank into it.

Deeper and deeper.

The quicksand of life pulling her down.

She reached her hand up to the faceless man, hoping he would save her.

"I want to set you free," he said as he watched her sink.

She tried to climb out of the hole she was lost in, but the sand was too heavy. She yelled, but her cries were muffled. The grainy substance filled up her mouth and chest.

She couldn't breathe.

She was suffocating, dying.

Dead.

Sydria jolted to a sitting position in her bed. Her chest collapsed hard with each gasp of air. She looked around the room, eyes blinking rapidly. The late afternoon sunlight seeped through her small bedroom from the window above her bed. Dust particles floated through the light in a tranquil way, contradicting her racing heart.

It was a dream.

Only a dream.

She wiped at the sweat that had gathered at her forehead, the moisture reminding her that the moment wasn't real even though the emotion behind it *felt* real. Sydria brushed a few strands of her black hair, which had fallen out of her braid, away from her face and reached for the glass of water on the nightstand. The cool liquid trickled down her throat, bringing a sense of calmness with it. She closed her eyes, searching for the meaning behind her dream.

Nothing.

There was nothing but useless facts in her mind. Everything personal to her was blank, not even a shred of a memory or a past. That part of her life was dark, like the blackness that filled her whenever she closed her eyes. Sydria should be used to it—used to not knowing who she was. She had woken up every day for the last three months with the absence of a history. All she knew was what her Aunt Edmay and Uncle Von had told her.

She was Sydria Hasler.

She'd been in a terrible carriage accident that had killed her parents.

She was lucky to be alive.

Sydria wished there was more to her story than that, but right now, there wasn't.

Her eyes wandered to the orange vial on the nightstand that Uncle Von had left for her. She turned the lid and squeezed the top of the dropper, sucking the liquid up into the tube. She held the dropper above her mouth. The glass skimmed the top of her tongue, and a bitter taste took over. The medicine was keeping her alive, keeping her heart beating as it should. She drank another swig of water, washing the drops away, and swung her legs over the side of the bed and slowly stood, tugging down the skirt of her lavender dress, letting the fabric fall to her calves. The walls of her bedroom seemed to be closing in on her the longer she stayed at her aunt and uncle's house. She needed some fresh air to quiet her racing heart and mind. She walked to her bedroom door and pulled it open.

Voices carried down the hall of the small cottage. She heard the bitterness in Uncle Von's voice as he spoke. "I would never choose to be stuck with you."

"And you think I like being *married* to you?" Aunt Edmay hissed back.

Sydria glanced down, playing with her fingers. The suffocating feeling from the dream returned. There was nowhere to go and no way to escape the feeling.

Trapped.

She always felt trapped.

"Don't use that word," Uncle Von snapped. "We're *not* married."

Then the front door slammed.

Sydria bit her lip, counting to thirty before she walked down the narrow hall and into the small living room.

Aunt Edmay looked up from where she sat on the couch, sewing a button onto Uncle Von's shirt. Her light brown hair had stripes of gray by her forehead, and the bags under her eyes seemed to get puffier each day. She blinked back her tears.

Next time, Sydria would count to sixty.

"Is everything okay?" Aunt Edmay asked expectantly.

Sydria couldn't tell her aunt that she'd overheard them

arguing again or that she'd had a bad dream—a dream that she thought was somehow connected to her past. She didn't want to upset Edmay. She'd done that once—told her aunt that she'd forgotten to take her medicine and that she'd had a severe headache. Deep lines of worry had crossed over her aunt's face. Sydria didn't want those worry lines to appear again—at least not because of her—so she lied.

"I'm fine, thank you. I just need some fresh air." Sydria's lips widened into a smile. It was the smile she'd been perfecting for the last three months—ever since she'd woken up from her coma—a smile that had nothing real behind it.

Her aunt sighed, almost like she was relieved that there wasn't something more she would have to deal with. "Don't be gone too long. I made split pea soup for dinner."

Sydria nodded. "Sounds delicious."

It didn't sound delicious.

It sounded like something Sydria wanted to gag on, but she didn't want to be rude. Her expression must have given her away because her aunt's brows dropped.

"The soup is all I've got. There's been no money since…" Her words trailed off, and she shook her head. "Well, it doesn't matter now."

She could finish the sentence for her aunt. There had been no money since *Sydria*.

She was to blame.

Von and Edmay had spent all their money caring for her when she was in a coma. She owed everything to them. Their small seaside cottage was her home now, and they were the family she would be indebted to for the rest of her life.

She crossed the room, looking back once at her aunt before she opened the front door and left. The sun was low in the sky, to the point that it nearly blinded her. She walked down to the beach, climbing over the black lava rocks that lined the perimeter until she hit soft sand. Cold water tickled her toes, and her eyes dropped to her feet. The waves were growing, reaching out to her with the evening high tide as she strolled down the beach.

The seashore calmed her restless mind as if she had walked side by side with the ocean her entire life, but that wasn't possible. Sydria had grown up in the kingdom of Northland, far away from the waves, the blue, and the delicate sand. When the carriage accident had happened a few months ago, her family had been traveling to Cristole to visit her Aunt Edmay. Luckily, they had only been a mile away from her aunt and uncle's house when the carriage had lost control. Uncle Von was a retired doctor and had saved Sydria's life. Her chest had been cut open by a piece of metal from the carriage, and the damage was severe. If Uncle Von hadn't been there, she wouldn't have survived.

Or so that's the story she'd been told.

Sydria's fingers glided up and down over her scar absent-mindedly. At first, she hadn't dared touch the large purple line that cut down her breastbone, as if her fingers could somehow split the raw skin open. But as the first days had turned into weeks and now months, the scar had become her solace, like a favorite blanket to a small child.

The wind picked up around her, causing a black strand of her hair to get tangled between her lips. She brushed it away as she moved forward. With each step, Sydria sank into the shore, leaving footprints in the sand behind her. She glanced over her shoulder, watching as the waves wiped away the traces of her steps until there was nothing but a blank canvas of sand. The visual seemed all too familiar—a sharp parallel to her life.

Empty thoughts swirled inside of her empty head. Time got lost with each push and pull of the waves until she noticed how dim the sunlight had become. She'd never walked this far down the beach, and she had the nagging feeling that she should turn around and go back. Aunt Edmay would be worried—maybe. Did people worry about their extended relatives whom they barely know? Maybe they weren't even her relatives. There was nothing about them that made Sydria want to claim them as her relations.

A way down the beach, sparks from a bonfire drifted into the air, mixing with the laughter of happy people. She paused for a minute, listening to the pleasant sounds. Had she laughed since she'd woken up from her coma? She'd done her fake smile, but she hadn't laughed. Her feet carried her forward, pulling her toward the carefree laughter as if something inside of her needed to know what happy people looked like.

Uncle Von and Aunt Edmay weren't happy. When they weren't fighting about their mutual dislike of each other, they spoke in harsh whispers about money, or the lack of it.

As Sydria got closer to the crowd, lava rocks jutted out from the ocean, grouped in piles. In front of her, a black wall of stone marked the end of the beach. The occasional green plant stood out against the cliff, cascading over the edges.

There was nowhere else for Sydria to go, but she didn't want to leave. She crouched behind the lava rocks, slowly crawling forward until she was as close to the group of people as she could get without being seen. The waves from the ocean crashed into the rocks, making it hard to hear, and every once in a while, droplets of water would land on her arms and cheeks.

She peered over her hiding spot. It looked like some kind of party. Everyone sat around the bonfire, twenty feet from the shore. Beautiful women leaned against the men, holding drinks in their hands while they flirted. At least Sydria assumed they were flirting—this was her first look at the skill post-accident.

A few of the men snuggled their women close, planting passionate kisses on their lips. Sydria looked away with embarrassment. She gave it a few seconds—how long do kisses usually last?—then she glanced back.

Still going.

Her eyes drifted to another couple, one that wasn't getting to know each other with their lips. The brunette with short, choppy hair flashed a sultry smile up at the man she sat by. The girl's hand went to his blonde hair, and she began twisting a piece around her finger. He wore navy shorts and a white button-up shirt, but only the bottom three buttons were fastened together. His arms wrapped around his knees, and his eyes were fixed into a glare as he stared at the fire in front of him. Everything about him seemed closed off, but that didn't stop the woman. The brunette's free hand went to his arm, tickling his skin where his sleeves were rolled up. This girl was a professional flirter—layering on flirting techniques, one on top of another. Sydria wanted to be impressed, but instead, she had the uncontrollable urge to scratch her forearm aggressively. After a few non-responsive seconds from the man, the girl placed her hand on his bare chest—the part that was exposed from the lazy way he'd buttoned his shirt. Her lips went to his neck, tracing kisses below his ear. Or maybe she was kissing his ear—ear kissing might be a thing.

The muscles on his face twitched like he wasn't happy about the way she'd sicced herself on him, but then he turned his face to the girl's, meeting her lips. His hollow kiss didn't match the way the other men were kissing their women. His hands remained around his knees, and his body was rigid. Something about his kiss reminded Sydria of the empty smile she'd been giving Edmay and Von for the last three months. Was this man hiding his unhappiness too? The brunette pressed her body into his, and frankly, Sydria was surprised they both didn't topple over from the woman's passionate aggression.

"Cheney," the blonde girl across the fire called out. She'd *finally* split apart from the large muscular man at her side. It was good to see her talk. Sydria had doubted she'd been getting enough oxygen. "Let's go walk down the beach." Her words were pointed at the ear-kissing brunette and the blonde-haired man.

Cheney pulled back from the man. "I'll go if *everyone* goes."

All eyes went to the blonde guy, and the entire scene paused, like if he moved, then the rest of them would move too.

The blonde girl held out her hand to the man she'd been kissing. "Kase is coming, so we'll all go."

The muscular man, whose name was apparently Kase, stood. He wrapped his arms around the blonde girl, and she let out a squeal as if he had tickled her. She was a cute girl—average height, a contagious smile, animated eyes, flowing long blonde hair. She reminded Sydria of someone, although she couldn't remember who. Maybe she had a friend back in Northland, a bubbly blonde who liked to kiss boys.

The blonde man slowly stood, and immediately the brunette looped her arm through his. His eyes darted to her hands like her touch had annoyed him, but then why kiss her? Cheney ignored his grumpy face, leaning into him even more. She couldn't be deterred easily. It was admirable to have that much determination and confidence. Sydria wondered if she'd ever been like that.

She wasn't like that now.

The rest of the group stood and followed the blonde's lead to go for a stroll. Sydria's heart picked up its pace. They would walk right past her. She slumped into herself, trying to become as small as possible. Her black hair would blend in with the lava rock she was pressed against, but there was nothing she could do to hide her lavender dress. She held her breath as the group walked by. No one seemed to notice her.

She was as invisible as she felt.

Once the group had walked far enough away, she stood, swiping at the sand on her skirt. She would wait a minute and then walk down the beach. The moment she passed them would be awkward, but there wasn't much she could do about that. It was her only way home.

Sydria hopped onto the rocks she'd been hiding behind, and carefully stepped across the sharp curves, stopping ten feet from the edge. It was as far as she dared go before she'd be in the wet zone from the crashing waves. The sky burst into a soft glow of oranges and pinks, reflecting the colors onto the rippling water. She looked out to the ocean, feeling the salty breeze brush against her cheeks. Her eyes pulled to something white bobbing up and down in the sea. She followed the white float to another one fifteen feet away and then another. A trail of buoys dotted across the water to the cliff across from her. She waited for the nearest wave to crash against the rocks, then she quickly stepped forward, trying to learn the purpose of the floats.

A black net was fastened to the side of the rocks, dropping down into the shallow water. Silver weights held the net in its place, swaying slightly with the force of each new wave. Sydria stepped back, turning her body away as the water crashed into the shore. The cold liquid splashed above her head, drenching her clothes and hair. She swiped at her eyes and bent over the edge again as a school of colorful fish swam past. Their bright yellows and reds stood out in the clear liquid. She smiled to herself. What if this was her first time seeing tropical fish? More colorful fish, every shape and size, darted out from rocks and coral. Then a turtle swam by and several stingrays. It didn't seem normal to have so many different types of sea life swimming in shallow water this close to the shore. If it had been a giant coral reef, Sydria would understand, but it wasn't. From where she stood on the rocks, she could only see a few coral formations scattered about.

She glanced at the net again; then it hit her. The sea animals were purposely kept captive in the small bay.

Trapped like her.

Sydria had to do something. She had to help free the

animals. She leaped forward as a wave crashed into the shore. Water sprayed over her, soaking her again, but she ignored it. She bent down, reaching for the bolt that the net was fastened to.

Then her hands paused.

Someone had obviously gone to a lot of effort to get all these fish into the shallow water. Was she really going to undo all of that? It seemed like the right thing to do, but then her thoughts drifted to a nameless person who might get upset that the sea life had escaped. What if Sydria got in trouble, or worse, what if she got Uncle Von and Aunt Edmay in trouble? She'd already been a nuisance to them. Nerves gripped her stomach, making her feel uncomfortable. She didn't like the idea of causing a problem or someone being mad at her. How was it that setting the fish free felt like both the right and the wrong thing to do?

A turtle swam by, tangling its foot in the net. The sea animal struggled, then finally freed itself. Sydria's heart broke. She had to release it—she had to release all of them. She began tugging at the knot again. When that one was untied, she reached her hand into the water, found the second knot, and began working on it. The next one was farther down, and Sydria had to lay down on her stomach to reach it. Her chest ached where her scar was, but she wasn't going to let her wound hold her back. A huge wave tumbled over her, and she stopped untying to brace herself against the rocks for when the tide retreated into the ocean.

She grunted, feeling the powerful pull of the water. She didn't have a lot of strength. Being in a coma for months will do that to a person. Uncle Von said it was called muscle atrophy, but right then wasn't the moment to lament her wasted-away muscles. She glanced out into the ocean. She had a few seconds before the next wave would come, and her hands worked furiously over the tie.

"Please!" she pleaded. This entire situation felt very *un*like her, but she was in too deep now.

"What are you doing?" a sharp voice demanded.

Sydria whipped her head around. It was the blonde man from earlier, and now his glare was fixed on *her*. He must've come back from the walk by himself because no one else was around. His expression held a mixture of confusion and irritation as he took in the situation. His grumpy stare darted to her legs, and Sydria's eyes followed. The water had pushed the skirt of her dress up to her thighs. It was the most unladylike position she could imagine. Her natural reaction would have been to save herself from disgrace by immediately pulling her dress down, but the next wave splashed over her, and she had to stop herself from being taken with it. Her bare legs scraped against the sharp rocks, and she let out a yelp as the rough edges cut into her skin. The water was so strong, and her weak muscles were tired. Just when she thought she couldn't hold herself back any longer, the man grabbed her waist, lifting her into the air as if she were as light as a seashell. His touch was warm, spreading through her wet clothes, and before Sydria knew what was happening, he'd cradled her in his arms.

She looked up at him. His features were angular and sharp, but in a good way—a way that made him look fiercely handsome. Light blonde hair curled over his ears and neck. Hazel eyes that complemented his golden complexion stared down at her with a thousand questions running through them. Then his gaze switched to the water, and he flinched. Sydria knew what that meant. She buried her face into him, her cheek rubbing against solid muscle.

She was skin to skin.

Cheek to chest.

Nose wedged between pectorals.

The position had Sydria questioning why the man didn't fasten all of the buttons on his shirt. That's what buttons were there for…to be *buttoned*. She shut her eyes tight as if it would take away the embarrassment of the situation. But she couldn't be embarrassed for long because another wave plummeted over them. She half expected the water to take his feet out from under him, but somehow, they were still standing. When the spray stopped, she lifted her chin, happy to put some distance between her and the curve of his pecs.

His lips pulled into a smile. It was small, but a nice look on him, regardless. Better than the frown he'd been sporting with his friends. "I can't figure out what you're doing," he said.

A cool breeze blew around them, reminding Sydria that her wet behind was out in the open. She pressed her hands against the man, wiggling her body until he lowered her to her feet. She tugged at her lavender dress, making sure everything was properly covered. Then she looked up at him. Would he be angry? His wide stance added to her rising fear.

She swallowed, pointing behind her. "The fish."

He nodded, glancing quickly out to the water. "Yeah."

"They're trapped."

He nodded again. This time more dramatically. "Yeah, so?"

Sydria puffed out a breath. "It's cruel."

"How is it cruel? They're still in the water." He looked over the shore. "And they have a huge bay to swim around in."

"That's not a huge place for some of those creatures. They can swim the length of the area in a few seconds."

The next wave pushed her forward, knocking her into his chest...*again.* His hands went to her waist, holding her up. Sydria didn't like having a stranger's hands on her hips. It felt too intimate—so did all the ways she'd experienced his upper body.

She took a step back, repositioning her feet so that she could stand without assistance. "Do you know why the animals are being held captive?"

He shrugged. "They're going to put them in the castle aquarium for display."

Her eyebrows bent. "An aquarium? Like a glass box?"

"Yeah."

She tried to shake off her annoyance at his indifference and focus back on the animals. "Trapping them in an aquarium is horrific."

He kicked his head back. "I don't know if it's *horrific*."

"It is horrific!" she stammered. "Why would they do that? Why would anybody purposefully box up an animal?"

"I don't know. That's just what they do." He shrugged again.

His casual shrugs seemed insensitive, but she remained calm. "Who is *they*?"

"Cristole Castle. The royal family."

"Well, it isn't right." Her skin felt flushed despite the cold water dripping down the side of her face.

The man lowered his chin, giving her a pointed stare. "Do you have a thing for sea life?"

"It's not about sea life. It's about the fact that they have no choice in their life. Who does King Marx think he is?" Sydria asked, hoping she'd gotten the king's name correct. She'd only heard her aunt and uncle talk about him and the McKane family a few times.

"I think he thinks he's the king of Cristole," the man responded slowly, watching her.

She shook his answer away. "Just because he's the king doesn't mean he can take something that isn't his and force it to leave its home, bring it to the castle, lock it up, and hold it hostage like he owns it." Her voice began to rise. "Maybe these animals don't belong here. Maybe they want to swim back to where they came from. Maybe the fish don't even know where they came from because King Marx swooped in and never gave them the chance to find their home, their family, or their people. And now—"

The man reached out and pulled her close as another wave hit them, stopping her mid-sentence. His arms wrapped around her back, and Sydria closed her eyes, relishing his closeness. It was nice to be protected, to be *hugged*.

Her eyes popped open.

What was wrong with her? This man was a *stranger.* He could be a murderer, for all she knew—slicing people open with his chiseled chest. She needed to stay focused on marine life. She pushed away from him and continued her speech. "And now," she said as if she'd never stopped, "these animals have to stay here in Cristole. Maybe they don't belong here. Maybe they belong in Northland."

"Are we still talking about the fish?" he asked. His expression seemed puzzled.

She raised her chin, fighting off the embarrassment growing in her chest. "What else would we be talking about?"

"I'm not really sure."

"Sea life," she confirmed as if it were obvious. Sydria turned her head, glancing quickly over the net before she met his gaze again. "Someone should tell the king that these animals need to be freed."

His hard expression softened into something she hadn't seen from him yet. "Somebody *should* tell the king that."

"Right." She nodded. "Maybe if he knew, he wouldn't keep an aquarium anymore. Do you think he'd listen?"

His eyes scanned over her. "Don't you recognize me?"

"No." Sydria straightened. "Should I?" This was exactly the type of situation that kept her up at night—people expecting her to remember them when she didn't. "Have we met before?"

He shook his head. "I don't think so."

"Then why would I recognize you?" Her voice came out harsh, and she instantly felt terrible. She shouldn't take her memory loss frustrations out on him.

"I guess you wouldn't." He stared back at her with a blank expression.

If he wasn't going to stop her, then she needed to continue

untying the knots. "I need to remove the nets before your friends come back." She looked out at the waves. The space between them was getting longer. If she got into the water, she could probably get the rest of the knots untied, and then she could dive down and push the weights off the bottoms of the nets. She took a step forward, but he grabbed her arm.

"Wait."

She turned to look at him, bracing herself for his anger, but his eyes were unreadable. He looked behind him down the beach. It was still empty. Then he glanced back to her. They stood there for a moment, him holding onto her arm as they stared.

"Let me do it," he finally muttered. He kicked off his shoes and handed them to her. "Hold these." Next, he pulled his shirt over his head. Sydria glanced away. It seemed like the respectful thing to do. She was already more acquainted with his chest than she should be. And he was hopping in the water for her—well, her *and* the sea animals.

He scaled the rough rocks with his bare feet, like he'd done it a million times before, and dropped into the water, resurfacing a second later. He sucked in a long breath then went under. Sydria peeked over the side of the rocks, watching him untie the knots through the foam sloshing against the rocky edge. He held his breath for a long time then came up again for air. His chest moved up and down, and he gave her a miffed expression.

"You're doing a good thing," she reassured.

"Right," he grumbled before taking in his next breath and sinking down. After a few seconds, he came up again. "It's untied. Now what?"

Sydria pointed to the net. "You'll have to push the weights off the bottom." He nodded, sucking in air to go under again. "And," she said, stopping him, "you'll need to pull the net out of the water. If you leave it loose, the fish might get tangled in it."

His teeth clenched, and his annoyed eyes bore into her.

She shrugged her shoulders innocently. "You'll be a hero."

He sighed, adding a wry smile. "I'll bet." Taking a deep breath, he gracefully dove forward, kicking his foot, sending a splash of water into the air. His muscled arms cut into the water and pulled back, slicing through the liquid as if he were a fish himself. He was a good swimmer. Did Sydria know how to swim? She watched his strokes and his leg kicks, and she thought she did.

He pushed the weights off the bottom one at a time, gathering the large net in his arm as he swam to the next one. His breathing was labored, and his strokes slowed the longer he was out there. An overwhelming sense of gratitude washed over her. There was no way Sydria could have done all that by herself.

When he reached the other side, he threw the net on the rocks and lifted his body out of the water. He looped the net around a few big boulders so that it wouldn't fall back into the ocean and turned to look at her.

His tall physique, long arms, and broad shoulders had him looking like he was meant to live in the water instead of walk on land. He waved his hand out in front of him. "You're free now," he called to the fish. "Go back to where you came from. Swim to Northland."

Sydria laughed at the soft tone of his voice and the way he'd joked. He sent her a big smile from across the bay then dove into the water, swimming back to her.

"They're going!" she said, pointing at the animals as they explored the area outside of the bay. "Look!" She glanced down at the man, fully expecting him to be watching the fish too, but his eyes were pinned on her. His expression was veiled, and she fidgeted with her fingers, not sure what else to do. "Aren't you happy they're free?"

He raised his eyebrows, letting out a small laugh. "I don't know. I'll tell you tomorrow." He hoisted himself onto the rocks in front of her. This time, Sydria didn't look away. She watched each curve of his arm muscles move as he lifted himself until he stood directly in front of her. He was a fit man. There was no denying that. Tall and trim but with enough defined muscles it was obvious that looking good was important to him. His abdominal muscles weren't chiseled perfectly. They were more unassuming, taunting her with glimpses of their cut edges each time his breath went in and out. Blonde hair hung down his forehead, and he shook his head so water didn't drip into his eyes. When that didn't work, he lifted both hands to his hair, brushing it back from his face. The movement made his biceps on his arms and the lats on the side of his back pop out. It was like there was a spotlight on his rounded arms and sides. Those muscles were front and center—the main event. She watched him, feeling nervous. What was she supposed to say now? The fish were free. His shirt was off. She was staring. Her dress was wet and possibly see-through. It wasn't the typical kind of situation Sydria was used to, as far as she knew.

Her body shivered, and he nodded his head toward the fire. "Come on. Let's get you warm." He grabbed her elbow. The heat of his touch emanated a different kind of warmth that slowly moved through her bloodstream. He helped her across the rocks until they were on the sand.

Sydria handed him his shirt and shoes. "Thank you for your help. I hope you don't get in trouble because of it."

He laughed, something light and deep. "I hope I don't either."

Her eyes widened. "Could you really get in trouble? Do you know the king?"

His mouth shifted into a crooked smile. "I'm sure I'll be fine." He sat down close to the fire, sitting in the same position he'd been in earlier, with his arms wrapped around his knees. Except this time, he was shirtless.

Sydria slowly knelt beside him and winced. The sand irritated the scrapes from the rocks, causing her to reposition herself.

"Are you hurt?" he asked.

She shook her head. "I'm fine." She pulled the fabric of her damp skirt over her legs to cover the ugly scratches, but he tugged at the skirt.

"Let me see."

Sydria held the hem firm at her knees, refusing to let him look at the cuts on her thighs.

He raised an eyebrow. "I'm trying to help you."

"Thank you. That's very kind of you, but my uncle is a doctor and can see to them when I get home."

"Okay." He smirked.

They sat in silence for a moment as the crackling fire burned around them. Sydria bit her lip, unsure of what to say to the man. Since the accident, she hadn't had that much practice conversing with people. For the past three months, she'd only been with Uncle Von and Aunt Edmay. Occasionally, Von's friend Otis would come by, but there was something about that man and his gray eyes that sent Sydria hiding whenever he was there.

"Do you always go around rescuing animals?" the man asked.

She was glad he'd spoken first. But of course, it wasn't a question she could answer. Did she go around rescuing animals? She had no clue. "I'd like to think I do."

His light brows furrowed.

It was an odd answer, and she wished she could take it back. She'd give a more generic answer to his next question, something that he'd be expecting. "You and your friends seemed to be having a good time." She felt his eyes on her but kept her focus on the dying flames.

"You were watching us?" he asked, amusement in his voice.

She had been curious about them, a group of people

around her same age, living a life that was so different from her own. She turned to him. "It looked like a party. Are you celebrating something?"

He let out a harsh breath. "There's nothing to celebrate."

The orange glow from the fire danced across his face and his toned arms. "Is that why you were in a bad mood?"

"What made you think I was in a bad mood?"

"Well," she didn't know how to say it. "The other couples were quicker to…um," she looked down momentarily, trying to find the words, "*enjoy* each other's company than you were."

He gave her a sideways glance, and one eyebrow raised. "Couples?"

"Yes." She pulled her knees close to her chest, hugging them tightly. "Isn't the brunette your girlfriend?"

"I don't know what she is, but she's not my girlfriend."

Sydria tilted her head. "Then why did you kiss her?"

He shrugged. "Because she wanted me to."

"But you didn't want to?"

The corner of his mouth lifted. "I can think of worse things."

"So you were pretending to be interested?"

"Does that bother you?"

It didn't bother her. She could relate, but maybe he was offended by her questions. She straightened. "Sorry. I shouldn't have mentioned it. It's not appropriate or any of my business."

He laughed. "It's okay. Most people don't think I'm *appropriate*."

She glanced away, biting back a smile. "She likes you. If that's any consolation."

"Cheney?" His chin rested on his arm as he considered her words. "Nah, she likes the *idea* of me."

"What's the *idea* of you?"

"You know." He shrugged. "She likes who she thinks I am."

"Who does she think you are?"

"I don't know. The man I've shown her. But she's wrong." He stared at Sydria for a long moment, his eyes holding a seriousness that resonated deep inside.

"Then who are you?" It was the same question Sydria had been asking herself every day for the last three months.

His hands dropped, and he leaned back against them. "I see what you're doing." His lips eased into a smile, and the seriousness in his eyes vanished.

"What?" Had she said the wrong thing again?

"You use the high of rescuing innocent animals to get people to tell you their deepest, darkest secrets."

"Oh," she breathed out. He was joking. "Is that your deepest, darkest secret…that you're pretending to be someone you're really not?"

He looked back at her. "Haven't you ever played a part, hidden who you are to please the people around you?"

He'd described her life every day since she'd come out of the coma.

He shrugged again. "Maybe everyone is pretending. Are any of us being who we want to be, or are we just being some filtered version of ourselves?"

The filtered version of herself was all Sydria had.

"I don't even know who I am or who I want to be," she said, holding his gaze.

"I hope you figure it out." There was a softness in the corners of his eyes that she never got from Von or Edmay. She glanced away, not sure how to process the stirring in her stomach.

She watched the fire for a moment, letting silence soak in around them.

"I feel trapped." She finally said, her eyes slowly drifting back to his. "That's why I wanted to set the fish free. I can't help myself, but at least I could help the animals in the bay."

"Why do you feel—" Laughter in the distance pulled his

gaze behind her, and Sydria stood before he could finish his sentence.

She looked anxiously around the beach. "I need to hide." Her voice sounded panicky. That was a new tone she hadn't experienced yet.

"Why?"

She didn't know why. All she knew was that the thought of talking to such a large group of people made her uncomfortable. "I need to hide! I don't want anyone to see me."

"Okay," he said, standing. "But why?"

Her breath came out deep and heavy. "I…I…" She couldn't get a hold of her breathing. "I don't know. I just do."

He looked around before gently pulling her over to some of the rocks hidden from the firelight. "It's okay." His words were soothing. "Everything's going to be all right."

She hid behind the boulders, holding her knees to her chest.

"Are you going to be okay?" he asked. "I don't want to leave you if you're not all right."

She sucked in two breaths and nodded. "I'll be fine."

The voices were getting closer. He hesitated for a moment, as if he wasn't sure what to do, but then he turned around walked away.

"Thank you," she whispered, "for freeing the animals."

He looked back at her. Glowing fire illuminated his face and his simple smile. "I did it for you."

Marx

Marx leaned down, picking up his damp shirt. He threw it over his head as he walked to greet his friends. He used the term *friends* loosely. There was his younger sister, Dannyn—he supposed she was a friend—then his personal guard, Kase Kendrick. And Warren Bradshaw, the son of a High Ruler, Cheney Cordova, the daughter of one of the wealthiest men in Cristole, and then an entourage of people from affluent families whom his father had decided years ago should be his friends.

He looked over his shoulder to make sure the girl wasn't visible. No one would be able to see her from her spot between the rocks. It was probably for the best that she was hidden. If his friends had found him with her, Marx never would've heard the end of it. She was way too beautiful to go unnoticed and unmentioned—a little fragile but beautiful, nonetheless.

When Marx had first seen her standing on the rocks in her flowing lavender dress, he hadn't known what to think. It was like she had appeared out of nowhere. Then she'd lain down on her stomach, and for a moment, he'd thought she was trying to bodysurf, which would have been weird. But nothing could've prepared him for a marine life rescue mission. In all honesty, Marx had never once paid attention to sea life, or any animal, for that matter. The fact that he had orchestrated the rescue of an entire bay was pretty much laughable. But the girl had looked so, so…well, stunning, helpless, determined. How could he not help her? Her black hair had been tangled into a long braid that fell down her back. Her skin was tan like it had been touched by the sun every single day. Black eyebrows and lashes added to her delicate features. But it was her dark eyes that had gotten Marx in the end. They'd gazed up at him with so much concern; he would've rescued every single house pet in all of Cristole if it would have made her happy. Marx smiled to himself. Helping an unassuming woman like that had to be crossing off a life goal he hadn't even known he'd had.

A life goal that he would love to repeat.

And for once, Marx didn't feel like a complete failure. He had done something good—something someone was proud of. It wasn't like he wanted a medal for his gallant act of kindness. His younger brother, Palmer, used to do things like that all the time. It was the kind of guy he'd been. But it wasn't typically the type of guy *Marx* was.

"Where did you wander off to?" Dannyn asked. His sister's blonde hair bounced around her shoulders as she skipped forward.

Marx shoved his hands in his pockets. "I've just been here."

"You left me all alone," Cheney said, aiming her smile at him. She combed her fingers through her short brown hair as she sauntered toward him. The sway of her hips bugged him, causing him to frown.

It's not that he didn't like Cheney. He just didn't like her like *that*. Sure, there had been times over the last few years that he'd given her the impression that they were more than friends. Tonight was one of those times. Before this evening, their most recent kiss had been nearly two months ago. Marx had been looking through Palmer's old stuff, rummaging through awards and keepsakes. Sometimes he was numb to the pain of his brother's death, and other times the wound was open wide. Cheney had found him at his lowest, when the sorrow was accessible. In a moment of weakness, he'd let her comfort him. It had only taken a few seconds of her lips on his for Marx to know that she couldn't take away the guilt of Palmer's death.

Nothing could take that away.

But Marx had been lonely, so he'd given in, something he rarely did. Cheney had been the only girl he'd kissed recently, and by recently, he meant in the last two years. He wasn't the type of guy who went from one woman to the next. He'd learned early on that he wasn't invested in relationships—or the women who wanted them—as much as they were. Instead of breaking hearts, he'd decided not to get involved, to keep his distance. He wished he'd done that with Cheney.

She stopped right in front of him, glancing down at his shorts. "Did you get in the water?"

"Just a quick swim." He didn't feel the need to explain his rescue excursion.

His mood soured again. For a brief moment, with the mysterious woman, he had been his real self, and things hadn't seemed so bleak.

"We should go back," Kase said, looking up at the darkening sky. "It's getting late."

Dannyn wrapped her arms around his waist, pulling him close to her. "You're not as fun when you switch into 'soldier mode.'"

Kase tilted his head down to Dannyn, provocatively raising a brow. "You, of all people, should know how much fun I can be."

Marx rolled his eyes. He wasn't thrilled that his little sister was messing around with Kase Kendrick. Kase was his friend and a good enough guy, but was he a good enough guy for Dannyn? Ever since Palmer had died, Dannyn had gone from one guy to the next like it was her way of coping with her grief —a temporary crutch she leaned on. Marx wasn't about to take that crutch away and watch her tumble to the ground. But he wasn't going to let a guy like Kase break her heart either.

"Kase, why don't you go on ahead and make sure the pathway is clear," Marx said. Kase raised his eyebrows. Marx had never cared about his personal security as king nor had he ever asked Kase to make sure the pathway was clear, but he wanted to put some space between his friend and his little sister.

"Sure," Kase said, unlocking Dannyn's grip.

As the other men worked on putting out the fire, Marx glanced over to where the woman was crouched behind the rocks. If his group stayed at the beach, she wouldn't be able to leave. "Let's go."

Dannyn jumped on Warren's back, pulling on his brown ponytail, letting him give her a piggyback ride.

Cheney copied Dannyn, and before Marx knew what was happening, he had two legs straddling his back and two arms wrapped around his neck. He glanced in the direction of the woman again. For some reason, he hated knowing that she had a front-row view of him carrying Cheney around. Surely the woman would know he wasn't carrying Cheney because he wanted to. Somehow, she'd seen right through him.

2

Sydria

Sydria made her way back to her aunt and uncle's cottage. Her pace was faster than usual. She'd never been out this late and hoped that she hadn't worried them. The hot summer air coated her body like a warm blanket, and she looked forward to peeling off the damp clothes that irritated her skin. Sydria pushed the cottage door open, and immediately Uncle Von stood from his seat at the kitchen table.

He raised his half-moon glasses back up so they rested on the bridge of his nose. The light above the kitchen table shone down on his bald head. "Where have you been?" he asked. A heated expression crossed over his face.

Sydria's tongue felt heavy, and she looked at Aunt Edmay for some help. "I took a stroll on the beach."

"A stroll?" Uncle Von asked. "A stroll doesn't keep you out all night long."

Sydria's shoulders dropped. "I went a little too far and lost track of time." She didn't understand where her uncle's anger was coming from. She was a twenty-one-year-old woman—at least, that was the age they'd told her. She didn't necessarily have to answer to him.

He scooted his chair back and paced the small rectangular kitchen. "When we couldn't find you, we sent a message to St —" He stopped walking, and his hand went to his chin."To Otis."

Why would they send a message to their friend Otis? Sydria had only met the man a handful of times and had learned quickly to avoid him. His beady eyes were constantly on her, watching, assessing.

"When he comes, he'll be furious that we lost you." The hand rubbing his chin shifted to his glasses, adjusting their position again.

"She's not lost," Edmay chimed in. She still sat on the couch in the same position that Sydria had left her in a few hours ago.

"I don't understand why your friend Otis would be upset about my absence," Sydria said, walking farther into the room.

Her aunt and uncle exchanged glances. They seemed to do that nearly every time Sydria asked a question, making her suspicious.

"It doesn't matter now," Uncle Von said, dismissing her with the flip of his hand. "Otis will be here soon."

Sydria looked down at her wet clothes. "I'm going to go change my dress."

Uncle Von shook his head and turned his back to her. She peeked at Aunt Edmay, who nodded as if giving her permission to be excused. She walked out of the room and rounded the corner. Uncle Von's whispers followed behind her until she shut the door to her room. She leaned her back against the wall, looking up at the peeling paint on the ceiling. If only she could remember who she was, then everything in her life would be different. Uncle Von and Aunt Edmay wouldn't treat her like she was broken, and she wouldn't have to stay here. She could go home to Northland. She sighed and began pulling off her clothes, replacing them with a dry blue dress. Edmay had been so excited when she'd brought the colorful clothing home. She'd gone on and on about how it was the first time working-class people could wear dyed clothing. Sydria had stared at the bright clothing, guessing by Edmay's reaction that it should have been a monumental moment for her—her first time wearing colored clothes—but something about the colorful dresses felt familiar. She combed through her wet hair, dragging her fingers through the tangles. A heavy knock pounded on the front door of the cottage.

Otis.

If Sydria had it her way, she would stay in her room the rest of the night. She didn't want to see Otis, but she knew her aunt and uncle would expect her to come out of her room and greet him, and she didn't want to let them down. She stilled herself then slowly opened the door.

"Do you not know the seriousness of the situation?" Otis's sharp voice cut out.

"Of course, I know the seriousness," Uncle Von said. "I, out of anyone, have been with the girl the longest."

She paused outside her door. Something about their conversation urged her to stop and listen.

"If we lose her, we will all be ruined," Otis lashed out.

Ruined.

That was a peculiar word choice.

"Don't you think I know that?" Uncle Von said.

"Well, then you should be taking better care of her, watching her."

"I don't want to do this anymore," her uncle said. "I *won't* do this anymore."

"Neither will I." Edmay's bold statement was betrayed by the quaking in her voice.

"You don't have a choice," Otis hissed. "If you don't keep this up, I will destroy you."

"You've already destroyed me!" her uncle spat. "I'm sick of your empty threats."

"There's nothing empty about my threats. You can count on me ruining your life like I've done with the others."

Sydria bit her lip as her heart raced. Otis's words didn't sound like something a friend would say to another friend. There had to be more to this story than what Von and Edmay had told her. There had to be a reason why Otis was so worried about *her* specifically. She could try asking her aunt and uncle more details about him, but they would change the subject like they always did when it came to her past.

Thick tension crowded the small house. Sydria wanted to recoil to her room and pretend like she'd never heard this conversation. Their words were too much for her foggy mind. Even if she tried, she'd never be able to make sense of the meaning.

"It doesn't matter now," Otis said, letting out a frustrated breath. "Things will change tomorrow. You only need to hang on a few more days."

"She won't remain with us?" Aunt Edmay asked.

Where else would I go?

Otis barked out a laugh. "We didn't save her from dying so that she could be a working-class girl here with *you*."

Sydria couldn't see Aunt Edmay's expression, but she could imagine her sinking into herself the way she always did when Otis visited them.

"Make sure you don't lose the girl between now and when I come back tomorrow." The front door creaked as it opened. "We're so close to finishing this." The door slammed shut, and the room went silent.

Sydria slowly retreated to her room. She was so confused by what she'd just heard. Heavy questions raced in her mind and there was no way she could get the answers she needed. Nothing was as it seemed or as she'd been told. There wasn't anyone she could trust. She felt trapped by the strict rules Von and Edmay imposed and by her unfamiliarity with the land surrounding her. But right then, she was held captive by her lack of knowledge. She wasn't like the beautiful fish she'd seen at the beach. No one was going to free her from her miserable life.

3

Commander Stoddard

Stoddard leaned his back against the jagged cave wall. Outside, waves thrashed against the rocks; their loud thundering blended with his beating heart. He looked to the cave's opening, hoping King Marx McKane would arrive soon. His eyes blinked rapidly several times, as if he could make the man appear.

Where was he?

Reaching out to the Cristole royalty had been a risky move, but for the last nine months, ever since he'd been driven out of Tolsten, there'd been a massive target on Stoddard's back. Everywhere he went, he was constantly looking over his shoulder. In each crowd, he saw the faces of King Adler and his persistent daughter, Princess Myka. Their blue eyes taunted him, telling him they were coming to get him, shouting at him that he needed to pay for what he'd done. He couldn't sleep at night. When he closed his eyes, Adler stood above him with a pillow, waiting in the shadows to suffocate him with it...like Stoddard had done to him.

He needed to remove the target and place it on someone else's back. That's where King Marx came in. It was Stoddard's last chance. His other plans had blown up in his face. He had to salvage the situation now, pivot so it all wasn't for naught.

Stoddard wiped his sweaty palms on his pant leg. Once he revealed his cards—gave up the identity of his hidden weapon—it wouldn't be a secret anymore. There was always the chance that King Marx would turn him in to the Council of Essentials, but if he did, Seran would die. Stoddard had already given Doctor Von the order. If he didn't return from this meeting, Von was to kill the girl.

The muscles on his face ticked, and his lips crept into a crooked smile. That would be an ironic outcome for the girl who was already considered dead.

But Stoddard was confident Cristole would want what he had to offer. Now that Princess Myka had become the queen of Tolsten and had married Commander Drake Vestry from Albion, the bond between New Hope, Tolsten, and Albion was unbreakable. Their iron clad friendship created the strongest three-way alliance since Desolation. Their kingdoms' relationships ran deeper than the usual stuff alliances were made of. Drake Vestry was King Ezra Trevenna's best friend, and because of everything that had happened at Ezra and Seran's wedding a year and a half ago, Ezra had become like a son to King Bryant. Where did that unbreakable alliance leave the other four kingdoms? And what could the other kingdoms do to make sure they retained some of the power?

Stoddard had the answer.

He always had the answer.

"Show me your hands!" a voice called out, causing Stoddard to jerk his head to the entrance. A Cristole soldier dressed in a navy-blue uniform stood with his arms stretched out in front of him. The barrel of the soldier's gun was pointed right at Stoddard.

He could easily pull out his own gun hidden in his gray jacket, but that wasn't why he was here. Slowly, he raised his hands, keeping his voice calm even though his skin crawled with nerves and excitement. "I'm alone and unarmed," he said.

The soldier stepped inside the cave with his gun outstretched. Two other guards followed behind, shining hand lights deep into the darkness.

Stoddard knew the protocol. After all, he'd been the commander of the Tolsten army for the last twenty years—the highest military position there was. With his knowledge, he could run circles around these less-experienced soldiers. It was laughable that they had their guns pointed at *him*. But King Marx would never enter the cave until his guards made sure everything was safe.

He straightened and lifted his chin as the first soldier stepped in front of him. The guard flipped Stoddard's jacket open and grabbed the gun that was hidden inside.

"You won't be needing this," the soldier said as he tossed the gun to the man behind him.

Stoddard shrugged, placing a confident smile on his lips. "No, I'm sure I won't. In fact, I'm sure King Marx and I are going to become good friends after this meeting."

The guard lowered his brows. "I doubt that." He turned over his shoulder, speaking to the men behind him. "Tell the king everything's clear."

One of the men nodded and left. It would only be a moment before King Marx was there. Stoddard puffed out his chest as his anticipation grew. It felt good to be in control again, to be planning something that would change the course of the Council of Essentials.

The light at the opening of the cave dimmed as a group of men passed through. In the middle of the pack stood King Meldrum McKane, the former king of Cristole and Marx's father. Stoddard scanned the other faces, searching for King Marx, but he wasn't there.

Was this some kind of trap?

The letter he'd received confirming their meeting had been signed by King Marx. Stoddard still had it. He'd read it again earlier that morning.

He licked his lips nervously. "Where's King Marx?"

"Marx won't be joining us today," McKane said as he walked toward him. With each step, his features became more visible. He was a tall and skinny man with an angular nose. The remaining few strands of his light hair were combed over on top of his scalp, attempting to hide the baldness that increased with his age.

Stoddard flicked his eyes around the cave to the soldiers. "The information I'm offering is for the king."

McKane laughed, something light that had a mocking undertone to it. "My son doesn't run the affairs of Cristole. I do. Any information that you have for him goes through me."

Maybe it wasn't a trap.

It wasn't that surprising that Marx was only king in name. It was widely known that Meldrum McKane had wanted his younger son, Palmer, to be the king. When that hadn't worked out, he must've decided to keep ruling Cristole himself, using Marx as a front.

"All the better," Stoddard said, lifting his chin. "I don't know your son, but I have a prior relationship with you."

McKane shook his head. "I wouldn't say that we have a prior relationship."

Stoddard had met the man several times over the years when McKane had been the king of Cristole, but they had never spoken. McKane had only been interested in speaking with King Adler, not his commander. Things were different now.

"It's not our relationship in the past that I want to talk about. It's our relationship in the future that interests me," Stoddard said.

McKane clasped his hands behind his back. "And what

makes you think I want to have a relationship with a criminal? You must know that every other kingdom is looking for you. Perhaps I should turn you in to the Council of Essentials."

This was Stoddard's chance—the moment he had been rehearsing in his mind for the last few weeks. He squared his shoulders, a small gesture that showed his opponent that he wasn't scared. "You could do that. The Council might praise you at first, but eventually, they'll forget about you and Cristole. The three most powerful kingdoms are aligned, and they don't need you to change the way this world is going."

"The three most powerful kingdoms?" McKane raised his eyebrows.

"Yes. New Hope, Albion, and Tolsten. You're outnumbered...powerless."

"I would hardly say I'm outnumbered. There are still four other kingdoms left."

"King Davin in Enderlin will vote with the other three. The status quo has changed, and you and your son have been left behind."

"And you think you can change that?" McKane huffed.

"I know I can." There was enough confidence behind Stoddard's expression to sway even the biggest skeptic.

"I'm listening," McKane said after a moment.

"What if I told you that I had a weapon that could change your fate with the Council of Essentials?"

McKane shook his head. "I'm not interested in weapons. That was King Adler's dream."

"Not a literal *weapon*, rather something so important to New Hope that it would change the future of the world we live in."

McKane took in a deep breath as he considered his words. "And what do you want in return for this *weapon*?"

A slow smile pulled across Stoddard's lips. "What everyone wants. Money. Power. Prestige. Protection."

"You're asking a lot, for a criminal," McKane said.

"Let's start with the basics first. Protection and money. The power and prestige can come after you've used the weapon to your liking."

"Don't play coy with me. I need to know what kind of weapon we're talking about before I would ever agree to make a deal with you."

"Naturally," Stoddard said with a devious smile, "but I would prefer to tell you in private." His eyes flashed around the cave full of guards.

"Very well. Leave us," McKane ordered, waving a hand to dismiss the guards. Once the two men were alone, he turned to Stoddard. "This had better be good."

Stoddard smiled. It thrilled him to finally tell someone the secret he'd been holding on to for almost two years. Something this big practically screamed to be revealed.

"Princess Seran is alive and I have her," he said plainly. His eyes danced as he watched McKane's expression turn to disbelief.

"Bryant's daughter?" McKane asked.

"Yes." Stoddard's smile widened.

"That's impossible. My son, Palmer, saw her dead body lying in a casket two days after the wedding."

"That was her body, but she wasn't dead."

McKane laughed again, but this time the mocking tone behind it dug into Stoddard.

Stoddard's eyes narrowed, and his fists tightened. "Clearly, you're not the man I thought you were. You lack vision and imagination. Perhaps, it would have been better to deal with your son, after all."

McKane's degrading smile faded into stone. "Don't insult me."

"Don't insult me either," Stoddard said, jutting his chin out. "Respect. Admiration. Awe. Those are what you should be feeling toward me right now. I alone have pulled off the biggest deception of our dispensation. So big that you can't even wrap your head around it."

McKane rubbed his chin. "Princess Seran? Alive?"

"Not only is she alive, but she doesn't have a clue who she is."

"She has amnesia?"

"Kind of. Let's just say that the doctor who kept her alive has created a way to block out certain memories."

"That's impossible," McKane sneered.

"Is it?" Stoddard smirked.

"How, then? How are you blocking her memories?"

Stoddard enjoyed seeing McKane stumped.

"Doctor Von is an amazing chemist and created a drug that blocks the neuron connectors in the brain. Think of it like a drawbridge. The medicine he created blocks the pathway between the brain and the neurons causing isolated or induced amnesia. We've selected what we want her to know."

"How can you select *what* you want her to know?"

Stoddard lifted his eyebrows. "Do you really need to know every last detail of how we did this?"

McKane's eyes narrowed to a slit. "I need to know if it worked."

"I wouldn't be here if it hadn't."

"So you replaced her old memories with new ones?"

He shook his head. "No. We can't replace memories or rewrite them, only make them lost inside her mind so that she can't find them. We didn't block everything. She still has most of her knowledge. We only blocked things associated with her past, who she is, and where she came from."

"And what do you want me to do with a princess everyone believes is dead?" McKane asked.

Stoddard thought he'd be meeting with King Marx, but now that this deal hinged on King McKane, he needed to change his tactic—manipulate the plan in a new direction, a direction that hit Meldrum McKane right where he was the weakest. "For years, New Hope has looked down on your kingdom. Cristole has never been good enough for King Bryant. Even your son, Palmer, wasn't good enough for Bryant's precious daughter. Now is your chance to change that." He lifted a calculated brow. "Wouldn't you like to put King Bryant in his place? Settle the score from years ago?"

King Meldrum McKane

McKane looked back at Commander Stoddard. There wasn't a trace of joking on his expression. His chin lifted high; pride beamed from his eyes. He had Princess Seran, had a doctor who had created a new drug, and he was ready to strike a bargain.

Years ago, McKane had wanted the princess, but Stoddard was right. Bryant had tossed him over. McKane could still remember the discussions like they'd happened yesterday. It was his last Council of Essentials eleven years ago.

McKane stepped in front of King Bryant just as he exited the front doors of the Appa Ruler's Mansion.

"Bryant," McKane said with feigned surprise. "Are you leaving so soon?"

King Bryant tilted his chin down, frowning slightly. He'd been avoiding McKane the last few days of the Council of Essentials and was clearly upset that he'd been cornered.

"The Council is over," Bryant said. "It's only natural that I would go back home to New Hope."

"I'd hoped that we could finish our conversation about the marriage alliance between your daughter Seran and my younger son, Palmer. Perhaps we should sign a formal agreement before you leave."

His weight shifted, and he glanced away. "I don't think a marriage match between my daughter and Prince Palmer is a good idea."

McKane raised his eyebrows. Was that why Bryant had been avoiding him? He didn't think Palmer was good enough for his daughter? "Palmer would make an excellent husband. I believe he and the princess are about the same age. And Palmer will become the next king of Cristole."

Bryant shot his brown eyes back to him. "None of that concerns me. It's the alliance with your kingdom that I'm not interested in."

McKane reared back. They'd already discussed what the alliance would entail. They would become allies. Vote the same way. Trade with each other. Their militaries would support each other. What more could Bryant possibly want?

"The details of the alliance are solid," McKane said.

"It's not the details." Byrant looked away. "It's the kingdom."

"What's wrong with an alliance with Cristole?"

Bryant pursed his lips. "Did you really think I would consider an alliance with Cristole instead of aligning with a more powerful kingdom? I've been talking with King Carver, and I've decided to match Seran with his son, Ezra. It's more advantageous."

McKane's jaw stiffened. "You went behind my back and made an alliance with the kingdom of Albion?"

"You're the one acting like we had an agreement. I never planned on aligning with you." Bryant ran a hand through his brown hair, giving McKane the sense that this entire conversation set him on edge.

"What could a marriage to Ezra Trevenna and Albion possibly offer you besides a war with Tolsten?" he scoffed.

"It's better than being tied to you. You and your family bring nothing to the table. You're insignificant to me." Bryant stepped around him, heading for his waiting carriage. "But I don't have to explain myself to you."

McKane followed him. "How dare you!"

Bryant didn't stop.

McKane's anger flared, and he pointed his finger at Bryant's back. "I won't forget this. I'll find a way to make you pay for the fact that you passed over my son and insulted the kingdom of Cristole."

Bryant turned and rolled his eyes. "You wouldn't dare mess with New Hope and now Albion." He shook his head once then entered his carriage.

McKane watched the horses trot away, pulling the New Hope carriage behind them.

Bryant was wrong. McKane would dare mess with them.

"Well?" Stoddard asked, bringing McKane back to the cave and their conversation.

"What if someone recognizes her?" he asked, still thinking through the possibilities.

"You know as well as I do, that only military and royalty travel to different kingdoms. The chances of someone recognizing her are slim. Besides the Council of Essentials, how often do you go between kingdoms?"

"Never," McKane said.

Stoddard tilted his head. "And if I lined up every other royal, do you think you would recognize all of them?"

McKane shook his head.

"See? You have nothing to worry about. So do you want to make a deal?"

King Bryant's dismissal of Cristole eleven years ago had made aligning with other kingdoms difficult for the past decade. McKane had lost his footing within the Council of Essentials. For years now, he'd had to fight for respect for himself and his kingdom. His people had suffered because trade deals hadn't been made. New Hope and Albion had become the power players, and McKane was sick of it. Every member of the Council knew that Bryant had overlooked him—that Cristole wasn't good enough for New Hope. Not to mention the fact that Palmer wasn't good enough for Bryant's daughter. There had been no one better than Palmer.

No one.

"Yes. We have a deal." McKane straightened. "I do have a few ideas of how I could use Seran to benefit me and show King Bryant that he didn't get the last word after all."

"Excellent." Stoddard held his hand out in front of him.

McKane wouldn't be slighted by King Bryant again. He would show him it was a mistake not to align with Cristole in the first place. But as he shook the criminal's hand, he wondered if *he* was the one making a mistake.

4

Sydria

The hot afternoon sun beat down on Sydria's back as she hung laundry on a line to dry. She stuck her bottom lip out, blowing her hair away from the sweat that had gathered on her forehead. The summer heat smothered her lungs. Being from Northland, she wasn't used to the humidity in the air or the high temperatures of Cristole. And her weak muscles weren't used to the manual labor of her daily chores. Aunt Edmay had had to show her how to do everything from hand-washing clothes to planting a garden and making dinner. For some reason, Sydria didn't remember how to do any of that, but she could remember all fifty states from pre-Desolation America. She would trade in her useless educational facts for more practical memories if she could.

Stomping hooves turned her head to the dirt road. Otis rode toward the house, pulling the reins of his horse at the last second. He leaped off the animal and barely glanced in her direction as he pushed the front door of the cottage open.

A tight foreboding settled in her bones. She had hoped that Otis wouldn't come back, had hoped that he hadn't solved the situation—whatever that meant. Something was off with him and the way he treated Von and Edmay. There were too many inconsistencies for Sydria to sift through. The answers felt obvious, but she couldn't piece any of it together.

She arched her back before bending down for another one of Aunt Edmay's shirts. Uncle Von leaned his head out the door and called for her. "Sydria, we need you inside."

That was quick.

They had skipped the small talk and gone straight to the part about her.

Her stomach constricted. She didn't even know what she was nervous about, but she knew whatever Otis had to say couldn't be good. She dropped the shirt back into the basket and sucked in a deep breath as she walked toward the house. The glaring sunlight outside made everything in the kitchen seem dark until her eyes had a chance to adjust.

Otis and Uncle Von stood in front of the cupboards, watching her.

"Sydria, Otis has some exciting news for you," Uncle Von said, but the excitement didn't reach his eyes.

She turned her head to Otis, studying him. He was about her same height, bald, with dark gray eyes that made her insides coil.

"What is it?" she asked.

Otis folded his arms across his chest. "As you know, your aunt and uncle risked a lot to save you. For months, they've worked tirelessly to keep you alive, and a large amount of money has been used to purchase the medicine that keeps your heart beating."

"I know that," Sydria said. How could she not? Aunt Edmay and Uncle Von never passed up a moment to tell her that her presence there had cost them a lot. "I'm grateful for everything they've done."

"Are you grateful?" Otis asked.

She stood taller, slowly raising her shoulders back. "Of course, I am."

"How grateful?"

She eyed Uncle Von and Aunt Edmay, but they didn't meet her stare. They seemed content to let Otis run the conversation. She shifted her eyes back to him. "I'd do anything for them." She'd thanked them every day, worked tirelessly around the house and in the gardens without complaint. No one could say she hadn't proven her gratitude.

"If I gave you a chance to repay them for their kindness, would you take it? Would you do the smallest of favors?" Otis asked.

She wanted to say that it depended on what he asked of her, but how could she? Sydria was indebted to them. And they were the only link to her past. She nodded her head slowly. "I would do what I could to repay them."

"Good." Otis's lips turned upward into a rehearsed smile. "You're to be married."

To be married?

Sydria repeated the words back to herself, trying to grab ahold of their meaning. That wasn't the kind of favor she'd been expecting. Something more like find a job in the market. Skip a meal every single day. Move out. Those were the types of *favors* she had expected.

Not a marriage.

Her brows lowered. "I don't understand. How does that help Edmay and Von?"

Otis clasped his hands behind his back, tilting his head to the side. "This isn't just any marriage. You are to marry the king of Cristole."

"Why would the king of Cristole want to marry me? I'm a nobody."

"King Marx wants to marry a working-class girl to show his people that he values everyone. Not just the ruling class. And in return, he's agreed to compensate your aunt and uncle very generously."

"Aren't there plenty of other working-class women who

could marry the king?" her words came out sharp. What was wrong with the king that he had to pay someone for a wife?

Otis shook his head. "None that he wants."

Her hand went to her chest where her scar was. "But why would he want me? I'm not even from Cristole."

Otis's lips raised. "Your mother was."

No one had told Sydria that before.

"In fact," Otis continued, "this marriage was your mother's idea, the entire reason you were traveling to Cristole in the first place."

Her heart pounded with this new information.

"You see, King Marx made an announcement that he was looking for a working-class wife." Otis glanced at Edmay. "Your aunt wrote to your mother and told her. When your mother found out, she sent a letter to the Cristole royalty, entering your name into the running. I guess King Marx liked the idea of marrying someone from another kingdom who also had ties to Cristole because he selected you."

Sydria didn't believe him. Her gut told her *not* to believe him.

"What's in it for you?" There had to be a reason why Otis was there negotiating all of this.

He shrugged innocently. "Only a small finder's fee."

Finder's fee?

Sydria glanced around the room to her aunt and uncle. "So I'm to be sold?"

"Don't look at it that way," Aunt Edmay said from her place on the couch. "This is a huge honor, *and* you'd be helping us out. Don't you want to help us?"

Was this manipulation? It felt like it, but she did *owe* them.

Otis raised his shoulders. "And don't forget that your mother wanted this."

Sydria shook her head. "What if my memory comes back in a few days or weeks or months, and I remember the life I had before I came to Cristole? If I'm married to the king, I won't be able to leave and go back home."

"Why would you want to go back home when you could be the queen of Cristole?" Otis asked.

Her hard eyes went to him. "Because I don't belong here." There was a constant longing inside of her, an ache to go *home.* She couldn't explain it, but everything inside of her knew this wasn't where she was meant to be. "Besides, I don't even know who I am. How can I be the queen of a kingdom when there are basic things that I don't remember or understand about life?"

Otis waved her words away with the swoop of his hand. "The king doesn't need you to be a ruler. He just needs someone to look good by his side."

"Perhaps we should get him a puppy, then."

Otis glared at her. "A puppy isn't the same as a wife."

"It sounds like he doesn't want a wife, just an ornament."

"Either way," Otis raised an eyebrow, "you will be the one fulfilling that role. It's what your mother wanted."

"Well, my mother isn't here anymore. I'm sure there are other available women he could choose from."

"Please, Sydria," Uncle Von pleaded. "We're desperate. We have no money left." He glanced at Edmay. "We've given everything we have to save you."

Her focus snapped to Von. "You're a doctor. Can't you go find work and *earn* money another way?"

"I, uh..." Von stammered.

"He can't work in Cristole," Otis broke in. "He's been banned from the hospitals for using unorthodox medical practices." He walked to Uncle Von's side like some sort of manipulation tag team. "Isn't that right, Von?"

"Uh, yes. I can't practice medicine anymore."

Lies.

Everything they told her felt like lies.

Sydria shook her head. "Surely, there's *something* else we can do for money."

Von dropped his eyes from her. "We have no other options."

"I can work," she volunteered, knowing in the back of her mind that her weak health might make that difficult, but she was determined not to be sold to a king in some kind of weird marriage arrangement.

"We're giving you the opportunity to marry a king. You would be fulfilling your mother's dream," Edmay said. "It's not like we're asking you to do something awful."

It was awful.

The fact that her aunt was trying to convince her to go through with it was another kind of awful, unless she wasn't really even her aunt. She shook her head. Why would Edmay pretend to be her aunt? It was a stupid thought. Aunt Edmay was probably saying all of that because she felt threatened by Otis. Maybe Uncle Von owed him some money, a debt that he needed to repay. But it wasn't Sydria's debt.

She squared her shoulders. "No, I refuse."

"Why?" Otis scoffed.

"For starters, I don't know him."

"You don't know anyone," Otis snapped, the sting of his words crumbling some of her defenses. "This marriage will elevate you to a queen. The arrangement has already been made—by your parents."

She lifted her chin. "I need more time to remember who I am."

"You may never get your memory back. It's time for you to move on and build a future."

It was her biggest fear, not knowing, not ever getting her past back. She shook her head. "I won't marry him. I can't."

Otis's gaze hardened. "You don't have a choice. It's this, or you're out on your own, and I know as well as you do that you have nowhere else to go."

"You'll kick me out on the street if I don't marry the king of Cristole?" She glanced at Aunt Edmay.

Her aunt looked down at her fingers. "It's not that we would kick you out, but we can no longer support you financially."

Sydria's chest tightened. Her aunt spoke out of fear. What did Otis have on them? Whatever it was, the consequences of it had seeped down into her own life.

Trapped.

Her memories were locked somewhere inside of her brain. She was trapped in the wrong kingdom, and now she would be trapped in a marriage that she didn't want. The unfairness of the situation was enough to collapse her to her knees, but she stood tall, some innate response inside of her to not let anyone see how upset she was.

"The papers have already been signed," Otis said. "The king has given you some leeway because of your accident, but if you don't go through with this marriage, then you will be in breach of the contract and be thrown in jail."

Her choices were limited. She didn't have anywhere else to go. She didn't have any money, and if she had any skills that would get her a job, she didn't know what they were. Even if she could find work, her body didn't have the stamina for hard physical labor, and if Otis was telling the truth, she'd be thrown in jail if she didn't marry the king.

She lifted her eyes, meeting Otis's.

"Well?" he demanded.

His logic and the entire situation were absurd, and yet, there was something about it that resonated deep inside of Sydria as if an arranged marriage was her fate no matter what. Maybe Otis was telling the truth. Maybe this felt familiar because her parents *had* wanted this for her. She tried to look at the situation objectively, but she couldn't. She shook her head and went back out the front door. True or not, she wasn't ready to agree to anything.

5

Marx

Marx walked down the hall of Cristole Castle, heading to his room. He had spent the entire day hiking and planned to take a shower to rinse off the salty sweat that coated his skin. He'd have to tell his secretary to send up dinner.

Ahead of him, the light from his father's office shone into the hall, creating a perfect rectangular shadow on the marble floor. Marx sighed. He had hoped to avoid seeing his father, but now he'd have to walk right past his office. There was a chance that his father wouldn't notice him, but Meldrum McKane was the type of guy who noticed *everything*.

Marx kept his head down, picking up his pace. Two strides would be all it took to get past his office.

One.

Two.

All clear.

"Where have you been?" his father asked from inside his office.

Marx closed his eyes and sucked in a deep breath before backing up. He leaned his head through the opening, placing his hands on the doorframe. "Some of us went hiking."

His father raised an eyebrow. "Did Dannyn go?"

Marx shifted his weight. "Yes, she was with us."

"I don't like it." His voice was stern. "I've told you before. I don't want Dannyn hanging around you and your friends."

"She's twenty-two. I think she's old enough to decide whom she wants to hang around with. And it's good that she's with me. I can protect her."

He lifted his chin. "Like you protected Palmer?"

Marx's jaw turned to stone. He'd walked himself right into that one. "That was different."

"Nothing's ever different with you," his father said, tightening his eyes. "You've been reckless since the day you were born, without a care for how it affects others."

"I don't see how going hiking is reckless."

"It is reckless when you have a kingdom to run."

"I don't have a kingdom to run. You're doing it for me." He tried to hide the bitterness in his voice.

"I'm only doing it for you because you're too irresponsible to do it yourself."

"You've never given me the chance to do it myself," Marx replied.

His father rolled his eyes in response.

Marx shook his head. "Whatever you say, *Your Majesty*." He pushed off the door frame and turned to leave.

"Wait." His father's deep voice stopped him in his tracks. "There's something else we need to talk about."

"Listen, if you're going to chastise me for all of the mistakes from my past or suggest that I'm incapable, then I think I'll just pass for the night."

"Blast it, Marx! This is important. Not everything is about you and your sordid past."

"Then what's it about?"

"Come in and shut the door," his father said, gesturing with his head for him to enter the room.

Marx looked up at the ceiling. Conversations with his

father had been strained as far back as he could remember, but things had gotten worse during the last year since Palmer's death. In some ways, Marx couldn't blame his father for his indifference toward him. In other ways, it was his deepest wish that his father would love him the way he'd loved Palmer. Ever since he was a little boy, he'd been trying to win his father's favor.

"Look what I made," Palmer said, pointing to his sandcastle on the beach. The structure had several levels to it, and a row of seashells circled around the entire thing.

His father glanced up from the papers in his lap, and he grinned at Palmer. "Well, that's impressive." He hopped up from his spot on the blanket, leaving the papers on the colorful fabric. "I need to see it up close."

Marx stopped digging in the sand, watching his father admire every last detail of Palmer's castle. "I made something too," he said, trying to pull his father's attention to him. Marx hadn't built a sandcastle. Instead, he'd made a racetrack through the sand.

His father didn't even look in his direction, still focused on Palmer's castle.

Marx stood and looked around. His eyes jumped to the rocks hanging over the water. He bet his dad would be impressed if he climbed them. He ran over to the cliff and started pulling his eight-year-old body up the side. He wedged the tip of his foot into a small hole, supporting his weight so his fingers could find another place to hold. He climbed higher and higher until his dad and Palmer were fifteen feet below him.

"Dad!" Marx called. "Look at me! Look how high I am!"

His father shifted his gaze to the rocks and immediately the smile reserved for Palmer switched to a frown. "What do you think you're doing?" He stomped over to the side of the cliff. "Get down from there, right now!" he hollered.

Marx's own smile faded. He didn't understand why his dad was so mad. "I thought you'd like it," he said as he began lowering himself down the rocks.

"You thought wrong." His father placed his hands on his hips. "You're always doing things like this. Why can't you be more like Palmer and just build a sandcastle?"

"He made a racetrack," Palmer said, pointing to where Marx had been digging.

He glanced at his brother. Palmer's eyes were hopeful, as if he thought he could sway his father's anger away from Marx, but his father dropped his hands and shook his head as he walked back to the blanket, muttering the entire way about how he always caused trouble.

Marx took a deep breath, pushing the memory out of his mind. He reluctantly stepped into his father's office and closed the door behind him. He wasn't going to sit down. Sitting encouraged a longer conversation, and Marx didn't want that. He wasn't staying. He stood with his arms folded across his chest.

"What do you want to talk about?" he asked, giving his father a pointed stare.

"I've negotiated a deal."

"Okay." Marx shrugged. "What kind of a deal?"

"You're to be married." The simple way his father said it alarmed him. There was too much ease and confidence behind his voice.

A surprised laugh escaped out of his throat. "Married?"

His father's face remained even.

"To whom?"

"To someone who is extremely valuable to our future and the future of Cristole."

Marx shook his head, thinking through every other kingdom and their eligible brides. Queen Myka had just gotten married, and there wasn't anyone else in the other kingdoms that he could think of that his father would be this excited about.

"All you need to know is that marrying this woman will make sure that Cristole has a power position when it comes to the Council of Essentials and our alignment with the other kingdoms."

"How?" If she wasn't the daughter of an already existing king, then who was she?

His father crossed his legs, relaxing into his chair. "You need to trust me."

"I don't trust you."

"That's the biggest difference between you and Palmer," his father said.

"Palmer wouldn't have married some woman without a little explanation first. I want to know the details."

"The explanation is that I want this to happen, and therefore it will. Those are your details."

"If you like this arrangement so much, why don't you marry her?" Marx gave his father a stony glare.

His father skipped over his immature remark. "All you need to know is that this marriage is in your best interest as well as the kingdom's."

"If you don't want me to know, what's going to keep me from learning the truth when I meet her? Won't it be obvious?"

"No. Nothing will be obvious," he said with an eerie smile. "The girl doesn't *know* who she is."

"What does that even mean?" Marx asked as his brows lowered in confusion.

"She was in a carriage accident and suffered memory loss."

His chin dropped. "Amnesia?"

"That's right."

Their conversation had gotten stranger by the second. "You want me to marry a girl who doesn't have any memory or know who she is?"

"Is there a problem with that?" his father questioned.

Marx threw his hands in the air. "I can think of a few problems."

"Look at it this way; if she has no memory, she doesn't know what a disappointment you are."

His father had him there. But that wasn't enough to agree to this insane marriage. "I'm not going to marry some girl when I don't even know who she is or how it benefits us."

"You don't have a choice."

"Of course I have a choice. *I'm* the king."

"You're not the king. You're a puppet—my puppet—and you'll do as I say," his father snapped.

He dropped his arms to his side, closing his fingers into a fist. "I'm not your puppet."

"You've allowed this to happen."

Marx didn't want this, hadn't asked for *this*.

"You don't take your role as king seriously, leaving me to pick up the pieces along your trail of mistakes. Meanwhile, you gallivant around the kingdom like some teenager who hasn't learned to become a man."

Marx gritted his teeth. "If you think I'm such a terrible king, then why did you force me to run in the election?"

"I had no other choice," his father said, looking away. "You made sure of that."

"Right." Marx nodded. "We all know you wanted Palmer to be king."

"I did, but I at least thought you'd be better than this."

"Well, I'm sorry to disappoint you." That seemed to be the theme of Marx's life, disappointing his mighty father.

"You've disappointed this entire kingdom." He straightened in his chair. "But now is your chance to make it right."

"I don't see how marrying a random girl is going to magically make me a great king. It won't fix anything."

"It fixes everything." His eyes dropped to his desk as his fingers skimmed across the glossy oak top. "You owe me this." His fingers continued to brush along the ornate edges of the desk in front of him. "All I'm asking you to do is put your name on paper with hers."

"So I never have to talk to the woman?"

"I didn't say that. For my plan to work, she must fall in love with you. Ideally, she'd give you a child. The more ways we can bind her to you and our kingdom, the better."

"Why would she ever love me?"

His father raised an eyebrow. "There has to be something redeemable about you that she can fall in love with."

"I don't *want* to make her fall in love with me. I don't even want to marry her." Marx hated being left in the dark, and this was too big of an event not to understand the details. "I'm not going to do it unless you tell me who she is."

His father glanced up. "It's *your* fault we're in this situation. It's *your* fault that you are the king and not Palmer."

Marx shifted his weight, knowing what his father was implying—that Palmer's death was on *his* hands.

His father was right.

He was responsible for Palmer's death.

"You'd be doing this for Cristole," his father said with a sigh, "and for *me*. This marriage is important to me. I've never asked anything of you, but I'm asking now. Will you do this and finally make your father proud?"

Finally make his father proud?

That's all Marx had been trying to do his entire life.

His mind raced through all the moments where he'd sat and watched his father beam at Palmer, pat him on the back, and say to him *I'm so proud of you, son.* Marx had always wondered what it would feel like to have his father say those same words to him. Deep down, he longed for that. It wasn't that Meldrum McKane was incapable of being a proud father. He was just incapable of being proud of *him*.

Marx looked at his father, studying his light brown eyes that matched his own. What did it matter if he got married? It wouldn't mean anything to Marx, but if it meant something to his father, maybe he could suffer through it. And it would be a good way to escape the expectations of all the women in the kingdom like Cheney—the women who wanted him to be something he wasn't.

"Fine," he said, shooting his eyes to the ground. Even as he conceded, he doubted that he could ever do anything that would actually make his father proud of him.

"You'll thank me for it later," his father said.

Marx doubted that. He turned his back to leave.

"Marx?" his father called after him, but he didn't stop.

"Plan the wedding," he said as he walked out of the room.

"Good." His father's voice reached down the hall to him. "The wedding will take place tomorrow."

Tomorrow?

A sick feeling filled his stomach.

Marx picked up his pace, as if he could somehow outrun his inevitable future.

Meldrum McKane

"You're getting to bed late," Malory said as she rolled over to greet McKane in the dark. "Did I wake you?" he asked his wife as he lifted the sheets wide enough to get his body into bed.

Malory sat up, leaning her back against her satin pillow. "No, I wasn't sleeping. I can't stop thinking about Marx and the wedding." She turned her head to face him, the moonlight from the window highlighting her delicate features. "Are you sure we're doing the right thing? I thought we said we were going to let *him* choose his wife."

McKane wanted to close his eyes and go to sleep, but he needed his wife on board with the marriage if he was ever going to be able to convince Marx to take it seriously. He reached his hand up, using his thumb to trace his wife's cheek.

"Darling, I'm worried about Marx too. That's why I arranged this marriage."

She sighed. He would need more to convince her, but he couldn't tell her the real reason. He couldn't tell her the girl Marx was marrying was the assumed-dead princess from New Hope and that he planned to use her to get revenge on King Bryant.

Bryant had overlooked their family eleven years ago. He'd turned his nose up to a marriage alliance with Palmer, as if Ezra Trevenna was so much better than McKane's youngest son. Nobody was better than Palmer. Now, Bryant would pay the price for his complete dismissal of them. If the princess became the queen of Cristole, fell in love with Marx, gave him a child and heir, then she'd be tied to Cristole forever. When she found out her true identity, her life in Cristole would be so set in stone that she wouldn't want to go back to New Hope. She'd be McKane's bargaining chip to get into the good graces of the Council of Essentials, to gain the power that was rightfully his. Every kingdom would want to align with Queen Seran. She'll elevate Cristole to where it should have been before Palmer's death and before King Bryant had slighted them all those years ago. New Hope would be bound to Cristole forever, and Bryant would be forced to open up his circle and include the McKane family in it.

It was the perfect plan.

Unless Stoddard inserted himself and ruined everything. Perhaps McKane shouldn't trust him, but he was too excited about his plan to change his mind now. Besides, Stoddard had nothing left. He wouldn't ruin this. All he wanted was the money.

McKane drew a soft smile. "Marx needs a woman who will influence him, help him leave his recklessness behind, and show him how to be a good king."

"I don't see how another woman will be able to change

him when his mother couldn't." Her chest filled up with air then she let out a long breath.

"You've done all you could." He dipped his chin lower so he could see into her moonlit eyes. "It's time to try something else."

"And you think this woman will be a good influence on him?" she asked, swiping away a lock of light hair from her face.

"Darling, you're going to love her. She's everything that we want our son to marry."

Aside from the fact that she doesn't remember who she is.

"Okay. I trust you."

McKane's smile widened. "Then why do you still look so sad?"

Moisture glistened in her eyes, and one tear dropped. "I just…I can't afford to lose another son. With Palmer gone, I can't lose Marx too."

McKane reached for his wife, cradling her in his arms. "I know," he said, patting her back as he hugged her close. "Don't worry. We won't lose Marx over this marriage. Everything will work out for the best. You'll see."

A shred of doubt hovered over his words. McKane didn't know exactly how every part of his plan would work out. When the time came, what would he tell New Hope? He didn't want the Council to question whether Cristole had been involved in Seran's supposed assassination and kidnapping. Everyone thought she was dead, so when she showed up alive and well, it would be obvious that someone had lied. McKane had to make sure Cristole came out looking innocent. He drew in a deep breath. There was still plenty of time to work out the details. The first step was getting Marx to marry the princess. Then he would figure out everything else.

6

Marx

Several hard knocks banged on Marx's door, serving as his warning. Three seconds later, the door to his room opened, making him close his eyes even tighter. He hugged his pillow to his head as footsteps swept across the marble floor. His secretary, Elsbeth, was headed to the window. The curtains swooshed open, and a blast of light filled the king's suite. Marx tugged at his gold comforter, throwing it over his head to block out the bright rays.

"Your Majesty," Elsbeth said. "It's time to wake up."

Marx ignored her as if his sleep was so deep that his secretary's voice and the sudden intrusion of light couldn't jerk him from it.

"Your Majesty," she repeated. "It's well past ten in the morning and time for you to wake up."

Marx sucked in a deep breath and pushed the covers off of him. He looked at his secretary. She was an unconventional choice for the job—old with no training—someone his father would disapprove of, which was exactly why Marx had chosen her, that and the fact that she'd been his maid when he was a child, and she knew how to handle him.

"I would prefer it if you didn't wake me up until well past noon," he said.

She shook her head, swaying the gray bun on top of her head. "You have things you need to do today."

As far as Marx knew, his day was clear…besides getting married, but he wasn't going to count that. That was on his father's to-do list, not his.

"Were you able to talk to the castle seamstress about putting a team together for the clothing drive?" Marx asked, sitting up higher in his bed. It was a new project he'd been working on. At the recent Council of Essentials, Marx was the one who had proposed that clothing dyes be essential for everyone. His proposition wasn't about colored clothes. It was about the choice. Since he'd become king, Marx felt like he'd lost all of his freedoms. He couldn't live the way he wanted, do the things he wanted, and it bugged him.

The working-class people had lived that way for years, even down to the simple fact that they couldn't wear the color of clothing they wanted. Being able to wear colored clothes wasn't going to change lives, but it was a start. It was a freedom given back to someone who had lost the ability to choose. But just because the choice was available now didn't mean everyone could afford it. That's where Marx's clothing drive came in. He wanted to provide new colored clothes to impoverished working-class families. From now on, they only had to wear muted colors if they *wanted* to, not because somebody had told them they had to or because they couldn't afford anything else.

"I did talk to the castle seamstress, but," Elsebeth's voice dropped, "your father would not allocate the funds necessary to make the project happen."

Marx looked up at the ceiling and the large wood fan that slowly spun around above his bed. It didn't make sense. His father wanted him to be a king, to do things for the people of Cristole, but whenever he tried, the man was always behind the scenes stopping his plans. Even Marx's good intentions weren't good enough for his father.

He glanced back at his secretary. "Fine. Take money out of my personal account to fund the project." He didn't need the money anyway.

"Very well." Elsbeth fought back a smile, a small sign that she approved. "Would you like me to let the newswriters know about your project and how it's being funded? Gain a little positive press?"

"No." That wasn't why Marx was doing it. Other people in the ruling class liked to brag about their generosity in order to gain public favor, but that wasn't his goal. The aim was to help people any small way he could. Besides, a little positive press couldn't change years of disappointing everyone. The only reason he'd been elected as king was because Palmer had just died and the entire kingdom felt sorry for the McKane family. Marx was known as the reckless son that didn't take anything seriously. He'd had the label so long he didn't know if he'd created it himself or if his father had. But now, it was his identity, and who was he to set everybody straight? Even if Marx tried to reverse the rumors, to shout from the rooftops that that wasn't who he was, would anyone believe him?

Marx was the guy who didn't let people in, keeping everyone an arm's length away. Only Palmer and Dannyn knew the *real* him. They knew that he had ideas and dreams about Cristole, things he wanted to do to make a difference, but somewhere along the line, he'd lost the confidence that he could make it happen, that there was more to him than being a disappointment. His father was a big part of that. If only the man saw him the way he'd seen Palmer.

Now he had to marry some woman—another thing for him to fail at. No doubt she was somebody important. His father would never marry him off to someone insignificant. She was a pawn in his father's game, just like he was.

He didn't even want to interact with the woman. He

wanted to avoid her at all costs. She'd be better off without Marx ruining her life too. But that's not what his father wanted. He wanted Marx to make her fall in love with him. His father's words from the night before skidded through his mind.

Will you do this and finally make your father proud?

He was set up for failure.

Elsbeth tossed some clothes out on the bed. "There's a High Rulers' meeting at eleven o'clock that you need to attend—"

"*Should* attend," he corrected her. Marx had stopped going to those meetings months ago when he realized the High Rulers were still directing their concerns and questions to his father, not him. It was another reason for his father to be upset with him.

She lifted her brow. "Then your mother is hosting a luncheon at noon, with the head of Cristole's extended education, that she would like you to pop in on."

"Tell my mother I'll stop by, but I'm not staying," he said, fluffing the hair at his neck with the palm of his hand. He actually liked the meetings on extended education, especially since that subject was near and dear to his mother's heart, but today he didn't feel like sitting through an entire meeting. Call it depression over his forced nuptials, but Marx needed to release the frustration coiling in his stomach.

"And then King McKane has requested that I block out your entire afternoon and evening for a separate event," Elsbeth said.

"My wedding?" he sneered. "How long does that take?"

A knock sounded, saving Elsbeth from answering. She whisked around, heading for the door. "Thank you," she said, taking a tray of food from the servant. She carried it over to his bed and placed it on his lap. Her eyes lingered on the bruise on his bare chest, a token from their hike yesterday when a tree branch had hit him.

Marx raised an eyebrow at his secretary. "Elsbeth, I have a feeling the only reason you wake me up early is so that you can see me without my shirt on."

She rolled her eyes. "Young man, don't flatter yourself. I may be old, but I can still remember changing your diapers."

Marx liked how Elsbeth called him out on his antics. "Well, I have a different idea for my itinerary this morning," he said as he sank his teeth into a strawberry.

"And what would that be, Your Majesty?" she asked.

"Tell Kase and the boys to ready the personal transporters. I'm in the mood for some racing."

Elsbeth narrowed her eyes as if she disapproved. "Don't you think you have more important things to do today besides racing?"

"I *am* doing the important things. I'm getting married later. What could be more important than that?"

She shook her head.

Yes, getting married was *so* important that Marx needed to leave the castle for a bit to wrap his head around it.

Sydria

Sydria stood in the middle of the small bathroom in her aunt and uncle's house. She leaned her face closer to the mirror, rubbing her hands under her bloodshot eyes. She hadn't slept at all last night. How could she, when she was being carted off in a negotiation that she couldn't stop?

Sydria had lain awake last night, staring into the blackness. She had thought through all her different options. She could run away. That was the most logical thing to do. But the logic of that situation fell apart in her mind, giving way to her fear. Where would she go? How would she survive? She didn't have any street-smarts to rely on. She couldn't even remember her own birthdate. So she stayed in bed, watching as dawn slowly illuminated the day. She considered about begging, crying, pleading with Edmay and Von. But it was useless. They wouldn't change their minds. Sydria had brought the subject up at dinner the night before after Otis had left. But they maintained that this was a great honor, that her mother had wanted this for her, and that *this* was the reason she had come to Cristole in the first place.

How could Sydria go against her mother's last wishes?

Was it even true? Or were Von and Edmay feeding her more lies?

It was all so confusing.

As the last bits of sun crept into the sky, a new idea popped into Sydria's head. What if she took her concerns to the king? She could plead with him to stop the marriage, vow to be a servant in his castle for a few years…until she remembered who she was. The money she earned as a servant could be sent back to Von and Edmay. She'd be able to solve all of their problems. The king could find another working-class girl to marry. The plan hinged on the king being a reasonable man—or on her own persuasive powers. Did she have that kind of fight inside her?

She braced her hands on the sink in front of her and lifted her chin to the mirror. She didn't recognize her long black hair or her dark eyes. A stranger stared back at her. Shouldn't the curves of her face and the brown flecks in her eyes be something she remembered? She looked away, disappointed again by the fact that even seeing herself didn't help jar her memory.

Sydria's hand went to her chest, and her eyes glanced back at her reflection. She parted the collar of her shirt, opening it wide to where her scar was visible. What would a man think about her ruined skin, about the jagged purple line that marred her chest? No man would be satisfied with a disfigured wife, especially a king. She squeezed the fabric of her collar closed and shut her eyes. She had to stop this wedding. This couldn't be her future. People without pasts cling to the promise of a happy future.

Sydria wasn't about to give up on her happy future.

She took one last look at herself in the mirror and hoped that she was strong enough to stop this wedding. It didn't matter that her mother had wanted it. *She* didn't want it, and that was enough to keep fighting.

7

Marx

Marx nodded at Kase and Warren riding next to him on their personal transporters. The speeding machines funneled wind into their faces, blowing their hair back. He smiled at his friends in a way that let them know they were about to lose the race. Marx leaned his chest closer to the handlebars and pushed the lever forward. His tires spun faster as the machine kicked into a higher gear, sending a spray of sand out from under the wheels. His fingers clutched the handles tighter as he steered his PT forward into an enormous sand dune. He drove upward, not knowing what was on the other side of the steep hill. His heart raced as he approached the top. His machine lifted into the air as if it were weightless, drifting gracefully through the sky. A rush of adrenaline tied his stomach into a thrilling knot as he looked at the thirty-foot drop below.

Everything seemed to happen in slow motion. The nose of the PT dove forward as Marx floated through the air. The longer he waited, the more complex the landing was going to be. At the last second, he pulled the machine up as fast as he could, lifting the nose. His tires hit the ground and skidded on the smooth sand. The impact was enough to throw him off his machine and roll his body several times until he came to a halt on his back. His chest heaved up and down as his eyes squinted against the harsh sun. Thinning white clouds slowly sailed through the blue sky above him, painting a portrait of serenity.

But serenity was the last thing Marx felt.

"Are you trying to kill yourself?" Kase asked as he leaned over him.

Marx's eyes shifted to his guard. "Nah, I was trying to impress you." He added a cocky smile to his answer.

Warren's head popped into view, lining up with Kase's. "If you would have landed it, then I would have been impressed."

Kase straightened. "There's a rumor going around that you're getting married today."

"I wish it were a rumor," Marx said, closing his eyes.

"I never thought I would see the day that the lazy king would get married," Warren laughed. "I assumed marriage would be too much effort for you."

Marx didn't like the term lazy or what it implied. He wasn't *lazy*. He was indifferent. He had to be. The second Marx allowed himself to feel or get invested in his kingdom, his father would do something to take it all away. That's how it had been his entire life. Things were easier this way.

"It's not a real marriage, though." Marx heard the teasing in Kase's voice and opened his eyes in time to catch his mocking smile. "Or is it?"

He gave him a pointed stare. "No. It's not a real marriage, just some political move my father conjured up."

"It doesn't mean you can't have some fun with your wife, assuming she's attractive," Warren joked.

Marx nodded half-heartedly. Why exactly was he friends with these guys? The reasons were getting less and less apparent the older he got.

Kase reached his hand out to help him up. "So who is she?

The daughter of a High Ruler or a relative of another monarch?"

Marx took the outstretched hand and pulled his body up to a stand. His muscles ached and protested with the movement. "I don't know who she is." And, at this point, Marx didn't care. He would live his life, and the woman would live hers. Their lives would be parallel to each other, intersecting just enough to keep his father off his back.

8

Commander Stoddard

Stoddard paced back and forth in front of Doctor Von's cottage, waiting for the transporter from Cristole Castle to arrive. Marrying Princess Seran off to King Marx was working out better than he'd expected. The princess was pliable and easy to manipulate. It hadn't taken much to get her to agree. Her submissiveness was a welcome change from all the years he'd had to deal with Princess Myka in Tolsten.

Once they arrived at Cristole Castle, Stoddard would turn Seran over to King McKane, who, in return, would hand him a large sum of money. Doctor Von and nurse Edmay would get their cut, enough to ensure that they kept their silence about the situation. But the rest of the money would go to him. He was the one who deserved it.

There were times that Stoddard doubted the money would be enough. He'd wanted so much more for himself. He'd wanted to take over all the kingdoms, to show the conceited rulers that they weren't better than him, that he could toy with their lives and their emotions just for the fun of it. He had wanted to be a part of the dramatic moment when they all realized Princess Seran was still alive, see the shock on their faces, but he had to alter his plans now that he didn't have

Tolsten's weapons. Things had to change after Queen Myka had destroyed the cache of weapons. Stoddard had narrowly escaped that night with a drugged Seran with Von and Edmay to care for her. Now, the Council of Essentials were chasing after him. Handing Princess Seran over to Cristole in exchange for money, was the best option he could think of. It would be his consolation prize. Money instead of power; but using the money to continue hiding would have to be good enough.

Doctor Von stepped outside, shutting the door behind him. "She's almost ready," he said.

"Did you give her enough supply of the medicine?"

"I gave her everything I had. It should last her several months. And with the money that we're getting from McKane, I'll be able to make more."

Beads of sweat collected at the base of Stoddard's neck, trickling down the cavity of his back. "Are you sure she'll continue taking the medicine?" Her memory loss was crucial to McKane's plan.

"I don't see why she wouldn't. I've told her that the medicine is the only thing that's helping her stay alive, helping her heart keep regular, rhythmic beats."

"If she were to stop taking it, how long before her memory would come back?"

Von paused as if he were calculating something in his head. "There would be some side effects to going off the medication. I imagine it would only take a couple of weeks before everything would come back completely."

The sweat dripping down his back seemed to intensify. After today, Stoddard would be long gone with his money. If the princess stopped taking her medicine and remembered who she was, she'd be King McKane's problem, not his.

Sydria

"Do you have everything you need?" Aunt Edmay asked as Sydria walked into the front room. A small bag hung down from her hands, resting against her thighs. She nodded at Edmay's question. She didn't own anything so packing for a life-changing event was relatively easy. She wondered where all her belongings went after the carriage accident. Surely Sydria hadn't traveled from Northland to Cristole without a suitcase, but when she'd asked her aunt about it, she'd shrugged the question away.

There were no traces of her past life, no letters from her mother addressed to Edmay, no belongings that she could associate with the story they'd told her. There was no evidence to support anything. It was almost as if Sydria had appeared out of thin air or had been plucked out of the ocean.

"Well, good luck now." Aunt Edmay pulled her into a quick hug, then stepped back. "I hope everything works out for you."

Sydria raised her brows. "You're not coming with me?"

"No, my job is done. I've done all I was supposed to do."

Her job was done?

Was Edmay no longer her aunt? Did she no longer consider herself the sole person Sydria could count on? She had so many questions for the woman standing before her, her only blood relative, but her aunt avoided her stare. Edmay didn't even care enough to see her own niece to Cristole Castle and watch the wedding she was forcing her to go through with. Unless she wasn't really her niece.

Sydria lifted her chin. "Thank you," she said.

Edmay glanced up and nodded, visibly pleased with herself and all she'd done for her.

But Sydria wasn't thanking Edmay for saving her from dying or even thanking her for letting her stay there the last three months. Sydria was thanking Edmay for that moment of clarity. If Edmay's job was done, then so was Sydria's. She wouldn't think of Von and Edmay again. From that moment on, she was no longer in their debt. When Sydria convinced the king to call off the marriage, she would no longer feel obligated to the two people who had made this her future.

They weren't her family.

They didn't really love her.

If they did, they wouldn't be selling her off to the highest bidder without the slightest look back. Even if the story was true about her mother wanting this marriage, it still didn't make up for the fact that Sydria didn't want it. Didn't she have a say in her life?

She smiled at Edmay, something so sweet it could only be fake. "I hope you're happy with your decisions." Edmay's expression fell and her lips parted to speak, but Sydria cut her off. "You're the one who has to live with them. Not me." She stepped forward, placing her hand on Edmay's shoulder. The woman's lips pursed, and her eyes trembled with fear.

Von swung the front door open. "The transporter from Cristole Castle has arrived."

Sydria glanced at the woman one last time, then threw her shoulders back, for no one other than herself, and stepped outside.

The transporter was parked on the dirt path in front of the house. Its oversized rubber tires seemed too big for the dusty road that usually only carried horses and carriages. A Cristole guard stood next to the sleek vehicle. His heavy navy uniform was much too thick for the hot climate.

Otis held the transporter door open for her. "You're doing the right thing," he said.

"Doing the right thing for who? You?"

Something was off with Otis. He was more than her aunt and uncle's *friend*. He had ulterior motives, but Sydria didn't have time to figure out what they were. She was in self-preservation mode now. The people who had claimed her as family had proven that they didn't have her best interest in mind. From that moment on, she couldn't trust anyone but herself.

Otis's thin lips slithered into a smile. "Yes, for me…and everyone else, of course. You're mother would be so proud."

She had the urge to slap him across the face. She didn't even know who her mother was, but her gut told her that she wouldn't be proud. Instead of the dramatic slap, Sydria managed a curt smile and ducked inside the transporter. The smell of rich leather sparked empty memories to life in her mind as she scooted across the bench seat to the other side of the vehicle. If she married the king, this would be her mode of transportation for the rest of her life, no more carriages. Her mind tried to conjure up all of the negative things about riding in a carriage, but she couldn't remember anything. All she could imagine was how easy and convenient transporters were. But their convenience didn't matter. She wasn't going to marry the king. She was going to find a way out of this mess.

She turned her head to Otis and Von, situating themselves onto the bench across from her. "Have I ridden in a transporter before?" she asked.

Von gave a sharp glance to Otis.

Otis quickly spoke up. "Of course not. How could you have? You were born into the working class."

Sydria nodded. "Right."

Could she even believe him?

She gazed out the tinted window as they pulled away from the cottage. Besides walks along the beach, this would be the first time since waking up from her coma that she'd been anywhere. Nerves shot through her body. There were so many things to fear. What if her plan didn't work? She'd be in a new house with a new life and a new husband. It would be quite a monumental day—such a contrast to the monotony of the last three months.

"How long will it take to get to Cristole Castle?" she

asked, watching the waves in the distance crash into the beach.

"Only a few minutes," Otis said as he tugged at his black pants.

She'd had no idea that she'd been living that close to the castle. In a way, the proximity comforted her. Maybe she could still walk along the shores of the beach that she'd grown to love.

Sydria rested her chin on her hand, watching as the dirt road winded and turned until they came upon a white stone wall lined with tropical plants and cacti. The transporter came to a stop in front of an iron gate. Her breath caught as the guards slowly pulled the gates open.

"Will the king greet us?" She wanted to prepare for whatever fanfare waited for them at the end of the drive. One thing was for sure—she wasn't going to let anyone see how scared she was.

"I doubt it," Otis said, chuckling to himself.

Something about his laugh unsettled her, and she realized she hadn't asked one question about the man she was supposed to marry. "Is the king a good man? Is he kind?"

Otis tilted his head toward her. "He's a king, isn't he? That should be *good* enough." He turned his head away from her, exchanging a look with Von.

Being a king wasn't *good* enough for Sydria.

They passed a row of palm trees as they drove down the path. The transporter rolled to a stop in front of four large white pillars. Sydria smoothed her hair out and tried to calm her haphazard breaths. Her door swung open, and a guard's hand waited. She hesitated for a moment.

"Well?" Otis said next to her. "Are you getting out?"

A part of Sydria wanted to stay inside that transporter and beg the driver to take her far away from there, but a royal driver would never disobey his king, so she placed her hand in the guard's, letting him pull her out of the vehicle.

"Thank you." She straightened and turned toward the castle, expecting to see the king and a line of people. Instead, there was one woman who looked to be in her thirties. Her dirty blonde hair was pulled back into a simple bun highlighting hollow cheekbones. She smiled back at Sydria and even added a slight curtsey.

That was new.

Sydria had never been bowed to before.

She glanced up at the towering walls of Cristole Castle. The limestone sparkled in the sunlight, making it seem like the entire house was built out of tiny crystals. Every piece of the building was white, from the large balconies to the ornate swirls carved into the window trim. Lush green plants with exotic flowers lined the steps up to the front of the castle. The entrance was open where there usually was a door, allowing her to see inside to a white marble foyer. At the other end of the entry was floor-to-ceiling glass windows.

The guard gestured her forward to where the woman stood.

"Where are all the doors?" Sydria asked, still gaping at the elegance of it all.

The woman laughed as she looked behind her at the open entryway. "The weather here makes it so we don't need doors, but rest assured there are doors and closed-off wings of the castle. Not everything is open."

"Oh," Sydria said, her voice barely over a whisper. It was probably a stupid observation. She'd only been there thirty seconds, and already she'd shown how naïve she was.

"You must be Miss Sydria Hasler."

Sydria stared blankly back at the woman. Nothing about her given name felt familiar. "Yes, I am."

"My name is Idella, and I'll be your personal assistant."

"My personal assistant?" Sydria raised her eyebrows. "For what?"

The woman laughed, looking at Otis and Von like Sydria

had said something hilarious. "My dear, for anything you need. Technically, I'm your lady's maid, but I've never liked the term *maid*, so I'm not going to use it."

Sydria nodded, trying to wrap her head around the fact that she had a maid. The entire thing seemed surreal.

Idella glanced at the guard. "Take these men to King McKane's office." The man turned, prompting Otis and Von to follow him.

She turned her head, watching as they walked away. She wondered if she'd see them again. Did she even care if she saw them again?

"Come, my dear," Idella said as she whisked around in the opposite direction. "We have much to do."

Sydria stumbled to keep up with the woman. "When will I meet King McKane?"

"Right before the wedding."

Sydria tried not to let her surroundings distract her as she followed after Idella, but everything was so white and fancy. She knew she was in a castle, but did the royal family have to live such a luxurious life? It seemed a little excessive compared to the way she'd been living for the last few months.

"I thought King McKane would greet me when I arrived—you know, since we're to be married." She hoped she'd meet the king before the wedding so she could strike a bargain with him.

Idella abruptly stopped and turned over her shoulder, causing Sydria to nearly bump into her. "You're not marrying King McKane."

Sydria's brows lowered. "But I thought—"

A brisk laugh barked out of Idella. "You're marrying his son, King Marx McKane. King McKane is already married to the queen mother."

"But you called him king."

Idella began walking again. "King McKane was the previous king. He's already served his time, but he keeps the same title. And we also use the title of *king* for Marx since he's the current king of Cristole."

"I see." Sydria needed to get the name of the groom right—a rather significant oversight. The man wasn't going to let her out of the marriage if she didn't call him by the correct name. Or…maybe he would. Perhaps then he'd see how ludicrous this whole arranged marriage was. "Do King McKane and the queen mother live at Cristole Castle?" Maybe she could convince one of them to call off the wedding, soften them to her cause.

"Yes, they live here. As well as Princess Dannyn."

Dannyn? The girl from the beach the other night?

Sydria couldn't believe she was a princess. She was pretty enough to be a princess, but she lacked a kind of refinement that Sydria had expected princesses to have. Did that mean that one of the men at the beach the other night had been King Marx? She shook her head, doubting that the king spent his evenings sitting on the beach stealing kisses. Surely he had more important things to do.

"When will I meet all of them?" she asked. Sydria didn't rightly understand her eagerness. Two nights ago, at the beach, she'd cowered at the thought of meeting new people. Now, she couldn't get it done fast enough. But this situation was different. She needed these people to free her.

"Dear, there will be plenty of time for everything. Right now, we need to focus on cleaning you up before the wedding this afternoon."

Her eyes widened. "The wedding is this afternoon?"

"Yes, ma'am. In a few hours."

"Why so soon?" Sydria asked.

Idella turned over her shoulder, giving Sydria a warm smile. "Why wait?"

There were only a few reasons why a wedding would happen quickly. Sydria had no clue how she knew that, but she did. Quick weddings usually happened if the bride was with child, or if something about the wedding agreement wasn't entirely legal, or if the couple was madly in love and couldn't wait. Since it wasn't the latter and she wasn't pregnant—well, not that she knew of—there must have been something with the agreement that could be contested.

"It's such a beautiful day for a wedding." Idella had a dreamy look in her eye that made it seem like she thought this wedding was some kind of fairytale ending for Sydria.

This was not a fairytale.

This was a nightmare.

They climbed a white marble staircase that led them to an open-air hallway suspended above the luscious garden below. The cool air inside the castle vanished, replaced by the humid, muggy heat outside. Sydria looked up at the blue sky, hoping there was another corridor for when it rained. The hallway led to another wing of the castle, and the cool air covered her skin as they left the outdoor heat.

"This is the queen's suite," Idella said, holding the wood door open for her.

Sydria stepped inside, and the grandeur of it took her breath away. The room was a mixture of white marble and limestone like the rest of the castle, accented with maple beams. It had large windows with several potted plants on the floor in front of them. Besides the white, everything was decorated in mauve, from the flowing curtains to the feather comforter. Mauve couches faced the sliding glass windows that led to the balcony with a view of the ocean.

If there were a way for Sydria to keep the bedroom without having to actually marry the king, she'd do it.

"In here is your bathroom and the queen's closet." Idella disappeared into that part of the suite. On the opposite side of the room next to the bed was another large door that was closed. Sydria found herself wondering where that led. "My dear, are you coming?" Idella asked as she popped her head around the bathroom door frame. "We need to get you cleaned up."

Was there a smear of manure down Sydria's dress that she didn't know about? Because that was the second time Idella had talked about cleaning her up. It was a little annoying, considering she'd spent extra time readying herself that morning. Idella flashed another warm smile, and Sydria's annoyance flew away with breeze of the ceiling fan.

"Where does that door lead?" She asked, pointing to the closed door she'd been wondering about.

"That door leads to the king's suite."

Sydria's steps paused. "We have connecting doors?"

Idella nodded.

"Why?"

"Probably because once you get married, you're supposed to have connecting lives…even at night." She wagged her eyebrows up and down.

Sydria stared at the woman. There was nothing about the situation that warranted eyebrow wagging.

"Now, come on." Idella waved her over to the bathroom. "We're pressed for time."

Sydria reluctantly walked the rest of the way to the bathroom and sat down on the velvet chair that faced the large mirror. She silently watched as Idella brushed through her black hair.

"What do I need to know about King Marx?" Sydria asked.

So that I can get on his good side and convince him to call off this wedding.

"Is he an amiable man? Someone who listens to others' opinions?"

Idella sighed. "He'll find his way…eventually."

What did that even mean? Could the woman be any more vague?

"Are you implying that the king is somehow lost?"

Idella paused brushing and looked off in the distance, caught up in her thoughts. "Marx McKane has always been a little lost, but the last year-and-a-half since Prince Palmer died have been hard on him."

Sydria looked at her maid through the mirror. "Who's Prince Palmer?"

"He was Marx's younger brother." Her maid shook her head with pity. "They were best friends."

That was sad.

Sydria had lost her parents, but she didn't know or remember them, so it was a different kind of pain. Losing a brother—someone who was a best friend—would be devastating.

"King Marx needs something to help ground him. I suppose that's where you come in."

Despite the king's loss, Sydria had no intention of *grounding* him. Whatever *that* meant.

"Don't worry, dear. The king will be a good man. He just needs a little nudge in the right direction."

Will be a good man…meaning that he *wasn't* a good man now.

Fabulous.

No wonder the king needed to purchase his bride. He probably couldn't get anyone else to agree to marry him.

It sounded like this was a marriage *and* a service project.

9

Sydria

There was something odd about walking down the halls of a foreign place wearing a wedding gown. The simple silk dress hung over Sydria's body, sweeping across the floor. The dress's neckline showed off her collar bones but was high enough that she wasn't self-conscious about her scar peeking out. As she followed Idella, she noticed how the dress blended with the white marble floor and walls. She could press herself up against the walls of the castle, and no one would be able to find her. Perhaps that could be part of her escape plan if convincing the king to call off the marriage didn't work.

"Where are we going?" Sydria asked her maid.

"It's time to meet the royal family," Idella said.

This would be her chance. She wiped her damp hands on the sides of her dress as Idella opened a wooden door, ushering her inside the room. She took a deep breath and stepped in, hoping that she would make a good impression. The room was empty.

"You can wait here, in the greeting room." Idella closed the door, leaving Sydria all alone.

How appropriate. The royal family had an entire room devoted to occasions like this—*greeting* people they'd purchased. She looked around, taking in the crystal chandelier hanging from the ceiling, the pristine couches, the greenery, the dark oak coffee table, and large windows.

Sydria didn't dare touch anything for fear that she might get a smudge on the perfectly white room. She stepped toward the windows, hoping to catch a glimpse of the ocean. She glanced down to a beautiful courtyard full of pink flowers and lush green bushes. In the center of the yard was a large cylinder wrapped in glass with bubbling water inside. Fish of every kind swam through the blue water in a circular motion, around and around. So this was the royal family's aquarium.

She pressed her hand against the glass window as she watched the fish, each of them in its own kind of cage, on display for everyone to see.

Her eyes watered, and she blinked back the moisture. It seemed silly that something like that could upset her so much, but the aquarium mimicked her life in a heartbreaking way.

"Miss Hasler?" a voice said behind her.

Sydria jerked around, glancing at the man and woman watching her.

"I see you've found our aquarium." The man beamed. He looked to be in his early fifties, tall and thin. His light hair and his sharp features commanded attention. "Isn't it incredible?" he asked.

The aquarium wasn't incredible. She hated it, but at the moment, all she could think about was pleasing the man who seemed so pleased with his glass fish cage. "It's lovely."

"I'm Meldrum McKane," he said.

Sydria quickly curtsied out of respect.

"Please, don't," the woman next to him said. Her light hair was tucked back from her face into a regal twist. She wore a pink blouse decorated with two oversized pink buttons and a fitted pink pencil skirt. "You're going to be family," the woman said as she smiled up to King McKane. "Actually, you're going to be queen."

Sydria's stomach twisted together into a giant knot.

The woman smiled warmly, reaching out to her. "I'm Malory McKane, Marx's mother. Oh my! That's a lot of M's." She giggled, then grabbed Sydria's hands and held them. "We are so pleased that you're here."

Sydria held hands with the queen mother, forcing a smile, because that is what the queen mother wanted—she could see it in her light brown eyes.

"Yes," King McKane said, wrapping an arm around his wife's shoulders, which seemed odd because his wife was still holding *her* hands. "We want you to feel welcome at Cristole Castle."

"Thank you." Sydria pulled her hands away, clasping them together so there could be no more spontaneous hand holding. She didn't want to be touched anymore. "I was hoping to meet with the king before the…" She couldn't bring herself to say the word.

"I'm sure you do want to meet him, and we *want* you to meet him." The queen mother smiled nervously at her husband. "I promise we're not hiding him from you on purpose. He's running late."

"Don't be worried," the king interjected. "He's excited about your wedding."

"Thrilled!" Queen Malory added.

"Thrilled?" Sydria coughed.

That was not what she wanted to hear. She opened her mouth to speak, to tell them that she didn't want to go through with this, to find out if her mother had really set this up for her, but the king spoke first.

"We'll give you a minute to get prepared for the ceremony."

Sydria looked down. She was wearing a wedding dress. Wasn't she already prepared?

Queen Malory squeezed her arm.

The woman didn't know how to keep her hands to herself.

"You look absolutely beautiful. I'm so excited." She leaned into Sydria. "I packed some tissues in my pocket because weddings always make me cry."

Sydria blinked. Was the queen mother insane? This wasn't a real wedding. Unless the woman meant to say arranged —*arranged* marriages always made her cry. Sydria would understand that sentiment.

"Come on, Malory," King McKane said, pulling his wife away from Sydria. "Let's give Miss Hasler a minute."

Sydria watched as the royal couple exited the room. She had wanted to talk to them about the absurdity of it all, but she hadn't.

She had folded under pressure faster than a pre-Desolation lawn chair.

Marx

"IT LOOKS LIKE YOU'VE HAD SOME FUN, YOUR MAJESTY," Louden said as he grabbed the handlebars of the personal transporter from Marx and rolled the machine into the castle's garage. Louden took care of the castle's vehicles, making sure the solar panels were charged, filling the tires with air, fixing the hydraulics whenever Marx rode them too hard.

"Don't worry." Marx placed his hand on the servant's shoulder. "I didn't break anything this morning."

"That's a relief, Your Majesty." Louden glanced behind him at another PT with its engine open. "I still haven't fixed the machine you wrecked last week."

"I wasn't talking about the PT. I was talking about myself. *I* didn't break anything." He shrugged. "I would check the PTs solar panel. I think I cracked it when I crashed."

Louden shook his head as he chuckled. "I should have known."

Marx grimaced. "Sorry, I make your job harder."

Louden swiped his hand over the sand that covered the PT. "It keeps me busy."

"Well, thank you."

"My machine is perfectly intact," Kase said as he parked his PT next to where Louden had parked the other vehicles.

"That's because you drive like a grandma." Marx punched Kase in the shoulder as he walked by.

"No," Kase said, jogging to catch up to him. "I, unlike you, don't have a death wish every time I go for a ride."

They walked stride for stride toward the side door at the same time two men exited the front of the castle twenty feet away. The first guy, a bald man with glasses, dropped into the back of the waiting transporter, but the second guy, another bald man but much shorter, paused by the door of the vehicle. He studied Marx. An eerie look full of prideful secrets swept across his face. His lips slowly etched into a smile.

"I know that guy," Kase said.

Marx stared back at the stranger. "Who is he?"

Kase scratched the back of his neck. "I can't remember where I've seen him."

The man dipped his head to Marx in acknowledgment then climbed into the transporter.

Kase groaned. "That's going to bug me until I remember who he is."

Marx kept walking. "I've never seen him before."

He pulled the door open, and there stood Elsbeth. Her arms were folded, and her foot tapped against the floor. Her lips pressed together so tight they weren't lips anymore, but a white slash in the middle of her face. Marx had seen this expression many times before as a child, and he'd experienced the scolding that followed it.

"Miss me?" He tried to layer his question with his most charming smile, but her flashing eyes told him her anger wouldn't be easily overturned.

"You were supposed to be back hours ago. King McKane has been looking for you. The wedding is to begin soon."

"I'm here. Everyone can calm down," Marx said as he walked through the door. "I'll go shower."

"Miss Hasler is waiting for you in the greeting room," Elsbeth said.

He drew his brows together. "Who's Miss Hasler?"

Elsbeth tilted her head toward him. "You're *bride*."

Kase chuckled next to him, slapping him on the back as he walked past. "See you at the altar, lover boy."

Marx glared at his friend, swiping a hand through his tangled hair. He looked at Elsbeth. "Am I supposed to meet her or something…before the wedding?"

"Yes. Miss Hasler would prefer it."

Miss Hasler would prefer it.

Marx rolled his eyes. Miss Hasler was probably like all the other women he'd encountered in his life. Women like that didn't care about the man. They only cared about the title of the man, and unfortunately, Marx held the biggest title of them all—*king*.

He didn't know what difference a thirty-second introduction would make. They would still be strangers when they said 'I do.' But he was a little curious. Okay, he was *a lot* curious.

"Fine," he muttered, changing his direction. "I'll go meet her."

"Like that?" Elsbeth questioned.

Marx looked down at the dirty clothes that he'd worn to go racing in. He didn't look like much of a king. Maybe this Miss Hasler would take one look at him and change her mind. In fact, that was a brilliant idea. He might not be able to persuade his father to give up on this idea of an arranged marriage, but there was nothing his father could do if Miss Hasler called it off herself.

"Maybe Miss Hasler likes the rich smell of body odor," Marx said as he raised his eyebrows. "Besides, it's not my clothes that charm the women. It's this face." He pointed to his fake smile.

Elsbeth shook her head and huffed away. She was too easy to upset.

Marx stepped into the greeting room, and his gaze was immediately drawn to the back of a woman in an elegant white dress. Her shiny black hair fell straight to her lower back. She stood in front of the window, her focus on something outside.

"There must be something really fascinating down there." It wasn't Marx's most charming line, but he wasn't trying to win her over. Technically, he'd already won. The wedding was in less than a half-hour.

The woman whipped around, and instantly her dark eyes widened. "It's you." An element of surprise filled her voice, the same surprise that made his own heart skip a beat. "What are you doing here?"

She was Miss Hasler?

Marx was supposed to marry *her*?

His eyes glided across her face and down the length of her body. Two days ago at the beach, she'd been beautiful, albeit wet. But today, with a little help from everything the castle could offer, she looked absolutely stunning. Light makeup had been added to her eyes and lips, complementing her olive skin. Her hair was shiny and perfectly straight. The white silk dress she wore skimmed over her body in a way that seemed unfair to every other woman out there.

Her eyebrows lifted as if she was contemplating whether he was mute. Marx cleared his throat, trying to kick himself out of whatever weird gawking trance she'd put him in. "What am I doing here?" he said, repeating her question. "I live here." Wasn't it obvious? She'd been expecting the king, and now Marx was there.

"Oh."

"What are *you* doing here?" he asked, even though the situation already made sense to him.

"I don't really know what I'm doing here." She lifted her shoulders. "I mean, I guess I'm here waiting for King Marx."

He nodded, slowly walking toward her. Clearly, she hadn't put together that he was the king. Maybe it was his dirty clothes that had thrown her off. "What business do you have with the king?" He should probably tell her who he was, but for some reason, he liked keeping this secret, even though it would only last for twenty-six more minutes.

"Right now, my only business with the king is to tell him what I think about his stupid aquarium." Her eyes darted to the window.

"Right." Marx placed his hands in his pockets, standing beside her in front of the window. "Are we back on the aquarium thing again?" It would be a long and painful marriage if this girl didn't have something more to talk about besides fish and sea turtles.

"Yes, we are." Her back straightened—good posture had never looked so *good*. "This aquarium is completely unacceptable, and I plan on letting the king know how I feel about it as soon as I see him."

He wasn't about to tell her who he was now.

She turned to face him. "I'm supposed to be meeting the king here, but he hasn't shown up."

"Maybe he's too scared to come because he knows you're going to let him have it for his aquarium."

She pursed her lips together, trying to hide her small smile. "No, I'm going to let him have it for not meeting me."

"I'm sure he has a good reason," Marx said, defending himself.

She smoothed her dress. "It doesn't matter. I don't need to meet him to know what kind of a man he is. I've already heard all about him."

The air escaped Marx's chest. He'd liked being the good

guy with her. The guy that rescued animals and rendered thanks. The other night at the beach, she'd seen the real him, but now that would all be tainted.

"Well, it was good to see you again." He turned to go. There was no reason to stay and convince Miss Hasler he wasn't as bad as everyone else had made him seem.

"Where are you going?" she asked, taking a step after him.

"I have somewhere important I need to be." He didn't want to be late for his wedding.

"I suppose I'll see you around, then." She smiled. "I'm Sydria, by the way."

Sydria Hasler, my soon-to-be wife. Yes, I got the memo.

"I didn't catch your name."

He shook his head. "I didn't offer it." Then he ducked out of the room before he had to actually tell her who he was.

Marx walked down the hall, disappointed by how things had ended with her. He couldn't believe that the woman he'd seen on the rocks by the beach the other day was the same woman his father wanted him to marry. His father had said that he'd thank him someday for the arranged marriage. He must have been proud of the striking bride he'd bargained for on his son's behalf—as if that was all Marx cared about. But there was more to it than that. Something about the girl and the situation didn't add up. His father had alluded to the fact that his bride would put Cristole in a power position with the Council of Essentials, but Marx had a hard time believing that Sydria Hasler had anything to do with the Council of Essentials. Besides her beauty, she seemed so innocent and fragile—not someone his father would be excited about. He didn't know what Meldrum McKane was up to, but he planned to get to the bottom of it.

10

Sydria

"He never came," Sydria said as she followed Idella down the white halls of the castle.

"That's the king for you. But don't worry, he'll make a good husband once he's grounded."

Grounded.

There was that word again. At this point, Sydria half-expected the king to have wings and fly into their wedding.

"Still," Idella shrugged as she walked. "I didn't expect him to jilt his bride before the wedding."

"He didn't *jilt* me." Sydria straightened. "He just didn't *meet* me."

"Well, no matter. You look beautiful, my lady." She stopped walking and tugged on Sydria's shoulder until she turned around. "Now for the veil." She pushed a comb into the top of Sydria's head, letting the white netted fabric fall behind her, then she pulled one layer over her. "I wasn't going to hide your face, but since the king couldn't even be bothered with coming and meeting you beforehand, I think we should. Let him guess about your beauty."

She blew the material away from her mouth. "I'm sure I don't care if he finds me beautiful or not." That wasn't exactly true. Something inside of her hoped she was pleasing to the king, even if she had no plans to actually marry him.

What was Sydria going to do now? She was wearing a wedding dress, on her way to the chapel. Everything would have to be so *dramatic*. She'd have to stop the wedding in the middle of the ceremony. The guests would be shocked. The king would be angry. It was really going to turn out ugly—not the kind of situation she wished to endure, much less be the cause of.

Idella placed her hand on the doorknob in front of them. "Are you ready?"

Her heart raced. "What? Now?"

"Yes, now."

The air in her lungs froze, making her chest heavy.

"This is the castle chapel. What did you think was happening?" Idella asked.

"I don't know, but I didn't think..." Her voice trailed off as Idella slowly opened the large wooden door. There was nothing Sydria could do. She didn't have time to prepare her thoughts on how she would interrupt the ceremony. Should she do it at the beginning or let the officiator get started and then cut him off?

An aisle split the room down the center with wooden pews on each side. At the front was a marble dais with a gold tapestry hung on the wall behind it. In the middle of the platform stood a middle-aged man with a receding hairline, making his forehead more prominent than it really was. The buttons on his shirt pulled apart where his stomach had gotten bigger than what the fabric could hold. The man smiled at her with his yellowed teeth, and Sydria grimaced.

Oh heavens! Is that King Marx?

Her heart banged wildly in her chest, adding to her rising panic.

"Is that—"

"That's High Ruler Grier," Idella whispered. "He'll be the one performing the wedding."

Sydria's breath released. That was a relief.

She scanned the rest of the guests in the room, looking for her soon-to-be husband. King McKane and Queen Malory sat in the first row, staring back at her. The queen dabbed at her eyes with a tissue. The wedding hadn't even started yet, and the woman was crying. Seated next to the queen mother, King McKane gave Sydria a calculated look, assessing his son's purchase. Did King Marx's father approve of his son paying for a bride? If she really had been *chosen* from obscurity like Otis had said, had King McKane and Queen Malory helped make the choice?

King McKane's lips curved into a smile. His smile wouldn't be there for long, once Sydria stopped the ceremony.

Besides the three of them, the room was empty. Maybe King Marx would be a no-show, and Sydria could pretend this day had never happened. Or she could look back on it like it was some sort of school-day field trip where she learned about how the rich and royal lived.

The side door to the chapel opened abruptly, and the blonde girl from the beach rushed in, on the arm of the man she'd been kissing that night. The man escorted her to the seat next to the queen mother.

Princess Dannyn.

"Sorry we're late," she whispered a little too loudly. King McKane gave his daughter and the man a reprimand with his eyes.

A soft violin began to play, and suddenly Idella nudged Sydria from behind. "That's your cue."

She stepped her foot out in front of her, stopping the nudge. "How can that be my cue? There's no groom."

"I don't know. I just know you're supposed to walk down the aisle once the music starts." Idella gave her another forceful nudge, and before Sydria knew what was happening, she was halfway down the aisle. The entire thing was ridiculous. What was she even walking toward? And she didn't know what to do with her hands. They moved restlessly in front of her. Why hadn't Idella given her a bouquet to hold? A bride should never be without a bouquet of flowers. What kind of wedding was this?

Sydria's pulse knocked around inside her chest, and she wiped her clammy hands together. A flash of a memory bolted through her mind. Not a memory, but a sensation like she'd done this before, like she'd walked down an aisle feeling helpless. Her mind wandered to her dream from the other night. Had that been some kind of premonition? She wanted to explore the thought, but there was no time. She'd arrived at her destination. She stood on the dais…alone.

Was she to wed herself?

At this point, marrying herself didn't sound too bad.

The music stopped, and Sydria's eyes wandered to the High Ruler, but he looked at King McKane.

King Marx had been running too late to meet her. Now he was late for the wedding. Who's late to their own wedding, even an arranged one? Maybe he was hurt, kidnapped, or better yet, maybe he'd fled the kingdom. Anything to get out of the marriage. Was it possible that he didn't want this marriage either?

No, he wanted it.

He'd *paid* for it.

The awkward waiting stretched on. How long were they going to make her stand there before someone said something?

The room was silent—painfully silent. Who would be the first to speak? Sydria guessed it would be the former king.

There was a commotion at the side door and footsteps. She turned her head in the direction of the disturbance, and there he was, walking toward her. Her eyes widened as she gaped at his freshly showered *familiar* face. His blonde hair fell to his brows and wisped to the side. He wore a dark, fitted suit, and his hazel eyes were fixed on her.

Her heart seemed to explode inside of her chest at the groom's reveal. She felt confused and stunned. Puzzle pieces from their last two encounters now fit together. She probably should have known he was the king when he'd entered the greeting room twenty minutes before the wedding…or at least considered that he was a candidate.

King Marx stepped onto the dais and stood next to her. A mixture of mint and soap filled the air around her. So what if he smelled good? Sydria would count that as a win for herself. She had no desire to be married to a smelly man for the rest of her life.

Nevermind.

This wasn't an actual ceremony. She wasn't really going to marry the mint-smelling king.

"Very good," High Ruler Grier said. "We can begin. As is the custom set forth by the Council of Essentials—"

"Sorry I'm late," King Marx whispered as the High Ruler rambled on. "I had to feed the fish in my aquarium."

Sydria pursed her lips, keeping her head and her eyes focused on the High Ruler.

"I suppose it was too much to ask that you show up on time to your own wedding," she whispered.

He stepped closer, his shoulder brushing up against her arm. In a way, she liked that she had a prior relationship with the king. It could only help her cause. But he'd lied to her about who he was.

Twice.

"You lied to me," she whispered.

"I don't recall lying to you."

"You didn't tell me you were the king."

"You didn't ask."

She turned her head slightly. "Why would I think to ask if you're the king?"

"Well, this is Cristole Castle, and you were in the greeting room waiting for the king."

"I didn't think the king would forgo bathing before meeting his wife-to-be."

"I've showered now."

Yes, his wonderfully delicious smell made that plenty obvious.

King McKane cleared his throat loudly behind them, no doubt letting them know that their whisperings during the ceremony weren't appreciated.

She lifted her chin, training her focus back to the High Ruler.

"I've known King Marx since he was a small child…" High Ruler Grier said as if this was a real wedding that needed sentimental remarks scattered throughout.

"Are you disappointed that I'm the king?" he whispered closer into her ear, sending a small ripple of chills down her neck and arm.

She rolled her neck to stop the sensation. "I'm disappointed in a lot of things right now."

"The aquarium?"

"Yes, that's one of them." She kept her gaze forward, not wanting to get in trouble again.

"My suit?"

"What?" she eyed him briefly. "No."

His dark suit jacket pulled across his broad shoulders and chest, fitting snugly around his arm muscles as if each measurement of the jacket had been made to fit his body perfectly.

"I really wanted to wear a blue suit, but my secretary set out this dark one, and I was already late, so I didn't change." He shrugged, and because he stood so close, Sydria felt the movement roll down her arm. "I just got out of the shower." He tilted his head toward her. "I would've asked you to join me, but I was in a hurry."

Sydria snapped her gaze to him.

An amused smile filled his lips. "I'm kidding."

She lifted her chin, looking back at the officiator. As the High Ruler spoke, his eyes narrowed in on King Marx as if he disapproved of his whisperings.

She gave the High Ruler an apologetic smile and whispered back to the king. "Do you mind? We're in the middle of our wedding."

"I don't mind." He shrugged, the movement rubbing against her arm…*again*. "It's my wedding. In fact," he raised his index finger to High Ruler Grier, "can you give us a moment?" He said it loud enough for all the guests to hear—all four of them. He gently grabbed her elbow, pulling her off the dais.

Sydria's face flushed with embarrassment as she looked back behind her at the bewildered expressions following their every move.

King Marx led her to a closet off the side of the dais. He pulled her into the small room, shutting the door behind them. They stood in complete darkness as his hand grazed the wall looking for a light switch. The switch clicked, and a blast of light filled the area.

Hazel eyes studied her. His chest and face were mere inches from hers, and Sydria tried to take a step away, but her back hit against a shelf.

She looked around nervously. "What is this room?"

"A broom closet."

This had to be the strangest wedding ever.

"We need to talk," he said.

This was her chance to get out of this marriage.

"Is this wedding your way of getting back at me for the whole aquarium thing?" he asked.

"What?" Her jaw dropped. "I'm being forced into this."

His brow raised. "Forced?"

"Do you think I would willingly choose to marry a man I've never met?"

"Technically, we have met."

Sydria thought back to the first time she'd seen the king. "Where's the girl you were kissing the other night?" she asked. "I believe you called her Cheney."

His lips puckered out. "I have no clue."

"You have no clue who she is?"

"Of course I know *who* she is. I just don't know *where* she is."

"You were kissing her, and now you're marrying me?"

He let out a long sigh, his minty breath filling the air around her. "It would appear that way."

"Why are you marrying me?" she asked, finding some confidence.

"I'm being forced as well."

She paused, taking in his words. "Who's forcing you?"

His stare shifted to the door. "My father."

"And I'm being forced by my uncle." And Otis and Edmay, but he didn't need all the details. She didn't even know if the details were true.

So it wasn't Marx who had paid for her. It was his father. The fact that he was a victim like her changed things. Sydria found herself feeling sorry for the man, sorry for whatever was going on in his life that had made his father arrange a sudden marriage to a complete stranger.

"I'm glad it's you," he said, looking into her eyes. "I mean, I don't know you, but anyone who cares that much about marine life can't be that bad of a person."

A slight blush heated her cheeks. This wasn't the direction she needed the conversation to go.

"And," he continued, "I like knowing that you're being forced into this marriage like me. It puts us on the same side."

She studied the green in his hazel eyes and the way his lips twitched as he spoke, as if the words he'd said had made him a little nervous.

Sydria needed to end this now. She glanced down, swallowing as she tried to gather the words.

"I need you to trust me," he said, pulling her gaze back up to his. There wasn't a hint of joking in his eyes. "Trust that I'll find a way for us to get out of this marriage."

Her brows drew together. "Are you suggesting that we actually go through with the ceremony?"

"What else would we do?"

Suddenly, Sydria didn't know. Could King Marx figure everything out *after* the ceremony? For some reason, that seemed a lot easier than her causing a big scene. If they went through with the wedding, that didn't mean any of it was real. If the king didn't want it and she didn't want it, maybe they could find their way out *together*. That kind of resolution might be better for her in the long run than her trading her future away to be a servant in the castle, which was what she had been prepared to do.

But could she really trust King Marx?

Sydria peered up at him. "What man are you?"

His eyebrows raised. "Excuse me?"

"Are you the man who shows up late to your wedding, or are you the man who frees the fish?"

It was a silly question but his answer would tell her a lot. Her maid had implied that King Marx was irresponsible in some way. Could Sydria trust a man like that? She'd had her own experience with him on the beach. She couldn't explain it, but the man she'd met that day hadn't seemed like a guy who would break his promises. Her gut told her that if he said he'd get her out of this marriage, then he would.

Something serious crossed through his eyes. He shifted his weight, causing his leg to brush up against hers, sending a warm feeling down to her toes.

"I'm the man who frees the fish."

They stared at each other, both considering their options until Sydria finally spoke. "Then I agree."

His lips twitched, but he didn't release his smile. Instead, he offered her his hand. "Shall we?"

She looked down at his hand, knowing that she should feel more nervous than she did. She was trusting her own instincts. The same instincts that told her Otis, Von, and Edmay weren't giving her the full story. She nodded, placing her fingers in his. The warmth from her toes funneled up to her chest at the softness of his touch.

King Marx opened the door to the closet and escorted her back to the dais. Sydria could feel the weight of every eye on them as they walked, but she didn't have the nerve to meet any of their stares. The situation was too embarrassing.

They stood in front of the High Ruler. "You can continue," King Marx said

The High Ruler slowly nodded back at them. "As I was saying…"

The wedding was back on.

Sydria hoped that she'd made the right decision. She hoped that King Marx wouldn't let her down.

He said he was the man who frees the fish. I have to trust that.

An image of the ridiculous aquarium passed through her mind, and she silently chided herself for not including that in their agreement. She needed to up her negotiating skills if she was going to make it at the castle.

"Do you have the rings?" The High Ruler asked.

Sydria didn't have a ring. She didn't even have a bouquet of flowers. This was a low-budget castle wedding.

The king turned to his left and grabbed two rings from an older woman with a graying bun who must have been standing there the entire time, but Sydria hadn't noticed her. Marx cleared his throat, looking at Sydria expectantly until she realized he needed her hand. She lifted it up and held her breath as he slowly slipped the diamond onto her ring finger.

It was so big and clear. They probably could have used *that* in the closet for some light.

Oh, no. We left the closet light on.

What kind of a person thought about closet lights when they were getting married?

"Do you like it?" he whispered.

She fanned her fingers out in front of her, focusing on the ring. "It's a bit gaudy and pretentious, but I suppose I only have to wear it for a little while," she whispered.

Her words probably should have offended him, but instead, he smiled, and Sydria found herself tucking her lips together, suppressing her own smile.

King Marx handed her a simple gold band and extended his fingers. "I think this is the end," he said softly.

Her heart raced. "I think so too." Her hand brushed over the top of his as she slipped the ring down the length of his finger. A flow of heat crept up her neck to the tip of her ears, and she jerked her hand away.

High Ruler Grier straightened. "Seal your marriage with a kiss," he said.

Sydria stiffened at the simple phrase. Slowly her eyes met his. King Marx pivoted so he faced her. He raised his eyebrows as if he found the situation amusing. His hands went to the corner of her veil, gently lifting the netting over her face.

Sydria's heart pounded at an unnatural pace. Marriage or no marriage, she wasn't going to let him kiss her, especially not in front of all of these people. She spun, intending to walk back down the aisle as fast as she could, but the king still had a hold of her veil. Her neck jolted back as the netted fabric pulled tight. She felt like a fish on a hook and her face flushed with so much embarrassment she thought she might die. She was mortified by her current situation, but she wasn't about to slow her pace. She pushed forward, causing the comb in her hair to snap, sending her body forward as her veil yanked off behind her.

The few wedding guests looked at her with wide eyes and slightly open mouths. She rushed down the aisle, but Marx caught up to her. Was he going to swing her around and force her to kiss him?

No.

He looped his arm through hers.

"At least let me walk you back down the aisle," he said into her ear, causing a sharp shiver to spread over her neck.

She lifted her chin, swallowing back her pride. "Fine."

11

Marx

They exited the chapel into the hall. "I've never had a woman so determined not to kiss me," Marx said as he handed her back the veil.

"I…" she shook her head, avoiding his gaze. "I didn't kiss you because I don't know you."

He reached his hand out in front of her. "Marx McKane," he said, introducing himself.

She eyed his proffered hand before slipping her delicate fingers inside his grip. "Sydria Hasler."

"It's nice to meet you, Sydria." Marx didn't pull his hand away. He didn't want to.

"This doesn't mean you'll get your wedding kiss now."

"We don't even need the kiss."

Her brows lowered as if she didn't understand.

"I don't know about you," he said, shoving his hands in his suit pockets, "but I'd consider that a successful wedding."

"You would?" Her lips grew into a shy smile.

"Definitely. When we started the ceremony, we didn't even know each other, then during it, we somehow managed to have a fight in a closet, make up, and agree to marry each other."

She let out a small laugh.

"It was a very productive twenty minutes," he said with a glint.

Dannyn exited the chapel, stopping right in front of them. "That was the most awkward wedding I have ever seen. Who stops the officiator to have a mid-ceremony broom closet conversation?" She smiled at Sydria. "Hi. I'm your new sister-in-law."

"Hello." She straightened, extending her hand to Dannyn. "I'm Sydria Hasler."

"McKane," Marx muttered. Both women looked confused. "Technically, your name is Sydria McKane now."

She swallowed. "Right."

"I can't believe my son is married!" His mother squealed as she swept through the door. She grabbed Marx and pulled him into a tight hug, sniffling the entire time. Was his mother really crying over his fake wedding to a woman none of them had ever met? He looked at Dannyn for confirmation, but she rolled her eyes.

His mother released him from her death grip and turned to Sydria, who took a step back, probably fearing that the queen mother would choke her in to a hug. "Oh my dear, welcome to the family." Sure enough, his mother leaped forward, pulling her new daughter-in-law's head down to her chest, hugging her tightly. Sydria bent over awkwardly as her cheek smashed against his mother's bosom. She stood unmoving, arms to the side, eyes wide.

Marx doubted there was a more awkward hug between two women in the history of time.

"Mother." He sighed, prying Sydria from her grip. "She doesn't want to be hugged by you and your chest. You don't even know her."

Sydria shot him a grateful look as she backed away.

"Well, we can't wait for you to tell us all about yourself," his mother said.

Sydria's face paled.

Did his mother not know about the amnesia? Because there wouldn't be a lot for Sydria to tell.

"Malory, don't make her nervous. I'm sure this is all very overwhelming." His father smiled sweetly, taking Sydria's hand and kissing it.

Wow.

He was really laying on the charm thick for this girl. Whoever she was, his father wanted to impress her.

Marx had been curious before the wedding about his mysterious bride, but now his curiosity was at an all-time high. He felt something for the woman. Not love or anything like that, but a sort of protectiveness, like he needed to rescue her from this marriage and his father more than he needed to rescue himself.

His mother clapped her hands together. "I couldn't be happier about this wedding!"

Couldn't be happier that her son had been forced into a marriage with a woman he didn't love? It was crazy. But that was his mother, always pretending that everything in their family was perfectly fine.

He'd learned how to pretend from the best.

Marx caught Sydria's eye, and though he didn't know her, he could've sworn she was as baffled by the queen mother's happiness as he was.

"Let me escort you into the courtyard." His father offered Sydria his hand. "We have a small gathering setup with our close friends to celebrate the marriage."

Sydria's eyes darted to Marx. She wasn't asking for permission. It was more like she wanted him to save her, like he was the person who would watch over her and make sure everything would be okay. It was an odd position to be in, since this was only the second time they had met, but he liked the role.

"Father, why don't I escort Sydria into the courtyard? She is *my* wife, after all."

My wife? Did I really say something that stupid?

Had Marx turned into one of those men who only got married to pretty women so they could show them off on their arms?

"Yes, of course." His father smiled, obviously pleased by the idea. His father took Sydria's arm and made a show of handing her off to him.

Marx looked down at their two hands joined together, but Sydria immediately released the grip and looped her arm through his. Arm looping was a less intimate gesture, and clearly this bride and groom were not going to be intimate in any form of the word.

Marx led her down the hall, his parents and younger sister trailing behind them. With each step toward the courtyard, Sydria's body tensed.

This was going to be a disaster. She hadn't even been able to stand the idea of meeting his friends at the beach the other night. How was she going to react to a room full of the most prestigious people in Cristole?

"How many people will be at this gathering?" Sydria asked, no doubt thinking the same thing he was.

"I'm not sure. I didn't know it was happening until right before the ceremony. My father must have set it up."

She audibly swallowed and then Sydria's shoulders rolled back. Her chin lifted, but her trembling fingers on his arm told the real truth. She was nervous. Marx didn't blame her. Functions like this were always stupid, and everyone made a point to stare. He'd take control of the situation, show her how to handle the crowd.

Marx stepped over the threshold to lead her down the stairs, but a tug on his arm pulled him back. He glanced at Sydria, fully expecting her to say that she wasn't going to go into the courtyard or that she needed to take a moment so that she could throw up in the nearest vase or something. Instead, she stood tall, with confidence flowing.

"Wait for the introduction," she whispered.

His eyes went to the herald, standing by the entryway.

Right. The introductions.

How did Sydria know about that?

The herald's voice echoed through the courtyard, and the crowd hushed. "Introducing His Royal Majesty, King Marx, King of Cristole, and Her Royal Majesty, Queen Sydria."

All eyes turned to them, and it was Sydria who stepped forward first, as if she'd done this moment a hundred times before. She looked regal, classy, and surprisingly like a queen.

Marx fumbled with his step, trying to keep up with her. He'd never walked into a room with someone on his arm before. He'd made a point *not* to. The newswriters liked to gossip about his relationships—the ones he didn't really have. Entering a room with a woman on his arm was the quickest way to start a rumor. It was kind of nice to have Sydria there with him—someone to split the focus with. But it only took a second for Marx to realize that no one was staring at him. All eyes were pinned on the gorgeous woman at his side.

There was a refinement about her that didn't make sense. She'd gone from a nobody to a queen in a matter of minutes, as if she were born for the role. Or maybe she'd been training for this moment her entire life, and that was why his father was excited about Marx marrying her.

His eyes darted around the room. He had to decide quickly who he wanted to introduce her to first. There were the High Rulers, men who were all his father's friends. He didn't want to give them the honor. He could take her over to his mother's friends, but they were all the wives of the High Rulers. Dannyn's friends were all clumped together. That seemed like a good choice. He assumed Sydria was about their age, and if she was acquainted with them, it might make her time at the castle a little more bearable. Then he saw Cheney

—and her glare—standing in the middle of the group of girls. It wasn't like Marx and Cheney were in a relationship or anything. Still, her sour expression conveyed her sentiments about his very recent nuptials, and Marx had no interest in dealing with that right now.

His only choice was his group of friends. They were going to have a great time with this situation—the loner king finally married. Marx might as well get it over with.

He led Sydria over to them. "Come meet my friends."

She kept her same stiff posture and straight face as the circle of men opened to greet them.

"Gentlemen, may I introduce you to my wife, Sydria," Marx said.

There it was again.

My wife.

It was like he couldn't stop saying it. It rolled off his tongue way too easily.

Kase turned to Sydria first, his eyes glossing over. "Your Majesty, it's, uh…um, I—I am…"

The entire group watched in agony as Kase tried to get the words out.

"You're Kase Kendrick," Marx finished for him.

"Yeah." Kase laughed nervously, still lost in Sydria's eyes. "I'm the king's personal…"

"Guard," Marx said, finishing his sentence for him again.

A small glimmer of amusement showed behind Sydria's trained smile. "Officer Kendrick, you are the epitome of focus and discipline."

Had Sydria just made a *joke*? The thought did something funny to Marx's stomach.

Kase smiled, thinking she'd given him a compliment, and he took her hand, bowing to kiss the top of it. As he straightened, he gave Marx a look that said he'd hit the jackpot when it came to beautiful brides, so much so that Kase had turned into an idiot in front of her. Marx couldn't argue with Kase's stare or the impressed expression on his face. Sydria was one of the most beautiful women Marx had ever seen, but he hoped there was more to her than that.

He needed more than beauty. He needed an ally to get them both out of this mess.

"Your Majesty," Warren said, bowing before her next. "I'm Warren Bradshaw, and I don't believe King Marx knows what a treasure he's married."

Sydria's dark eyes flashed in his direction. "I don't think he does."

Marx swallowed, a pathetic attempt to stay composed. Her gaze was enough to completely undo an entire army.

Warren took her hand and kissed it. "I will have to remind him daily how lucky he is."

Marx's lightly snorted in disgust. It was one thing watching Warren flatter women they'd grown up with, but it was another thing to watch him turn his tricks on Sydria. She deserved better than that. At least he assumed she did from what he knew of her.

"Gentlemen, may I steal my brother for a minute?" Dannyn asked as she approached the group.

Marx looked at Sydria. He didn't want to leave her alone in her first thirty minutes of wedded bliss, but she nodded back at him.

"I'm sure your friends will take good care of me," she said.

Without another thought, Warren offered her his arm. "Can I accompany you to the drinks, Your Majesty?"

"Certainly." Sydria gave Marx one last look before looping her arm through Warren's, allowing him to whisk her away.

Irritation boiled inside of him as he watched Sydria leave with his friends.

"When I went to bed last night, my brother was a single man. When I woke up this morning, he's suddenly to be married to some random girl. What am I supposed to think about that?" Dannyn asked.

Marx sighed. "If I had known this was happening, I would have told you."

She folded her arms, raising an eyebrow up as if she wanted more information than that.

"What?" he shrugged. "Obviously, this was Dad's idea."

Dannyn peered across the room to Sydria. "Why her?"

"Your guess is as good as mine. I don't know anything about her."

"She's pretty. Very refined."

Marx glanced at Sydria, noticing the proper way she carried herself.

"How come I've never met her before? Who's her family?" Dannyn asked.

All of her questions made him feel like he was on the defense. "I don't know who her family is."

"Where's she from?"

Marx shook his head. "I don't know. I doubt she even knows that."

"Of course she knows where she's from," Dannyn scoffed.

"Didn't you hear?" He gave his sister a sideways glance. "She has amnesia."

Dannyn's nose scrunched together. "Amnesia? Why?"

"Apparently, she was in an accident, and now she doesn't remember anything."

"That explains how they convinced her to marry you," Dannyn joked. "Your wife has amnesia." Dannyn broke into a giggle then immediately covered her mouth. "That's terrible," she muffled through her hand.

Marx rolled his eyes at his sister's immaturity. She always laughed at the most inappropriate things. But, despite his best efforts, a small laugh choked out of him too. He tried to hide it with a cough.

"She doesn't know about your crappy reputation?" Dannyn asked, her laughter growing.

Marx shook his head, making his sister laugh even harder.

"The poor girl, she could be from some remote village in Cristole, thinking she's so lucky to be marrying the king." Her words were broken up by her stifled giggles. "She doesn't know any better and if she did, she doesn't remember." At this point, his sister was laughing so hard she was hanging on to him for support as if she might collapse to the ground from laughter.

"Very funny," he muttered. "As if you're one to talk."

Dannyn sucked in a deep breath, calming herself. "Well, maybe our entire family is messed up."

It definitely felt that way.

"Sorry. You know I love you." She straightened. "I'm sure your wife will love you too."

I wouldn't be so sure about that.

"What was with the pause during the wedding?" Dannyn asked, changing the subject at the perfect time before Marx had to explain that this wasn't a real marriage. "I thought you were going to call the whole thing off."

"Nah, we were just talking about the weather." He'd been surprised by her hesitation to marry him. Yes, she didn't know him, but she would instantly become a wealthy queen. Her reluctance suggested she didn't care about that stuff. She seemed more concerned about *who* Marx was. Not *what.*

Dannyn raised her eyebrows. "You were talking about the weather?"

"Yep," he said, keeping a straight face.

"I can't believe you're not going to tell me." Dannyn rolled her eyes in annoyance. "You've known her for one hour and me your entire life."

Marx glanced at Sydria. She was his wife. His loyalty was to her now, for better or worse.

Sydria

Sydria sipped her drink slowly, letting the fizzing bubbles tickle her throat. She hadn't had champagne since she'd woken up from her coma, but she must have had it before because the citrus taste reminded her of…what? She shook her head, frustrated by the blank space inside her mind.

"Queen Sydria, you must not be from Cristole. I would have remembered if I had seen a beauty like you before," Warren said. He was an attractive man in a rugged sort of way. His brown hair was long and pulled back into a knot at the base of his neck. A short brown beard covered his face, contrasting his light blue eyes. His smile was suggestive, and the way he leaned in close to Sydria said that he was a man with few boundaries.

"Do you always flirt with your friend's wives?" Sydria asked, deflecting his question about where she was from.

"I don't know." Warren laughed. "None of my friends have ever been married before."

She glanced across the room at King Marx. "And why is that?"

He dipped his shoulder into her, lowering his voice into a husky whisper. "None of us have ever found anyone as charming as you."

Flattery.

So this was the male equivalent of flirting. She'd seen how women flirted the other night. Cheney had been much more touchy than Warren was, but perhaps that had something to do with the fact that Sydria was a married woman and the queen.

The queen.

Something about that seemed right.

Being there in the castle, wearing the fancy dress, and mingling with party guests made her feel more comfortable than she'd felt since her accident. It was almost as though she was *meant* to be a queen—meant for this lifestyle.

Now Sydria was crazy.

She sipped her drink again, chastising herself for thinking such stupid thoughts.

"Queen Sydria?" the queen mother said behind her. "Would you join me? There are a few people I would like to introduce you to."

She was glad to get a break from Warren and his heat-filled stares. "Certainly." She nodded at Warren. "If you'll excuse me?"

Queen Malory smiled back at her as Sydria walked toward the group of women gathered together.

"Ladies," the queen mother said, "this is my daughter-in-law, Queen Sydria."

Daughter-in-law? The queen mother was really living in a fantasy world.

The women dipped into curtsies.

"Sydria, these are my friends." Queen Malory gestured to the women. "They're the wives of the High Rulers. You'll want to become closely acquainted with them. I always say that they're the ones who get things done around Cristole."

Collectively, the women let out a fake laugh at the queen's remark.

One of the women, wearing colorful feathers as a hat, spoke up. "As queen, you'll learn very quickly who your friends are."

"Or how to influence your husband to get what you want," another woman in a fitted peach-colored dress said.

The women laughed again like they all had access to some inside wives' joke.

"I hadn't heard that the king was getting married," a new woman said. Her tone was more accusatory. Then Sydria noticed Cheney standing next to the woman. Her jaw was tight and her glare, cutting. They both had the same brown hair and light brown eyes. The woman was clearly Cheney's mother.

Sydria opened her mouth to speak but didn't know how much King Marx or his father wanted them to know.

"It was a last-minute decision," the queen mother jumped in. There was a jittery smile on her face, as if lying made her nervous. "Queen Sydria wanted to be sure before she agreed to marry my son."

"He does have a reputation," Cheney's mother said, and another group chuckle broke out around her.

"And where are you from, Your Majesty?" the feathered hat lady asked.

Finally, a question Sydria could answer. "Northland."

"Were there no suitable kings in your kingdom to marry—you had to come all the way down to ours?" Cheney's glare deepened.

Sydria lifted her chin to the girl. "I suppose there wasn't."

"Is your father a High Ruler in Northland?" another woman wearing gold swirls asked.

"Where are your parents?" Cheney asked, going on her tiptoes as she looked around the room. "I don't see them here."

"They're not." Sydria held her challenging gaze. "Unfortunately, my parents have passed away." That was the first time she'd said that out loud. The finality of her situation took her breath away.

She had no parents.

Cheney scoffed. "So you have no family? No siblings?"

"What do you like to do in Northland?" the woman in peach asked. "I've heard there is a lot of snow up there. Very different from Cristole."

Golden swirl woman leaned forward, lightly touching Sydria's forearm. "Do you ride horses?"

"Do you like adventure?" the feather hat woman asked. "King Marx is known for his adventurous side."

Each question came at her like a bullet, shooting down any confidence Sydria might have had.

"If you'll excuse me, I'd like to get some fresh air." It was a stupid thing to say. They were already outside *in* fresh air, but Sydria needed to escape.

As she left the courtyard, she heard Cheney say, "King Marx might act interested right now, but then he'll get bored, and eventually he'll move on."

She looked back to see Cheney's menacing smile.

Marx

"I CAN'T BELIEVE YOU GOT MARRIED," Kase said, lifting his glass up to his mouth. "I have to be honest—my mind went blank when Sydria was in front of me." He shook his head. "Like nothing. There was nothing there. I was mush, lost in her dark eyes."

Marx gave Kase a sharp glare. "I don't know if I should be irritated with you for drooling over Sydria because she's my wife or because you're in a relationship with my sister. But either way, I'm irritated."

"Forget about me," Kase said. "You'd better watch out for Warren."

"Thank you for the obvious," he said dryly. "But I don't think the queen is interested in someone like Warren." The truth was, Marx didn't know what Sydria was interested in. He *hoped* she wouldn't be interested in someone like Warren.

Marx glanced around the courtyard, looking for her. He would have thought her white dress would stand out, but all he saw were colorful suits and dresses mixed together with exotic plants and flowers.

"There's something I need you to do," he said, turning back to Kase. "I need you to investigate Sydria's background."

"Why? Don't you trust the arrangement your father made?"

"Not in the least," Marx said, still searching the room. It shouldn't matter where Sydria was. If she'd fled the castle, that would be a dream come true, but that didn't stop his eyes from scanning every inch of the garden. He gave up looking for her and shifted his focus to Kase. "I want to know everything about her. Who she is and why my father thought a marriage to her was a good idea."

Kase scoffed. "All it takes is one look at the woman to know why marrying her was a good idea."

"No. There's more to her than just a pretty face, or else my father wouldn't have made the deal."

"I know you have a tense relationship with your father, but can't you ask him why he made the deal?"

Marx rolled his eyes. "Is anything easy with Meldrum McKane?"

Kase shook his head and took a sip of his drink.

"Sydria said she was forced into this marriage by her uncle. We'll start with him," Marx said.

"Okay. I'll dig around, see what I can come up with."

12

Sydria

Sydria pressed her hips into the stone balcony, staring below at the vast ocean. Her hands rested on the limestone railing, and the short train of her dress lifted behind her with the ocean breeze. Pink streaks were painted across the evening sky as the sunlight faded. She wished she could walk along the sand, feel the grainy softness between her toes, but there was a cliffside standing between her and the beach.

She hadn't stopped the wedding like she'd planned. She was in uncharted waters now without the slightest clue how to navigate.

"I take it you don't like wedding parties?"

She looked over her shoulder, catching a glimpse of King Marx walking up behind her. His blonde hair raised with the wind, and the last bits of sunlight danced off his hazel eyes, bringing out their striking green hue.

Sydria turned back to the water. "How did you find me?"

The king stopped beside her, hands in his pockets, head forward. "It wasn't hard. You asked about ten servants and guards how to get to the beach. I followed your trail."

"I can't get to the beach," she said. "This is the closest they'd let me go."

"Castle rules." Marx shrugged.

They stood in silence for a moment, watching the waves below them.

"Now what?" she asked, glancing up at him.

"Well," a slight grin played on his lips, "we missed our wedding dance, so I guess this marriage is doomed for failure."

"Wasn't it already doomed for failure?" She bit her lip, holding in a smile. There wasn't anything funny about the situation she was in.

"Oh, come on. I really thought we had a fighting chance."

They stared at each other for a moment, each of them on the verge of letting a real smile escape.

"How old are you?" she finally asked.

He raised an eyebrow, the innocent action adding to his charm. "What does that have to do with anything?"

"I'm just wondering why a man in his mid to late twenties would still require his father to make his marriage arrangements."

"Ooof," he grunted. "You went straight for the insult. I thought we would get to know each other a little bit before that happened."

She smiled in an attempt to soften her blow. "This is me trying to get to know you."

"Well," he looked out at the crashing waves, "my father and I have a complicated relationship that I wouldn't expect anyone to understand." He shook his head. "I don't even understand it. I let him force me into this marriage because I feel like I owe him and"—he hesitated like he wasn't sure he should finish his thought, but he did anyway—"I wanted him to be proud of something I did."

Sydria appreciated his honest answer. "I shouldn't be so hard on you. My uncle and his friend said my mother made the arrangements before she died, and I had no choice but to believe them. I owe my uncle a lot too."

"Why?" His expression had turned serious, and he leaned in, ready for answers.

Eye contact was a terrible thing when she was about to tell him something important. "I was in a carriage accident three months ago, and I lost most of my memory."

The gauntlet had been dropped.

Would he run away in fear or stay and engage?

"Were you aware of that before you married me?" She had his full attention, so naturally, she decided to look away.

"I was aware." His voice was softer than she'd expected. "But I still don't understand how memory loss lands you in an unwanted marriage or why you owe your uncle anything."

She raised her shoulders. "My uncle saved my life. The carriage accident happened a mile from his house. He was trained as a doctor and was able to save me. His entire life savings went toward my recovery and medication. They have nothing left, and you…well, your father was the highest bidder."

He nodded…*slowly*. People only nodded slowly when they were trying not to show how appalled they were by the revelation they'd just heard.

The entire situation was so humiliating.

Sydria had been sold.

"Let's get this straight," Marx said. "Your uncle told you that your mother made the arrangements before she died?"

"Yes. She died in the carriage accident. They said I was traveling from Northland to Cristole because I had been chosen to be the queen of Cristole."

The line between his brows deepened. "Who chose you?"

"I thought you had, but I guess it was your father?" She said it like a question.

"Yes, this scheme has my father written all over it."

"They said you were looking to marry someone from the working class and that it was a huge honor that I was chosen."

"None of that is true, as far as I know."

"That's what I was afraid of," she said.

King Marx turned around, leaning back against the ledge so he faced her. He crossed his legs out in front of him. "The way I see it, we have two choices."

She met his gaze. "And what might those be?"

"We can resign to our fate. Go on as strangers who are married but who barely talk. Or we can right the wrong that has been done to us."

"How would we right the wrong?" she asked.

"Do you want to be married to me?"

Her eyes dropped.

"Be honest." A soft laugh puffed out of him. "I won't be offended."

She looked up, shaking her head.

"Good. I don't want to be married to you either." He grinned, provoking a shy smile out of her. "So let's end this marriage."

Sydria couldn't believe what she'd heard. "You can end it just like that?" This was working out so much better than she'd anticipated.

"Not really." He tilted his head back and forth. "Obviously, there is a lot going on behind my back that I don't know about. We need to figure all of that out first."

"But you're the king, so you *can* figure it out, right?"

"I can't do it alone. I'll need your help."

"My help?" Her hand went to her chest. "What could I do?"

"My father wants this marriage to work, and he won't be satisfied until it does. So…" he dipped his head closer to hers, "you would need to go along with it, pretend like we're happy and falling in love." Her eyes widened, and he quickly added, "For now, just until my father is convinced. Meanwhile, we'll figure out who you are and where you came from and why everyone wants this marriage."

"I know where I came from. I'm from Northland."

King Marx frowned. "That's the thing—there has to be more to your background story than that. My father would never marry me off to a working-class girl from Northland. There would be no advantage to that."

Sydria's throat tightened. "I thought the same thing. Why me?" Her hands gripped the railing. She had very few things she knew about her life, and what she did know, King Marx challenged. "Everything is so confusing. I don't know who is telling me the truth and who isn't. And I can't figure out why anybody would lie to me in the first place, so maybe they are telling me the truth and I'm just being dramatic." She sighed. "I just want to know *who* I am."

His eyes softened. "You can trust me. I'll help you find out the truth."

He seemed so confident in his plan. "And then?"

"Once we know who you are and where you're from, we can use that information to free ourselves from this marriage."

"So you'll help me figure it out?" She bit her lip, trying to find the caveat in his proposal. "And once you do, you'll let me walk away?"

He nodded.

"And I can go back to where I'm from?"

"I'll even provide the transporter to take you wherever you need to go."

A self-conscious laugh escaped, and she turned her head away. "You really must not want to be married to me."

He moved his head toward hers, catching her eye. "It's not you. I just…" It was his turn to look away. "I just don't think I'm suited for marriage."

"Oh."

There was an awkwardness lingering between them, something heavy that hadn't been there earlier. The sound of waves tumbling into rocks eased the silence.

"So do we have a deal?" he asked, pulling her attention to him.

It was everything Sydria had wanted. She could find out the truth, find out who she was, get out of the marriage, and return home. All she had to do was pretend that she was falling in love with King Marx enough to convince his father.

She would be a fool not to make this deal.

She stuck her hand out. "Yes. We have a deal."

King Marx smiled. He really should smile more. He was quite attractive when he did. He shook her hand, solidifying their agreement.

"So this is a fake marriage?" she reiterated, and for some reason, neither of them dropped their hands.

"That's right," he said. This wasn't a simple handshake anymore. *This* was akin to handholding. "We already know that I'm good at pretending to be what people want, but how good are you?"

Sydria swallowed, dropping his grip. "I don't know."

"I guess we'll find out."

There was another one of his easy smiles.

13

Sydria

Sydria sat on the velvet bench in her room as Idella brushed through her long black hair, readying her for bed. She reached for the orange medicine vial, going through her nightly routine of dropping the liquid onto her tongue. She looked up through the mirror, noticing the way Idella watched her.

"What did you think about King Marx?" Idella asked. She'd waited an entire twenty minutes before she'd said anything. That was some amazing restraint.

"He's different than I thought he'd be. There was a kindness about him that I didn't expect."

Was it kindness or selfishness? The deal they'd struck benefited him too. So maybe he was looking out for himself.

"I think you're ready." Idella set the brush down on the vanity counter. "I laid out a nightgown for you."

Sydria glanced at the bed and the silky white gown that was strewn across the mauve comforter. It looked more like an undergarment slip than pajamas. The front was cut low in a deep V, and the straps were narrow and thin, only a little wider than a piece of string. She didn't know what was typical for a queen to wear to bed, but that nightgown seemed to miss the mark, especially considering the modesty guidelines set forth by the Council of Essentials.

Where had that piece of information come from? Modesty guidelines? She shook the thought away and pointed to the slinky gown. "You want me to wear that to bed?"

A big grin spread across Idella's face, and she nodded excitedly. "Isn't it gorgeous?"

"It seems a little fancy for sleeping, and it's missing some crucial pieces of fabric."

"You're not going to be wearing it that long," Idella said, and Sydria thought she saw the hint of a blush tint her maid's cheeks.

Her brows drew together. "Why wouldn't I be wearing it for long?"

Idella looked away, her blush deepening. "Because it's your wedding night, and the king will be joining you soon."

Her mouth went dry.

She'd agreed to pretend like this marriage was real, and real married couples had wedding nights.

"Thank you, Idella. That will be all." She didn't have the heart to tell her maid that she was absolutely not putting on that nightgown and that she was absolutely not allowing King Marx to enter her bedroom. Her maid beamed with enthusiasm as she curtsied, then she rushed out of the room.

Sydria paced back and forth, not sure how to handle the situation. She and Marx hadn't set up any boundaries regarding their relationship. Was physical touch a part of it? Was kissing a part of it? Were wedding nights a part of it? Her stomach churned. How could she have been so foolish as to not set the parameters? Another negotiation failure.

She glanced at the wooden door that led to the king's chamber. In a few minutes, he'd probably knock and expect something more from her than she was willing to give.

Sydria walked straight to the door between their two rooms and opened the one on her side, purposefully knocking loudly on his. She was ready to draw the lines before Marx had a chance to cross them. She needed to spell out the terms of their relationship—the things that they hadn't discussed—and it needed to happen before he ever stepped foot in her room.

Yes, it was best that she got out in front of his expectations before it was too late.

Marx

MARX DIPPED HIS HEAD UNDER THE COOL SHOWER WATER, rinsing the soap out of his hair. The day had started off badly. He'd gone racing in the morning, trying to run away from the realities of his life, but somehow, everything had ended better than he'd expected.

Out of all the women his father could have chosen for him to marry, Sydria Hasler was about the best option he could have ended up with, not because she was beautiful—although she was—but because she wanted something. She desperately wanted to know who she was. She'd said as much the first time they'd met. At the time, Marx had thought she was speaking figuratively, but her literal predicament worked to his advantage. They both needed something. He wanted his father to think that he'd tried with this marriage before ending it and she wanted her identity. They could help each other.

It was the perfect scenario. As long as Marx could make his father believe that he was complying, he'd be able to gain the upper hand, and maybe for once in his life, he would be able to control his own destiny.

He turned off the faucet and rubbed the water out of his eyes. As he slid the shower door open, a knock pounded on his bedroom door.

"Come in," he yelled. It was probably Elsbeth.

He grabbed the towel from the golden hook on the wall and wrapped it around his waist, tying it in a knot so that it stayed put. Outside the bathroom, the door clicked shut. Marx wiped his wet feet on the plush shower mat and ran his fingers quickly through his hair so that he at least looked presentable. Not that Elsbeth cared.

"What do you need?" he asked as he walked out of the bathroom.

He stopped walking and stared blankly at the woman before him.

Cheney stood in the middle of his bedroom. Her eyes took in his wet torso and his undressed state. Her lips curled into a smile that Marx didn't like.

"How did you get in here?" he asked. He'd never had a woman in his chamber before.

"You told me to come in." Her smile lifted higher.

"No, I mean how did you get past the guards?"

"Kase let me in." She skimmed her fingers over the back of the white linen couch.

He was going to kill Kase for behaving more like a friend than a guard. "What are you doing here?"

"Is it really so difficult to guess?" There was a sensual tinge to her voice that made Marx uncomfortable, especially when he was pretty much naked. He looked down at his bare chest and towel. "Let me go change first."

"There's really no need," she said, adding a smile. "I don't mind."

"I mind." He moved to go back to his closet when another knock sounded at the door, causing him to turn back around. Who was here now?

"I think it came from this door." Cheney pointed behind to the wooden door that separated the king's suite from the queen's.

Marx reached out. "Wait. Don't open it." But he was too late. Cheney was already swinging it open.

Sydria's eyes locked with Cheney's, then her gaze shifted

to Marx and his bare chest. Her jaw dropped five feet to the floor.

This looked bad.

"Oh, I'm sorry!" Sydria said, stumbling back. "I didn't know that—"

"You don't have to apologize." A satisfied smirk flittered across Cheney's lips. "Can *I* help you with something?" Leave it to Cheney to act like she owned the place.

"No." Sydria swallowed. "What I came to say can wait until tomorrow."

Marx rubbed his forehead. This may be a fake marriage, but he intended to approach it with fidelity. He hadn't gotten off to a good start, at least from Sydria's perspective.

She backed up from the door. "You guys enjoy your night." She closed her side, and the bolt clicked into place.

Cheney shrugged as if she couldn't understand why Sydria had behaved so weirdly. She shut his side and locked it, turning back to him. "Where were we?"

Marx placed his hands on his hips. "You were just about to leave. That's where we were."

Her smile drooped into a frown. "That's it? That's all you have to say to me after you married some stranger?"

He lowered his head. "I should've told you beforehand. I only found out last night."

"And?" she pressed.

"What do you want me to say?" He didn't like seeing Cheney upset. "It's not like I chose this."

"I know." She folded her arms across her chest. "I heard my father talking with your father. I know, obviously, that this is an arranged marriage. But what does it mean for us?"

Marx furrowed his brows. "There is no *us*."

She shifted her weight. "I guess I always thought that you would come around, that there would be an *us* someday."

"I'm sorry if I led you to believe that, but it's not going to happen, especially now that I'm married."

"But this isn't a real marriage."

He felt the same way, but he wasn't going to tell Cheney that. He didn't want to encourage her. "I'm going to try to make this marriage work, and I need you to respect that. It's what my father wants."

"But if *you* don't want it, then what's the problem with us continuing?"

"I want it too," he lied.

She stood there, shaking her head as if she didn't believe his words.

"You'll come back." She walked toward the door. "You'll regret her, and you'll come running back to me."

She left the room by slamming the door.

Marx smoothed his damp hair back from his face.

Bravo.

Somehow, he'd managed to hurt *two* women's feelings in a matter of five minutes.

He needed to set things right with Sydria, let her know that he hadn't invited Cheney to his room and that he hadn't let her stay. He opened his side, lifted his knuckles, and paused. He looked down. Was he really going to knock on her door dressed in a towel?

No.

He had boundaries.

He shut the door between their rooms.

Marx would apologize tomorrow.

14

Sydria

"I'm glad you invited me here tonight," she said, slowly walking toward him. She made a conscious effort to sway her hips, to lace her eyes with passion, to smile in a pleasing way even if it didn't feel right.

"I'm glad I did too." His voice was quiet. "You are my only future."

She stared back at the nameless, faceless man as darkness closed in around her.

You are my only future.

You are my only future.

Wind whipped around her. The floor beneath opened up, and suddenly she fell through the vortex into blackness.

Sydria closed her eyes, trying not to think about the dream she'd had last night and what it meant. It probably didn't mean anything, just some version of her own wedding night nightmare. She reached out in front of her, grabbing the strawberry jelly on the table, and spread it across her toast. Idella had set up breakfast for her on the terrace outside the royal sitting room. She looked up at the white canopy above her head, grateful for the shade it provided. The heat of the day had already started to creep in.

"Mmm." She sighed as she took a bite of the toast. She'd missed the taste of strawberry jelly. It must have been something her mother had made back home in Northland. If that was even where she was from.

She was glad the king wasn't there. She didn't know if she could face him after stumbling upon him and Cheney together in his room last night. What had Sydria been thinking? It was laughable, really, that she had assumed the king had wanted to spend his wedding night with her. He probably had a plethora of women he could choose from.

Sydria was nothing to him.

Thank goodness for that.

Things were exactly how she wanted them. She hadn't wanted to spend her wedding night with King Marx either, but still, a pang of hurt poked around inside of her, enough that Sydria had tossed and turned the first hour after she'd lain down to sleep. Then her mind had conjured up that dream. And, to make things worse, Sydria couldn't stop thinking about Cheney. Sydria had never been the jealous type, at least she didn't think she had, but there was something about Cheney that brewed envy deep inside of her.

Sydria shook the feelings away. This was the perfect situation. Her responsibilities to the king would be simple—even more so if nothing physical was included.

The glass door to the terrace slid open, and King Marx walked out, wearing light blue dress shorts and a tight pink v-neck shirt. Sydria choked on her toast at the sight of him.

He smiled down at her, completely unfazed by the awkwardness of the night before. He was probably used to several people in the castle knowing about his nightly extracurricular activities.

"Good morning," he said, pulling out the chair next to her and sitting down.

She finished chewing the bits of toast she'd just so gracefully choked on. "Good morning."

He reached out for the juice, bringing the bottle to her cup first and pouring her some.

It was a kind gesture that didn't go unnoticed.

"What do you have planned for your first day as queen?" he asked, filling his plate with food.

Were they really not going to talk about the night before?

"Uh…Idella said I'm going to have tea with your mother and sister."

"Ooh, that sounds intimidating." His eyes went wide.

"Is it intimidating?"

"Nah, I was just joking. The women in the family are very easy and pleasant."

"What about the men?" She raised her eyebrow. "Are they easy and pleasant?"

He looked at her with a playful gleam. "Some of the time."

"I…uh." She glanced at her plate of food, trying not to focus on how cute the gleam in his hazel eyes was. "I also have a dress fitting with the castle seamstress later this afternoon to get my wardrobe designed." That was one appointment Sydria was excited about.

"I think I'll join you for that."

"You want to come to my dress fitting?"

"I'm not going to turn down a new suit, and maybe we can get a matching outfit made for when we make our first official appearance as man and wife."

"Oh, okay." Matching outfits seemed a little juvenile, but Marx was the king, so he could do whatever he wanted.

He rolled his neck around, rubbing the side of it. "I kinked my neck. I must have slept on it wrong last night."

"Perhaps it had something to do with your nightly activities with Cheney," she said sweetly, sipping her juice.

Marx smiled. "That was a little bit of a rough transition, but okay. Here we go. We are hitting this topic head-on." He turned to her more fully. "I'd like to apologize for last night. I want you to know I did *not* spend the night with Cheney."

"This is a fake marriage, so the rules are different. It's none of my business if you did or you didn't." Sydria feigned disinterest as she slathered a fresh layer of strawberry jelly on her toast.

"Fake marriage or not, I wouldn't let her stay. And I didn't invite her to my room in the first place. In fact, no woman has ever been in my room before."

"I didn't ask if they had."

He lifted his brow, somehow pulling off a relaxed charm. "You wanted to ask," he said.

"No, I didn't."

"It seemed to me like you did."

She turned to him, raising her eyebrow. "No, I didn't."

"Maybe just a little bit." His thumb and his index finger squished the air between them together until there was only a small space.

Sydria shook her head.

Marx pointed to himself. "To me, it seemed that you wanted to ask, but okay. Anyway, I'm sorry. I hated thinking that I might have hurt your feelings."

He hated thinking that he'd hurt her feelings?

King Marx was good at apologies.

Sydria kept her focus on her toast, not wanting to give him any reason to think that she was interested in his love life, but inside she was smiling. Could insides smile? If they could, hers were beaming.

"Why did you knock on my door last night, anyway?" he asked.

"No reason."

"There had to be some reason for you to unlock your door, open it, and then knock on mine."

Yes, it did seem like a lot of effort to take those steps. She was going to have to ask him her question.

She sat back in her chair and folded her arms across her chest. "There were a few terms of our agreement that we didn't discuss. Like, for starters, my maid set out a very elegant but skimpy nightgown for me to wear on my wedding night."

"Do you want me to fire her for that?" he asked, trying to pull off a serious expression.

Sydria shook her head. "Why would she do that?"

"She probably did that because she thought you and I were going to spend the night together." He rested his chin on his hand, completely calm. Did anything ever ruffle this man?

"Why would she *think* that?" She looked at him accusingly.

"Because that's normally what married couples do."

"These are the terms I'm talking about." She pointed back and forth between the two of them. "*We* are not a normal married couple, and *we* will not be doing anything like that."

"I never said we would."

She lifted her chin, feeling a bit of relief. "I didn't know that. We hadn't talked about it yet."

"We do need to have *some* physical contact, though." A slight smile crept up his mouth. "Or else no one will believe that we're falling in love."

"What do you suggest? Hand-holding?"

"Yes."

"Hugging?"

"Yes."

She cleared her throat. "Kissing?"

His lips worked into a bigger smile. "I think yes."

"I think not," she said a little too emphatically. "You already saw what happened when you tried to kiss me at our wedding."

"I can't be blamed for that. It was a command…*seal the marriage with a kiss.* Who doesn't obey commands?"

"Well, kissing is not part of our deal."

"Are you sure? I think that it would add a nice touch to our facade."

"I think not," she said again.

"Tell you what," Marx said as he sat back in his chair. "I won't kiss you until you ask me to."

Sydria leaned forward, so her eyes could meet his. "I won't ask you to."

A smile cracked through his relaxed front. "Okay." He had a *We'll see* expression on his face that she wanted to slap away.

Instead, she straightened, adding more jelly to her toast. "Good. I'm glad we got that all situated."

"Me too." His smile seemed to widen as he stared back at her. "Well," he finally said, scooting his chair back so he could stand. "I have a lot of things to get done today. So I'll see you at the dress fitting."

"Wait." Her hand went out. "What am I supposed to tell your mom and sister?"

"About what?"

"Are they supposed to know that we're," she lowered her voice to a whisper, "*pretending*?"

Marx leaned down, resting his palm against the table in front of her so that his warm words tickled her neck and shoulder as he spoke.

"I think not." He leaned his head even closer to her cheek. He seemed to have this pretend relationship thing down to a science. Too bad there wasn't anyone there to witness his performance. "We're supposed to be convincing my father that we're falling in love. So I would strongly advise that we don't tell my mother or sister that we're faking it."

She gave a stiff nod. "My thoughts exactly."

His hazel eyes held hers. Why wasn't he backing off? She'd given him his answer.

"Have a good day, Queen Sydria." He pushed off the table and walked to the door. The air around Sydria lightened, and she breathed easier with the space.

"Oh," he said, pausing right before he left, "I almost

forgot. If we're going to figure out who you are. I need to know your uncle's name."

"Von Nealman. He and my Aunt Edmay live in a seaside cottage a few miles from here."

He nodded. "Also, I'd like to know what exactly you *do* remember."

"I remember—"

He held up his hand. "No, like, write it down on a piece of paper, and we'll talk about it later."

"Okay. I'll do that."

He nodded again, then left the terrace. Sydria resettled into her chair, picking up the strawberry toast. She stared at it for a moment before dropping it back down onto the plate. She was too anxious to eat. It was because Marx was digging into her past. Not because he'd been close enough for her to realize how good he smelled. That freshly showered scent was still lingering around her, leaving her stomach swirling.

15

Sydria

Sydria sat in the middle of the royal sitting room, waiting for the queen mother and Princess Dannyn to arrive. She watched in silence as the giant wood ceiling fan circled, blowing a soft breeze over her.

"Sorry, I'm late," Dannyn called, rushing through the door.

Sydria jumped from surprise.

"I slept in," she explained as she plopped down on the couch.

Tardiness must be a family trait.

"Then I stopped by my mother's room, and I guess I stayed too long." She kicked off her shoes, tucking her legs under her.

Sydria looked at the door. "Isn't your mother joining us?"

Dannyn tugged at her dress, pulling it over her legs. "No, she said she has a headache."

Sydria's expression filled with concern. "Is she going to be okay?"

Dannyn swatted the air in front of her. "She's fine. In my opinion, she's kind of a hypochondriac. It's a recent thing."

"Oh."

The two women stared at each other for a moment. Without the queen mother, this meeting was going to be unbearable. What was Sydria going to say to a princess? She couldn't think of a single thing. Instead, she leaned forward, taking a sip of tea from her cup on the coffee table.

"You know, my brother really is a good guy," Dannyn said.

They were going to start right off with the marriage. Apparently, small talk wasn't necessary.

"I mean, he was a *better* guy before Palmer died, but we all were better back then."

Sydria held her teacup frozen in mid-air. Her muscles tensed. They were also going to jump right into the dead brother conversation. She had assumed something like that would be addressed in a couple of weeks.

A slight smile touched Dannyn's lips as she spoke. "Palmer was our brother. The youngest child. From day one, he was always my parents' favorite—the hero child. The attention my parents gave him bugged me, but not Marx. He adored Palmer, and the two of them were inseparable."

"What happened to him?"

"He died a year and a half ago. Right before the election."

Sydria lowered her cup to the table as she listened. She was glad Dannyn was telling her all of this. Everyone in the kingdom probably already knew, so it was good for her to be up to speed.

"Palmer was supposed to be king."

"Instead of Marx?" That surprised Sydria, especially since Marx was the oldest son.

"Oh, yes! That's what my father always wanted. Like I said, he was the hero child, but it was more than that. Palmer played better to the crowd. He wasn't reckless like Marx and me. His head was on straight, and being the king of Cristole was important to him. He'd already been campaigning before he died. Once he was gone, my father had to hurry and put forth Marx for the election."

"Why did you need someone from your family to become the monarch? Why couldn't you have ended your father's reign and moved on?"

Dannyn laughed. "It sounds pretentious, really, but when you're used to a certain lifestyle, used to royalty and the prestige that comes with that, you don't want to give it up."

"So Marx took his place in the election and became king?"

"Yes, even though he didn't want to. Palmer had always been the face of the royal family. The people loved him. He had so much charisma and natural leadership. Right before the election, my father sent him abroad to Albion for the infamous wedding."

Sydria had no clue what wedding Dannyn was talking about, but she didn't want to interrupt and ask questions yet. She wanted to know how the story ended.

"After that, he went to the kingdom of Appa to negotiate a trading deal. He traveled all over Cristole. The election was his."

"So what happened?"

Dannyn's expression dropped with her eyes. "Three weeks before the election, Palmer drowned. It shouldn't have happened—one of those freak accidents. Marx was with him. He did everything he could to save him."

Emotion filled Sydria's eyes. She didn't know if she was upset over the loss of Palmer or on Marx's behalf.

"Marx has had the hardest time dealing with the grief." Dannyn laughed to herself, which seemed like an odd reaction. "Or maybe I'm having the hardest time or my mother. Who knows at this point? All of us have been pretty screwed up since it happened."

"I'm so sorry for your family's loss." That was a terribly stupid thing to say in a moment like this, but Sydria didn't know what else to say.

Dannyn gave her a sad smile. "Thanks." She slapped her hands against her thighs. "So there you have it, the sordid details of the McKane family history. Have I scared you off?"

"No." Sydria shook her head. "At least you *have* a history."

"True, but all of my memories are tragic."

Sydria laughed. "They can't all be tragic."

"Some are good, I guess." Dannyn looked her over. "So you have no memory?"

"I remember some things. Small facts and details of life, but I don't remember anything related to me—what my family was like, what my personality traits are—it's weird how everything personal to me is gone."

"What do you think about all day if you don't have any memories?" Dannyn asked, clearly intrigued.

"I don't know. I suppose I make new memories and think about them. Or I think about how other people act and respond in situations, mostly wondering if that's how I should be behaving too."

Dannyn's smile changed to something sincere. She was no longer the free-spirited princess, but a vulnerable woman. "We can make new memories together. I'm in the market for a sister."

"So am I." Sydria smiled, and for a moment, the emptiness inside of her felt a little smaller, until she remembered that none of this was real. Dannyn wasn't really her sister.

"Perfect." Dannyn's genuine smile glowed. "We can trade clothes and talk about our love lives. I think that's what sisters do."

"Does that mean I can ask if Kase is your boyfriend?"

"Oh, Kase. He's trouble and definitely not good for me. It's a heartbreak waiting to happen."

"Then why do you let it continue?"

Her lips curled upward into a mischievous grin. "Some heartbreaks are worth it."

Sydria nodded, giving her a half-hearted smile. She didn't understand what Dannyn meant, but she hoped one day she would.

16

Marx

Marx pretended to read the most recent newswriter as he sat in a linen chair in the royal sitting room, but really his focus was on studying his mysterious wife across the room. Sydria stood on a platform that had been brought into the room along with three-paneled mirrors. The castle's wardrobe design team hovered around her, measuring her body. Marx wasn't stealing glances at her because she looked good with measuring tape held snugly around her waist. No, he was immune to his wife's attractiveness. Why? Because she wasn't really his wife. And he could not be attracted to his fake wife. Instead, he examined her like an investigator would an unsolved mystery. Her gaze shifted to him, and he jerked his head forward, zooming in on an article in the paper about the season's crop prediction.

Very fascinating stuff.

He glanced back at her, trying to convince himself that the article was more fascinating than the way Sydria smiled at Paula, the castle's seamstress, and her team as they brought out colorful fabric.

"This is gorgeous," Sydria said, pointing to a gold silk roll. "I think we should pair this fabric with the black sheer lace you showed me earlier. The dress should have a fitted bodice." Her hands went to her ribcage and carved down the curves of her body. "And with a slight mermaid bottom fanning out. That style would really work with this material."

"Your Majesty, that's an excellent idea," Paula said, taking notes while Sydria spoke.

"And what about chartreuse?" Sydria asked. "I haven't seen a fabric panel with chartreuse."

His brows pulled together, deepening the lines on his forehead. What did a working-class girl from Northland know about the color chartreuse or mermaid cut dresses? Had Sydria been some kind of fashion designer in her previous life?

"Your Majesty, your style and tastes are exquisite," Paula complimented.

Yes, they are. And, very expensive.

Sydria shrugged as she ran a finger down a pool of leather. "I've never seen fabrics like these before. We don't have them where I come from."

Marx's interest was piqued. He watched as the smile dropped from her face as if it had suddenly dawned on her that she didn't actually know where she'd come from. The more he saw of her, the more he knew she hadn't come from a poor family in Northland.

"And what about you, Your Majesty?" the seamstress asked, looking directly at him. "What clothing would you like to have made?"

Marx flipped the newswriter paper closed, leaning forward. "I'll take the usual, a fitted suit with a colorful tie." He stood and walked toward Sydria. "Give me something that matches what the queen has ordered."

Sydria smiled over her shoulder at him, and his stomach filled with butterflies.

What on earth was happening?

He'd only ever experienced butterflies doing something dangerous, jumping off the side of a cliff, surfing in the ocean.

"Which dress of the queen's would you like to match?" Paula asked.

"It doesn't matter, whichever dress she likes best."

Sydria reached for his arm, pulling him toward her.

The butterflies intensified.

Was this part of the pretend story?

Their bodies faced each other, splitting the small space on the rounded podium. Marx placed his hands softly on her hips for…*stability*. He didn't want to fall off the platform. Sydria was close enough for him to smell the hints of gardenia in her perfume and see the soft pink gloss coating her lips.

She turned her head, looking at their reflection. "You know, Paula, I think the king would look really good in a tapered pant."

He met her eyes through the mirror. "A tapered pant?"

"Trust me."

His gaze drifted to her shiny lips, hesitating a moment too long, then shifted up to her eyes. "I do trust you."

"The pants shouldn't be so tight that the king looks ridiculous," she said, looking at Paula, "but something fitted, and then what if the hem ended a little shorter and we matched his tie with a colorful patterned sock?"

"I love it!" Paula exclaimed as she furiously took notes.

Marx raised an eyebrow. "Where are you getting these ideas?"

She shrugged, and a little bit of the glimmer from her eyes was lost with the action, making him regret that he'd ever asked the question. "I don't really know, but I've seen it before in a picture. I think."

"Pictures haven't existed since Desolation," he said, watching her reaction.

She glanced behind him, lost in thought. "It must have been a pre-Desolation picture, then."

How would a working-class girl get a hold of a pre-Desolation picture?

She turned to the seamstress with a fake smile—the genuine one from moments ago was lost. "Thank you, Paula. I'm pleased with what we've come up with today."

Sydria stepped down from the podium, walking out of his grasp. Marx had never been so aware of the empty space around him as he was in that moment.

Paula tried to curtsy between her notepad and the swatches of fabric in her hand. "It's been our pleasure, Queen Sydria. These dresses should be ready in a few days." She turned to Marx. "Your Majesty, I also wanted to let you know that we've ordered the fabric for your clothing drive. With the money you donated, we were able to get enough fabric to clothe all of the families in the three poorest provinces—every family that said they were in need."

Marx scratched his ear, glancing quickly at Sydria. He preferred that she not hear about his clothing drive. The project meant a lot to him, but it would come across as vain to someone else—like he only cared about people in his kingdom looking good. It was too late to keep things under wraps. Sydria's eyes were fixed on him.

"Uh, thanks, Paula. That all sounds great."

Paula's eyes went serious. "What you're doing is really special, Your Majesty. Even if King McKane doesn't agree." She dipped again in front of them both and followed her team out the door.

"Well," Marx breathed as he stepped off the podium. "That was fun."

"What was Paula talking about?"

He pointed over his shoulder. "Oh, that? That was nothing."

Sydria's eyes dropped. "Sorry. I shouldn't have asked. It's not my place to know the workings of your kingdom."

Marx had somehow managed to hurt her feelings by trying to escape his own embarrassment.

"It's not that," he said. "I don't care if you know the workings of the kingdom." He rubbed the back of his neck. "I'm just a little embarrassed because it's not a big deal."

Her dark brows lifted, and her lips softened. "You're embarrassed? I didn't know kings get embarrassed."

Marx didn't *usually*, and he couldn't explain why he was now. He shoved his hands in his pockets, trying to exude confidence. "They don't."

She leaned back against the couch. Her hands rested behind her. "Then what's the project Paula talked about?"

He walked toward the table where he'd been reading. "Like I said, it's not a big deal." She lifted her eyebrow as if she wasn't going to stop asking until he told her. "I wanted to make sure every family in Cristole had access to a few colored clothing items." He pulled out the chair in front of him, sinking down into it.

"That sounds like a big deal to me."

"It's not."

"Why?"

"Other monarchs worry about solving hunger, or transportation issues, or detonating deadly weapons. I'm worried about colored clothes."

She dipped her chin, giving him a pointed stare. "I bet you're worried about more than colored clothes."

There was more to his project than colored clothes, but Marx wasn't going to tell her all the reasons. How do you tell your stranger-wife that your life isn't your own, that you long for the freedom to choose, and that those longings have led to the clothing drive?

"Looking good is kind of my thing, especially looking good in colored clothes," he deflected.

Sydria folded her arms across her chest. "I don't believe you. That's just a front you're putting up."

"A front?"

"Yes. What you say to hide your real motivations."

How did she do that? How did she see right through him?

He drummed his fingers on the table in front of him, feeling an overwhelming push to open up to her. "You're right. It's about more than looking good. It's about giving people the right to choose. Giving the working class more freedom to be who they want to be."

"I love that." Sydria smiled. "*That* makes your project a big deal."

Marx felt his embarrassment flare. "I don't know about that."

"Having the freedom to choose and be who you want to be is a big deal to me, even if it starts with something as simple as colored clothes. I don't know who I am, but I know that I don't want anyone else telling me who I have to be. What you're doing is amazing."

A slow warmth spread through Marx's chest. He hadn't experienced a feeling like that in a long time. Palmer had usually been the one to believe in him, see the underlying good, and make him feel like he had something important to offer. He had taken so much of Marx with him when he died.

"Thanks," he said. He scooted his chair into the table, ready to change the subject and the feelings burning inside his heart. "Now, then, do you have a list of memories for me?"

"I do." She walked to the side table and grabbed a small flowered notebook. "Idella gave me this book to write in." She smiled with pride as she looked down at the front cover like she'd never had a notebook of her own.

Marx shook his head. He couldn't quite figure her out.

She pulled out the seat next to him and sat down, opening the notebook to the first page, and began reading. "My name is Sydria Alyson Hasler. I'm twenty-one years old. My parent's names are—"

"Wait," Marx said, holding up his hand. "Is that stuff *you* remember or stuff you've been told?"

"Stuff I've been told."

"How do you know if it's true or not?"

"I guess I don't." Her countenance fell, and he hated it.

"Let's start with something you remember on your own. Something that no one has told you."

"Okay." She fidgeted with the pen that had been tucked inside the middle of her notebook. "My favorite food is a rack of lamb served with mustard shallot sauce."

"That's what you remember?" Marx couldn't help the amusement in his voice.

She nodded.

"You can't remember your name or anything about your life, but you remember mustard shallot sauce?"

Her dark eyes glared back at him. "Is there a problem?"

Marx tried to contain his laugh, he really did, but it came out despite his best efforts.

"Are you laughing at me?"

He covered his mouth with his hand, coughing the laughs away. "No."

Sydria bit her lip, trying not to smile, and an adorable crease appeared between her dark brows. She looked very appealing when she tried to be angry.

"Are you seriously making fun of someone with amnesia?"

He shook the remains of his laughter away. "I think you should know something about me before we go any further. I'm not a good person."

Sydria swatted him on the shoulder, but it was nice. He didn't have any complaints.

"You're not a bad person." She lifted her shoulders. "It *is* kind of funny."

"All right, let's continue on, and I promise I'll be on my best behavior," Marx said, gesturing for her to keep going. "What else do you remember?"

"Playing with dolls. There was always a prince and princess, and they would get married and live happily ever after."

"Do you remember anything about where you grew up? Was it snowy? Were there lakes? Mountains?" If she could remember a physical landmark, that might help pinpoint which kingdoms they should focus on.

"I see glimpses of it all. Water sloshing around, green fields, snow-capped mountains, cliffs on the edge of the ocean. I don't know what is real or what my mind made up." Moisture filled the brim of her eyes. "It's all very confusing."

Marx's chest collapsed. Was he pushing her too hard, too fast? He gave her a gentle smile. "I bet it is confusing. Don't worry, though. We'll figure it out." He placed his hand on top of hers. "Together."

She glanced down at their interlocked hands, causing Marx to jerk his away—nothing had ever moved so fast. Things had gotten too real. *He'd* let them get too real. "I have some things to do this afternoon." He abruptly stood. "I'll see you tonight at dinner."

Sydria looked up at him with hesitation. "Is there another party?"

"No, just dinner with my family. Although, that might actually be worse."

"Will Dannyn be there?" she asked.

"I assume so. Did your meeting with her earlier go well? I heard my mother didn't show up."

"It was just Dannyn, but I think it went well. I really liked her carefree personality."

"That's Dannyn for you." Marx paused for a moment. "Keep working on the things you remember, not the things someone told you."

She nodded her head. "I'll do my best."

17

Marx

Marx twisted his swivel chair back and forth as he stared out his office window. Green palm trees lined the yard leading out to the majestic ocean.

Elsbeth sat in the white chair on the other side of his desk, taking notes. "What if the cook doesn't have any lamb available for dinner tonight?"

Marx shifted his stare to his secretary. "Then he needs to find some. It's very important to the queen."

Her expression scrunched to displeasure. Usually, Marx didn't have an opinion on the menu at the castle.

"I didn't know Queen Malory even liked lamb."

He shook his head. "Not that queen. The *other* queen."

"And do we care what the *other* queen likes?" she asked.

"She's my wife, isn't she?"

Elsbeth narrowed her eyes. "Yesterday, you didn't want to marry her; today, you're planning a special dinner for her."

"What can I say? I'm a good husband." He gave his secretary his most charming smile.

"I don't know what you're up to, but I'll find out," she said, standing. "First, I've got to go talk to the cook."

"One other thing." He paused his swivels. "I want you to free all the sea life in the castle aquarium."

"Excuse me?"

Marx spoke slower as if that would help ease her shock. "I want you to free the fish—"

"I heard you the first time," she snapped.

"Then what's the problem?"

"We can't empty the aquarium. Where are we going to put all the fish?"

He gestured to the window. "How about the ocean?"

"Is this because of the *other* queen?" Elsbeth's stern glare made him feel like he was being punished for something.

"She has a name, you know."

"I'm aware," she said dryly. "Your father isn't going to like it."

He raised his eyebrows. "Her name?"

"The aquarium."

"This doesn't concern my father."

"Since when did you care about sea life?"

Marx brought his fingers to his chin as if he were really thinking over the timeline. "Since about four days ago."

Two knocks hit the door. "Your Majesty, you wanted to see me?" Kase stood outside his office.

"Yes," he said, leaning forward. "Elsbeth was just leaving."

His secretary scowled as she turned to go.

"Thank you, Elsbeth," Marx called after her. "You know you love me."

Kase turned over his shoulder, watching as she shut the door behind her. "I still don't understand why you chose such a grumpy secretary."

"Elsbeth? She's like a teddy bear."

"A grumpy teddy bear," Kase said under his breath. He took the seat she'd vacated.

"I found out the name and location of Sydria's uncle and

aunt," Marx said. "I want you to pay them a visit, see what you can find out."

"Whatever you want," Kase said.

It was time Marx found out more about his wife.

Sydria

King McKane stood at the head of the dinner table, raising his glass. The queen mother, Princess Dannyn, King Marx, and Sydria all stared back at him with their own glasses lifted. The golden bubbles inside each cup danced up to the top.

"I'd like to take a moment to officially welcome Sydria to dinner, to Cristole Castle, and to our family," Meldrum McKane said. He lifted his glass a little higher. "To Sydria!"

The others around the table repeated his sentiments. "To Sydria!" Then they each took a sip.

Sydria dropped her eyes. It was odd to suddenly be the center of attention, to have people toast to *her*.

McKane sat down in his chair, and immediately a team of servants placed plates of food in front of them. Each dish had a silver lid covering the top, preserving the heat from the meal inside. The head waiter nodded, and at the same time, each servant lifted the top off of his plate. A familiar smell wafted up to her as Sydria looked down—a rack of lamb drizzled with mustard shallot sauce.

"Dinner is served," the waiter said.

Sydria turned to Marx, but he was already watching for her reaction.

His eyes glowed with delight. "Wow, what a coincidence," he said.

She bit back her smile, not believing this was a coincidence even for a moment. The plan was to pretend like their marriage was going well, but a gesture like this was made *behind* the scenes. Its purpose didn't benefit their fake relationship.

"It smells delicious," the queen mother said.

Sydria picked up her fork and knife and cut a small piece of the tender meat. She swirled it around in the sauce and took a bite. Pepper, cream, and onion filled her tastebuds, bringing with it the feeling of excitement over a special occasion. It tasted as good as her mind remembered.

She had *remembered* something.

"How is it?" Marx asked.

"It's amazing."

"I'm glad you like it."

She looked deep into his hazel eyes, the light of the room bringing out the brown circle of his irises. "It's the sweetest thing ever."

It *was* the sweetest thing anyone had ever done for her.

He leaned in closer, whispering against her cheek. "Are we talking about the lamb right now?"

Her heart skipped a beat. "What else would we be talking about?"

Marx's easy smile grew as he leaned back to his spot.

"Sydria, we want to get to know you better," McKane said, pulling her from whatever moment she'd shared with Marx. "Although, we realize that might be a bit of a challenge for you, with your recent condition."

Marx's fingers closed into a fist, and he gave her an apologetic expression.

"Your memory might be gone, but I'm sure you still know your likes and dislikes," King McKane said.

That was the thing. Sydria didn't know what she liked or disliked. It felt like all of that had been erased with her memory. She'd lost her entire identity.

She swallowed. "I'm not really sure—"

"Come on, Dad. This is only Sydria's second night here.

Let's not bombard her with questions." Marx gave his father a pointed stare.

"Since we can't talk about Sydria," Dannyn said, "why don't we talk about Marx?" Her expression turned smug.

"Actually, I think we should talk about Dannyn." Marx exchanged a playful glare with his sister. "Did you know Dannyn used to kiss the walls?"

"I was like three years old," she defended.

"No, I think that lasted until you were about nine."

"Nine!" Dannyn exclaimed. "Do you know how old that is?" She looked at the queen mother. "Mom, help me out here."

"It did seem to last a while," her mother said with a grin.

Sydria laughed. "Why did you kiss the walls?"

Marx twisted in his chair so he faced her. "My sister liked to play pretend, and the walls were her prince charming."

Dannyn raised her shoulders. "Every princess needs a prince to kiss, and since there weren't any, I improvised."

"It was funny at first," Marx said.

Dannyn cut in, finishing his thought. "But then Palmer started doing it too. And that's when things got weird."

The entire family stiffened at the mention of Palmer.

Marx cleared his throat. "Palmer was my younger brother. He passed away a little over a year ago."

Sydria nodded, feeling the thick tension that had replaced the lighthearted story.

Dannyn shoved a bite of food in her mouth while simultaneously talking. "I already told her about Palmer," she said between chewing, "so everybody can relax. We don't need to go through all of that right now."

Relief colored Marx's expression. "Oh."

"It's not like Marx was some saint. I may have kissed the walls, but Marx destroyed the entire castle landscaping one summer," Dannyn said, bringing things back to normal.

"That's a bit of an exaggeration," Marx said as he relaxed into his seat again.

Dannyn ignored him, diving into the story. "Marx and Palmer found an old pre-Desolation stop sign. They spent the entire afternoon hammering a hole through the top of the metal. Then they got some rope from the castle garage and tied the stop sign to the back of Marx's horse."

"Why?" Sydria asked, looking between the two of them.

"They wanted to drag the sign around. They dragged that stop sign around the castle grounds, whacking trees and bushes, chopping off the heads of flowers." Dannyn looked at Marx. "Do you remember that?"

"I remember that Palmer blamed it all on me."

"I remember that too." The queen mother laughed. "You had to work that entire summer out in the garden to replant all the bushes you destroyed."

"While Palmer got to play all summer with his friends," Dannyn added.

"I don't recall Palmer being a part of that situation. I only remember Marx," King McKane said, glancing around the table.

Sydria noticed Marx's eyes drop.

"Oh, Palmer was definitely a part of it," Dannyn said, taking another bite of her food. "What other stories can I tell about Marx?" Her question prompted him to look up again and smile.

Sydria spent the next hour listening as Dannyn and Marx swapped stories from their childhood. She envied the way they could recall each memory so easily, like it had only happened yesterday. She didn't know how family dinners usually went for them, but there was a lightness in the air. A burden had been lifted off their family, for a moment, as they laughed and reminisced. Even Meldrum McKane seemed to be having a good time.

She looked around the dinner table, and all she saw was a

family, not royalty. A part of her wanted to slip into the role of a daughter-in-law, to allow these relationships to become her relationships. And if she wasn't careful, something like that could easily happen.

Family dinners with Von and Edmay hadn't been like this. Sydria felt more loved and wanted on day two with the McKane family than she ever had with her aunt and uncle. But despite all of that, Von had saved her life. Why would he do that if he didn't care for her even a little bit?

She needed to stay focused on remembering who she was, on finding the truth, and hopefully remembering whatever family she still had left.

If there were any.

Marx

"DINNER WAS FUN," Sydria said as they walked out of the castle and into the garden. The waves below seemed louder than usual, crashing against the rocks.

"Yeah," Marx said. "I thought so too."

His family hadn't had a dinner like that since Palmer had died, but somehow Sydria's presence had pieced them together again, even if it was only for a night.

They stopped at the balcony, looking down over the moonlit cliff.

"I'm sorry if my father made you feel uncomfortable about your memory."

"It's okay. I don't blame him. No one, including myself, knows what to do with a person who has no past. It makes getting to know me kind of hard." She turned to face him, the wind pulling strands from her dark hair and blowing them back from her face. "I wish there was someone I could ask, who could tell me everything I need to know about myself. What I like. What I don't like. The things that are unique about me."

"You don't need somebody to tell you all of that." He smiled back at her. "Just be the woman that you want to be. Like what you want to like."

She gripped the railing. "That's easier said than done."

"Why?"

"Shouldn't you take your own advice?" Her tone was flat.

"How so?" Her boldness amused him.

She brushed a lock of her hair behind her ear. "When we met on the beach, you said you were pretending."

"Oooh, look who's calling me out," he said, bumping her shoulder with his own.

"Shouldn't *you* be the man you want to be?"

"You got me there." He laughed.

"See," she said. "It's not that easy."

"Well, if you're looking for someone to tell you who you are, I'm the man for the job." He pushed off the railing and walked over to a stone bench on the other side of the balcony. The smell of flowers filled the air around him.

"What do you mean?" she asked as she watched him.

"I've got a great imagination." He patted the seat next to him, hoping she'd join him.

Slowly she walked over, sitting down on the edge. "What can your imagination do for me?"

"Let me show you." He sat up straighter, looking deep into her eyes in a playful way. "You are Sydria Alyson Hasler." He leaned in, whispering in her ear for dramatic effect. "Or so we've been told."

"You forgot McKane," she reminded him.

"Right. You are Sydria Alyson Hasler McKane. The queen of Cristole, married to the most charming and handsome man there ever was."

One dark brow lifted. "Is this going to be about you or me?"

"*You*," he dragged out the word, answering her question,

"have a soft spot in your heart for sea animals. You enjoy cumulus clouds."

She laughed. "Cumulus clouds? Really?"

"And brisk walks at dawn." She shook her head at his description. "You're passionate about passion fruit."

"I don't even know what passion fruit is."

"A rare delicacy," he whispered as a side note. "And you don't like green beans."

She crumpled her nose. "I hope there's more to me than that."

Marx swept his eyes across her face, and a rush of heat filled his chest. "You're honest. You mean what you say and say what you mean. You ask sincere questions. You're kind to others. You have these amazing convictions, and you stand up for what is right even if it isn't popular. You're beautiful, classy, and put-together." Sydria blinked back the emotion in her eyes and glanced away. "You get shy when you're the center of attention, but you can also shine in the middle of a crowd, lighting the room with your smile. And you bring out the best in people."

That was true for him. Sydria brought out the best in Marx, the way Palmer always had.

Her dark eyes shifted to his. "You've learned all that about me in a few days?"

Marx hadn't planned on saying anything like that. It had just come out.

His voice softened. "You're easy to know."

Sydria's hand went to her chest, rubbing the base of her neck. A strand of her black hair pressed against her lips. Marx slowly lifted his fingers, skimming them across her cheek. The touch of her smooth skin sent an eruption of chills down the length of his arm as he pulled the stray hair away from her lips and released it into the wind.

"It's actually split pea soup," she whispered between them.

"What?" he asked.

"I don't like split pea soup." Her lips donned a soft smile. "The verdict is still out on green beans."

"You'll have to let me know what you decide about them," he said, holding her gaze. Marx could see why Kase had been mesmerized. There was something about Sydria, about her eyes. A man could easily get lost in her beautiful, dark eyes. He couldn't let that happen to him. He'd learned from experience not to get too close to people. He usually ended up disappointing them. He stood, placing his hands in his pockets. It was time to flip into business mode.

He cleared his throat. "We need to talk about the next few days."

"What's happening in the next few days?"

"We have a lot of public events scheduled. There's a meeting with the newswriters to announce our marriage to all of Cristole. Dannyn is throwing us a party on the beach. My mom's planning a wedding reception for the ruling class. Things like that." He shrugged. "We need to sell this relationship at each of those events."

Sydria looked up at him. "What do I say to the newswriters?"

"I'll take care of it. Just defer all questions to me."

She nodded. "I understand. I'll be ready to pretend."

Marx was more than ready to pretend. For some reason, he looked forward to their game.

18

Doctor Von

"Nineteen, twenty, twenty-one." Von counted, raising the last vial of solution up to his eyes. "Twenty-one is an unlucky number." He breathed heavily, then kissed the small glass bottle for luck. He placed the bottle in his medicine box and fastened the lid shut, checking three times that it was closed tight. He looked around the empty bedroom that had been his home for the last three and a half months. He wouldn't miss the lumpy mattress, the stiff pillow, or the way he had to shimmy around the dresser to get to his side of the bed. The last nine months of his life had been the worst living conditions he'd ever had to suffer through, and it was all Commander Stoddard's fault.

He looked at the suitcase full of cash lying on top of the bed. He would recheck it, but he'd already counted it five times. The money was still all there. His problems would be solved now. He'd leave this cockroach-infested cottage and never look back.

"That's the last of it, besides my clothes," Edmay said as she walked into the room.

Pretending to be married to Edmay the last three months had been humiliating. A man as brilliant as him deserved privacy. Von couldn't stomach one more night sleeping in the same bed or house as his nurse, even if it wasn't real.

He swiped at the sweat on his bald head. He would never get used to the humid climate of Cristole. "I'll take these bags out to the wagon and wait for you out there." He picked up the suitcase on the bed, tucking his medicine box under his other arm. These were his last two items. The most important things he owned. They would be stored under his seat for the journey.

Before he could settle himself, he needed to drop Edmay off at her brother's house near the Appa border. He'd give her a cut of the money for her silence and be on his way. Von had run all the numbers in his head. He couldn't return to Albion or Tolsten. He might be recognized. Northland was too far away, and Cristole was too humid. The kingdom of Appa was his best option. He'd have to journey back to Cristole once or twice a year to supply Stoddard with more of Princess Seran's medicine, but he was sure he would be compensated for his work.

Von walked through the empty kitchen and out the door to the waiting wagon. He opened the bench and carefully placed his medicine box inside.

"Going somewhere?" a deep voice behind him asked.

Von startled, dropping his box the last three inches. The glass vials inside clanged together, but instead of checking if they were broken like he wanted to do, he turned to his visitor.

His hands trembled at the size of the man. Big muscles—an absolute brute. He didn't look like a Cristole guard. He wasn't wearing the typical navy uniform.

"Can I help you?" Von asked. He clenched the handle of his suitcase of money.

The man smiled as his eyes scanned the fully loaded wagon. "Are you leaving?"

Von slowly followed his gaze. It was evident that they had

packed up their belongings. There was a ninety-nine percent chance that the man couldn't be convinced otherwise.

"I am." He nodded, sending his glasses down his nose. His fingers lifted, pushing them back up.

The man reached his hand out. "I'm Kase Kendrick. I'm one of King Marx's guards."

Why was a guard here? Had Stoddard turned on him? Was he going to be taken to prison? Von calculated his chances for escape. On one side was nothing but flat ground and wide-open space. The other side was the ocean. He was trapped.

He licked his lips as he shook the guard's hand. "What do you want?"

Kase shrugged innocently. "King Marx sent me to invite you to the castle. He missed you at the wedding three days ago."

Von's heart rate sped up, pulsing through his neck. "Why would I be at the wedding?"

"Isn't Sydria Hasler your niece?"

"Yes." He'd answered too quickly. The guard was probably trained in detecting the facial twitches of liars.

"Aren't you the one who saved her life?"

He nodded again.

"Well, the king has some questions about her condition."

"What kind of questions?" Questions weren't part of Stoddard's plan.

"King Marx would like to know about Sydria's diagnosis and treatment."

"I would think her diagnosis was obvious. She has amnesia," he stammered.

"From a carriage accident?" Kase questioned, seemingly unconvinced.

"She must've hit her head."

"How long until her memory comes back?"

"The brain is a very complex organ." Von knew more

than anyone how complex the brain was. He'd put in a lot of effort to make sure the princess wouldn't remember anything. It was only a few months ago that he'd spent two weeks targeting her memories.

Von removed the IV drip he'd been using to keep the patient in a coma, replacing it with his new solution, the solution he'd named Isolated Amnesia. He'd purposely stopped the coma-inducing medicine forty-five minutes ago, and the patient was already starting to stir.

"Are you sure it's wise to take her out of her coma?" Stoddard asked. He looked at Nurse Edmay as if he needed her to confirm what Von had already explained to the commander. "What if she remembers us? Or this hotel room?"

"She won't." Von turned up the drip of the new drug to full capacity. "We'll block any memories she has."

Commander Stoddard nodded. "I'm trusting you, Von. If this doesn't work—"

"It will work," Von said. The truth was he didn't know if it would work. He'd done the math, researched what he could, but until he had a live patient, he wouldn't know for sure.

The loading phase of the drug was the most critical phase of all. This was when they could pinpoint memories to block. If they missed something during this time, Von wasn't sure they would be able to go back and redo it. This high concentration of a dose of the Isolated Amnesia drug might not be as effective again.

"Do you have the list of items?" Von asked.

Stoddard pulled out a folded paper from his pocket and held it up. "Tell me again, exactly what I'm supposed to do. I don't want to mess anything up."

"I'll do the first one so you can see." Von reached for the paper. He read the first item to himself and then leaned over the patient.

He jostled her arm, bringing her to more consciousness.

"Where am I?" she moaned.

Von got right in her face. "It's time to focus."

She lifted her eyelids open, barely able to keep them up.

"Who are you?" he asked.

She shook her head, thinking for a moment. "Seran."

"You're not Seran." Repeat it with me. "I'm not Seran Alyssa Haslet."

She waved her arm around, as if mesmerized by the needle sticking into the top of her hand.

"Focus," Von said again. "I'm not Seran Alyssa Haslet."

She squeezed her eyes tight then opened them again, looking back at him. "I'm not Seran Alyssa Haslet." Her words came out slurred, but it didn't matter. All that mattered was what happened inside her brain—that the thought 'Seran Alyssa Haslet' and the memories associated with it were piqued so that the drug could find the neuron connection and block it.

"Say it again," he said.

"I'm not Seran Alyssa Haslet."

"Good." He looked at Commander Stoddard, handing him back his paper. "You do the next one."

Stoddard's eyes were wide with worry. "This is going to take forever. How are we going to keep her subdued?"

"Don't worry about that. The new drug keeps her in a foggy state."

"What if we forget something?" Stoddard asked.

"I would say we err toward blocking more memories rather than less." Von nodded toward the paper. "Let's keep going while the drug is flowing."

Stoddard stood. He leaned over the patient, getting close to her face like Von had shown. "You are not the princess of New Hope," he said. "Repeat it with me. I am not the princess of New Hope."

The patient rolled her head around. "I am not the princess of New Hope."

Von looked at the guard standing next to the wagon. "In my professional opinion, her memory may never come back."

"Is there anything King Marx can do to help?" Kase asked.

He shook his head. "Right now, the only thing that can help is the medicine I left with Sydria. She must continue to take that for her heart. She suffered a significant puncture to her aorta. The medicine keeps her heart pumping and prevents blood clots."

Edmay walked out of the cottage holding her last suitcase. She stopped when she saw the guard and shot a concerned look at Von, but if they found any trouble, he would only be saving himself.

"If that's all the questions you have, we've got to get on the road. We have a long journey ahead of us."

"Sure," Kase said, stepping back from the wagon. "Do you have any intention of staying in touch with Sydria?"

"Of course. She's our niece," Von snapped, eager to leave.

"But just in case we need to get a hold of you, if Queen Sydria has a medical emergency or something, where will you be staying?" Kase asked.

"We're going west for a few weeks to Calicristole." His face twitched, and he wondered how good this guard was. Could he tell that Von had told another lie?

The guard smiled, the kind of smile that said he was trained in lie detection. "Enjoy your trip." He turned and walked to his personal transporter parked to the side of the cottage.

Dust swirled into the air as he sped away.

"What was that about?" Edmay asked as she stepped closer.

"King Marx is on to us." Von quickly put the suitcase on top of his medicine box and closed the bench seat, looking at his nurse. "We need to get out of here immediately."

19

Sydria

Sydria waited in the open-air suspended hallway for King Marx to escort her to the newswriter's interview. When she'd first arrived, she'd thought the outdoor hallway was strange, but the longer she lived there, the more she loved the unique features of Cristole Castle.

She watched a red bird pick at a leaf on a tree, wishing the meeting with the newswriter was already over, but it hadn't even started yet. Her body temperature rose. She should probably walk back inside, get out of the summer heat, but the sound of the waves down below comforted her thrumming heart.

Maybe the interview wouldn't be so bad with Marx by her side. Lately, he seemed to make everything better.

She turned to the sound of footsteps approaching.

"Sorry I'm late," Marx said, joining her in the middle of the bridge.

"I'm getting used to it."

He reached out to her like he might kiss her cheek. Their heads tilted back and forth for a moment, neither one of them sure which direction they should go, until he settled on an awkward arm squeeze.

Sydria hoped they wouldn't be that awkward in front of the newswriter.

Marx looked out over the garden to the ocean. "You know, this outdoor hallway is my favorite part of Cristole Castle."

"I like it too."

He smirked. "I always thought it would be a great place to kiss a beautiful woman."

A puff of air broke through her lips. "Uh…"

"Don't worry. I wasn't talking about right now. We can't even get a simple kiss on the cheek right."

She laughed, grateful for the way he eased the tension between them.

"Shall we?" he asked, offering her his arm the way he always did.

Sydria slipped her hand through, walking with him. She liked the way the side of his body pressed against hers as they moved together.

"You're nervous," he said. "I can tell."

"I'm a little nervous," she eyed him, "but I'm up for the challenge."

"Is it a challenge to act like you're falling in love with me?" There was an amused look in his eyes.

Not as big of a challenge as I thought.

"We'll find out." She grinned playfully, hoping to cover up her real answer.

"You have nothing to worry about. Remember, just defer all the questions to me."

They entered the royal sitting room, and a thin woman with auburn hair stood from her place on one of the couches. She curtsied. "Your Majesties."

Marx placed his hand on the small of Sydria's back, guiding her forward. The complexity of his simple touch was astonishing. The gesture went a long way to calm her nerves, but tangled her insides at the same time.

"Thank you so much for your time today. My name is Foys

Kaufman. I've met King Marx before," the woman said, speaking to Sydria, "but I haven't had the pleasure of meeting our new queen."

Sydria smiled at the newswriter as she took her seat.

"Isn't that the purpose of the interview?" Marx asked. He dropped into the cushion next to her, his hip touching hers, and he lifted his arm, resting it on the back of the couch.

Resting it *on* Sydria's shoulder, to be exact.

She did her best to ignore the sensations rippling through her body, but it was hard. Marx had a way of making sitting on couch look attractive. She felt every bit of his attractiveness, from his arm on her shoulder to his hip pressed against hers.

"First of all," the newswriter said, taking her own seat. "I want to congratulate the both of you on your marriage."

"Thank you," they said in unison.

"We were a bit surprised when Elsbeth sent the note about it," Foys explained.

Sydria gave an overdone nod in agreement, not having the faintest idea who Elsbeth was.

"I like to keep the newswriters on a need-to-know basis," Marx said.

"So this was a planned wedding?" Foys asked.

Sydria looked at Marx, deferring to him like it was her profession. That was the plan.

"Of course." He pulled his lips into a hollow smile, the one she'd seen him use with his friends on the beach the night they'd first met.

Foys scribbled something on her notepad. "Did you marry for love, or was this an arranged marriage?"

"Marriage shouldn't be a business transaction," he replied coolly.

That was an excellent answer. Marx seemed so calm and collected, as if the weight of the newswriter's questions couldn't affect him.

"Queen Sydria, the entire kingdom is wondering who you are," Foys said.

"Aren't we all?" Marx smiled back at the newswriter with so much sarcasm, Sydria almost laughed out loud.

"Tell us about yourself. Who is Queen Sydria?" Foys's eyes were fixed on her.

The room seemed to get warmer, and the rhythmic ticking of the ceiling fan above hummed deep in her ears.

Who is Queen Sydria?

Defer to Marx.

The fan got louder, pulsing in her ears, and her hands felt clammy even though they were resting in her lap.

"I love cumulus clouds!" she blurted with more excitement than the situation called for.

Marx turned his head to her. Amusement carried through his eyes as he dared her to continue.

Cumulus clouds? Why didn't I stick to the plan?

She looked at Foys, who seemed confused with her answer, so Sydria pasted on her showman's smile, trying to smooth things over. "Rather, I studied meteorology in Northland. Where I'm from."

Foys leaned forward. "Meteorology?"

She lifted her chin. "Yes, you know weather patterns. And clouds. Nimbus. Cirrus—"

"And, of course your favorite…cumulus." Marx smiled with a glint so goading she couldn't stop now.

"Yes, they are my favortie." Her playful expression matched his. "How could I ever forget about cumulus?"

Foys nodded. "Did you study anything else besides meteorology?"

"Education and politics." The answer rolled off her tongue easily as the image of a post-Desolation map of all seven kingdoms shot through her mind. It was quick, too quick for her to find the meaning behind it.

"What else can you tell me about yourself?" the newswriter asked.

Sydria's smile faltered as she tried to make sense of whether she'd experienced a real memory. "I…uh…"

Marx grabbed her hand with his free hand, letting their fingers intertwine. "Sydria has a soft place in her heart for sea life."

"You've come to the right kingdom, then." Foys smiled.

The spontaneous handholding set Sydria back. Her thoughts were on the warmth behind Marx's touch, but she managed to turn to the newswriter. "Yes, it appears so."

Foys looked between them. "And how did you two meet?"

"I'd like to answer this one." Marx closed his hand around Sydria's shoulder, snuggling her in closer.

She tried not to let the king's nearness break her, but his touch and his minty smell made it hard for her to concentrate.

"I'd had a terrible day," Marx began. "There was a lot on my mind, so I took a walk down the beach. When I got to the end, I saw a woman standing on the edge of the rocks. Her black hair was wet and blowing in the wind behind her. She wore a simple lavender dress, but no one had ever looked so elegant before."

Sydria's eyes slowly drifted across the side of Marx's face as he spoke. She studied every smooth angle of his features and the different shades in his light stubble; the golden complexion that painted his skin screamed of summertime. His usually unruly hair was styled in a messy but purposeful way. His voice rumbled against her arm as he spoke, filling the space between them, and Sydria heard *every* word.

"I didn't know what she was doing there, but I knew I needed to find out. I walked toward her, scared that she wasn't real but excited that she actually might be. When she turned around, her dark eyes captured me. I felt her stare in every beat of my heart. It was different from anything I'd ever felt before."

Foys leaned into his story, captivated by the words he spoke. If she leaned another inch closer, she would have fallen off the chair. "What happened next?" she asked.

Marx slowly turned his head, meeting Sydria's gaze. His eyes were a mixture of greens and browns and held an intensity she'd never witnessed before.

"She saw right through me," he said. "To the *real* me, and I knew I'd never be the same again."

Sydria swallowed. The warmth from his body, from his hand, from his words, filled her frozen mind. She was certain she'd never heard anything so beautiful in her entire life even if she *could* remember everything. His words were branded into her heart—it didn't matter if her mind kept them or not.

Foys melted into her chair, sighing with contentment. "That's a romantic story."

Marx held Sydria's gaze.

That was a story, Sydria reminded herself.

Marx was a good storyteller.

That was what he did.

He pretended—gave everyone the version of himself that he thought they wanted. He gave the newswriter the smitten king she'd expected. Someday, when Marx was actually in love, he'd be great at it.

And Sydria could only hope that someday, someone would say something half so lovely about her and actually mean it.

"Anything else you'd like to know?" Marx asked, turning back to Foys.

The newswriter asked a few more questions about how Sydria fit in with the royal family, their plans for the future, and if they had any policies they wanted to implement. Sydria sat silent. She smiled and nodded when she was supposed to, but mostly she let Marx do the talking. She didn't mind the questions. She liked being nestled against Marx.

"See, that wasn't so bad," he said as they walked down the

hall after the interview was over. "I thought you handled the questions like a professional."

She inclined her head. "Except now, all of Cristole will think I am an expert on the weather."

"That's your fault. You went rogue on that one."

"I panicked and said what you said yesterday."

"Look at the bright side. The weather in Cristole is always the same, hot with a few rainstorms mixed in. Anyone can be an expert on that."

Sydria looked away, curbing her smile.

"Your Majesty?" An older woman with stiff features and equally stiff posture rushed toward them. "There's a meeting scheduled with the transportation department starting in five minutes. Will you be attending, or shall I tell your father—"

"Thank you, Elsbeth." Marx stopped the woman.

So that was the Elsbeth the newswriter had mentioned. She must be the king's secretary.

He glanced at Sydria, and it was almost like he was embarrassed again before shifting his focus to the woman. "I would love to attend the meeting."

Elsbeth's eyes tightened. "Really?"

"Yes, really." Marx ushered his secretary forward. "We'd better go if we want to be on time."

"And do we want to be on time?" Elsbeth asked, her tone dry.

"I love punctuality," he exclaimed, looking over his shoulder at Sydria. "I'll see you later."

Sydria couldn't help but smile as she walked down the hall in the opposite direction. She crossed through the foyer, glancing at a maid cleaning the front of the giant windows on the other end. Sydria had lived at Cristole Castle for three days and still hadn't looked out the beautiful windows. She moved closer, peering outside to a direct view of the castle aquarium. She'd seen the glass cylinder from the greeting room the first day she'd arrived. But the foyer's vantage point provided a better view.

A team of six men and women stood around the glass container with hoses, nets, and smaller glass boxes. Sydria watched as a man carefully lifted a rainbow colored fish from the tank and placed it into a small container.

"What are they doing?" she asked the nearby maid, her eyes never leaving the scene below.

"King Marx ordered that the aquarium be emptied," the woman said.

Sydria's lips parted as she turned to look at the maid. "Why?"

The woman paused her cleaning long enough to look at her and shrug. "He wanted to set them free."

Her breath caught in the back of her throat, and she blinked slowly as she replayed the words in her head.

He wanted to set them *free*.

20

Marx

Marx looked down at the turquoise water fifty-five feet below him. The two-foot waves looked more like ripples from his vantage point. He'd come out to the cliffs early that morning to get away from the thoughts inside his head, to relax. The last four days since his wedding had been full of appointments, interviews, meetings. He didn't know what it was about marriage, but all of a sudden, he'd gone from careless to responsible. It was exhausting and, if he was honest, a little satisfying.

He repositioned his feet on the edge of the cliff, soaking in the anticipation before the jump. The sun beat down on his head and chest, mixing with the warm summer breeze. Sweat trickled between the muscles on his back as adrenaline coursed through his veins.

One.

Two.

Jump.

He dove forward, feeling the heavy wind against his body as he fell. His arms went above his head, creating a straight line from the tips of his fingers down to his toes. Excitement pulled inside his stomach as he dropped. He hit the water, the weight of it filling his ears and pressing against his back. His mind flashed to Palmer. Was that how his brother had felt—overpowered by liquid? He kicked his legs, forcing his body back up to the surface. Marx's head popped up into the air, and he sucked in a breath.

"You're crazy!" Kase's voice called to him.

He turned over his shoulder, seeing his friend standing on the beach. He flipped to his stomach and swam to the shore. When the water was shallow, he stood, sloshing through the swells.

"I've always hated heights." Kase looked up at the cliff Marx had jumped from.

"How did you know where I was?"

"Louden told me."

Marx puffed out a laugh. "Of course he did." Louden wouldn't give Marx a personal transporter to drive unless he promised he wasn't taking it racing. He'd barely fixed the hydraulics on the machines they'd taken out the other day.

He walked to where Kase leaned against a rock and laid down on the hot beach. Gritty sand stuck to the back of his body as his arms spread out wide. He closed his eyes, letting the scorching sun dry him off.

"I found out some things about your wife's family that I thought you might be interested in," Kase said.

Marx opened his eyes, squinting against the light. He hadn't seen Sydria since the newswriter's interview the day before. He wasn't avoiding her or the feelings she created inside of him. He'd just been busy. "What did you find out?"

"For starters, her aunt and uncle left town."

The lines on Marx's forehead creased. "For good?"

"It looked like it."

"Why would they leave when their niece lives only a few miles away from them?"

"I don't know, but I spoke with the owner of the cottage. Her uncle made no plans to return. They've only been renting that place for the past three months. Before that, I'm not sure where they were."

"Three months?" Marx sat up, placing his hands on his thighs. "Isn't that when Sydria's accident happened?"

Kase nodded.

"If she was critically injured, how were they able to move her to a new house?" Marx asked, thinking out loud.

"I don't think they could."

He looked at Kase. "Unless the accident happened right after they moved here."

"Possibly. But there's something else. Sydria's uncle, Von Nealman, was not the person who rented the house or paid for it. It was someone by the name of Otis Sutton."

"Otis Sutton?" Marx questioned. "Who's that?"

Kase shrugged. "Don't know, but I do know that there isn't a single record in Cristole that has Otis Sutton or Von and Edmay Nealman on it."

"So they're from another kingdom?" Marx had already guessed that much.

"Or they used made-up names."

Marx fidgeted with his lips as he thought, trying to make sense of the information.

"Remember the two men we saw coming out of the front of the castle the day of the wedding?" Kase asked. "Well, the first man was definitely Von Nealman."

"Maybe the second guy was Otis Sutton," Marx offered.

"I've seen the other guy somewhere before, but I don't recognize the name, Otis Sutton." Kase shook his head. "For some reason, I can't place where I've seen him."

"I'm sure it will come to you." Marx stood, brushing off the sand from his skin. "Keep digging into the uncle and the aunt, and I'll work on Sydria, see if I can get any clues from her on who this Otis guy is."

The two men began walking down the beach, side by side.

"When you talk to Sydria," Kase said, "ask her about the medicine she takes."

This was the first time Marx had heard of medicine. "What are you talking about? Why does she need medicine?" His voice came out harsh, and a panicky feeling pinched his heart.

"Geez, buddy. Calm down." Kase laughed. "It's something Von mentioned when I went to visit him. He said that Sydria needed to keep taking her medicine so that her heart would work properly."

Marx rubbed his face, hating the thought of Sydria with a broken heart…a literal broken heart. Not the kind that he typically caused in his family. "Okay, I'll ask her about that." They walked a few more feet before he added, "And maybe I will have the castle doctor take a look at her to make sure she's okay." He could feel his friend's eyes on him.

"Whatever you say." There was a laughter behind Kase's remark that bugged him.

The only reason Marx was so invested in Sydria was so that he could figure out who she was and send her back home. Then they could both escape the arranged marriage and move on with their lives the way they each wanted to.

That was the only reason—the only reason he was willing to admit to.

Sydria

Sydria opened the double doors to the balcony in her room and stepped outside, feeling the windless summer heat. White glittering stars dotted the night sky above her, and the sound of waves lulled her to a brief moment of peace. She peered out into the blackness. The ocean was dark, like her mind. She wrapped her arms around her stomach, tucking her hurts inside—the emptiness, the loneliness, the forgotten happiness.

"Looks like you had the same idea as me."

Sydria turned to her left. She hadn't noticed Marx when she'd walked outside. His balcony mirrored hers in size and shape. He wore a pair of cotton shorts and a plain white t-shirt. His hair looked damp from a shower, and his face was clean shaven. She hadn't seen him all day and had decided he must only want to see her when they were in public and could play out their fake relationship in front of people.

"King Marx, sorry if I disturbed you." She turned to go.

"Hold on," he said. "We're married. Remember? That means you can't call me *King* Marx."

"You're right," she said, glad that he didn't like the formality.

"Do you want some company?" he asked.

She pulled at the side of her silk robe, making sure it covered her nightgown and, more importantly, her scar. "Sure. I'll go unlock my door."

"There's no need," Marx said. He climbed up on the edge of the railing.

"What are you doing?" Sydria panicked. There were six feet between their two balconies and three stories to the cement ground below.

He balanced on the twelve inches of stone that capped the railing. "I'm going to jump across."

Her hands went out to stop him. "Are you crazy? You'll get hurt."

"You don't think I can make it?" His lips pulled into a cocky smile.

"I don't think you should try. What if you're overconfident in your abilities?"

"I know my strengths."

Sydria shook her head. She didn't like taking risks.

Marx lifted a brow. "Ready? One. Two. Three!"

She covered her eyes with her hands as he leaped across, hearing his feet land hard on her balcony, or maybe that was his body landing on the cement below. It was hard to tell, especially when her mind liked to imagine the worst.

There was silence.

"Are you dead?" she asked, keeping her eyes shut. If his body was splattered on the ground, she didn't want to see it. She had so few memories. Something like that would take up way too much space in her mind.

"You can open your eyes now," he whispered. His warm hands were on hers, pulling them away from her face.

Marx stood in front of her. His closeness stalled her breath, countering her quickened heart.

"I can't believe you did that," she breathed out.

"I do a lot of things you wouldn't believe."

They stared at each other, and Sydria began to wonder why they always found themselves in such close proximity, gazing into each other's eyes, when no one was around.

Marx broke the spell first, peeking his head into her room. "How do you like the place?" He stepped inside, and Sydria quickly followed, not sure what she was so nervous about. It wasn't like she had a secret diary lying open on her bed.

"I love it. It's a beautiful room." She fidgeted with her robe as she watched him glance around.

"I haven't been in here since my mother moved out," he said, turning to her.

"This was your mother's room?" Now she felt guilty that she'd been staying there. She didn't know why. It wasn't like Sydria was the one who had chosen which room to put her in.

"Well, her stuff was in here, but she always stayed next door with my father."

"Oh." Sydria felt the exact pattern of her blush as it crawled up her cheeks.

Marx must've noticed because his eyes sparked with amusement.

"I haven't seen you around," she said, trying to change the subject.

"Did you miss me?" There was enough seriousness in his expression that she didn't know if he was joking or not.

She smoothed the back of her hair. "I just want to make sure I'm fulfilling my end of the agreement. Am I playing the part of an in-love newlywed enough?"

"I see." He nodded, but she thought she saw a flash of disappointment in his eyes.

"Did you have a good day?" she asked.

He stared at her for a moment, and Sydria wished she knew what was hidden behind his veiled expression. "It's better now."

Marx spun around, walking farther into the room. He stopped at the vanity, looking over the items left out. He glanced back at her as he picked up the orange vial containing the medicine her uncle had given her. "What's this?"

"Medicine for my heart." Part of her wanted to snatch the bottle out of his hand and shove it under her pillow. It was silly. Taking medicine didn't make her a weak person, but for some reason, she was embarrassed.

He twisted off the top and lifted the dropper out, smelling the liquid inside. "Do you take this every day?"

"Yes."

"What happens when you run out?"

Sydria shrugged. "My uncle said he'd bring me more."

She watched as he put the lid back on and set the vial down on the vanity. "I've been looking into your uncle and your background."

"And?" she asked, eager to find out something new about herself.

He leaned against the desk, crossing his feet out in front of him. "Who is Otis Sutton?"

"I don't really know. They told me he's a friend of my uncle's. He visited the cottage every once in a while. And," she hesitated, "he stood to gain something from this marriage."

"I think he's somehow involved in your past too."

She let out a long sigh and walked to her bed, sitting down on the edge of the mattress.

"What's the matter?"

She looked at him, unsure if she would be able to explain her thoughts. "I was hoping I would have a simple past, that the pieces would come together easily, that every suspicion I've been feeling was just me being paranoid, but if Otis is involved, then nothing is simple."

"He may not be involved. It's a hunch right now."

Sydria glanced down at her hands. "The day before the wedding, I heard Otis talking with my uncle and aunt. He said that if they lost me, they would all be ruined. Then my uncle said he didn't want to do this anymore, but Otis threatened to destroy him if he didn't continue." She looked up at Marx, not sure what his response would be. "It all sounds so ridiculous. Perhaps I misheard."

"Don't do that." He straightened. "Don't doubt yourself. You're stronger and smarter than you think."

"You are the only person…" Sydria bit her lip. There was a gentleness in his eyes that got her every time.

"I'm the only person who…?" he prompted.

"You are the only person who treats me like there's more to me than a broken memory."

"Because there *is* more to you than a broken memory. Soon you'll see it too."

Sydria was almost scared to see it, to find out what kind of life was hidden inside of her. What if she didn't like the person she was or the life that she'd had?

"Well," Marx clapped. "I think I've taken up enough of your time. I should probably let you sleep." He turned to go back out the balcony.

"Why don't you go through the door?" she said, standing.

"My side is locked."

"You could always go through the front door of both our rooms."

"And have the guards see me leave your room?" He shook his head. "No. I would rather keep them guessing about what's going on in here."

"I don't know. It could help our cause if they thought you were leaving my room late at night."

His lips spread into a tilted smile. "I think me *staying* would help our cause more."

There was a part of her that wanted him to stay, just for the company. Sydria liked how she felt around Marx, liked the confidence he gave her, but him staying would further complicate their already complicated situation.

"I think not," she said with a playful smile.

"In that case, I'd better hop on over to my side. Good night, Sydria," he said as he ducked out of the room.

"Don't kill yourself when you jump back to your balcony."

"I won't." He popped his head back into the room for a moment. "My wife would miss me too much."

Sydria laughed.

She *would* miss him.

21

Sydria

After dinner the next night, the royal family gathered in the sitting room to play dice. Sydria was getting used to the McKane family and how good it felt to be part of something bigger than herself. She wondered if her own family had sat around like this, talking and playing games. It seemed like a regular thing, something that she should be able to remember.

What was wrong with her? Why wasn't she stronger than this? Why couldn't her mind drive through whatever blocked it and get to the other side?

Marx looked at her and raised his eyebrows, code for *are you all right?* Sydria pushed a smile onto her lips and nodded back at him.

"Marx," Queen Malory said, scraping the dice off the table and into her hands. "I've been meaning to talk to you about something."

"Okay." Marx leaned into the table, resting his cheek against his fist.

"What's wrong with the aquarium?" his mother asked. "Is it broken?"

Sydria eyed him. They hadn't had a chance to talk about it yet, and she'd forgotten to bring it up the night before when he had been in her room.

"Uh…" He straightened, releasing his arm out in front of him. "No. I had it emptied."

"Emptied?" King McKane scoffed. "Why on earth did you do that? Where did you put all the fish?"

"The ocean," Marx said. "Where they belong."

His mother dropped the dice onto the table, and every face went to his as they clanged around.

"You put them back in the ocean?" His father's voice rose. This was the exact reaction Sydria had been afraid of the day they'd met. "Why do you always do things like this? Do you have any idea what it took to gather and hold all of those fish?"

"I have a pretty good idea," Marx answered, avoiding Sydria's panicked eyes.

"I loved those fish," the queen mother said.

Dannyn picked up the dice and shook them in her hand. "Mother, you don't even pay attention to them."

Queen Malory frowned. "Yes, but I know they're there, all colorful and bright."

"I'm sure you'll get over the fact that they're gone," Marx muttered.

"What am I going to do with that space? It's the central focal point of the windows in the foyer."

"I'm sure you'll think of something," Marx said as he watched Dannyn take her turn.

"I don't understand why you would do something like that," King McKane huffed.

Marx glanced at Sydria. Was he going to tell his father that it had all been her idea? "I just wanted to do it."

"That's it?" King McKane snapped.

"Yeah, that's it." Marx looked at his father. "Someone told

me that it's cruel to keep wild sea animals in a box, and so I set them free."

King McKane glanced quickly at Sydria. He was on to them. He had to be guessing that *someone* was her. She braced herself, trying to come up with a rebuttal.

"I suppose that's your choice, then," his father said, dropping the subject.

It seemed odd that the second the king found out that it was Sydria's idea, he was no longer angry. But Queen Malory wasn't over it quite yet.

"Why is it cruel?" his mother asked. "We were enjoying them."

"Yeah, but do the fish enjoy it?" Dannyn asked.

The queen mother sighed. "I hate to have an empty aquarium sitting there. It's such an eyesore."

"Make it a solarium," Dannyn suggested.

Marx took his turn with the dice. "Better yet, a planetarium."

Dannyn smiled back at her brother. "An honorarium."

"No, a terrarium," Marx said.

Queen Malory beamed with excitement. "A terrarium! Sydria, you know about that."

"I do?"

"Yes, I read about it in the newswriter article. You studied...clouds." The queen mother frowned. "Oh, I guess it's not the same thing."

Marx shook his head. "Nope."

"Yes, a terrarium with butterflies," the queen mother said.

"Butterflies?" King McKane questioned. "I don't think we want to spend our money or energy on that."

"You don't have to. I will." She sat up in her seat. "I will, and Sydria can help me with the plants and butterflies."

She frowned. "I don't know anything about plants or butterflies."

"Sure you do. You know about the weather, so you'll be fine," the queen mother said, patting her arm. "We'll get started on the terrarium tomorrow."

Sydria looked at Marx for some help. He wasn't even trying to hide his smile.

22

Sydria

The next afternoon was the first big event since Sydria had married Marx. Queen Malory called it their wedding reception for the people who weren't their close friends. Party invitations had been extended out to the ruling class families in the surrounding provinces.

Sydria chose her new chartreuse dress to wear. It had a square neck and cap sleeves. The bodice was fitted, and the length ended below her knees. She'd always loved the way the bright color had complemented her dark hair and tanned skin. Could she count that as a memory?

The top and sides of her hair were slicked back around her ears, letting the black strands fall straight down her back. She completed the look with dangling sapphire earrings and a sapphire pendant.

It was showtime.

Sydria knocked on the door between Marx's suite and her own. Elsbeth opened the door, and Sydria gave the rigid woman a hesitant smile. Then her eyes darted to Marx across the room. He wore the fitted blue suit pants that Sydria had designed. The color matched her sapphire earrings, and the hem was shorter than normal, showing off the chartreuse socks that went with his chartreuse tie. He looked beyond handsome, and the fact that he'd worn what she'd picked out —trusted her in that way—made her heart skip with excitement.

Marx stood there, finishing the button on his cuff. But when he looked up, his movements paused. His lips parted as his eyes slowly glanced down her body and back up.

Then they closed—briefly.

There was a slight shake of his head, so slight that Sydria wasn't even sure it had happened. He opened his eyes, finding her once again.

"You look…uh." Marx was more rattled than Sydria had ever seen him. He cleared his throat. "You look incredible."

"Thank you," she said, biting her lip.

Marx's fingers went to his brow, rubbing it once before going back to the button that he couldn't seem to get fastened. He held his arm up. "Uh, Elsbeth, do you think you could get this buttoned for me? I can't seem to—"

"Focus?" his secretary cut in.

His hand went to his brow again, and he shook his head, letting out a rough laugh. "Thank you, Elsbeth, for finishing my sentences. Once again, you've proven your value. Now, could you come button this for me?"

Sydria shrugged. "I'll do it." She walked over to him. His fresh mint smell floated between them, and his hazel eyes drew her in.

He held his forearm up for her. Perhaps volunteering was a bad idea. She wasn't sure if she could steady her trembling hands long enough to actually complete the job. She tightened her fingers into fists before lifting them to the button.

Marx leaned toward her, still pulling her in with his gaze as his mouth slipped into a playful smile. "You are stunning to the point of distraction."

She knew the feeling.

Her fingers pulled the button through the small slit, and

she stepped back. "All done," she said, clearing her throat as she tried not to let his words go to her head. After all, he had to convince his secretary he was enamored with her.

He stuck out his leg, showing her his pants. "What do you think of my new suit?"

She smiled. "I really like it."

Who wouldn't when he was the one wearing it?

"What do you think?" she asked.

"It grows on me more each day." The serious look in his eyes made Sydria think he was no longer talking about his clothes.

"Are you ready for this?" he asked.

She raised her shoulder. "I think so."

"You're going to do great." He offered her his arm. "Shall we?"

Sydria wrapped her hand through as Elsbeth opened the door for them. They walked down the hall, and it wasn't long until the soft sound of violin music floated up to them, growing stronger as they approached the ballroom.

"Is the party not outside?" she asked.

"Nah, it's too hot."

She nodded as they rounded the corner to the ballroom. "Do you have any advice about how to handle the situation or the guests?" she asked, feeling her nerves grow stronger.

"High Ruler Bates has a wandering eye," he said in complete seriousness.

"Oh, like he cheats on his wife?"

Marx turned to her. "No, like one of his eyes doesn't follow the other. I never know where to look, so I keep to the center of his forehead."

They reached the top of the stairs, and hundreds of heads turned to face them.

"That's your advice? To look in the middle of some man's forehead?"

Marx smiled big, the smile that Sydria rarely got to see.

Marx

MARX'S ATTENTION TURNED to the room full of people below them as the herald boomed out. "Introducing His Majesty…"

"I like to start walking down the stairs as he's announcing," Sydria said, pulling him forward to the first step. "It cuts the time that people stare at us in half."

Marx gave Sydria a sideways glance. How would she know something like that? But now wasn't the time to ask. She was focused on descending the massive staircase. It felt as though he'd gotten a brief glimpse into her mind, a flash of her past; it wasn't the first time it had happened, but none of it ever made sense.

Marx looked back over the crowd. The herald finished their introduction as they reached the last step.

"See," she said. "That's much better timing."

The crowd parted as they walked through the giant room toward the dais. The ballroom had twenty-foot ceilings with wood beams running the length. The walls were painted white, blending seamlessly into the white marble flooring. White netted curtains swept across the walls from window to window and colorful plants sat in white vases at the base of each one.

Marx leaned into Sydria as they walked so that only she could hear. "I'm trying to figure out how you know so much about introductions and the timing of entering ballrooms."

"I don't know." She turned her head slightly, putting her cheek and lips in line with his.

Marx didn't pull away immediately.

He also knew a thing or two about timing.

Sydria swallowed and slowly moved her head and her gaze back to the front.

"Maybe you were a herald before you lost your memory."

She choked out a laugh and immediately tensed with embarrassment. Her free hand went to her lips then back down. He wanted to feel bad about her embarrassment, but he couldn't. He'd made the beautiful woman next to him laugh. How could he feel bad about that?

Marx escorted her to the podium and helped her into her seat. His mother and Dannyn sat in the chairs next to them, and he didn't miss the accusatory look in his sister's eyes, a look that said, *you like her.*

What was so bad about liking his wife?

Dannyn's look was confirmation that Marx was upholding his end of the bargain. He'd made everyone, including his sister, think that he was falling in love.

He nodded at his father as he took his own seat. The violin music started again, and the room exhaled. Chatter resumed, and the servants moved around the room delivering drinks. Sydria casually placed her hand on top of his.

Casually.

Like it was no big deal.

Like it didn't trip up everything inside of him.

The tripping feeling was an added bonus to their charade. If Marx had to pretend to be married, he might as well enjoy himself a little bit. He moved his hand so that their fingers were laced together on top of the plush armrest between them.

His father's words reverberated in his ears. "Things with Sydria seem to be going well."

Marx turned in time to see his father's smug smile—the *I told you so* of all expressions.

He gritted his teeth together, checking his pride and restraining himself from telling his father that he had a plan of his own. Whatever his father thought was going to happen, he'd do better not to be so cocky. Still, he wanted his father to feel secure with the marriage arrangement, so secure that he didn't notice Marx investigating the motives behind the agreement.

"Yes, father," Marx said. "Are you happy?"

Are you finally proud of me?

McKane laughed, his eyes blazing with satisfaction. "It proves that I'm always right."

He would usually be annoyed by an expression like that and by the fact that his father would never be proud of him no matter what he did, but there was an incredible woman at Marx's side, holding his hand, so things couldn't be *that* bad.

Sydria

Sydria felt like she'd met a thousand people and given a thousand fake responses to every person who bowed in front of her throne, eager to meet the new queen. She tried to be genuine, but how genuine could she be when she didn't know anyone, not even herself?

"It's almost over," Marx said when the last guest stepped off the dais. He squeezed her hand, pulling her to a stand.

"What's left?" she asked.

Dannyn poked her head between them. "The fun stuff!" She took her hand, dragging Sydria to a group of their friends. She recognized Kase, Warren, a few other girls, and, of course, Cheney. Marx followed after them, standing next to Sydria.

"Your Majesty," Warren said, "you've met so many people this afternoon. Do you think you'll remember a single person?"

Sydria gave him a reserved smile. "I remember meeting your mother, Lawna Bradshaw, and Kase's little brother, Kell Kendrick."

Warren raised his eyebrows. "I'm impressed."

"I guess I have a knack for remembering names," Sydria said.

"Except for your own," Cheney spoke under her breath, loud enough for Sydria to hear, but not Marx.

She met Cheney's scowl with a polite nod of her own,

wondering what Marx would have done if he'd heard. Would Cheney have gotten away with her joke?

The group broke off into smaller conversations, and Sydria found herself listening to Dannyn tell a story about the first ball she ever attended while the men talked about the new transportation system that was breaking ground in Calicristole. Halfway through Dannyn's story, Cheney walked around the group of girls, positioning herself on the other side of Marx. Sydria tried to concentrate on the details of Dannyn's story, but Cheney couldn't be ignored.

"Marx, your hair is getting so long." Her painted fingernails tickled the back of his neck, where his hair flipped out. "Come by my house sometime, and I'll cut it again."

There were two things that Sydria picked up on.

The obvious, that Cheney had cut Marx's hair before. For some reason, that knowledge grated on her in a way that it shouldn't. It wasn't like haircuts were an intimate thing, but they *could* be.

The second thing she noticed? Marx hadn't moved. He'd tensed, and his back stiffened, a clear sign that he was uncomfortable with Cheney's claw-like nails on his skin (the woman knew how to cut hair but not her fingernails?), but he hadn't stopped her advances. Even if he didn't like Sydria, which *he didn't*, he was still supposed to convince everyone else that they were in love.

Perhaps Sydria should do something on her own—make it clear that Marx was taken. Her chest constricted at the thought. Marx wasn't *hers*, and because of that, Sydria lacked the confidence to put the woman in her place.

"I like your pants," Cheney said, still tickling his neck. "Where did you get your new style from?"

"From my *wife*." Marx grabbed Cheney's hand and removed it from his neck and wrapped his arm around Sydria's waist, pulling her close.

She bit back her smile as ten thousand emotions rolled

through her body. She was elated that Marx had put on end to Cheney's advances and that she hadn't had to herself. But she was also melting from the gentle way Marx touched her, reassured her.

Their marriage might not have been real, but the feelings Sydria felt were.

The violin music stopped, and the sound of silverware clinking against glass silenced the room.

"I'd like to propose a toast." All eyes turned to King McKane standing in the center of the room with his glass held high. He smiled at Sydria. "To the new queen. The future of Cristole is in her hands."

The entire future? That seemed like a lot of pressure.

"To the happy couple!" McKane said, lifting his glass higher.

The ballroom cheered, and glasses were raised.

A similar scene played across Sydria's mind.

A different ballroom.

Different clothes.

Faceless people.

So many smiles.

But the *same* sentiments.

Marx tugged her hip against his. Sydria shook the feeling of familiarity out of her head and smiled at him.

This was their big moment—the perfect opportunity to show everyone and King McKane that they were, in fact, a happy couple.

"Kiss! Kiss! Kiss!" The room chanted.

Kiss?

Her eyes wandered up to his.

Marx's brows were raised. "I think the entire ballroom wants us to kiss."

"I hear them."

He slid his hand from her hip to her lower back. "You need to ask me first."

Sydria suppressed a smile. "No."

"I can't kiss you until you ask me."

The crowd seemed to get louder, and so did her pounding heart. They couldn't *not* kiss. Everyone expected it, but Sydria didn't care. It was more fun to play this game with Marx than the fake relationship game.

She shook her head. "I'm not asking."

His lips drifted into a smile. "It seems we're at an impasse."

She raised a challenging brow, making Marx laugh a little. Slowly he leaned forward, his mouth getting close to hers. The pounding in her heart stopped, replaced by dramatic stillness.

Sydria froze.

Watching.

Waiting.

Marx's lips skipped past hers, and Sydria's eyes closed as he gently placed a soft peck on her cheek. The fire behind his touch had her spinning. The crowd erupted in a mixture of cheers and boos as Marx pulled back and stared at her.

"Now for their first dance," King McKane called above the noise of the crowd. He gestured to the musicians, and a smooth melody began to play.

Marx pulled Sydria to the center of the ballroom as everyone else stepped aside. He looked at Sydria, some kind of emotion funneling through his eyes. "Do you know how to dance?"

"Yes."

He took her hand while his other arm wrapped around her waist. His whispers tickled the side of her ear. "Sorry, I had to ask. It was only a week ago that you were hiding behind a rock."

"That's a fair assessment."

They glided around the room in perfect harmony, everyone watching from the edges. She caught a glimpse of King McKane craning his neck to see them. Since they hadn't kissed, Sydria should do something else to convince him of their happily ever after. Perhaps she should rest her head on Marx's shoulder.

She had it!—the perfect thing.

Slowly her fingers began skimming the back of Marx's neck the way Cheney had been doing moments ago, but Sydria's tickles didn't look as natural as Cheney's had. Her tickles looked more like she was scraping her nails on the side of a chalkboard.

Marx leaned in. "Alert the newswriters. My wife has initiated neck caressing."

"It's awful, isn't it?" she whispered, stopping her scratches. "I don't know how to flirt."

He raised a playful brow. "Is it really that difficult to flirt with me?"

"It's not even that. It's that I don't know *what* to do."

He leaned in closer, and his lips brushed up against her ear as he spoke. "When you like someone, it's all about proximity." His hand tightened around her waist as he pulled her toward him, diminishing the gap between them. Sydria's heart pounded at full speed. "It's about getting the person as physically close to you as you can. So close that you become one." Her hands gripped his shoulders and neck tighter as he enveloped her with his arms, pulling her flush against his chest. "Because when you like someone, you don't want to let them go."

If proximity was what Marx was after, he'd achieved it. Their bodies meshed together. They moved as one with accelerated breaths and heated feelings. She clung to his suit jacket as they swayed together, lost on the dance floor.

The music stopped, and the crowd around them clapped in approval. They pulled apart, and Sydria eyes darted around the room at the smiling faces.

Another memory swept across her mind.

She'd done this before too.

Déjà vu.

"Let's leave the party on a high," Marx said, grabbing her hand.

She looked up at him. "What?"

His lips quirked upward. "Unless you want to dance with me again."

Sydria's hand went to her head. "Actually, I'm not feeling well. Can we leave?"

The memory had scared her, knocked her off balance. The details were fuzzy, but the feeling was so real.

Marx wrapped his arm around her waist, and an adorable touch of worry crossed over his brow. "Are you okay?"

She smiled up at him in the most reassuring way she could muster. "Yes, yes. I'm fine. Just ready to go."

"Then we're out of here."

He led her through the ballroom to the exit. She looked down at their interlocked hands, so grateful that he was by her side, that he had *stayed* by her side. That's where the déjà vu stopped. The dream had invoked feelings of disappointment and embarrassment. All Sydria's mind could feel was her partner getting farther and farther away from her, running toward the color red.

23

Marx

Marx paced back and forth, leaving a trail in the sand on the beach. The party had ended an hour ago, and he'd deposited his wife in her room to rest. Scattered cloud cover shaded the sky, making the sunset a hazy eruption of colors.

"I should have done more. I should have stopped Cheney immediately," Marx said, replaying the events of the day with his friend.

"Eh, it wasn't that big of a deal." Kase picked up a seashell and threw it into the waves in front of them.

"I'm a married man, and Cheney was tickling *my* neck." Marx threw his hands up. "Of course it was a big deal. I should have stopped her as soon as it started."

Kase paused his actions. "Sydria could have stopped Cheney, but she didn't."

"It's not up to her to stop it."

"I'm envisioning Sydria wrestling Cheney to the ground and yelling, 'Stay away from my husband!'"

Marx shook his head. "What?"

Kase's mouth tilted into an indecent smile. "I think the

entire room would have appreciated a wrestling match between two beautiful women."

He gave his friend a pointed stare as a warning.

Kase laughed as he bent down to pick up another seashell. "Well, if you're so upset about it, then why *didn't* you do something more to stop Cheney?"

"I don't know. I froze under pressure. But I should have defended Sydria and our marriage."

"I don't get it. I thought you didn't want to get married, didn't care about Sydria. Why do you care now that you didn't *defend* her?"

"It's the principle of the matter. I'm her husband. I should have proven my loyalty to her. Shown her some respect."

Kase shrugged. "You might be beating yourself up over nothing. Maybe Sydria didn't even notice. Or maybe she didn't even care."

That was the root of the problem.

Sydria didn't care about Marx.

Not in the way he had begun to care about her.

Sydria

"Can you believe the gall of that woman?" Sydria asked, walking the width of Dannyn's room.

"Gall," Dannyn said. "That's a great word." The princess was lying on her stomach on top of her bed, reading a newswriter. She wasn't actually *reading* any articles, just looking for the marriage announcements.

Sydria paused. "Dannyn, focus."

"Okay, okay." She pushed the newswriter aside and sat up. "I'm ready for girl talk."

"I know Cheney's your friend, but that doesn't excuse her behavior. Marx is a married man."

"Then why didn't you tell Cheney that?"

Why hadn't she told Cheney to stop tickling her husband's neck? Her shoulders slumped. "I didn't say anything because the thought of creating a big scene makes me uncomfortable. I'm the queen of Cristole. How would it look?"

Dannyn raised her eyebrows. "You've been the queen for a week."

"I'm still the queen."

"True."

Sydria leaned against the large white bedpost. "What would you have done if a girl was tickling Kase's neck right in front of you?"

"Oh, don't follow my example," Dannyn said, shaking her head. "I'm a mess."

"No, seriously. I want to know. What would a normal, self-respecting woman have done in that situation?"

"You're a normal woman." Dannyn smiled encouragingly, but Sydria leveled her with her gaze. "I mean, besides the fact that you don't remember anything." She pressed her lips together, making her cheeks look like a blowfish. "I don't know, I guess you could have said, 'Excuse me, I'm standing right here.'"

Sydria nodded. "Yes, in my haughtiest voice."

"Haughty." Dannyn smiled. "That's another good word. I feel like I'm getting smarter the more time I spend with you."

She ignored her, lost in her own thoughts. "Okay, so I should have marked my territory, claimed my man, leaving no doubt that Marx is taken."

"Yeah, that sounds good." Dannyn clapped. "That's what I would do."

Sydria spun around the bedpost, sinking down onto the mattress. "The problem is, I don't know if I'm confident enough to do that."

"Why wouldn't you be confident enough to do that? Have you looked in a mirror lately?"

Sydria rolled her eyes. There was more to confidence than looking good. She needed to *feel* good too. "Everyone looks at me like I'm broken because I don't have a memory or a past or anything that makes me interesting."

"The fact that you *don't* have a past makes you interesting. I mean, come on. Who wouldn't want to hang out with that girl?"

Sydria laughed at Dannyn's attempt at cheering her up.

"You are a gorgeous woman. Intelligent. Refined. Not to mention the queen of Cristole."

"I'm the default queen of Cristole, and everybody, including Cheney, knows that."

"Default queen? What does that even mean?"

"It was an arranged marriage." Sydria sighed. "No one believes I deserve the title."

"Then prove them wrong."

She wanted to prove them wrong. There was a lot of good she could do as queen, but she didn't know how long she would have the job. Was it really a good idea for her to take a big interest in kingdom politics even if she was interested?

"Listen, if you want people to respect you, give them something to respect," Dannyn said. "I know how great you are. It's time you showed everyone else." Her smile widened. "And in the process, my brother will see it too."

Sydria shook her head. "I don't care if your brother sees it."

"Yeah, right. I can see it in your eyes when you look at him."

Was that true, or was she just really good at faking it?

"I was a good sister tonight, huh?"

"You're asking the girl with amnesia who doesn't know how to act in social situations. But yes, I think you were great."

Dannyn waggled her brows. "We're quite the pair, aren't we?"

Sydria smiled, but in the back of her heart, she dreaded the day that Dannyn was no longer her sister. She liked her new life in Cristole and the people that were in it. The more attached she got, the harder it would be to leave.

24

Commander Stoddard

Stoddard opened the door to his apartment. Anger shot through him the moment he saw Doctor Von standing outside.

"What are you doing here?" Stoddard hissed. "I thought we weren't going to meet up again."

"Let me come in," Von said, leaning forward.

Stoddard stretched his neck with annoyance as he opened the door wider. He gave the doctor a cutting glare as he passed through.

"We weren't going to meet again," Von said as he surveyed the apartment.

There wasn't much to the one-bedroom space, but it was only temporary until Stoddard's beachside house was ready.

Von turned around, panic in his eyes. "I had a visitor."

"What kind of visitor?"

"The kind that comes from Cristole Castle—a castle guard."

Fear crept into the corner of Stoddard's mind. "You didn't tell him anything, did you?"

"Of course not."

"What did he want?"

"He was asking about the princess. About her accident, her condition, and her memory loss."

"Okay," Stoddard said, running through the possible reasons why a Cristole guard would be investigating.

"I think he suspects something," Doctor Von said. He fidgeted with his hands nervously.

Stoddard scoffed. "What could he possibly suspect?"

"I'm not sure." Von paced.

"You got your payout," Stoddard said. "Take the money and move on with your life."

The muscles on the doctor's face ticked. "That wasn't our deal or the deal that King Adler promised me. Adler promised that if I gave him my Isolated Amnesia medicine, that he would make sure it got in front of the Council of Essentials for every kingdom to see."

Stoddard rolled his eyes. "What is it with you and that medicine? Isn't it enough that you got an enormous amount of money?"

"If I wanted money, I could have gotten it on my own by selling my formulas. I don't care about the money." Doctor Von shook his head. "Isolated Amnesia could change the world. Do you know how many people this drug could help—people suffering from post-traumatic stress disorder? It could pinpoint the trauma in their lives and completely take it out of their mind. It's the most groundbreaking drug since Desolation."

Stoddard had forgotten about how weak Doctor Von was. He needed to be coddled every step of the way. "Listen, you need to be patient. Your drug will be released to the other kingdoms. All in due time." Stoddard didn't really care about Doctor Von or his medicine, but he told the man what he wanted to hear.

"Be patient, that's all you ever say—"

"Because that's what a project like this requires."

"I'm sick of being patient. I'm sick of looking behind my back, wondering if someone is coming after me."

"No one is coming after you."

"One of King Marx's guards already did."

"A few harmless questions," Stoddard said, dismissing his concerns.

Doctor Von secured his glasses into their spot on the bridge of his nose. "I thought you made the deal with the king. Why is he sending a guard after me anyway?"

"I didn't make the deal with King Marx. I made the deal with his father, King McKane."

The doctor began pacing again in his nervous way. "This is terrible." He threw his arms out. "Everything is going to blow up in my face."

Stoddard grabbed the doctor's shoulders, shaking the man. "You need to calm down."

His eyes twitched with fear. "How can I calm down? This was never the plan. Working with you was never the plan. I was supposed to be working with King Adler. None of this would have happened if he were still alive."

"Adler's not alive. I'm all you've got left," Stoddard snapped.

"No." Von moved his head sporadically. "I've got to get myself out of this mess."

"Don't do anything stupid." Stoddard shook his shoulders again as if that would knock some sense into the anxious man. "I'll go to Cristole Castle, talk to King McKane, tell him to keep his son in line."

"And what about my drug? Will you tell him about that?"

"I already told you. We must be patient about the medicine." Stoddard softened his voice, placating him.

"What if King Marx still comes after me? I don't want to be the fall guy."

"You're not the fall guy."

"How do you know?" Von asked.

"Tell you what, if our plans go awry, let's make Marx the fall guy. If we both stick to that plan, there will be two of us against him."

"What about his father? He's not going to turn on his son."

Stoddard smiled. "I'll take care of King McKane. Until then, I want your word that you won't blow up this entire project."

Von wiped at the bead of sweat trickling down his forehead. "Fine. You have my word."

"Good." Stoddard dropped his hands from Von's shoulders.

Doctor Von and his paranoia were a liability.

25

Marx

Marx walked out of the castle's garage carrying a yellow and blue surfboard under his arm. The morning sun was already hot on his skin. Sydria stepped out of the foyer with Dannyn by her side. Her long black hair hung around her shoulders, falling down over her chest. She wore a pink cotton summer dress that was loose and ended below her knees.

She looked breezy, casual, and adorable.

It was a great day to pretend to be in love.

"Who's ready for some fun?" Dannyn asked, bouncing up and down as she rushed to Kase. She went up on her tiptoes, kissing him on the cheek. Sydria watched their exchange, and then her dark eyes turned to Marx.

She cautiously stepped forward, placing her soft hand on Marx's forearm as she went up on her toes. His heart raced as he anticipated her smooth touch. Every muscle tensed when her warm lips brushed the side of his cheek. The kiss was quick—over as soon as it had begun, but its impact lasted long after. Marx would have to remember to thank Dannyn later for the example she'd set.

"Good morning," Sydria whispered, pulling away.

He smiled back at her. "Good morning. I hope you're feeling better than you did at the party last night."

"Yes, thank you. I'm fine now." She pointed to the fiberglass board under his arm. "What's that?"

Marx grinned. "A surfboard."

She nodded slowly, watching two servants fasten more boards to the top of the transporter in front of them.

"Do you know about surfing?" Marx asked, doubting that she did, but Sydria was full of surprises.

She shook her head.

"Surfing was a pre-Desolation thing. Not something you should remember." He lifted the tip of his board. "You use these boards to ride on top of the waves."

She looked back at Marx. "*You* do that?"

"I try to."

She bit her lip. "I probably won't."

"You don't have to do anything you don't want to."

Her lips moved into a small smile. "Surfing isn't part of our fake relationship?"

"Nope." He stared at her beautiful eyes for a moment before he came to his senses and walked his board over to the servants.

Dannyn turned to Marx. "The staff is going to follow behind us in the transporters. They have the food, the canopy, the blankets, everything we need to make our day at the beach the best day ever."

"I should've known when you said that you wanted to plan a celebration party for our wedding that what you really meant was that you wanted to plan a day to hang out at the beach."

Dannyn smiled over her shoulder as she strode away. "It's the perfect excuse."

"Are you ready to go?" Marx swung his leg over a personal transporter, turning the machine on.

"Are we going on that?" Sydria asked.

"You heard Dannyn. The transporters are full of supplies."

She looked the machine over with skepticism. "I'm in a dress."

"I think you'll be fine."

She bit back a smile. "But are you going to kill me on that thing?"

"I don't plan to."

"I suppose it's safe then."

Marx handed her his only helmet and helped fasten the strap under her chin, giving him the perfect reason to stare into her dark eyes again. He offered her his hand, pulling her onto the machine behind him. The position made her pink dress hike up a little, revealing long tanned legs that were currently straddling the seat. Her arms closed around his body, and the palms of her hands grabbed his chest as her body pressed against his back.

Marx wanted to thank whoever it was that had invented personal transporters—look him in the eye and shake his hand.

He owed this moment to him.

"Have you been on a PT before?" he asked as the bike lurched forward, causing her body to push against his even more.

She leaned in closer, creating a buzz of feelings inside his stomach. "Yeah, I convinced a guard to give me a ride once."

Had Marx heard right? The wind blew past them, but he'd thought he heard her say that she'd asked a guard to give her a ride on a personal transporter. Why did Sydria have a guard or have access to a PT? That seemed like a huge clue to the puzzle. He turned his face to the side, looking back at her, but she looked at the scenery whipping past them, as though she were completely unfazed by what she'd just said. So he let it go, tucking it away in his mind for later.

It only took a few minutes to get to the beach. He wouldn't have minded it if the ride had been longer.

Marx grasped Sydria's hand, helping her climb over the rocks. Once they were on even land, he didn't let go. The gesture felt too good, too normal. He was getting good at falling in love. Surprising for a man that who never before been invested in a woman.

They walked to where a team of servants worked, putting up a shade tent and spreading out blankets. The rest of their friends had already arrived and were stripping down to their swim garments. Marx glanced at Sydria. He'd forgotten to tell Paula to make her a swim garment. Not that it mattered. She probably wouldn't get in the water anyway.

"Did you see the surf today?" Warren asked, reaching his hand out to greet them. "We're going to get in some nice rides."

Marx reluctantly let go of Sydria to shake Warren's hand. He turned to the ocean, studying the waves. "Yeah, we'd better get out there before they break too far out."

He took off his shirt, throwing it aside. Then he turned his head, catching Sydria watching him. Her gaze was fixed on his chest, but the moment she noticed him watching her she glanced away. Was she checking him out? A satisfied smirk snuck across his lips, and he might have flexed his muscles a little, just in case she stole a second look.

Attraction was a *fun* thing.

"I'm going out surfing," he said, lowering his head to meet her eyes. "I'll teach you how if you want."

Sydria sat down on the blanket, pulling her dress over her knees. "I think I'll sit here and watch."

Marx bent down, whispering in her ear. "Surfing is all about timing."

"Timing." She gave him a sideways glance, keeping her smile under wraps. "I'll be sure to watch for that."

He picked up his board and walked to the water, glancing at his wife over his shoulder.

He was the luckiest man alive.

Sydria

The women were slower to get in the water. Dannyn and her friends took their time peeling off their dresses and pulling their hair back. They all had similar swim garments to the one Dannyn had given Sydria, black suits that came up high in the front and back with short cap sleeves, but the part of the suit that made Sydria nervous was the way it cut off at the top of the legs the same way undergarments did.

"This doesn't meet the Council of Essentials modesty guidelines," Sydria had said to Dannyn when she'd brought the suit to her room earlier that morning.

"Modesty guidelines? Who pays attention to modesty guidelines?" Dannyn had scoffed. "Besides, we'll be swimming. We can't be expected to wear long dresses in the water."

"Okay," she'd agreed. She didn't know why the modesty guidelines had felt so important to her.

Cheney bent down, picking up the surfboard closest to Sydria. "It's a shame you're too scared to try to surf." Her expression was full of fake pity. "I'm sure you'll have a good time here with the servants."

"I have a great view of my husband from here," Sydria said, adding the sweetest smile she could summon. "But good luck out there."

Cheney rolled her eyes and ran after the rest of the group.

Marx led everyone, holding his surfboard up as he skipped across the water until it was deep enough that he could throw the board forward. He dove after it and hoisted himself on top of the board, laying on his torso. He used his arms as paddles to get farther out into the waves.

"I have another surfboard, Your Majesty," one of the servants said. "If you'd like to join everyone."

Sydria smiled at the man. "Thank you. That's very kind of you, but I actually don't know anything about surfing. I think I'll watch first."

The servant laughed, skimming the water with his eyes. "The truth is, none of these people really know anything about surfing, except for King Marx. He's the one who discovered the hobby."

"How did he discover it?" she asked.

"A few years ago, a large box of artifacts was brought to Cristole Castle. When they were digging a new trench in Calicristole, they'd found the remains of a surf shop. Nobody at the castle cared about the box, but King Marx and Prince Palmer spent hours poring over the broken items inside. There were faded posters of men surfing, fragments of fiberglass boards, suits that they'd worn in the water to keep their bodies warm. Once King Marx saw those pictures, his adventurous spirit became addicted. He researched everything he could find about surfing and had the castle engineers make him his first board. It's taken a lot of practice, but the king's gotten the hang of it now." The servant shrugged. "Anyway, let me know if you want this other board."

Sydria nodded. She watched as a big wave moved toward Marx. He tucked the board and his head under the curl, letting the water spill over him. Once the wave passed, he resurfaced and continued swimming out to where more waves were folding over. The group spread out, sitting on their surfboards, with legs straddling either side. Cheney slithered her way next to Marx, hitting the water playfully, sending a splash toward him. That woman didn't stop. Marx nodded at something she said. Then his gaze and his head turned to the beach. Sydria couldn't tell exactly where he looked, but it seemed like she was the target.

As the next wave approached, several of them, including

Marx, lay down on their boards, using their arms once again to propel them forward. As the water peaked, Sydria held her breath, not knowing what would happen next. Marx dug himself forward, paddling, and just when she thought the wave would overtake him, he pushed his body up and tucked his feet under him, standing on the board. His knees bent, and his arms went out to the side for balance. The back of the surfboard was nestled at the top of the wave. Marx leaned into the wall of water, keeping his center of gravity on the board. He seemed to be floating, moving with the curling swell. He torqued his mid-section, swerving in and out, sending a spray of water in his wake with each cut of his board. His knees bent even more, and his body leaned over as he dropped one hand in the water, skimming his fingers across the white foam. Then he straightened and flipped his board into the wave like he intended to climb over the top of it.

Sydria smiled as she watched him dance with the water. She'd never seen anything so beautiful—well, in the three months that she could remember. He moved and bent as if he had some kind of control over the water, as if the ocean wasn't bigger than him. She'd never been more physically attracted to a man in her entire life. There was something sexy about Marx surfing, curving through the cresting tunnel. His long hair fell over his face, glowing in the sunlight, and his muscles popped and moved with each bend of his body. Sydria couldn't have looked away even if she'd wanted to.

As the wave fizzled out, Marx tilted the board, sending a spray through the air. Slowly, the board sank, dropping him into the water. The wave brought him closer to the shore, and he turned and looked at Sydria. She clapped her hands above her head, letting him know she'd seen his ride.

"Are you impressed?" he yelled to her.

"I suppose." She shrugged with fake indifference.

His grin widened as he floated with his board. "I guess I'll have to do it again, and better."

She laughed, not complaining one bit. She could watch Marx surf on repeat for the rest of her life.

He flipped his head behind him, looking for his friends. The others around him who had gone after the same wave hadn't had as much luck—or perhaps it was skill. Either the wave had passed them by, leaving them behind, or it had crushed them, tipping their boards over and sinking them into the water.

For the next hour, Sydria leaned back on her hands, watching as each person attempted to ride the waves like Marx had. Kase had one good ride, and so did Warren. Dannyn also caught a little wave before the nose of her board dipped in the water and tipped her over the front. But the majority of the group could not get up. She watched, comparing their movements to what Marx did. They were either too far in front of the wave, riding the white foam, or too far outside, missing it altogether.

Then Sydria remembered Marx's words.

It's all about timing.

Some of the women walked back to the beach, toting their boards with them.

Cheney's loud voice carried over the others. "Surfing is a lot harder than it looks. I'm not sure if women were built for an activity like this."

"Actually, there were professional female surfers before Desolation," Dannyn said.

"True. If anyone can do it, I'm sure I can." Cheney tilted her head, looking directly at Sydria. "I'll have to ask Marx for some private one-on-one lessons." The look on her face suggested she hoped for more than surfing lessons.

Sydria had had enough. Cheney was awful, and she wasn't going to be bullied by her any longer. She stood, and the women all turned their heads to her. She walked toward them, grabbing Cheney's board out from under her arm.

"What are you doing?" Cheney sneered. "You won't be able to get up."

"It's all about timing," Sydria said, walking to the water.

She was probably crazy.

Yes, she was most definitely crazy.

She wasn't even sure she knew how to swim, let alone surf, but Dannyn had said that if she wanted people to respect her, she had to do something they would respect. She stopped right before the water, dropped the board, and began pulling her dress up.

Marx

Marx sat on his board, searching behind him for his next wave.

"Is that your *wife*?" Kase called out to him. He looked at his friend, following his gaze to the shore, catching the last few moments of Sydria raising her pink dress over her head.

Marx's eyes widened as they slowly swept up her legs to her fitted swim garment—little was left to his imagination. His lips parted as Sydria lifted her chin, closing her eyes slightly. Both of her hands went behind her neck, twisting her black hair into a knot on top of her head.

Everything happened in real-time, but for some reason, Marx felt like time had stalled. His heart thudded to a slow drum as he drank her in. He would never be able to *unsee* this moment. It was like he was in the middle of a memory game, and he was definitely winning. His brain soaked in every detail of her, memorizing every inch.

"Watch out!" Warren called behind him, but it was too late.

A wall of water crashed over Marx, sending him flying forward. His board flew out from under him, hitting him in the head as his body was pushed under the surface. The water spun him around, swirling him in the undertow.

He probably deserved to get taken out by the wave because, at that moment, Marx needed something to bring him back to reality.

Sydria

SYDRIA SLID HER STOMACH ON TOP OF THE BOARD like she'd seen everyone else do. Her arms stroked through the water, moving her out to the waves. There was a good chance she would die out there. Marx had been taken out by a huge wave, and he was experienced. She could only imagine what would happen to her. She'd survived a carriage accident, but *surfing*… surfing would be the end of her.

There was a small part of Sydria that hummed with excitement. She was trying something new, unexpected—something that no one had *told* her she had to do. She was doing it because she wanted to.

Once she made it out to where the waves were breaking, she turned her board around, looking over her shoulder.

You can do this, she breathed.

She'd sat on the beach, watching the mistakes of everyone else.

It's all about timing.

In the distance, a wave gathered, picking up momentum.

This is the one.

She lay down, paddling forward as hard as she could. She didn't know if she would be strong enough, but she kept moving. After a few strokes, she turned her head and the sound of the water pushing toward her got louder. The rushing water tickled her toes and legs as it got closer.

Wait for it.

She felt a burst of speed and momentum, and her intuition told her to stand. She placed her hands on the board and popped up as quickly as she could. She stood there for a second, waiting for the wave to throw her off, but it didn't.

"I'm doing it!" she yelled to no one other than herself. The board wobbled, and immediately her knees bent, and her arms went out to the side to offset the shaking. The board swerved back and forth, and it was clear how inexperienced and naive she was.

"I don't know how to steer!" she yelled to the surrounding water. She was going to fall, and all she could think about was how humiliating it was going to be.

Then suddenly, Marx was behind her. He stepped on the back of her board, abandoning his own surfboard. Everything tilted and shifted with his weight, and for a moment, Sydria thought they would both tumble over, but he somehow gained the perfect amount of balance.

His chest was pressed against her back, and she looked over her shoulder, meeting his sharp jaw and hazel eyes. "What are you doing?"

Marx's focus was on the water, but he glanced down at her for a split second. "Steering."

She stood motionless, trying not to do anything that would disturb the stability. "Where did you come from?"

"I couldn't let you surf alone." He dropped his head, putting his lips next to her cheek. "I told you I would teach you how, didn't I?" Then his eyes jumped back to the wave.

His closeness.

His manliness.

His complete control of the situation set her heart off-kilter.

Goosebumps popped up along her arms and legs. Not because she was cold, but because Marx's skin was on her skin.

They rode the wave together until it started to die down. His arms wrapped around her waist, and before Sydria knew what was happening, they were both falling back into the water *together*. She came up for air, pushing the water out of her eyes and hair. Her feet kicked out, trying to find the ground below her, but she couldn't touch it. She wrapped her arms around Marx's neck while he held onto the surfboard with one hand. His other arm found its way around her waist.

Water dripped down his face, running into his cute smile. "You're a pro," he said as they bobbed up and down.

"I doubt that."

"I've never been so proud of anyone in my entire life." Marx's grip around her waist tightened, and she felt the slight tug of him pulling her closer so that her hips touched his. "My little surfer girl."

Something significant passed through his eyes. Sydria wished she knew what it was. She wanted to keep his gaze, to have him look at her like that every day. His stare made her feel strong, like she was so much more than what she believed on her own.

"Nice ride!" Dannyn cheered from the beach.

They both turned to see the entire group watching them, including a very upset Cheney. Her arms were folded, and she looked to be pouting.

Cheney's tantrum was more satisfying than it should have been.

"That was the cutest thing I've ever seen," Dannyn yelled, "but it's lunchtime, so you'll have to have your romantic moment in the water later."

Sydria smiled, feeling a wave of embarrassment fall over her. "I guess we'd better go have lunch."

"I guess so." Marx didn't immediately let go; it almost felt as though he didn't *want* to let go. "Hop on," he said, patting the top of the board. "I'll give you a ride."

"What? Do you think I'm a queen or something?" she said as she climbed on top, dangling her legs over each side of the board.

"Something like that." His lips grew into an amused smile as he looked over her. "Hold on tight," he said, pulling the board forward. "Unless you want me to rescue you again."

That's exactly what she hoped for.

Lunch was a spread of sandwiches and exotic fruits that only grew in the kingdom of Cristole. Everyone sat in a large circle on the blankets, eating, talking, and laughing.

It was strange.

A little over a week ago, Sydria had watched these same people do this same thing, but at the time, she had been an outsider looking in. Now, she was the one sitting next to Marx, but this time, he had a smile on his face.

"You've got fruit dip on your lips." He gently brushed his fingers across the side of her mouth.

"Thanks," she whispered.

His hand grazed the side of her arm as it dropped to the ground beside them.

"Can I take your plates, Your Majesties?" a servant asked.

Marx gathered the remains of Sydria's lunch and handed it to the young man. "Thanks, Gillson." The servant nodded and walked away.

Of course he knows the servant's name.

That was the kind of guy Marx was.

"What do we do next at a beach party?" Sydria asked, pulling one knee up to her chest. She didn't care what was on the agenda as long as she got to spend time with Marx.

"Whatever we want to do." His fingers wiggled through the sand, finding hers. He leaned in closer, pressing his shoulder against hers. His other arm rested on her knee. Sydria wasn't sure of her past, but she was definitely sure she'd never experienced this much skin-to-skin contact in her life.

The hot sun beat down on them, melting Sydria—or maybe it was Marx and his touch that melted everything inside of her.

She was currently on fire.

"It's hot," she said.

His face inclined closer to hers, and his gaze dropped to her lips. "Very hot."

"I heard it's a record summer." She rubbed the back of her neck, glancing once at Marx's lips too.

"You're the one who's studied the weather," he said, somehow getting close enough to skim the tip of his nose lightly across hers. His fingers brushed her bare leg, creating small swirls over her thigh.

Sydria puffed out a gentle laugh. His joke would have been funnier if she wasn't liquefying from his touch. Or if she could actually focus on a coherent thought.

"I can't seem to turn the heat down," she breathed between them, trying to somehow gain control over her racing heart.

One side of Marx's lips tugged into a half-smile. She saw it because her eyes kept drifting back to his mouth. "Are we still talking about the weather?"

She swallowed, but somehow her throat was still dry. "What else would we be talking about?"

He moved closer, filling the space between them with his breaths. "Nothing. Just the weather," he whispered.

Sydria's eyes shifted to his lips...*again*. "The sweltering heat."

"Yes, the heat."

It was the stupidest conversation she'd ever been a part of. She'd probably lost brain cells because of it, but at the same time, it was the best.

His mouth got closer. Was he going to kiss her?

"Marx?" Cheney said, clearing her throat above them.

Sydria jumped back. How had they gotten so close? People didn't usually sit that close unless they were together. A couple. In a relationship. None of which they were.

When it came to faking their physical attraction, they were nailing it.

"My skin is burning," Cheney said.

Apparently, Sydria wasn't the only one feeling the effects of the record-breaking heat.

Cheney flopped her hand forward, revealing a white tube. "Can you put sun blocking lotion on me?" Her lips puckered together, creating a pouty expression.

Marx stared at her blankly. "I'm not sure what you need help with," he said flatly. "You can reach every part of your body that's exposed to the sun."

Cheney's swim garment was almost exactly like Sydria's. It covered her front and back, high enough that only her arms, chest and neck would need the lotion, and logically, Cheney could reach the front and back of her legs on her own.

"But," Marx said. He stood, reaching for the lotion, causing Sydria's heart to plummet into the depths of her stomach. Was he really going to lather Cheney up right in front of his *wife*? Fake or not, that had to be crossing some sort of spousal line. "My back is getting burned." He took the bottle, turning to Sydria. "Hey surfer girl," he said with a playful expression, "would you mind putting some blocking lotion on me?"

"Sure, darling." Sydria stood, surprised by her use of the word *darling*, but she was new at this, and improv wasn't her thing.

Cheney's mouth dropped, and she shook her head before turning and walking away.

"Poor girl," he said, watching her walk away. "She can't get it through her head that she doesn't stand a chance."

"Why doesn't she stand a chance?" Sydria asked, feeling a little bad for Cheney.

Marx shook his head as if it were obvious. "Because I'm already married to the most incredible woman ever."

Sydria let out a self-conscious laugh.

"Now," he said, placing the bottle in her hand. "Weren't you going to help me protect my skin?"

"Oh!" Her eyes widened. "You really want me to do that?"

Marx tapped his finger over his mouth like he was thinking. "Do I want my wife to rub lotion over me?" He paused, looking at her with a gleam. "Yes, I do."

Sydria rolled her eyes. "You're taking advantage of the situation."

"I don't think so. You agreed to this." He nodded to the rest of their friends. "If you don't want to, I can always ask Cheney to come back."

"Fine," she said, reaching for the bottle.

Marx had a smug expression as he slowly turned around.

Sydria flipped the lid up and pounded the bottle against her open palm, feeling nerves flitter through her stomach. She was going to need a pep talk to get through this.

Okay. I'm going to touch—no, rub—this lotion on Marx. My hands are going to be all over him. It's not a big deal. This is part of the agreement. Just get in and get out.

Touching was not one of her strengths, but she mentally visualized the task at hand.

She pounded the bottle against her palm one last time and looked down. There was a glob of lotion in her hand so big she would have to apply sun blocking lotion to everyone on the beach to get rid of it.

Marx cleared his throat, no doubt wondering what was taking her so long.

Sydria dipped her index finger into the liquid and brought it up to his right shoulder blade, lightly rubbing the lotion into his skin.

Marx glanced over his shoulder at her and raised his brows. "Are you finger painting?"

"No!"

"At this rate, it's going to take you all day. How about you use more than one finger?"

Sydria knit her lips together, holding in her smile. She was being ridiculous. She'd given herself the pep talk. She could do this. She smeared the lotion on her right hand and began smoothing it into his skin. Marx's body relaxed as she ran her hand over every contour of his back. She started at his neck, working her way down to his defined shoulder blades and the perfect V shape his muscles created in the center of his back. Then her fingers slid around his lats—the muscles that she'd become acquainted with the first day they'd met. Her hand glided to his waist, and he dropped his neck, breathing easy.

"That's more like it," he said.

Sydria smacked his lower back. "All done!"

He turned around, his cocky smile encouraging the flame inside of her to burn out of control. He peeked at the pile of lotion still in the palm of her left hand. "I don't think you're all done. You better do the front too."

"You can reach your chest on your own."

"Yeah, but it's more fun when you do it," Marx said as he leaned in, sending a shiver down her body.

Was it fun?

The butterflies in her stomach said it might be.

"Fine, but only because I have extra lotion on my hands."

By the look on his face, Marx didn't believe her excuse.

Neither did she.

She rubbed her palms together, spreading the rest of the lotion out between her fingers. Slowly she raised both of her hands up to him, placing them on the top of his shoulders. Sydria felt his eyes on her, felt his breathing go ragged, but she refused to look him in the eye. Her hands slowly slid to his chest, and his pectoral muscles tightened as she massaged over them. Her fingers ran over the ridges of his abs and around to his sides, smoothing over the top of his skin. Applying sun blocking lotion felt more intimate than anything Sydria had ever done before. The thought of Cheney doing it popped into her mind, and she instinctively stepped closer to him. She was glad she was the one caressing his chest, not her.

After all, Sydria was married to the man.

Kind of.

Her hands rested on his hips, and she looked up. "All done," she whispered.

Marx's eyes blazed. "That might have been the best twenty seconds of my life."

Hers too.

That night, Sydria lay in bed thinking back through the day. The lines between real and fake were blurry. Feelings were real on her part, but probably not his. Except that they had shared some very real moments together. Maybe his feelings for her were changing and growing too. She hoped they were, but she couldn't plan on it. She had to tell herself Marx was pretending. That's who he was. That's the deal they'd made. He was living up to his end of the bargain. If she didn't think that way, she'd end up getting hurt.

Sydria understood now what Dannyn had said.

Some heartbreaks were worth it.

She understood, but did she really believe it? Part of her still wanted to protect herself from the pain and embarrassment, almost like she'd been there before—been hurt before. From now on, she'd hold up her end of the agreement and keep everything between them professional—as professional as fake-falling in love could be. She could enjoy Marx, but she couldn't let herself *love* him.

Marx

Marx lay in his bed, letting thoughts of Sydria creep into his mind. Actually, the thoughts of her weren't *creeping*. They were more like a pre-Desolation freight train, crashing through, shattering everything that was there before, filling up every inch of his brain with her.

He smiled and hopped out of bed, walking to the door between their two rooms. He unlocked the latch and opened the door—hers was still shut.

Was he going to knock?

If he did, what would he say to her when she opened it?

No.

He closed his door, leaving it a crack open. Just in case Sydria needed anything.

Needed *him.*

The more time he spent with her, the more she took away all of his reasons not to care.

But caring was dangerous. Whenever Marx started to care about someone, he ended up letting them down.

He didn't want to let Sydria down.

It was time to rein things in, make sure there wasn't anything real behind their pretend game.

No problem.

Marx had spent his entire life not letting anyone in, not feeling anything. He could easily do that with Sydria.

Everything was under control.

26

Marx

Morning sunlight filled the king's suite as Marx knocked on the door between their two rooms.

"Come in!" Sydria called.

Come in? Why wasn't her door locked?

Marx twisted the handle and pushed the door open, examining the lock on his way through. Surely there must be something wrong with it.

"Good morning," Sydria said. "Did you sleep well?"

He was still perplexed by the whole her-door-is-unlocked situation, but he looked up. Sydria sat in the middle of her bed, legs crossed, with her notebook in her hand. She had on a pair of *his* athletic shorts—rolled up at the top to fit her waist—and one of *his* oversized t-shirts. The neck of the shirt was too big, so it hung off the side of her shoulder. There was a lot of bare shoulder real estate being shown. The shorts exposed more leg than women typically showed. And to make everything worse, her dark hair was piled on top of her head in a messy but attractive way. Once again, she looked incredibly appealing. He brought his hands to his face, rubbing his eyes.

"Is everything okay?" she asked. The kindness in her voice killed him.

So did her outfit.

And her hair.

And her smile.

And her innocence.

He was dead.

"Yes!" He looked up, trying to add a chipper tone to his voice that he definitely wasn't feeling. "Everything is going as planned."

It was going as planned.

Marx just hadn't planned on his heart going *against* the plan.

"You know," Marx said, scratching his head, "while I have you here, I should mention that there are a few things that I would appreciate you not wearing. You know, things that make it hard for *us* to keep this relationship fake."

Sydria raised her dark brows. "Okay."

"For example, what you're wearing right now."

"This?" She picked up the fabric of the shirt. "But this is your shirt."

"Right. You're never allowed to wear that again."

"My wardrobe isn't complete." She tilted her head. "And don't you have a ton of shirts like this?"

"It's not about the shirt. It's about how the shirt looks on *you*."

"Oh."

"And, while we're making a list, that chartreuse dress you wore to the party the other night? You're not allowed to wear that again. Remember the physical boundaries we set? That dress isn't helping me meet those boundaries."

Sydria dipped her chin as a slight smile formed on her lips.

"And the swimming garment from yesterday. Don't ever pull that out again. Just burn it."

Her slight smile grew to something more—something adorable.

"And I don't know if you still have it, but that lavender dress I saw you wearing at the beach the day we met is out, a definite no." He placed his hands on his hips, pleased with how he was handling the situation.

He was clearly in control.

"I see," she said.

"What about me?" Marx asked. "Is there anything you'd prefer I not wear, you know, because it makes things too hard for you?"

She pressed her lips together, raising her shoulder—the shoulder that was bare and exposed because she was wearing an illegal shirt. "It's not what you wear that makes things difficult, but what you *don't* wear. Maybe you could button your top buttons a little more and not take your shirt off so much."

"Of course."

Had she said that because she thought he looked good without his shirt on, or because she was repulsed by him?

It has to be that she thinks I look good, right?

"But then, it's not really the things you wear that make me attracted to you," Sydria said. "It's the things you *do*."

He turned his eyes back to hers. "What do I *do*?"

"The mustard shallot sauce."

Marx nodded.

"And." She bit her lip. "The aquarium."

He scratched his ear. "Right."

"Why did you do those things?"

He shrugged. "Because I wanted to make you happy."

Her smile widened. "You did."

Forget about the list of clothes he'd rattled off. Sydria smiling like that should be outlawed.

Everything was confusing now.

Muddied waters.

Blurred lines.

Marx had to glance away. He was only two minutes into operation 'Don't Fall for Your Wife,' and he wasn't going to blow the mission now. That glowing smile wasn't going to be his undoing.

"Anyway." He cleared his throat, stepping back and bumping into the couch. He looked behind him at the sofa as if the collision was somehow the piece of furniture's fault. "What I really came to tell you was that I made you an appointment with the castle doctor."

"What for?"

"I thought we should get a second opinion on your condition. See if he has any thoughts on your memory loss or if he has another solution for your heart besides your medicine."

Sydria's hand went to her chest. "That's nice of you."

"Not nice," he said, backing out of the room, "just part of the plan."

The plan he was executing perfectly.

He made it to the door. "I'll meet you in the royal sitting room after lunch." Marx didn't even wait for her response. He left the room, shutting the door behind him. He took a deep breath.

So much for reining things in.

Sydria

SYDRIA SPENT THE MORNING RIDING HORSES with Dannyn. She hadn't been sure she even knew how to ride horses, but the second she hopped onto the saddle, her body took over, and a feeling of skill and confidence filled her. They rode down the long stretch of the beach nestled below the castle, the same place Sydria had walked when she'd lived with Von and Edmay. It was interesting how the more time she'd spent at Cristole Castle, the less she'd thought about them. There had been days that they hadn't even crossed her mind. She thought about dropping into their cottage and visiting them, but what good would it do? Sydria had decided the day they'd sold her that she would never think of them again, that her obligation was over.

Besides, the life she lived now was a thousand times better than the one she'd had with them.

The women nudged the horses into a full gallop. The wind blew around them, and splashes of ocean water sprayed into their faces with each stomp of the horses' hooves. Dannyn led Sydria through a path up the rocks to dry land as they made their way back to the castle grounds. They slowed their horses to an easy trot, giving the animals a rest.

"It's beautiful here," Sydria said.

Dannyn looked out at the ocean. "It is, but I've never been anywhere else, so I couldn't say if there's something better."

"I can't remember anything else, so I couldn't tell you either."

Both women laughed.

They rode a few more paces before Sydria spoke again. "You've really never been anywhere else?"

"I've traveled all over Cristole, but I've never been to another kingdom."

"Do you like being a princess?" Sydria asked.

Dannyn smirked. "You know me, I love being the center of attention."

"I'd be perfectly happy out of the spotlight."

Dannyn continued chatting as a splash of a moment colored Sydria's dark mind.

Green grass.

Mountains.

Dark curly hair on a nameless face.

"You don't like the spotlight?" the nameless face said.

Sydria closed her eyes, trying to squeeze more out of the memory.

"Are you scared to marry me?" he asked.

The wedding popped into her mind.

Flowers.

Dark curly hair.

Dread.

Then everything went dark again.

"Sydria?" Dannyn asked. "Are you okay? You look pale."

She shook her head, smiling back at her. "I'm fine. I just…"

She couldn't tell Dannyn about the memory she'd had.

How do you explain to your sister-in-law that you think you might already be married to someone else?

Marx

MARX STEPPED INTO THE ROYAL SITTING ROOM. Dannyn and Sydria sat on the couch talking. They hadn't noticed him yet, which gave him a second to see them interact together. He leaned against the doorframe, watching as they laughed and smiled at each other. Marx's heart expanded. They were the only two women he'd ever cared about besides his mother. He'd been unprepared for this fake relationship. He'd had no idea Sydria would touch every place in his heart. If Marx knew who she was, where she came from, then maybe he could understand the feelings growing inside of him, maybe he could *allow* them, but he didn't know that. He hoped Doctor Moore would be able to answer some of his questions.

He cleared his throat.

"Look, Sydria, it's your long-lost husband," Dannyn said. She gave a knowing smile to Marx and stood, stretching her arms out. "You two have fun together. I'm going to go take a nap."

"A nap?" Marx questioned. "It's one o'clock in the afternoon."

"Isn't this usually when you wake up?" Dannyn teased as she walked past him. She hit her shoulder into his arm on her way out.

Sydria stood too. "Have you really slept in until one o'clock?"

Marx placed his hands in his pocket. "If it's going to make you think less of me, then my answer is no. I'd never do that."

The truth was, he used to do that all the time. But lately, he'd actually attended the meetings that he was supposed to. He'd dove headfirst into his responsibilities as king, to the surprise of everyone around him. His father had bristled when Marx had walked into the High Rulers meeting a few days ago. But then the High Rulers had addressed *him*, not his father. They had looked him in the eye when asking questions or addressing concerns. It was as if they finally took Marx seriously, like they no longer viewed him as the reckless young man from his youth. It was amazing what a marriage could do for a man, the way it could mature a person in a matter of a week and a half.

"Did you have a good morning?" Sydria asked, walking toward him.

That was the second time she'd asked him a question like that.

Nobody had ever asked Marx about his day or how he'd slept.

Nobody had ever cared that much.

"Uh, good. I sat in on a few meetings. What about you?"

"Dannyn and I rode horses along the beach."

Marx lifted his brows. "You ride?"

A shy smile formed at the corner of her mouth. "At first, I wasn't sure if I could do it, but once I hopped on the horse, everything came back to me. Almost like muscle memory. I'm actually quite skilled."

Riding a horse wasn't exclusive to the ruling class. Sydria could have learned to ride anywhere. It wasn't necessarily a clue to her past, but Marx noted it anyway.

"Great," he said, trying to keep his voice even. "Are you ready to go see Doctor Moore?"

She swallowed and glanced down.

"Hey," he said, running his thumb across her cheek. "You have nothing to be nervous about. We're just trying to gain more information."

She looked up, nodding. "I know."

Marx wished he could reassure her, but the truth was, the more he got to know her, the more he was scared to find out who she really was.

27

Marx

Marx nervously drummed his fingers on the side of his armrest, waiting for Sydria and Doctor Moore to enter the room. He'd been waiting in the medic hall for over an hour as the doctor examined Sydria. Had she been his real wife, Marx would have demanded that he be in the room during the examination. Part of him still wanted to demand that, but he knew it was unlikely he would win that argument.

The door swung open, and the doctor ushered Sydria into the room. He closed the door behind them. Doctor Moore was heavy set, but rather than make him seem overbearing, it complemented his jovial nature. He had thick brown hair and big cheeks that added to his charm when he smiled.

He gave a quick bow toward Marx. "Your Majesty," he said. "Thank you for waiting."

Marx stood, helping Sydria into the seat beside him as the doctor pulled out his own chair behind his desk and sat down. He scooted forward, but because of his sizeable abdominal area, he only made it about an inch before he couldn't get any closer.

"Well," Doctor Moore said, looking between the two of

them. "I've examined the queen, and I find her to be in excellent health."

Marx looked at Sydria. "That's great."

"There are some lingering side effects of her coma," the doctor said.

"She was in a coma?" Marx questioned.

He'd never heard that.

"Yes. According to Her Majesty, she was in a coma for several months after the accident happened."

Marx would have to revisit that topic with Sydria another time.

"Okay, so the side effects?" he said, trying to get back to the doctor's original point.

"Her muscles have weakened, but I can tell with a proper diet and physical activity that she's gaining her strength back, and there doesn't appear to be any permanent damage."

"Good," Marx said, wrapping his brain around that. "What about her heart?"

"Yes, the queen mentioned that she takes medicine daily to keep her heart working properly. She thought her uncle had said that it was also to protect her against blood clots."

"That's correct," Sydria said.

"We did a chest X-ray, and although she has a large scar and scar tissue, I don't see any lasting effects from her accident. In fact, everything that I've found from my tests would suggest that her heart is working as it should."

"Could that be because I'm taking medicine, and if I weren't, then your tests would show something different?" Sydria asked.

"Possibly," Doctor Moore said, resting his elbows against his desk. "But we really wouldn't know that for sure unless you stopped taking the medicine."

"Do you suggest she stop taking it?" Marx asked.

"It's hard for me to say without speaking to her uncle directly. I'm not sure what the medicine is doing, but if it's not harming her, and like I said, I see no issues with her health, then I don't see why she couldn't keep taking it."

Marx leaned forward in his chair. "What about her memory loss?"

"We did a scan of her brain as well. I couldn't see anything in the scans that indicated there was any brain trauma. But the brain is a very complex organ. There's so much we don't know about it. Therefore, I have no conclusive evidence that her memory will or will not come back."

No conclusive evidence? What was Marx paying this man for?

"Although, the queen did mention that she's been having a few small flashbacks."

Marx looked at Sydria again. More information he didn't know.

"You've been having flashbacks?"

Sydria shook her head. "Just a few. Nothing helpful."

"I think the flashbacks are a good sign that eventually everything will come back."

Marx felt a rush of relief. "That's excellent."

Sydria smiled, but her smile was unconvincing.

What was she hiding behind those dark eyes?

"Now, since this is the first time that I've had the chance to meet with the queen since she arrived in Cristole, I want to get a feel for how everything else is going."

"Okay." Marx nodded.

"How are the marital relations going? Any problems there?"

Was Doctor Moore also trained in marriage counseling?

Marx raised his eyebrows. "I'm sorry. What marital relations?"

Doctor Moore glanced between the two of them and cleared his throat. "You know, the consummation of the marriage."

"Oh." Marx laughed, though nothing was funny.

Sydria pointed back and forth between them, shaking her head. "We haven't—"

"We haven't mastered things yet, but we'll be sure to ask if we have any questions," Marx said, his tone a little too high.

The doctor tried to keep his face expressionless, but if Marx had to guess, he would say he'd lost some of Doctor Moore's respect because of this conversation.

"If there are any problems in the future with that area of your life, please feel free to address them with me."

"Thank you, doctor," Sydria said graciously.

How was she not mortified?

Marx was.

Doctor Moore didn't say it out loud, but the look in his eyes said that he questioned Marx's manhood.

He stood, ready to leave the doctor's tiny office that seemed to be closing in on him by the second. "I think that's all we had." He escorted Sydria out. He couldn't leave the medic hall fast enough. He made a mental note to tell Elsbeth to hire a new doctor to examine him from here on out so that he wouldn't have to face Doctor Moore again.

They walked down the hall. He didn't know where to go, but he didn't want to leave her.

"Would you like to go for a walk?" he asked.

"Sure."

Marx led Sydria through the castle and up a back stairway until they were outside.

"Are we on the roof?" she asked.

He nodded, leading her to the east side where the view of Cristole was the best. Beyond the lush trees surrounding the castle was a never-ending view of the kingdom.

"Wow," Sydria exclaimed. She rested her hands on the limestone barrier that surrounded the roof. "I've been so busy looking back at the ocean, I've never seen what's out beyond the castle."

"It's easy to focus on what's behind us," he said. "I've been guilty of that." He watched her every expression, waiting with bated breath for her dark eyes to fall on him.

"Me, too. I've been so wrapped up in my past, I haven't thought about the possibilities of my future." Her gaze slowly met his.

"What do you want in your future?" It was a question he probably shouldn't ask. He might be disappointed with her answer.

Sydria shrugged. "Someone who will sit and watch the waves with me until they stop."

Marx smiled. "That seems doable enough."

She glanced away, shyness taking over her expression.

"Just so you know," he said, wanting to clear the air, "I had to say that back in Doctor Moore's office."

Her head lifted. "Say what?"

"You know, the whole consummating the marriage thing."

"Oh," she said, suppressing a smile.

"Doctor Moore is my father's doctor, and if word got back to him that we haven't...you know...our entire plan might be ruined."

That, and my reputation.

"True."

Marx raised his shoulders. "I never think about consummating the marriage." He tilted his head back and forth. "I mean, not *never*. It's not like I've *never* thought about it." He threw his hands out as if he were guilty. "I've thought about it. Okay? But I don't *think* about it. Unless *you* want to think about it, then we can."

Sydria smiled.

Why couldn't Marx keep his mouth shut?

He scratched the back of his neck. "I mean, do *you* ever think about it?"

She laughed.

"Just kidding. Don't answer that question." He glanced out at the view, freaked out by the last ten seconds of his life. "So, good news from the doctor, right?" That was his not-so-subtle way of changing the subject.

"I think so." Sydria raised a shoulder. "But we really didn't learn anything new."

"Sure we did. We learned that you're in excellent health." He peeked back at her. "And we learned that you have a scar."

"I already knew that."

"I didn't."

"It's not usually something I tell people."

"Where is it?"

"Somewhere you can't see."

"Come on! I'm your husband," he joked.

"My *fake* husband."

He couldn't argue with that.

"We also found out that you've had some memories."

She pulled back on the railing. "A few."

"Do you want to tell me about them?" He watched her face closely, looking for any sign of hesitation. "You don't have to if you don't want to."

Her dark eyes shifted to his. "I want to tell you about them, but they don't make sense."

"Maybe I can help you figure them out. I have an excellent imagination. Remember?"

"Okay." She turned her body toward him, leaving one hand on the stone wall. "I've had a recurring dream that I'm standing at a wedding." She paused. There was the hesitation he'd been looking for. "My wedding."

"Is it *our* wedding? Perhaps a nightmare?"

She smiled. "No. At this wedding, I'm sinking and suffocating, and I feel like I can't get out. And then that's it."

"Do you know who you're marrying?"

"Maybe. There have been other dreams. Dreams with a faceless man. He has dark curly hair, but every other detail is fuzzy."

Great. A faceless man. Who can compete with that?

"What is the man doing in your flashbacks?"

"Nothing, really. Sometimes he walks away from me. Sometimes he asks me questions."

"What do you think it means?"

"I don't know. Usually, my dreams and flashbacks are tied to certain emotions—happiness, fear, anxiety. But lately, I'm starting to wonder," she bit her lip the way she always did when she was nervous, "if I'm already married to someone else."

It was a gut punch.

No, a *throat* punch.

The karate chop of all punches—something that hit the windpipe, knocking the air right out of Marx. It was a possibility he'd never thought about, but it didn't make sense. Why would his father arrange something with a woman who was already married?

He forced a smile. "Are you worried that you're cheating on the faceless man?"

"No, that's not my concern."

"Because we'll get you back to him once we figure out who you are. We can find him." Marx tried to ignore the burning jealousy inside his chest. Sydria wasn't his, but he didn't necessarily want her to be somebody else's.

"Maybe he doesn't exist." She sighed. "Maybe these are just random dreams that my mind conjured up and not memories at all."

"Maybe." Marx put his hand on her shoulder. "But don't worry, we'll figure it out."

"Thank you for not freaking out on me," she said.

Oh, he was freaking out—*inside*—but he didn't plan on letting Sydria see that.

"What happened to Palmer?" she asked. "You never talk about him or how he died."

Marx's expression sagged as he thought back to that day and the guilt that followed him everywhere. He wanted to tell

Sydria what happened, but if he let her in, let her see the *real* Marx McKane, what would she do? Would she be disappointed with him like everyone else? If she really knew him, would she still like him?

His gaze met hers. Her eyes said that it didn't matter how many times he'd messed up, or how many things he'd done wrong in his past. She would forgive him. Her kindness was unconditional. She loved with her whole heart, and at that moment, Marx wondered what it would be like to have *all* of Sydria's love, not fragments of it or facades of it, but her whole heart.

Marx bet it would feel amazing.

He looked down, shuffling his feet against the cement floor. He was ready to show her a side of himself that she'd never seen before.

"Palmer and I went rock climbing. There was this new place that I'd heard about. An island of rocks west of here with a narrow space, a slot you could climb through. I wanted to try it out. So we rode our PTs an hour down the shore and paddled a raft out to the island, about two hundred yards offshore." He looked up, skipping his eyes over the view of Cristole. "The rock formations were amazing, and just like we'd heard, there was a slot between two rocks only wide enough to fit our bodies. We started free climbing. We didn't need any ropes because the space was so narrow. I got ahead of Palmer." He shrugged. "I'm competitive and didn't want my little brother to think that he was a better rock climber than me. There was a grinding noise, and Palmer yelled out in pain. He'd placed his hand in a crevice, causing a boulder to shift, pinning his forearm, and crushing his fingers." Marx glanced quickly at Sydria but kept going with his story. "I climbed down to where he was and tried to help him, but I couldn't lift the rock off his arm. After a half-hour of trying, we noticed the water had started to rise. The tide was coming in. I didn't want to leave him, but I needed help." Emotion filled his eyes as he thought back to that day. "I panicked, but Palmer remained calm, reassuring me that he'd still be there when I got back. He said there was no one that he'd rather have rescue him than me." He shook his head, remembering that moment like it had just happened. "I climbed down, took the raft, and paddled as hard as I could back to the shore. I rode my PT to the nearest town and brought back as many men with me that I could. I was only gone forty-five minutes, but by the time I came back, the tide had come in, and the water had risen so high, he was submerged." He let out a sharp laugh. "Four inches. That's all I needed. There were four inches from the top of the water to his nose."

He looked at Sydria, unable to hide the bitterness from his eyes. "How does a grown man—an experienced swimmer, hiker, climber—drown in four inches of water?"

Sydria placed her hand on his arm, squeezing tight. "I'm so sorry, Marx."

He shook his head. "I shouldn't have left him. I should have stayed there with him and done whatever I could to get his arm free."

"You had no choice," Sydria said. "You needed to get help."

"No, I should have done something more."

"It was a freak accident, nobody's fault."

"My father blames me."

"I'm sure he's looking for a way to cope with his own grief." Her other hand went to his cheek. Her touch was soft and soothing. "He doesn't really blame you."

"I wish that were true."

"I don't blame you," she said, peering into his eyes.

Her simple words impacted Marx's heart more than anything else had in his entire life.

"Thank you," he whispered.

"We're both a little banged up and bruised."

His eyes swept over her face. "I guess so."

Marx loved the ease of conversation that he shared with Sydria. She asked pointed questions, but the sincerity behind her questions made it easy to open up to her.

Everything with her was easy.

Everything but figuring out her past.

28

Marx

Marx hadn't slept. Every time he closed his eyes, he saw Sydria marrying another man. Not just any man, a *faceless curly-haired* man.

Curls?

Was this guy five years old?

He stomped down the halls of Cristole Castle, ignoring the chirping birds and golden sunrise. He made his way to his father's office. For the last few days, he'd wanted to talk to his father about who Sydria was, but their schedules hadn't aligned. Marx wasn't willing to wait for the right moment any longer. He passed his father's secretary, Lance, and headed straight for the door.

"Your Majesty," Lance stood, reaching his hands out. "The king said he didn't want to be disturbed right now."

"I'm the king," Marx grunted as he pushed his father's door open.

Meldrum McKane glanced up from a paper on his desk. "You're up early," he muttered.

Marx slammed the door behind him. He went to the desk, leaning his hands against it. "I want to know who she is."

"Who?" Smugness pulled across his face as if his father didn't know exactly who they were talking about.

"Tell me who she is and where you found her."

"We've already been through this," his father said, crossing his leg over his knee. "You're on a need-to-know basis."

"Well, I need to know now."

"Why?"

"Because she's my wife, and I deserve to know what I'm dealing with."

"You deserve to know?" he raised his eyebrows. "Why do you deserve to know?"

Marx straightened, resting one hand on his hip. "She's had a few memories, flashbacks, and I want to know what they mean."

His smugness deflated. "What kind of flashbacks?"

"I don't know, but she thinks there's a chance that she could already be married. So I'm asking you, is Sydria married to somebody else?"

"Already married?" His father spun his chair, facing the window. "That's ridiculous. Of course she's not already married." He eyed Marx. "Sydria must be confused. Keep doing what you're doing. Keep her happy, and everything will work out."

"That's all you have to say?"

"Yes." His father's lips pressed together.

Marx knew that was all the information he was going to get from his father. His jaw stiffened, and he turned to leave.

"I'm glad to see you care so much," his father called after him.

Marx kept walking.

He did care.

But something in his gut told him to trust Sydria's resurfacing memories over his own father.

Sydria

SYDRIA SAT WITH DANNYN IN THE ROYAL SITTING ROOM. She had her notebook on her lap and a pen in her hand, jotting down details of every dream she'd had. Every clue to her puzzling life. But it was hard to concentrate. Her mind kept drifting to Marx and the way he'd opened up to her the day before about Palmer. His wounds had been on full display. The vulnerable look in his eyes had made her own heart soften with compassion. He carried so much weight, harbored so much guilt. He needed a little grace—someone to forgive him and tell him that he wasn't a bad guy.

Sydria thought back to Idella's words on their wedding day.

Marx McKane has always been a little lost, but the last year and a half have been hard on him. He needs something to help ground him. I suppose that's where you come in.

At the time, Sydria hadn't understood the meaning behind Idella's words, but now, those words gave her purpose. Each day with Marx, Sydria found a little bit more of herself. She wasn't scared anymore of the life inside her. He made her want to fight for it, to become the best version of herself, and she hoped she brought out the same feelings in him.

"I'm supposed to go to this boring meeting," Dannyn complained. She was stretched out on the couch across from her.

"What's the meeting about?" Sydria asked.

"Jobs or something stupid like that."

"Jobs?"

"Yeah, you know." Dannyn changed her voice as if she were impersonating a man. "How can we create more jobs for the people in Cristole? Blah, blah, blah."

Sydria let the pen drop into her notebook. "Dannyn, that's important stuff."

"I'm sure it's important for somebody, but not me."

"You're the princess, and because of that, you're held to a higher standard. You have obligations to the working class to make sure they have the best quality of life they possibly can."

"What about my quality of life?" She threw her hand out.

"I think your quality of life is pretty good." Sydria snickered.

"I never know what to say at these meetings."

"I'm sure you have great ideas of how you can help the people."

"I really don't. But," she sat up, "I do have one great idea. Why don't you go to the meeting for me?"

Sydria reared her head back. "Why would I go to the meeting?"

"Because you're the queen. If I have to be at the meeting, then you should have to be there too."

"I don't know. I wasn't invited."

Dannyn swung her legs around, so they touched the ground. "Are you going to wait to be invited, or are you going to walk in and show them you're the boss?"

"But I'm not the boss."

"You are. You're the queen."

The queen situation was temporary, but maybe she didn't want it to be temporary. Maybe she could actually be a good queen. A strong desire pressed within her chest, the desire to help people, to solve problems, right the wrongs. She didn't know where the feeling had come from, but it felt familiar. Was it a part of the old her—the Sydria that wasn't a stranger in her own skin?

She could attend the meeting to see what would happen. She didn't have to say anything. She could sit there and listen, and maybe a memory would spark to life, something that explained the pounding in her chest.

"I think I will attend the meeting," she said, getting up from her chair.

"Really?" Dannyn seemed surprised.

"Yes. You're right. I should be there."

"You're going to be late."

"I'll hurry. Where is it at?"

"The main meeting room next to the royal offices."

Sydria walked briskly down the hall, her shoes clapping against the ground as she went. She rounded the corner and rushed through the door to the meeting room, then her footsteps halted. She looked around. There was a large oval conference table that fit at least twenty chairs around it. Every single seat was already taken.

"Pardon me," she said.

King McKane glanced at her. "Sydria, are you lost?"

She swallowed.

Was she lost?

She was a fool for thinking that she belonged at a meeting about the kingdom of Cristole.

She hesitated, balancing between who she thought she was and who she might actually be. The pounding in her heart increased, and she lifted her heel to take a step back when Marx stood up from the head of the table.

"She's not lost," he said. He gestured for her to come in. "She's the queen of Cristole, and she's here for the meeting."

His warm hazel eyes fixed on her.

How did he do that? How did he squash down every one of her insecurities and find strength buried inside?

"Come in. We'll make room for you." He signaled for the men beside him to move over, and he grabbed an extra chair from the corner of the room, placing it next to his.

Sydria nodded at all the faces and pairs of eyes looking at her as she made her way to her seat.

"Now that the queen is here, we can officially start," Marx said, helping her scoot her chair in. "We're gathered here to talk about how we can increase the jobs in our kingdom and positively impact the security of our people. I asked each High

Ruler to give me a report on the employment statistics from the provinces they rule over."

"When did you do that?" King McKane asked.

Marx shot a pointed stare over to his father. "A couple of weeks ago."

King McKane raised an eyebrow but didn't say anything.

Sydria turned her focus to Marx. He wasn't looking at her, creating the perfect opportunity for her to study him. He was dressed in dark pants and a cream button-up shirt, but of course, the top two buttons were left undone. His sleeves were rolled up casually, exposing the veins on his forearms. Blonde hair swept perfectly away from his face, and his jaw had a trace of light stubble running across it. His tone was deep and confident. It was his *business voice,* and it made Sydria's heart unravel.

She had thought the surfing version of Marx was attractive—okay, she *still* thought that side of him was attractive—but this other side, the version of him where he commanded a room, added another layer to his sexiness.

He was the chocolate cake they'd eaten at dinner last night—a Cristole delicacy—layered with cream filling, moist cake, chocolate mousse. No layer was better than the other, but all of them combined...well, that made the most perfect dessert Sydria had ever tasted.

"Let's start with High Ruler Bromley and work our way around the table," Marx said, nodding at the older man, and then he sat down, giving Bromley his own time to speak.

Marx's hand rested on top of hers, but his focus remained with the High Ruler. Sydria's eyes drifted to their joined hands. The movement was intentional, but would anyone in the room take her seriously if she was cuddling in the corner? She pretended to shift in her chair, moving her hands to her lap. It didn't take long before Marx's fingers found hers under the table, and she fell victim to his touch. Sydria curbed her smile, trying to focus on what Bromley said. Each High Ruler around the table took a turn, sharing information they'd gathered from their province.

When everyone had spoken, Marx turned to her. "Sydria?"

Her eyes grew. "What?"

"Do you have anything to add?"

"I only planned on being a spectator, not an active participant in the meeting."

"I'm sure you have an opinion."

"I just moved to Cristole."

"So?"

She glanced around the room, unsure if she should speak her mind, but the feelings inside her grew stronger, giving her confidence she hadn't known she had.

She lifted her chin. "I think if you want to create job security here within your own kingdom…within *our* kingdom," she corrected herself, "then we need to stop purchasing so many items from other kingdoms. Obviously, there will be some situations where trade is necessary, when we can't manufacture what we need. But in most cases, we can. For example, I believe it was High Ruler Pearson who mentioned that we're sending money over to the kingdom of Appa for timber."

High Ruler Pearson nodded. "Yes, a very large sum."

"As I understand it, the climate in northern Cristole would be perfect for tree farms," Sydria continued. "If we could find space within a northern province to start growing our own trees for timber, it would provide jobs for our people, and it would keep the money of Cristole inside our own kingdom."

Her eyes moved to Marx, and he smiled—the big grin, the grin that he usually only reserved for when they were alone. But in a way, it felt like they were alone, like the whole room had disappeared and only he saw her—the real her, even if she didn't see it yet.

"You're incredible," he said, shaking his head, then he

turned to the rest of the room. "Isn't Queen Sydria incredible?"

The room seemed to nod and smile in unison, but all Sydria could feel was the thrill of his compliment.

"High Ruler Pearson, since you're over a northern province, I want you to make this project happen," Marx said. "Find the acreage."

"Of course, Your Majesty," Pearson agreed. "I'll look into our land options and get back to you—"

"No, don't get back to me." Marx looked at Sydria. "Report back to the queen. It was her idea. She'll be in charge of the project from here on out."

High Ruler Pearson nodded. "I look forward to working with you, Your Majesty."

"What other ideas for job security do we have?" Marx asked the group.

But Sydria was stuck on chocolate cake, on the layers and layers of hidden sweetness that made her feel like she couldn't live without it.

Marx

"You wanted to talk to me," Kase said, popping his head into Marx's office later that afternoon. "What did I do?" he asked as if he were in trouble.

But it was Marx who was in trouble. Every second he spent with Sydria, he became more invested. She was attractive even at meetings about job security. He needed to find out who she was. He didn't know what was brewing between them, but he couldn't go on like this with so many unanswered questions.

"Do you have any new information about Sydria, her uncle, or Otis Sutton?"

Kase shook his head. "Everything I try leads to a dead end. Nobody around here has heard about the carriage accident. There was no record of any newswriter reporting it or the deaths of her parents or the carriage driver. There wasn't even a record of a disaster crew coming in to help clean up the accident or haul off the destroyed carriage. Nobody has heard of Von and Edmay Nealman or Otis Sutton. You said he was some kind of doctor. Well, not a single hospital in Cristole has ever employed him. It's as if they dropped out of the sky and landed in Cristole."

It was definitely starting to feel that way.

"And I found out that Sydria was in a coma, so the carriage accident didn't even happen three months ago," Marx said.

"That might explain why no one knew about it. I can broaden my timeline and see if anything new comes up."

"I also have another lead you can look into." Marx hesitated. "I think Sydria is married."

"I know. I was at the ceremony."

"No." Marx shook his head, disgusted that his friend couldn't keep up. "Not to me. I think she's married to someone else."

"But she's also married to you," Kase said slowly.

"Sort of." Marx brought his hand to his head, rubbing his forehead. "But if she was already married, then my marriage to her doesn't count."

"That's great news."

"Why is that great news?" he snapped. It felt like *awful* news.

"Because I thought the entire point of this investigation was to find out who she was so that you could get out of your marriage to her."

Marx swiped the air in front of him, swiping Kase's words away with it. "No, the point of investigating is so that we can help Sydria."

"Okay," Kase said, drawing the word out as if he didn't believe Marx at all.

"So I need you to find this guy," Marx said.

And then I can fight him to the death.

"What guy?"

"Her husband!" Marx groaned, looking over Kase. "How are you my personal guard when you can't even follow a simple conversation?"

"Nothing about this feels simple," Kase muttered under his breath.

"Here's what we know," Marx said, "he has dark hair and curls."

"Curls?"

Marx rolled his eyes. "I know."

He already hated the man.

"He has to be someone prominent that my father would be interested in. So let's start with the royal families, High Rulers, commanders, important people in each kingdom who might have attracted my father's attention."

Kase stiffened. "Wait. What did you just say?"

"Important people in—"

"No, before that." Kase's eyes lit up with excitement. "You said *commanders*."

"Yeah, so?"

Kase slapped the desk in front of him. "I know where I've seen Otis Sutton before."

"Where?"

"Tolsten House." Kase laughed. "Except his name isn't Otis Sutton. It's Oliver Stoddard, *Commander Stoddard.*"

Marx's mind worked quickly, trying to place the significance of that name.

Commander Stoddard. Tolsten. Escaped.

"Are you sure?"

"I'm positive. The guy I saw at Cristole Castle the day of your wedding is Commander Stoddard. When I was in Tolsten working as an operative, I spied on him. All the other operatives kidnapped Princess Myka, but I stayed behind to transfer letters to and from Tolsten House. I can't believe it took me this long to figure it out."

Why was Marx's father working with the enemy of the Council of Essentials? And more importantly, what was Sydria's role in the whole thing?

"What happened to the commander after the operative mission?" Marx asked.

"The other kingdoms stopped pursuing him. As far as I know, only Tolsten is trying to find him, and now we know where he is."

"*Knew*...we knew where he was, but that was almost two weeks ago. Stoddard could be anywhere by now."

"It's all coming back to me." Kase shook his head, laughing again. "After Stoddard killed King Adler, he escaped with a doctor, a nurse, and a woman. According to Queen Myka, the woman was immobile. They lifted her into the transporter."

Marx's heart stopped.

Sydria.

"At one point, I'd heard that Queen Myka believed that the woman Stoddard had was her mother."

Marx's brows dropped. "Her mother?" Unless Sydria had given birth at three years old, there was no way that was possible. Marx's mind spun with other scenarios. "Sydria could be Myka's long-lost sister. Did King Adler have any other children besides Myka?"

Kase scratched his chin. "Not that I know of, but I could find out."

"What does Queen Myka look like? You worked with her on the operatives' mission."

"I wouldn't say that I *worked* with her. Mostly I just kidnapped her," Kase said. "But she has dark hair and blue eyes. She was pretty, could definitely pass for Sydria's sister. Or," Kase shot his hand up, "What if Sydria is married to

Commander Stoddard and she came to Cristole Castle as a spy?"

"That's ridiculous," Marx scoffed.

"Why? It's no more ridiculous than you saying she could be Myka's hidden sister."

"Sydria isn't spy material, and wasn't the commander bald? She's married to a guy with dark curly hair, remember?"

"Oh, yeah. But still, I should tighten security around you, and by that, I mean *have* security around you more regularly. We can't risk her having open access to you."

"Sydria isn't a safety concern."

"I wouldn't be so sure. Anyone associated with King Adler and Commander Stoddard can't be trusted. Just in the last two years, they've been involved in an assassination and a major weapons conspiracy."

"I'll worry about my safety around Sydria. You worry about finding out who she is."

Kase frowned. "If you say so."

"Maybe you should go to Tolsten to get answers since you already have an established relationship with Queen Myka and King Drake."

"Yeah, an established relationship of mutual dislike. Drake is the only operative Queen Myka liked. I don't think she'd be too happy to see me."

Marx sucked in a deep breath. "Well, do whatever you have to do, but find me some information on Stoddard and who Sydria *really* is."

His father had been so confident that this alliance was beneficial for Cristole. There had to be a good reason his father trusted Stoddard.

29

Sydria

Sydria sat out on the terrace with Dannyn and her friends, making notecards for sick children. Queen Malory was hosting a ball that night in honor of the ill children around Cristole. It was a nice gesture, but Sydria wondered if the money spent on the ball could have been given directly to the sick children and their families.

"Kase is leaving me," Dannyn said, slamming her pen down dramatically.

Sydria looked up from the card she'd been writing, and Dannyn's friends gasped.

"What?" Cheney said. "How could he end things with you?"

Dannyn leaned forward. "Not *leaving* me, leaving me. He has to go to Tolsten for a little bit."

"What for?" her other friend, Truby, asked. She was thin, with the perfect amount of freckles showering her face.

"I don't know." Dannyn rolled her eyes. "Something important Marx wants him to do."

"When does he leave?" Cheney asked.

"Tonight. After the ball. How am I going to go for that

many days without him here?" She flopped her hands down, jostling the table. "I'm going to be so bored."

"You'll miss his company?" Sydria said as she drew a smiley face at the bottom of the note she worked on.

"No! I'll miss his lips."

The other girls laughed, and Sydria had to fight to keep her growing blush from getting too out of control, but of course, Cheney noticed it. Since the sun blocking incident, Cheney had mostly kept to herself. Until now.

"Come on, Sydria," she said, tucking a strand of her short brown hair behind her ear. "Don't be so appalled. It's just a kiss. Or does Marx not want to kiss you?"

She straightened. "I'm not appalled. I believe a lady doesn't kiss and tell."

Her mind opened up.

Triggered.

Where there had been darkness a second ago, now there was a sliver of light.

A girl with blonde hair. *Maybe they've already kissed.*

Then her own shy smirk. *A lady never tells.*

Sydria couldn't explain it, and she never knew how to recreate it.

Her hand shook slightly as the memory faded out of her mind. The other women continued talking around her, not noticing her falter.

Sydria had kissed somebody before. If she thought she was married, then yes, she'd kissed a man. But she had no recollection of it. No memory of how to do it or what it felt like.

She thought about Marx.

What would it feel like to have his lips on hers?

It never would happen…not unless Sydria *asked* him to kiss her.

Marx

Marx tugged on his black suit jacket, looking at his reflection in the mirror. Normally, he dreaded attending one of his mother's balls—a room full of pretentious people who cared more about whom they could impress than the children they were supposed to be honoring. But tonight, his stomach hummed with anticipation.

Marx hadn't seen Sydria all day. He missed her.

The way she smiled.

The way she moved into a room.

The way she talked.

The way her kind eyes offered reassurance whenever he needed it.

Everything about her, everything she did, was beautiful.

He knocked on her door.

"Come in!" she sang out.

Marx smiled.

Her door wasn't locked.

He didn't know why that one little gesture meant so much, but it did.

He pushed the door open, slowly revealing his *wife*.

Sydria stood facing a three-paneled mirror. Her hair was coiled into a bun at the top of her head, topped with a golden crown decorated with emerald stones. She wore the mermaid-cut dress that she'd designed with Paula. The dress was gold with a layer of black lace covering the top of it. The fabric pulled tight around Sydria's body, fanning out at the bottom with a short train. It had long sleeves and a high neck. But the best part, the part that Marx died over, was the open back. The keyhole showed off a perfect oval of her smooth skin and delicate lines, starting from the base of her neck, ending at her lower back.

She turned over her shoulder slightly, pinning him with her dark eyes.

His breath caught.

She was striking.

Elegant.

Alluring.

Devastatingly appealing.

Words couldn't describe.

Marx took his time running his eyes up the length of her body, soaking in every inch of her beauty, until his greedy stare met hers.

"You're beautiful," he said.

She demurred, turning her head back to the mirror.

He walked to her, so much purpose in each step until he stood behind her. He leaned in close, smelling her freshly applied gardenia perfume.

"I like your dress," he whispered. His finger went to the base of her neck where the back of her dress was open and slowly traced a line down the curves of her spine.

Sydria turned her head, putting her cheek against the tip of his nose. "Are you finger painting?"

He laughed as his hands closed around the sides of her arms, and his tone came out husky. "We might need to add this dress to the list of things you're not supposed to wear."

"Pretty soon, I'll have nothing left to wear," she breathed out.

He pulled her in closer, feeling her back against his chest. "Would that be so bad?"

It was her turn to laugh, something soft and throaty that drove him crazy.

"Your Majesty," Idella said, rushing into the room. "I found the earrings I told you about."

Sydria startled and tried to pull away, but Marx held her close.

"Oh!" Idella said when she saw them. "I, uh…"

"Idella," Marx said, glancing at the maid through the mirror. "Isn't my wife beautiful?"

"Yes, Your Majesty. I couldn't agree more."

Sydria smiled back at his reflection. "My husband isn't so bad either."

Marx *blushed*.

He didn't even recognize himself.

This was so unlike him.

He was the guy who'd never been impressed by a woman, the guy who had been deemed a jerk because he never would commit.

But with Sydria, he was all in.

Sydria

Queen Malory's Children's Ball wasn't what Sydria had expected. There were no children, no parents of the children, no information about how a person could help or donate money to the children. It was a regular ruling class party.

Sydria had wanted to stay by Marx's side, to feel his heated touch on her skin as he ushered her around the room, but the queen mother had insisted that she meet some of her friends. It didn't matter where Sydria was. She felt the gravity of Marx's stare the entire night. His look sped up her heartbeat, and thoughts of his hands on her body made her stomach toss with anticipation.

Was this what it felt like to fall in love?

The buzzing stomach.

The smile that wouldn't stop.

Feeling flushed.

Trembling hands.

The emotional pull.

Active senses.

It all mixed together, creating the most exciting feeling Sydria had ever felt in her life. There was no way she'd ever experienced this before because if she had, she wouldn't have forgotten.

Maybe that was why her dreams and memories were all tainted with an edge of sadness—she didn't feel like she'd loved the man she'd married. The fringes seemed perfect, but the core was suffocating.

Maybe she didn't want to know about her past. She was content to stay like this…with Marx.

Sydria sipped her drink, pausing at the appropriate time to smile and nod with the rest of the women at some story Truby told.

"Shew!" Warren slurred, walking toward them.

Sydria glanced up. Was he talking to her? His finger was pointed at her.

"You!" he said again with a little less garble. "You did it!"

Truby paused her story, and all the women stared back at him. Warren didn't look upset. He seemed completely intoxicated. He tripped on his feet, but somehow he was still standing when he got to Sydria's side.

"Shew robbed me of my best friend," he mumbled, leaning in too close to her as he spoke. "And nowah…now I'm miserable and alone."

Sydria took a step back from him. "I had no idea you and the king were so close."

"The king's not close with anyone." Warren twirled his finger out in front of Sydria before running the tip down the length of her arm. "So here's what we're going to do. Here's the plan." He flashed her a dazzling, albeit lopsided, smile. "You dump Marx and run away with me." He wagged his eyebrows up and down at her.

Sydria opened her mouth to speak, but a warm, gentle hand on her arm stopped her.

Marx.

He lightly pulled her to him. "Let's get out of here."

"She's running away with me," Warren chirped as Marx tugged her away.

"She's mine, and I have no intention of letting her go."

The deep, rough tone of his voice and the heat in his stare made Sydria's heart squeeze.

He swept her away, and she let him. She would feel a pull toward Marx even if he wasn't leading her, hand-in-hand.

"I can't keep my eyes off of you," he whispered into her ear, raising bumps over her skin.

"I noticed," she said, exhaling.

His lips brushed up against the side of her face as they moved into a smile. "I like knowing you noticed me."

She swallowed, trying to control the way her body reacted to him.

They exited the ballroom and walked down the dim hallway, stumbling upon Dannyn and Kase. They were pressed against the wall, a tangle of arms and legs as their lips locked together.

"Get off my sister," Marx said, pushing his friend's shoulder as they walked by.

"Marx!" Dannyn condemned.

"You're just jealous," Kase said, coming up for air.

Sydria was indeed jealous.

Her eyes widened as Kase's lips found Dannyn's again. Thank goodness Marx was towing her away, or she might have stayed there to take notes.

She thought he would take her out to the garden, to the balcony that had become theirs, but her heart fell as he led her up the stairs to their rooms. She didn't know what she'd been expecting, but it wasn't this. For her, the night wasn't over.

He stopped between their two doors and turned to her. "You're killing me in that dress."

Maybe she *wanted* to kill him.

"And," he closed his eyes briefly before opening them again, "I'm trying to do everything I can to stay within our agreement, so you need to change, and I'll change, and I'll meet you on your balcony in five minutes."

The night *wasn't* over.

She bit her lip. "Okay."

They both stepped toward their own doors, keeping their fingers interlaced until the distance between them was too great and they were forced to break apart.

"Five minutes," she said, holding up five fingers even as her other hand twisted her doorknob.

Marx held up his hand too, throwing her a crooked smile. "Five minutes."

Sydria wiggled out of her dress by herself. Idella wasn't in her room, and she was grateful. She didn't need her maid seeing how completely head over heels she was. She flipped through her drawers looking for the perfect thing to wear, stopping when she saw Marx's oversized t-shirt and shorts.

She smiled.

Sydria was a vixen now.

She threw the shirt over her head, letting the neckline fall off her right shoulder, and she shimmied into his shorts, rolling the waist several times so it would fit her. She went to the vanity and pulled off the gold crown, shaking her head until her hair fell loose from the bun. She bent over the mirror, applying a clear coat of lip gloss, and took one last look at herself.

What are you doing, Sydria? This isn't real.

She shook the thoughts away and stepped onto her balcony.

Marx

When a man tells a woman he'll meet her in five minutes, a gentleman gives her ten.

Marx sat on the sofa in his room. His knee bobbed up and down as he checked the clock one more time.

It had been eight minutes.

Only two more to go.

Nerves piled up in his stomach—not *nervousness*—but a tangle of energy.

He pulled at the fabric of his linen shirt, trying to alleviate some of the heat coating his body. He'd purposely left the top three buttons of his shirt undone. Sydria had said that was illegal. So this was a strategic move. He couldn't go into the heart of the battle zone with a woman like Sydria and not have a few tricks up his sleeve. He would've gone to battle shirtless if he thought he could've gotten away with it.

We're just going to talk, Marx reassured himself. *I love talking.*

He had to keep his wants and expectations in line.

He raked a hand through his hair, releasing a drawn-out breath.

I. Love. Talking.

He glanced at the clock. Nine minutes. Good enough. He stood, practically running to his balcony. Sydria stood by the edge with both hands resting on the railing in front of her. Her dark hair mixed with the night sky, blowing aimlessly in the hot summer breeze.

Marx laughed to himself.

She'd worn his shirt.

She'd come with her own weapons of war.

Keep it casual, he reminded himself. *We're just talking.*

"Hey," he said.

Casual was his middle name.

She turned to him with a half-smile. She looked like some kind of goddess, illuminated by the full moon.

"Hey," she said back. The undercurrent in her voice made his throat go dry.

Marx's heart skidded in his chest, his body reacting to her without his permission. He walked to the edge. "I'm going to jump."

She turned her head away. "And I'm not going to watch."

He balanced on top of his own ledge then leaped across to

hers. The landing was rough, dropping him right in front of her. Or maybe the landing wasn't rough, and he did it on purpose. Either way, he was right where he wanted to be. He slowly stood, his body inches from hers.

Marx took her shirt between his fingers. "I thought we agreed you wouldn't wear this?"

Her dark eyes gazed up at him, and she shrugged. "We did." Her hands went to his collar, tugging on the open part of his shirt. "I thought we agreed you wouldn't leave your buttons undone."

"We did." His hands rested on her hips.

She smiled, drawing his gaze to her lips.

Talking!

Marx let go of her and took a step back. He was never going to survive this night if he didn't put some space between them. He walked over to the wall where a stone planter bench was mounted between the sliding balcony doors and hopped up, taking a seat.

"Did you have fun tonight?" he asked.

That was a good conversation starter, and tonight he was a conversationalist.

Sydria bit her lip, walking over to where he sat. She turned around, hoisting herself on the cement planter next to him. "Marx, I have a question."

Questions were good. Questions led to more talking.

She turned her head to him. "Will you teach me how to kiss?"

Not that question.

His breath escaped his lungs, and he stood. Was she serious? He must not have heard her right.

He eyed her. "I don't understand."

"I've never been kissed," she said. "I mean, it *feels* like I've never been kissed." She glanced down. "I'm not even sure I know how."

"Uh…" He laughed, rubbing the back of his neck. "What

are you saying?" He wasn't deaf, and he wasn't an idiot. Marx knew what she was saying, but he had to be sure *she* knew because once he jumped, it would be all over. He would be past the point of no return.

"I'm asking you to kiss me."

His lips slackened into a small smile.

"You are my husband, after all." She shrugged, a nervous movement that told Marx how vulnerable she felt. He'd do anything to make her heart feel safe.

He cleared his throat. "I *am* your husband." He walked forward, throwing his hands out to the side. "Who better to teach you how to kiss than your husband?"

Her smile widened as she gained confidence. "That's exactly what I thought. If anyone is going to teach me how to kiss, it should be my husband."

Man, she was adorable.

The logic sounded good to him. He didn't need to be asked again.

He stepped toward where she sat on the planter and slowly placed his hands on her hips, feeling the softness of her body. Sydria's legs widened, making room for him to get closer to her. Each of her knees rested against the side of his thighs.

Her brown eyes found his. "What do I do with my hands?"

"What do you want to do with them?

Slowly she lifted her arms, circling them around his neck. A rush of chills ran down his back, and his heart shook, beating with each second of anticipation.

"Then what?" she breathed between them.

He leaned down to her, watching the wonder of the moment unfold in her eyes. His nose skimmed the side of her cheek. "Then you close your eyes," he whispered.

Her breathing came out in hot bursts against his lips, and her chest moved up and down with his. Her tongue swiped over the tip of her lips as she closed her eyes.

Marx watched her, balancing desire with respect.

He brought his lips softly down to hers. His movements were slow and gentle. He did all the work, moving their mouths lightly together. His body floated as if he were free-falling off the side of a cliff—the thrill of the ride sending his stomach into swirls. A slow, sizzling heat spread through his veins as if her lips had erupted a volcano inside of him. His feelings were molten lava—slow and steady—inching through his body with each simple skim.

His fingers gripped her hips, and he pulled back, resting his forehead against hers. His breath was heavy, not from exertion but from excitement.

Marx had done what she'd asked.

He'd taught her how to kiss. It wasn't anything flashy or fancy. He'd kept things chaste, but he'd done it.

Time to end it.

Sydria

More.

Sydria wanted more.

She wanted to ride the high of their kiss, let it take her to a place she'd never been.

Marx pulled back, but she dragged him closer, tilting her head, finding his lips. He seemed unsure at first, but the slight parting of her mouth broke his resolve. His hands dug into her sides, closing the gap between their two bodies. Sydria felt every curve of his chest and his arms as he enveloped her in his strength. She wrapped her legs around his waist as her hands drifted between his shoulders and the back of his hair.

Her lips reacted to his—moving, exploring, discovering him. Their bodies melded together in a push and pull of passion. Sydria was lost in a timeless dream, the kiss intensifying with each passing second. Explosive feelings spilled out from every pore of her body. She'd never felt so alive. It was as if a new heartbeat had been put inside of her. She was no longer a shadow of a person. She was restored, better than before.

The kiss accelerated.

Sydria wanted it to.

She *wanted* Marx.

Her hands slipped under the collar of his shirt. It was his own fault. He was the one who had left his buttons undone. Her fingers grazed over his shoulders, making their way to his chest.

Marx slammed on the breaks, pushing her body off his.

He stepped back. "The kissing lesson is over," he said through sharp breaths.

Everything stalled but Sydria's racing heart. She stared back at his handsome face, at his messed-up hair and his passion-filled eyes.

"Did I do it wrong?"

He swallowed, shaking his head. "You are more than skilled in the art of kissing. I think you taught me a thing or two, so I'm going to go," he said, already backpedaling to the ledge. "Because honestly, I can't stay here and be a responsible human being." He jumped across to his own balcony without looking back.

Sydria watched Marx duck into his room. A mixture of disappointment and happiness swelled inside of her. She hadn't wanted him to go, but the fact that he *had* to leave—had to leave because he'd felt the same undeniable attraction that she did—made her heart leap.

She dressed for bed, reaching for the medicine vial on her nightstand. She went to twist open the cap but stopped. Her heart felt stronger than it ever had before.

The fighter inside of her whispered *You don't need that. You're not weak like Von and Edmay thought.*

She opened the drawer to her nightstand and dropped the

vial inside, then she rolled over and lay on her back, watching the ceiling fan. She could hardly breathe as she replayed their kiss in her mind over and over again like the spinning fan above her.

There had been nothing fake about that kiss.

30

Commander Stoddard

Stoddard brushed a speck of dust off his pants and crossed one leg over the other. He looked around King McKane's office as he waited on the couch for the king to arrive. It was a large room with a nice view. He gritted his teeth, thinking about how a man as insignificant as McKane had become a king before someone as brilliant as himself. The injustice of it grated on him. Stoddard had worked and scraped for every little thing that he'd gotten in life, and the highest position he'd been able to achieve was the commander of the Tolsten army—never royalty. And now, he had to hide out from the Council of Essentials. It was maddening.

The door swung open, and King McKane walked into the room. Stoddard wasn't going to stand from his spot on the couch. Maybe he would have a few weeks ago when he had been trying to strike a deal with the man. But now, the deal had been struck. The money was in Stoddard's possession. He didn't need to stroke McKane's ego any further.

"I see you got my letter," McKane said, walking over to him. "I'm glad we made arrangements for me to get in contact with you again."

"In truth," Stoddard said, "I was going to come and pay you a visit."

"Why is that?" McKane sat down on the white couch across from him.

"Doctor Von had a visit from one of your son's guards."

McKane raised a surprised brow. "What did the guard want?"

"He sniffed around trying to gain information about the princess."

"Was Von stupid enough to tell him anything?"

Stoddard placed his arm behind him on the back cushion. "Surprisingly, no."

"So, what's the problem then?"

"The problem is, you need to control your son. We can't have him investigating the situation. Little things like visits from guards set off our fragile doctor, and when Doctor Von is nervous, the whole project is in jeopardy."

McKane skimmed his fingers over the armrest. "I will admit that my son is more curious about his wife's background than I anticipated. Usually, he doesn't pay attention to the details of anything in this kingdom. But lately, that hasn't been the case."

"You need to control him."

McKane clenched his jaw. "Why don't we focus on what you need to do?"

"And what's that, exactly?" Stoddard asked, shifting in his seat.

"The princess has had flashbacks, memories." McKane pursed his lips. "Not a lot, but the things she's remembering are concerning to me and my investment."

"That's impossible," he said. "I personally went through every detail of her life, blocking those memories. There's no way I missed something."

"Is that so? Then tell me how the princess remembers that she married another man."

Stoddard's muscles ticked with surprise. "She said that?"

"Are you accusing me of lying?"

"Should I be?" Stoddard asked.

Was this some kind of trap that McKane had worked up? Now that he had the princess, was he going to take Stoddard and turn him in to the Council of Essentials so that he could look like the hero? Stoddard wasn't about to let that happen. He fidgeted with the syringe in his pocket. He just had to figure out how to manipulate the situation in his favor.

"I paid you a large amount of money because you promised me a princess who wouldn't remember anything. I thought I had a few years to solidify her relationship with Cristole, to make her ties here so deep that she would never want to leave. If she remembers who she is right now, she'll go running back to Daddy, and I'll have a war on my hands. Her family will assume that I was behind her supposed assassination and kidnapping. King Bryant doesn't care for me or my kingdom. Never has. He'd take something like this and turn the entire Council against me."

"Listen," Stoddard said. "I'll talk to Doctor Von, and we'll get her memories all straightened out. Maybe we'll even do another loading phase of the medicine, build upon what we've already blocked out." He flashed a calming smile. "You don't have to worry about anything. We're on the same side here."

"Are we?"

"Of course we are. I want what you want. I want Cristole to become a power player within the Council of Essentials."

McKane's shoulders relaxed a little.

The manipulative magic Stoddard possessed was impressive.

"Give me some time to locate the doctor," he said, putting the finishing touches on the king. "And then you can formulate your next step in the plan."

Stoddard reached into his left pocket, covering his fingers

over the syringe. He stood, offering his right hand to McKane. The king eyed him but stood, shaking his proffered hand.

There was no time to lose.

Stoddard took his left hand out of his pocket, bringing it up to the king's shoulder as if he was going to pat him on the arm. He pushed the tip of the needle through McKane's clothes and skin. McKane's eyes widened in surprise, and he turned his head to the side where the prick had entered his arm. His gaze flickered to Stoddard.

"What was thaaaat?" he asked, his speech already beginning to slur. His body stumbled, threatening to topple. Stoddard quickly wrapped his arms around him, catching him from falling over.

"Yooouuuu!" McKane choked out. "I never…should…" his body tensed and cramped against Stoddard's as he gagged on his own words, "…have…trusted."

"No." Stoddard laughed. "You shouldn't have trusted me, and neither should your son." He gently lowered the king back onto the couch in a sitting position. His body was frozen, paralyzed.

McKane spoke even though his lips couldn't move. "Marx."

Stoddard bent down, meeting his gaze. There was nothing quite like seeing fear in an enemy's eyes. The entire moment reminded him of King Adler's death.

"Don't worry," Stoddard said. "I'll take care of Marx."

McKane's eyes widened, and his body convulsed.

Stoddard pressed his lips into a smile, watching as another king succumbed to death because of him. Why was that so satisfying? After a few more spasms, McKane was gone.

It was pretty anticlimactic.

Stoddard didn't need explosives or weapons to take down the Council of Essentials. He could do it by himself. One royal at a time. He went to the king's desk, picking up a newswriter, and walked back over to the couch. He positioned the king's leg so that it rested on his knee, and then he placed the newswriter in his lap. If anyone were to look in on the king, it would appear that he was relaxing on the couch, reading. By the time anyone discovered that McKane was dead, Stoddard would be long gone.

Everything had worked out perfectly. He had McKane's money and had gotten rid of any evidence that Stoddard was somehow involved. If the princess was remembering things, Stoddard needed to remove himself from the situation. By killing McKane, he'd eliminated the possibility that Cristole could turn on him. King Marx would be the fall guy now. He rolled his shoulders back and casually opened the door to the king's office, closing it behind him.

It's almost too easy to kill a king these days.

31

Marx

Marx flipped through the papers on top of his desk. He should be reading through the latest reports on the fire in the province of Colonias, but he couldn't concentrate. It wasn't like his mind couldn't focus on *anything*. He had no trouble thinking about Sydria's back peeking out of her dress the night before, or her hands running through his hair, her body against him, her soft lips lingering over his. Those things were easy to think about.

Too easy.

Marx had been dancing a fine line for a couple of weeks, teetering between their fake relationship and his real feelings. He'd been standing on the edge, a dangerous place to be, but instead of accidentally falling for Sydria, he'd jumped in—whole-heartedly. There was no point in drinking from the lie anymore. Last night, everything had become real.

In a normal situation, people would high-five him, congratulate him that he'd found the one woman whom he wanted to spend the rest of his life with, but nothing about this was normal.

Marx didn't know who Sydria was or what past life waited for her.

And there was a very big chance that she was already married to someone else. A piece of information that he'd forgotten about last night when he'd so willingly locked his lips with hers. In his defense, it was supposed to be a simple kissing lesson. Now it could be the title of a book, 'When Kissing Lessons Go Wrong.'

Or incredibly *right.*

He stood from his desk, walking over to the window. He drew in a breath, placing his hands on his hips.

Who was Sydria, and how had she gotten mixed up with Commander Stoddard? Marx hadn't mentioned Stoddard to her yet. He doubted that she'd recognize the name. Besides, was Stoddard really the one behind all of this, or was it King Adler?

Adler had always had weird things going on in the kingdom of Tolsten. The hidden weapons were proof of that. Marx wouldn't put it past the guy to have a hidden daughter as well—kept in secret for the last twenty-one years. Right now, that was the most plausible explanation.

There had to be a way to find out for sure who Sydria was. There had to be something that could jog her memory. Maybe if she saw a map of Tolsten or Queen Myka's name, her mind would be triggered.

It couldn't hurt.

Marx could take Sydria to the Cristole Castle artifact room, show her the map of the seven kingdoms and the royal families' records. He doubted it would work, but at this point, He was desperate. He couldn't be with Sydria, truly be her husband and share his life with her, until he uncovered the mystery of her past.

If his plan didn't work, if nothing in the artifact room sparked a memory, then he'd go to his father…again. He'd swallow his pride. Tell his father that he loved her and beg him to tell him who she was and put him out of his misery.

He didn't like that plan.

That's why it was Plan B, not A.

The fact that Marx was on a "need to know" basis, meant that his father had something nefarious planned. Did he intend to hurt Marx? Or worse, Sydria?

He needed to figure this out without his father so he could stop whatever was in the works.

He clapped once, pumping himself up.

It was time to go find out who his wife was.

Marx knocked on the door to the royal sitting room.

Knocked...on a door that was already *open*.

He was losing his mind.

Sydria turned around from her spot on the couch and looked at him. A timid smile crossed her lips as if she were as nervous to see him after their kiss as he'd been.

He leaned against the doorframe, keeping a safe distance from her until he could get his heart working properly.

"Hi."

It wasn't the most eloquent thing to say, but Marx was testing the waters, gauging how she'd react.

"Hi," she said back.

There wasn't much to her response—the data was inconclusive.

"You were holding out on me," he said with a smile.

Concern touched the tip of her brow. "About what?"

"If I had known all this time that you could deliver a kiss that kills, I would've never waited that long to kiss you."

She smiled, dropping her eyes to her hands. "Did it kill you?" she asked, glancing up through her dark lashes.

"Destroyed me."

"Me, too." Her smile grew, sending a flood of heat through Marx's body.

He straightened, needing to stop this conversation before he wound up on the couch next to her, kissing for the rest of the afternoon.

Although that did seem like a good option.

He shook his head. This was a perfect example of his focusing problems.

"Anyway, that's not why I'm here. I have some free time, and I was wondering if you'd like a tour of the artifact room."

"Are you trying to seduce me?" she joked.

Marx raised a brow. "With artifacts?"

"You never know."

Marx liked this teasing, flirty side of Sydria. It was definitely something he could get used to, but he was on a mission. He had goals.

He put his hand up in the air. "I promise to be a perfect gentleman throughout the tour and keep my hands to myself."

Sydria stood. "A *perfect* gentleman? How can I refuse that?"

They walked through the halls, slowly making their way through the castle until they were inside the domed room. Three arched, ceiling to floor, windows were on the room's outer wall, letting in plenty of light. Displays of pre-Desolation items were set up around the room and in rows running down the middle.

"How exciting," Sydria said as she walked through the open space.

"Yeah, there's a lot of amazing things in here. Cristole's artifacts probably look a little different than the other kingdoms since half of our kingdom lies within the pre-Desolation land known as Mexico." He pointed to a blanket hanging on the wall. "Hence all the bright colors."

Sydria studied the colorful wool blanket. "It's beautiful, but I wouldn't know the difference between Cristole's artifact room and another kingdom's since I've never been in another artifact room before." She turned away as she walked to the next display. "At least I don't think I have."

I wouldn't be so sure about that.

Marx remembered her mention of a pre-Desolation photograph when they had been with the castle seamstress.

But that was why they were there, to jog her memory even more.

"I want to show you something over here." He steered her toward the post-Desolation map of all seven kingdoms. "Surely you know what this is."

Sydria studied it, reading each word. "I've seen it in a flashback before."

Now we're getting somewhere.

"But it means nothing to me."

Marx's shoulders slipped, and his hope dropped, but he plowed ahead anyway. "You know, Tolsten," he pointed to where the kingdom was on the map, "had some crazy things happen to it in the last ten months. King Adler," he paused to see if a spark of recognition flashed through her eyes—it didn't, "had been building and manufacturing weapons of mass destruction for years without the Council of Essentials knowing about it."

"Why would he do that?"

"I don't know. He wasn't a good guy."

A frown crossed over her lips.

"He had a daughter, though, Princess Myka…Mykaleen." Again, he waited to see if she remembered something, but nothing happened. "Myka was the one who destroyed all the weapons. Her father died, and she ran in the election and became the first female elected ruler in over one hundred years."

"She sounds like a powerful woman. She must be an excellent leader."

"I've never met her, but I will at the next Council of Essentials in nine years."

"Have you met all of the other leaders?" Sydria asked, glancing over the map.

"Yeah, I've met the rest of the kings."

"What are they like? Are they good rulers too?"

"I guess it depends on how you would define a good ruler."

"Do they care about their kingdoms? Do they fight for what's good and right?"

"I think they try to, for the most part." He dropped his eyes to the floor. "But by that standard, I don't know that *I'm* a good ruler."

"I've seen firsthand that you're an excellent king. You don't give yourself enough credit. You care about your people, but for some reason, you don't like people knowing that. Your ideas are strong. You know how to command a room, and you keep your promises."

"You make me those things."

"No." Sydria shook her head. "You were those things long before I came along."

He wanted to believe that.

She stepped to the side where they had a list of each ruling monarch and their royal families. Marx leaned over her shoulder. Maybe if she saw Adler or Myka's name in writing, it would do something.

Sydria studied the paper, looking through the names. "What happened here?" she asked, pointing to New Hope where King Bryant's family line was listed. "Why is this one crossed out?"

"King Bryant's daughter died."

Sydria looked at him. "How did she die?"

"Well, it's actually a really sad story. She was killed at her own wedding. I guess the artifact keeper crossed her name out after it happened." He glanced to his own family, where a line was drawn through Palmer's name.

"That's too bad," Sydria said. "She had the same initials as me." She shrugged before moving on to the next display.

Marx froze.

He looked down at the paper.

Seran Alyssa Haslet.

Sydria Alyson Hasler.

He shook his head.

It was just a coincidence.

It had to be.

But things dropped into place in his mind, especially his last words.

She was killed at her own wedding.

Marx thought back to King Ezra and his dark head of curls.

No, it was impossible.

He stumbled backward. "I forgot something," he said. "I'm so sorry, but I have to go. Will you be okay here?"

Sydria's smile faltered. "I'll be fine, but are you okay? You look like you've seen a ghost."

Maybe he had.

"Yeah." He stepped toward the door. "I forgot a meeting I was supposed to attend. You know me," he said as he made his way to the exit, "always late. I'll see you later tonight."

She smiled. "I hope so."

Marx ran to his bedroom, knowing exactly what he was looking for. He went to his closet and pulled down the chest with Palmer's initials carved into the top. He fumbled with the lock and opened the lid. His fingers felt heavy as he sifted through Palmer's things until he found the letter. Marx's name was scribbled across the top in Palmer's handwriting. He unfolded the paper, scanning Palmer's words.

Marx,

I made it to Albion last night. The wedding is in two days, so I have plenty of time to spare. Who knows, I might even find a girl to distract me while I wait for the festivities. Albion is a nice place, but it's cold, and it's missing an ocean, so it's not home. Although, I'm hoping I'll have a chance to hike the mountains around here before I have to leave for Appa.

The other rulers I've met so far have been pretty decent. Dad was right. It's good for me to make connections leading up to the Council of

Essentials in a few months. I will say, I'm kind of regretting that dad didn't set up an arranged marriage between Princess Seran and me. She's a knockout. Just kidding. You know how I feel about arranged marriages. The princess is your type, though. Dark eyes, dark hair, tan skin with a smile that could bring down an entire kingdom. It's a good thing you didn't come to the wedding. You would have tried to steal the bride from Prince Ezra.

Tell mom I'm still alive.

Palmer

Marx let the letter fall to the ground. His breath felt heavy, and his mind struggled to keep up. Palmer's words rang through his mind on repeat.

Dark eyes, dark hair, tan skin with a smile that could bring down an entire kingdom.

The description was vague enough that he could have been describing half the people in the world, but somehow it made sense to Marx.

His mind raced through the other clues.

Her keen sense of fashion.

The mention of guards and PTs.

The way she knew how to wait for introductions when she walked into a room.

Her knowledge about government and politics.

His father's bitterness at being slighted from the marriage alliance years ago.

It all came together into a staggering realization. Could she really be Princess Seran?

She wasn't married, after all.

Sydria was presumed dead.

32

Marx

Marx walked to dinner. After the initial shock, he'd spent the rest of the afternoon researching everything he could find on New Hope, King Bryant, and his daughter. He'd gone back through the reports of the wedding and the circumstances surrounding Seran's death. It was widely speculated that King Adler was behind her assassination. Albion even said they had a co-conspirator who had admitted Adler's guilt and involvement. On top of everything, Ezra Trevenna had married Seran's step-sister, Renna. It was an awkward situation when the princess was dead. How much worse was it going to be when everyone found out she was alive?

Marx tightened his jaw as he thought about King Ezra. Seran had been betrothed to him half of her life. Did she love him? When she found out her true identity, would she wish that she was married to Ezra Trevenna instead of him?

The more Marx thought about it, the more his head and his heart hurt.

King Adler had done this.

How else could Sydria have ended up with Commander Stoddard? He was the leader of the Tolsten army—King

Adler's right-hand man. The entire situation seemed impossible. And if Sydria was Princess Seran, how had she lost her memory? And why had Seran's father, and her fiancé, and a room full of wedding guests, including Palmer, all thought she was dead…when she really wasn't? They'd even held a funeral for her.

Marx had so many questions for his father. He was the only person who could tell him for sure if his suspicions about Sydria were correct. Was his father somehow part of Sydria's attempted murder and kidnapping? Did he know who she really was? He thought back to the night before the wedding and the conversation they'd had in his father's office.

"She's someone who is extremely valuable to our future and the future of Cristole…All you need to know is that this girl will make sure that Cristole has a power position when it comes to the Council of Essentials and our alignment with the other kingdoms…You need to trust me."

It seemed like his father had known who she was, and it was going to take every ounce of Marx's strength not to lunge across the table and grab him by the collar, demanding answers. He'd have to wait until after dinner for that conversation.

Marx entered the dining room. The women were already seated, waiting to start. He kissed Sydria on the cheek, not missing his mother and Dannyn's surprised expressions. Sydria eyed him too, obviously unsure how to respond. Maybe he shouldn't have kissed her, but his mind was lost on other things.

"Where's Dad?" he asked, looking over at his father's empty chair.

His mother waved her hand out in front of her. "I went to get him for dinner, but he was sound asleep on the couch in his office, reading the newswriter. I swear, as much as he does that, we should put a mattress in there. I'm sure he'll come stumbling to bed later tonight."

Marx's jaw hardened. He wouldn't be able to talk to him. If he woke him up now, his father would be grumpy and groggy and not willing to give him the answers he needed.

"He's getting old," Dannyn said. "He falls asleep even when he's not reading the newswriter." She took a sip of her drink. "And he snores."

His mother looked at the head waiter. "Shall we start?"

Marx made it through dinner and games in the sitting room, only half-listening to the conversation around him about how difficult it was proving to be for his mother to get butterflies for her terrarium. Every once in a while, Sydria would look his way, questioning him with her eyes. Each time, he gave her a reassuring nod.

He was fine.

As fine as a person could be after finding out that the woman he loved was considered dead.

When the evening was over, they walked to their rooms hand and hand. He stopped outside their doors, turning to face her.

"My surfer girl," he said, brushing her hair back behind her ear. But that was the thing. Sydria wasn't *his* girl. She had an entirely different life from the one she lived there—an important life—one where she was needed and wanted.

"You were quiet tonight," she said, resting her hands on his chest. "Is everything okay?"

He forced a smile. "Yeah, I'll be okay."

But the truth was, Marx's heart was broken.

Not for himself but for Sydria. For everything she'd been through, for the years that she'd lost, for the life that had been stolen from her.

It wasn't fair.

He pulled her into his arms, hugging her tight. He never wanted to let her go. He wanted to keep her in Cristole and protect her from the world and the evilness it had shown her.

"Are you okay?" he asked. "I noticed you rub your head a few times during dinner and when we were playing games."

"I'm fine. It's a small headache." She wrapped her arms around him. "I'm glad you're okay too. I was getting worried that you regretted kissing me last night."

Marx pulled back so he could look into her eyes. He lifted his hands to her cheeks, gently stroking them with his fingers. "I regret a lot of things in my life, but I will never regret kissing you." He hesitated for a moment. "Or marrying you."

"I feel the same way."

Sydria McKane felt that way, but as soon as she found out she was Seran Haslet, she would feel differently.

She grabbed his hands from off her cheeks, holding them close to her heart. "Listen," she bit her lip nervously, "I'm not charming or flirty or anything like that, so I'm just going to come out and say it." She sucked in a deep breath, gathering courage. "Would you like to come in my room…you know," she glanced away like it was killing her to be so open, "and stay for a little bit?"

Marx knew what "stay for a little bit" meant. She wanted to repeat what had happened on the balcony the night before. He wanted that too. He wanted to kiss her more than anything. Sydria was definitely charming and flirty and everything like *that.* But he couldn't do it. Knowing who she was changed things, and Marx hated it.

"Thank you for the offer, but I'm going to decline."

The light in her eyes dimmed, and the air escaped her chest. He felt awful. If there was a way to take his words back, he would, but they were out there, floating between them like little knives pointed at her heart.

She pushed a smile onto her lips. "Of course." She shook her head, dropping his hands. "I totally understand." She reached for the doorknob and twisted the handle. She lifted her eyebrows as if she was trying to pass for bright and cheery, but he didn't buy it. "I'll see you tomorrow." Then she quickly escaped behind the door.

Marx dropped his head into his hands.

It was the story of his life.

He let down everyone he cared about.

"I'm going to decline!" Dannyn exclaimed, throwing her head back against her pillow. "Who says that to their *wife*?"

"I know. I'm such a jerk." Marx sat on the foot of Dannyn's bed. His feet rested on the bench at the end, and his elbows were propped up on his knees.

"I don't get why you turned her down."

Marx looked over his shoulder at his sister. "It's complicated. It's *really* complicated."

"It can't be *that* complicated. You're falling in love with her, and she's falling in love with you. What else matters?"

He twisted his body, facing his sister. "Why did you say that? Do you think she's falling in love with me?"

Dannyn rolled her eyes. "Please, as if you didn't already know."

"I don't know."

How could he possibly know? Their entire relationship was based on a lie, a sham, a charade.

"You two are adorable." She smiled. "It's like watching two awkward twelve-year-olds fall in love. Neither one of you knows how to act."

"I know how to act," he said, getting defensive.

"Really?" She tilted her head. "You just told your totally hot wife that you didn't want to come into her room and stay awhile."

He melted back into the bed, looking up at the ceiling. "I was trying to be the good guy."

"The good guy fights for the woman he loves. He lets

nothing stand in the way of being with her. If you know she's the woman for you, then fight for her."

Marx twisted his head so he could see Dannyn's face. "You know, you actually give pretty good advice."

"I know," she said. "I don't look smart, but I really am."

Marx knew what he had to do.

33

Sydria

Sydria woke early and dressed for the day. The dull pain in her head throbbed still. She assumed it was a side effect of not taking her medicine the last couple of days, but at least everything with her heart seemed to be okay. Well, not everything. Her heart was still wounded from last night.

She made her way to the royal sitting room, hoping Marx wouldn't be there. She still needed time to recover from the embarrassment. What had she been thinking, inviting Marx into her room? This was a *fake* marriage…at least, it was supposed to be.

She cringed every time she thought back to that moment.

Thank you for the offer, but I'm going to decline.

It was humiliating.

Had it been appropriate, Sydria would have curled up into a ball and gently rocked back and forth. That's how embarrassed she was. She'd only felt this kind of humiliation one other time in her life, a moment that she'd remembered yesterday morning. The memory wasn't the entire moment, more like the feeling of the moment. Standing alone in front of a large crowd. All eyes on her…waiting, whispering. Where had he gone? He was supposed to be there, with her. Even without the full memory, Sydria knew he'd gone after the color red. She was alone, and everyone knew it.

She shook the dark feeling away and rolled her shoulders back as she entered the sitting room. Dannyn sat alone at the table, eating fruit. She had a newswriter out next to her. Sydria exhaled, grateful she wouldn't have to face Marx yet.

Dannyn glanced up at her as she took her seat. "What can we do that's fun today?"

Sydria loved how full of life Dannyn was. "You know, you remind me of someone." She reached for the pitcher of juice and poured some into her cup.

Dannyn frowned. "How? I thought you didn't have any memories."

"I don't, not really, but yesterday I had more flashbacks than I've ever had. There was one with a blonde girl. She was happy and bright. I don't know who she is, but you remind me of her."

"Maybe she reminds you of *me*."

"Is there a difference?" Sydria asked.

"Well, I—"

"Your Majesty, Princess Dannyn?" a guard said, rushing into the room. "You need to come quick." The guard panted like he'd run the entire way.

"What's wrong?" Dannyn asked.

"It's King McKane."

A crowd of servants, maids, and guards stood around King McKane's office, watching as the medic team hurried in and out. Dannyn ran into the room, falling over her father's body as he lay stretched out on a medic board. The king's skin was a pale blue-ish color, and his body was stiff and rigid.

He was dead.

Queen Malory sat motionless on the couch next to her

husband, holding his cold hand. Marx stood by the window with his arms folded and his back to the room. He didn't even budge when they entered.

"How?" Dannyn asked through her tears. "How did this happen?"

Queen Malory was a statue. "He didn't come to bed last night. I found him here this morning."

Doctor Moore glanced at the queen mother, waiting to see if she would give more details than that. When she didn't, he turned to Dannyn. "We need to do an autopsy to be sure, but it appears the king had a heart attack."

"But he's so young," Dannyn said. "He's not even sixty yet."

Sydria's hand covered her mouth, and tears spilled down her face. She wasn't crying for McKane. She cried for his family—for Queen Malory, who would have to grow old by herself, for Dannyn, who would never get the chance to have her father walk her down the aisle or see her baby bounce on his knee, and for Marx, who never got to mend their broken relationship—to release the blame that hung over Palmer's death.

A dark, empty space opened up inside Sydria. The emptiness held so much. Raw pain that had been locked away in the deepest part of her heart spilled out of her. She saw flashes of her mother's funeral, her dead body lying stiffly in a casket. Long black hair had been situated over each of her shoulders. She wore a burgundy dress with matching lipstick painted on her lips. A small gold tiara rested on her head.

"Come now." A hand reached out to her. "It's time to close the casket."

Sydria tried to see the man's face. Her mind studied the hand, soft and manly, then slowly pulled back, giving her a better vantage point of the memory. She took in the man's slightly rounded midsection and expensive suit jacket. Her mind scanned up to his chest and then to his neck. Her heart raced. Would her mind let her see his face? She fought hard against whatever blocked the full memory.

Then she saw him.

His kind smile.

His thin nose.

His high cheekbones.

His brown eyes and hair that were a shade lighter than hers.

It was her father.

Her head spun as the memory swirled out of her mind.

Then blackness.

The opening had closed.

Sydria pressed against her forehead, putting pressure where the headache was.

"We'll take the king down to the medic hall and run some tests," Doctor Moore said.

Sydria tried to focus on what was happening in front of her. She'd have to think about the memory another time.

Dannyn sat back, and Queen Malory let go of McKane's hand so the nurse medics could take his body away.

"I'll let you know as soon as I know something," Doctor Moore said, following his nurses.

Dannyn scrambled to her feet, hugging her mother tightly. She sobbed in her mother's arms as Queen Malory stroked her hair. The queen mother was a rock, more composed than Sydria had ever before seen her. She'd been there before with Palmer, lost someone she'd loved deeply.

Sydria glanced at Marx where he stood at the window. She didn't care about last night or her embarrassment anymore. She walked to him, turning his body to hers. She wrapped her arms around him, pulling him into a hug. His arms unfolded and worked their way out, hugging her back.

"I'm so sorry," she whispered.

Marx buried his head into the side of her neck. His breaths were heavy, and his body trembled. His tears wetted her neck and hair, and his body shook. She held him tight, wishing she could take away the pain.

Marx

"I've never seen anything like this before," Doctor Moore said that night in the medic hall of Cristole Castle. "That's why I called you here."

Marx looked down at his father's body, stretched out on the table in front of him. His clothes had been removed, and a light cloth covered him from the waist down. Since his mother had discovered his father's dead body that morning, everything seemed blurry. It was like he was reliving the moments after Palmer's death, except this time, Marx was in charge.

"Have you finished the autopsy?" Marx asked.

"Not yet, but I don't think I need to." Doctor Moore pointed to a small dot on the side of his father's arm. "This is peculiar to me."

Marx leaned down, squinting his eyes. "I don't really see anything."

"From the outside, you wouldn't, but if you look at our body scans, you can see what I'm talking about." Doctor Moore opened the folder in his hand and held up a scanned image of his father's body. "The muscles around that spot have decayed away as if acid was dropped on them."

Marx looked at the picture, comparing the indentation in his father's muscle to where the dot was on his arm."

"And," Doctor Moore held up another scan, "if you look at the images of your father's brain, you'll see the same kind of decay."

Marx studied the scan, not really sure what he saw. He looked up at the doctor. "So what are you saying?"

"I'll know more once I open your father up, but I can say for sure right now that your father didn't die of a heart attack. His bloodstream was poisoned. I've never seen a drug this sophisticated before. It attacks the body, specifically the brain, in a matter of seconds."

Marx scratched his head, trying to work this information in with everything else. How would someone poison his father without anyone in the castle knowing?

"Thank you, Doctor Moore. You've been extremely helpful."

He left the medic hall and made his way to his father's office. His secretary, Lance, sat outside working on funeral arrangements.

"Lance, can you tell me my father's schedule yesterday?"

"Certainly, Your Majesty." Lance opened his top drawer, pulling out a notebook. He flipped back a page, scanning the paper. "Your father only had one appointment at the end of the day." Lance looked up. "A Mr. Otis Sutton came to the castle at King McKane's request."

Otis Sutton.

Or, more precisely, *Commander Stoddard*.

34

Doctor Von

Doctor Von shifted in his chair, rubbing his hands down his pant leg. He wasn't sure if he'd made the right decision coming here, but he was too far down the path now. He'd spent a lot of his money securing a transporter and had traveled for more than a week. His visit wasn't part of Commander Stoddard's plan, but Von had worked with Stoddard for almost two years now to know that there was always a fall guy. He wasn't there out of guilt. This visit was Von's way of making sure the fall guy wouldn't be him.

A woman around Von's same age popped her head out from the office. "King Bryant will see you now," she said, opening the door wide for him to enter.

Von closed his eyes, taking in a calming breath. He stood and walked to the door, clearing his throat on the way. King Bryant's office was decorated simply compared to what Von had seen from the other kings. There was a single desk, two leather chairs, and a black sofa pushed against the wall.

"Doctor Von," Bryant said, walking around his desk to shake his hand. They were about the same height but Bryant was rounder and Von was bald. "It's so good to see you."

Von's palms were slippery with sweat, but he shook Bryant's hand anyway.

"King Ezra said that you no longer work at the Albion Ruler's Palace."

"No, I don't."

Bryant gestured for him to sit down. "I was surprised to hear that," he said, walking around his desk and sitting in his own chair. "What made you leave Albion?"

"Actually, it the loss of Princess Seran that made me leave."

Bryant's brown eyes turned kind. "I'm sorry. Please know that none of us hold you accountable for Seran's death. You did the best you could to save her. There was nothing that could have been done."

Von nodded as he swallowed back the bile rising in his throat.

"So, what brings you to the kingdom of New Hope?" Bryant asked.

"I have some information about your daughter." He crossed his arms then uncrossed them, unable to get comfortable.

Bryant seemed confused. "What kind of information?"

He bounced his knee as he spoke. "What I'm about to tell you might come as a shock. Princess Seran isn't dead."

The king puffed out a small laugh. "I'm sorry, I don't quite follow what you're saying."

Von had anticipated this kind of reaction and the probability that King Bryant would not believe him.

The story was unbelievable. He could hardly believe it himself.

"Your daughter is alive. I saved her."

"That's impossible. I saw her dead days after the wedding. I buried her body next to her mother's."

Von shook his head. "You thought you saw your daughter

dead, but I had administered a drug that slowed her organs and vitals down so that she would *appear* dead."

"You did what?" Bryant's expression contorted. "Why would you—"

"King Adler made me do it," he burst out, dabbing his sweaty forehead with his handkerchief. "He *forced* me to do it."

Bryant didn't need to know that Von had been given a substantial amount of money—enough money that he could continue his research on the Isolated Amnesia project. Besides the cash, Adler had promised him that his drug would change the world, that he would bring it forward to the Council of Essentials.

That's all Von had ever wanted.

It was his life's work.

His baby.

His drug *could* change the world.

"King Adler was the one who had my daughter shot. Why would he want you to save her?" Bryant asked.

"The shooting at the wedding was staged. Seran was never supposed to die. The bullet was supposed to inflict a minor flesh wound. But when King Ezra pushed her out of the way, the bullet landed in the wrong spot. The wound was severe, but nothing I couldn't handle," he told Bryant matter-of-factly. "Once she was stable, I administered the medicine that made her appear dead. There were small hints and signs that a trained eye would've been able to pick up on, but you and your family were grieving. You missed all the signs."

The color drained from Bryant's face. "But I closed the casket. I watched them load it into a transporter in Albion and bring it to New Hope."

"King Adler had the transporters switched during your first stop along the journey."

Bryant stood and began pacing back and forth, shaking his head. "Switched the transporters?"

"Yes," Von confirmed. "The transporter with Seran's body

drove to Tolsten with me in it, watching over the patient. And the decoy transporter and casket went to New Hope." He held his hand up, remembering another detail. "I should also mention that we had a special casket designed for her body that circulated air, so there was no chance of suffocation while she was away from us. My job was to keep her alive."

He paused pacing, shooting a glare back at him. "If what you're saying is true, where is she?"

"That's why I'm here," Von said. "After King Adler died, Commander Stoddard and I escaped Tolsten House with your daughter."

Bryant's chest heaved up and down. "I remember the reports—a doctor, a nurse, and a mystery woman. That was *Seran*?"

"That's correct."

His breath faltered. "But the reports said the woman was immobile. Is Seran…okay?"

"Since the wedding, Seran has been kept in a drug-induced coma."

Bryant gasped, covering his mouth with his hand.

"It wasn't the initial plan, but Adler's illness and death changed things."

The king's hand drifted from his mouth to his chest. "Where is she?" he demanded again.

"Three months ago—" Von said, inclining his head, "I guess it is four months now—I brought your daughter out of her coma, under the direction of Commander Stoddard."

"What does the commander have to do with any of this?"

"When the weapons were destroyed, the princess was the only thing Stoddard had left to bargain with against the Council of Essentials."

"So, where is she? Does Stoddard have her locked up somewhere?"

"No. On the contrary. She's at Cristole Castle. She's the queen."

"What?" Bryant's voice rose. "What do you mean she's the queen?"

"Commander Stoddard sold the princess to the King of Cristole. He married her, and now she's the queen."

Bryant slammed his fist into his desk, making Von jump in his chair. "He sold her…like a prisoner?"

"She's not a prisoner." Von pushed his glasses back up his nose.

"If she's not a prisoner, then why doesn't she come home?"

"I invented a drug that blocks her memory. Isolated Amnesia," he said proudly. "She doesn't know *who* she is."

Bryant bolted across the room, grabbing Doctor Von by the collar and pulling him to a stand. "What have you done to my daughter?" he yelled.

The door to his office flew open, and his guard pointed his gun at Von, but Bryant didn't even acknowledge the man.

Von's hands went up in the air. "It wasn't me. They *forced* me." He blinked rapidly with fear. "I barely escaped. You were the first person I came to."

Bryant's eyes went to stone, and he shook him hard. "I should kill you!"

"You have to believe me. I swear." Von tried to convince the king. He hoped coming there hadn't been a mistake. Maybe he should have stayed in Cristole and trusted Stoddard. He needed to persuade Bryant that they were on the same team. "We can save your daughter, and I can bring back her memory. I promise!"

Bryant released his grip, and Von sank back into his chair, scrunching down with fear. The king looked at his guard. "Throw him in jail."

"Jail?" Von said in a panic. "I came to you. Told you where your daughter is. I'm your partner now."

Bryant shook his head. "You'll stay in the New Hope jail until you can be tried for your crimes."

Guards rushed toward him. Von looked around the room. There was no way out. This wasn't how things were supposed to go. King Bryant was supposed to be kind, understanding, thankful, not full of rage. They grabbed his arms, pulling them forcefully behind his back.

"Please!" He looked at King Bryant. "Don't do this. I can help you save her."

"Don't worry," the king said as he watched the guards drag him out of the room. "I'm going to Cristole to save my daughter myself. King Marx will regret the day he ever took advantage of her."

Von opened his mouth to speak, to tell King Bryant that it wasn't King Marx who had struck the deal but King McKane, then he remembered Stoddard's plan to pin everything on King Marx and he clamped his mouth shut.

He should have listened to Stoddard. He'd miscalculated. He'd risked everything by going to Bryant, and it had backfired. Stoddard had threatened to ruin him, but he had nothing left to lose now but his life. Von would have to revert to Stoddard's plan and hope it was enough to save him from being executed.

35

Marx

Marx was dressed in black. That's what people wore to funerals—the absence of color as a reminder that the person they loved was forever absent from their lives.

A group of fifty of his father's closest family and friends huddled around his casket on the west side of the castle grounds. His father would be buried next to Palmer. That's where he would've wanted to be.

The sweltering sun beat down on them, stealing their breaths. Some of the guests fanned themselves with their hands, trying to find a respite from the heat, while others dabbed at the beads of sweat pooling at their hairlines.

High Ruler Grier spoke to the group, reminding everyone what an accomplished man King Meldrum McKane had been. Dannyn stood on his left, eyes fixed on the green grass below them, and next to her was his mother. The queen mother had been stoic the last week since his father had died—different from how she'd handled Palmer's death. Everyone held their breaths around her, waiting for the moment her tough exterior would crack. It was only a matter of time.

Sydria squeezed his right hand once, then dropped it. It was enough to let him know she was there if he needed her.

She'd been amazing over the last several days. She'd planned and coordinated every last detail of his father's viewing and funeral. And she'd kept the queen mother distracted by working on the butterfly terrarium with her. She hadn't even been asked to help. She'd seen a need and had fulfilled it. Marx wondered if she would've done all of that if she knew the truth about his father, about how he'd conspired with Commander Stoddard to keep her away from her life and family back in New Hope. At least, Marx assumed his father had conspired with Stoddard. He'd never know for sure. The answers to every question Marx had had died with his father, and he hated him for it.

Not true *hate*.

Marx loved his father. He only wished that his father could've loved him the way he'd loved Palmer.

"And now," High Ruler Grier said, looking over the crowd. "As we lay to rest our dear husband, father, friend, and king in this cold, cold grave..."

Dannyn glanced at Marx at the mention of the word cold. There was nothing *cold* about the day or the grave. A trickle of sweat rolling down Marx's back confirmed that.

"...we take comfort knowing that King McKane is laid to rest next to his beloved son, Palmer. The coldness of the grave..."

Dannyn hiccuped a laugh, quickly covering her mouth. Anyone else might have passed it off as a sob, but she had definitely laughed.

"...and the cold chill of death—"

Dannyn laughed again, and this time Marx did too. He cleared his throat, trying to cover his tracks. How many times was Grier going to say the word *cold* when it was one hundred and ten degrees outside?

Dannyn looked down again, silently shaking with giggles. It was literally the most inappropriate time to laugh, and yet, Marx couldn't help himself. It wasn't even that funny, but if

Marx didn't laugh, he would completely fall apart. He dropped his head, placing his hand over his forehead, hoping to pass his laughter off as sorrow.

Marx felt Sydria shift next to him. Whatever feelings she'd had for him before this moment would surely fade.

Who laughed at their own father's funeral?

But beyond the laughter, once Sydria found out who she really was and what his father had done, she wouldn't want anything to do with Marx or his family.

All the guests had gone home, the food had been cleaned up, and the lights in the castle were turned down low. Marx and his family sat in silence in the royal sitting room, lost in thought.

"Well, it was a long, lovely day," his mother said, standing from her chair. "I'm exhausted. I think I'll go to bed."

Dannyn looked at him with a worried look in her eyes. "Mom, I'll go with you." She stood too, wrapping her arm around her mother's shoulders. "Good night, you two," Dannyn called as she walked out of the room with his mother.

Sydria sat on the other end of the couch, rubbing her temple with her fingers. She had on a simple black dress, and her hair was tied back from her face into a ponytail. She looked beautiful. Marx hadn't spent much time with her over the last week, partly because they'd both been so busy and partly because Marx knew what was coming. As soon as she found out who she really was, she'd leave him. There would be a hole so deep inside his heart, he didn't know if he'd be able to survive.

Marx had no right to love her. She wasn't his, not really. She'd go back to New Hope.

But not tonight.

Tonight, she was his wife.

He leaned over, reaching for her arm, pulling her to him. Her dark eyes peered into his as she curled up next to him on the couch. She rested her head on his chest, snuggling in close, and all Marx wanted to do was stay with her forever.

"Are you okay?" she asked.

"I am now." He wrapped both his arms around her. "Are you okay? I've noticed that you haven't been feeling well sometimes."

"I've had a few headaches this past week."

Marx tensed, dipping his chin down to see her better. "Why didn't you tell me?"

"It's not a big deal, but it's sweet that you've noticed."

"Of course I've noticed. Let's meet with Doctor Moore tomorrow to see if there's anything that can be done."

"Okay." She nodded against him.

"You were great today…and this last week." He kissed the top of her forehead.

"It was nothing."

"It was *everything* to me."

They sat in silence, holding each other. It was only a matter of time until Sydria would ask him about their deal. The entire charade of their fake relationship had been to prove to Marx's father that they were falling in love, but now that his father was dead, they didn't need to keep the pretense up. And now that Marx thought he knew who she was, she could go home.

It was over.

There was nothing left to keep her here.

Marx should tell her right then. He waited for the words to come.

Nothing.

Maybe he didn't have to tell her yet.

Maybe they *could* stay like that…just for a little bit longer.

36

King Bryant

Bryant rolled the transporter window down as his guard approached. The soft morning sunlight spilled into the vehicle, as did Cristole's humid temperatures.

"Your Majesty, Cristole Castle is in sight," the guard said. "We'll be there within a half-hour."

Bryant nodded. "And what about the New Hope army?"

"I received word that our men are in position to surround the castle, ready for battle if necessary."

"Excellent. Let's not waste another moment." Bryant rolled the window up, bobbing his knee nervously up and down as the transporter began to move forward again. He'd never stepped foot in the kingdom of Cristole before, and after this incident, he hoped he'd never be back. There had been a time, eleven years ago, when he'd entertained the idea of aligning with Cristole—of marrying Seran to one of McKane's sons.

He balled his fists. The McKane family had found a way to make the marriage happen without his consent, and they were going to pay for it.

Bryant didn't know what to expect when he arrived at the castle. He'd sent some guards ahead to gain some intel. Part of what Von had said was true. Marx McKane had just married a mysterious woman. But the most interesting piece of information that his men had found was that Meldrum McKane was dead. Marx had probably killed his father so that he wouldn't find out about Seran. That was a stretch, but at this point, Bryant didn't put anything past King Marx.

Would Seran be bound? Held as a hostage? Suffering? He closed his eyes as he thought of the possibilities and all the things his precious daughter had gone through.

He hated that he hadn't been there to protect her, to save her.

But he was here now, and he wouldn't let anything stand in the way of rescuing her.

He was prepared for war or whatever it took to bring her safely back home. King Marx would pay for his part in this. He was a ruler, a member of the Council of Essentials. Bryant held him to a higher standard; Marx's punishment should be more severe.

Usually, Bryant was the epitome of wisdom and stability. But when Doctor Von had said that Seran was still alive, something inside of him had snapped. His years of wisdom and righteous discipline meant nothing in this situation. He didn't care about being rational. He cared about getting justice for his daughter.

Bryant had always put his kingdom first, but now his daughter came first, and he didn't care about the consequences. Diplomacy, mercy, kindness—it was all gone. The father inside of him wanted to pull his gun out upon arrival at the castle and shoot the young king right in the heart.

Do to him what had been done to Seran.

37

Sydria

Memories came back in spurts, erupting inside Sydria's mind more and more each day. It had been over a week since she'd stopped taking Von's medicine, and her heart seemed to be beating fine on its own, but the severe headaches hadn't stopped. They'd only increased. Sometimes her vision blurred, sometimes the room would spin, sometimes the pain was so great she vomited. She thought about going back on the drug, just to make the headaches stop, but she didn't want to lose the memories she'd gained—there had to be a correlation between the medicine and her flashbacks.

When Sydria had lived with Von and Edmay, she'd forgotten to take the drug one day, and her mind had opened slightly. At the time, she hadn't made the connection, but now, things were starting to piece together. She wondered if Von knew that the medicine for her heart suppressed her memories, an accidental side effect. At this point, she preferred the headaches over a completely empty mind.

Sydria had filled in a lot of gaps, mostly things from her childhood. She knew the curves of both of her parent's faces. She saw herself on the beach chasing waves. She saw her old dollhouse and a crown she'd made out of flowers for a doll. There was a beautiful black stallion that she'd ridden. A large bedroom filled with nice furniture and fancy colorful clothes. There were teachers and private tutors. Piano lessons. Violin lessons. Dancing lessons. Her childhood had been made up of the most expensive things. But beyond the materialism, she'd felt loved.

She wondered if the people in her dreams were looking for her or at least missed her. The more her mind opened up, the more she knew with certainty that Von and Edmay hadn't told her the truth. She wasn't a working-class girl from Northland. And the memory she'd had the day King McKane died hinted that her mother had passed away years ago. She doubted Von and Edmay were even related to her—the feelings of love that she'd felt in her memories didn't match the way Von and Edmay had treated her. Why would they lie to her, trick her? What was in it for them?

There was still a lot Sydria didn't know, including her own name or the names of anyone else. Everything that she'd seen had been short clips, choppy memories, blurry moments, but she'd remembered them.

That was a good start.

She wanted to tell Marx about her flashbacks, but right after his father's death hadn't been the time. She'd sworn Idella to secrecy about how bad her headaches were. Marx had picked up on it a few times. He always could tell when she wasn't feeling well, but she'd brushed it away. She didn't want anyone to know how much pain she was in. Sydria had finally come to a place where everyone didn't view her as broken. If people knew about her headaches, the looks of pity would return to their eyes, and the strides that she'd made at building a life would all be erased.

Sydria sat on the edge of her bed, waiting for Idella to bring her a cup of water. She'd had a terrible migraine all night long, but it had started to fade.

"Are you sure you want to go down to breakfast?" Idella asked, handing her the glass.

She nodded, drinking the cool liquid. "Yes, I'll be fine. Besides, I'm worried about Queen Malory. Now that the funeral is over, she won't have anything to think about or keep her mind busy. I don't want her to be all alone."

"Fine." Idella sighed. "But I wish you'd let King Marx know how much you're suffering."

"I will," Sydria said.

She didn't know where she stood with Marx. There were times when everything between them felt so real, when she felt love pouring out of his eyes. Then other times, he seemed so distant.

It was the distance that scared her.

All Sydria wanted was to be with him.

Marx

MARX SAT AT HIS DESK, STARING AT A BLANK PAPER.

How do you write someone and tell them that you think their daughter is still alive?

His head fell into his hands.

Did he even want to write the letter?

Once he sent it, there would be no turning back. He'd have about a week for the letter to get to New Hope and then another week for New Hope to come to him.

Two weeks.

That was all he'd have left with Sydria.

He would have two weeks to figure out how to tell her who he thought she was.

Two weeks seemed like nothing when he wanted a lifetime with her, but it had to be done. Marx picked up the pen and began writing.

. . .

King Bryant,

"Your Majesty!" Commander Tindale said, hurrying into his office. The commander wore navy Cristole pants and a white shirt. A weapons belt was slung around his waist, and his usually calm exterior appeared anxious. "My men spotted transporters and personal transporters on the horizon."

Marx's brows bent. "How many?"

The commander gulped. "Hundreds."

"Hundreds?" Marx stood from his chair, scrambling to his window. In the distance, a line of PTs drove toward the castle, their tires churning dirt into the air creating a giant cloud of dust. Behind the PTs was a row of black transporters, all making their way to Cristole Castle.

"Their flags and uniforms look to be from New Hope," his commander said.

Fear rumbled through Marx's body.

"Find Sydria," he said. "And my mother and sister. And pull the alarm to gather the king's guard."

"What about the approaching transporters? We don't have nearly enough men here to fight them off."

"We won't be fighting them. I know why they're here." Marx turned to his commander. "I was too late."

"What's happening? What does their visit mean?"

"It means Queen Sydria isn't from Northland."

Sydria

Sydria was surprised to see both the queen mother and Dannyn dressed and down at breakfast. She'd assumed they would spend the day in bed, leaning into their grief.

Queen Malory greeted Sydria with a smile. "Good morning," she said cheerily.

Sydria smiled back, then looked at Dannyn, who shrugged, as if she thought her mother's behavior was bizarre too.

She pulled out a chair and sat down.

"Marx said they can't find Kase," Dannyn said. "When my dad died, he sent word for him to return home from Tolsten, but they haven't been able to locate him on the road or in Tolsten."

Sydria patted her arm. "I'm sure they'll track him down soon."

"Probably not." Dannyn sighed.

All three women jumped as a loud sound blared through the castle.

"What's that?" Sydria asked, lightly covering her ears. "Is it a fire?"

"No." Terror took over Queen Malory's expression. "It's the alarm for the king's guard."

"What's happening now?" Dannyn stood, slamming her napkin down on the table. "Doesn't everyone know my father just died? I can't take any more craziness."

A team of guards filed through the door. "Your Majesties, Princess Dannyn," the head guard said, glancing at all three women. "King Marx has asked that you come with me."

"What's going on?" The queen mother stood, her voice trembling as she spoke.

"The castle is under siege," the guard said.

Queen Malory fainted.

Dannyn gripped the table for support.

Sydria stood motionless as her mind exploded with a memory.

"I hope you can forgive me someday, but I want to set you free. Set us both free."

A gunshot.

Blood.

A stolen breath.
She was dying.
Dead.

38

Marx

Against Commander Tindale's advice, Marx opened the Cristole Castle gates, allowing several PTs and two transporters into the grounds.

Marx stood on the front steps of the castle with his commander and a line of guards behind him.

"Your Majesty, we're already surrounded. Why would you give them access to the middle of our stronghold?" Commander Tindale asked as they watched the vehicles drive down the lane.

"Because I know what they're here for."

Tindale shook his head. "You're a foolish man. Ready your guns," he yelled to the soldiers behind him.

Marx turned over his shoulder. "No!" he said, looking at each of his men in the eyes. "Put your guns down. We will not fight them."

"But sir—" Tindale pleaded.

Marx leveled the commander with a hard glare. "Do *not* engage."

The line of PTs pulled into a circle around the transporters. The riders got off their machines with guns drawn. They ducked behind their PTs, using them as shields in case shots were fired. Another team of guards with guns stepped out of the second transporter, pointing their weapons directly at Marx as they built a wall in front of the first transporter.

The door opened, and King Bryant stepped out.

His eyes seethed. He didn't look like the same wise ruler Marx had met at the Council of Essentials, but Marx couldn't blame him for his impassioned change.

"I want my daughter!" he commanded.

Marx nodded at the guard at his side. "Go get Queen Sydria."

"Yes, Your Majesty," the guard said, then he quickly escaped back inside the castle.

Tindale and the other soldiers looked at him in disbelief.

"Your castle is surrounded," Bryant said. "If you try anything, my men will attack."

"There's no need for that. We're prepared to cooperate fully."

King Bryant nodded slightly. Marx studied the man. He saw traces of Sydria in the small things the king did, the purposeful way he held his shoulders back, the way he lifted his chin, refusing to show weakness.

Regret and guilt filled Marx's empty heart the way they always did. He should have told Sydria who he thought she was. Now she'd find out with hundreds of eyes on her. Holding that information was the cruelest and most selfish thing he'd ever done.

But he wouldn't be selfish anymore.

He'd set her free.

Sydria

Sydria paced back and forth in the small safe room, worrying about Marx. Was he okay? What was happening out there?

The door opened, and all three women turned.

"King Marx has requested Queen Sydria to join him," the guard said.

The queen mother sat up from where she'd been resting on the small couch against the wall. "To go where?"

"I can't say," the guard said.

"Then I'm going with her." Dannyn stepped forward.

"No." The guard held his hand up, stopping her. "Only Queen Sydria."

Sydria glanced at Dannyn. "I'll be with Marx. It'll be okay."

She followed the guard down the halls of the castle, unsure what was waiting for her. They rounded the corner to the castle foyer. A line of soldiers stood on the front steps guarding the door, or the lack thereof. Every head seemed to turn over their shoulders, looking directly at her. She sucked in a deep breath, trying to still her nerves. The line of men split in the middle, letting her pass through. Her eyes caught Marx's. His lips were turned downward, and his hazel eyes were glazed over with sadness. She stepped toward him, searching his face for the answers she needed to calm her racing heart. Her head turned to the courtyard, and her throat went dry. A circle of soldiers with guns drawn surrounded two transporters, and in the middle stood the man she'd been dreaming about for the last week.

The man she guessed was her father.

Her pulse quickened as she studied him. He seemed older than the version in her dreams, but his brown eyes were the same. Emotion filled every part of him. Tears dropped steadily down his face, and his hand went to his quivering mouth.

"It's you," he said through his sobs. "It's really you."

She slowly nodded.

"You're alive," he cried out, cautiously stepping forward.

Had he thought she was dead?

He waved at his men. "Put your guns down." When they hesitated, he called out again. "Stand down!"

The circle of soldiers did as he asked and lowered their guns.

He walked toward her. She stepped to meet him, still studying his face.

"You're my father?" she asked.

"Yes, I'm your father," he said through his cries. He reached out, slowly bringing her into a hug. The tangy smells of frankincense and musty pine filled her senses, sparking a familiarity inside her heart. She wrapped her arms around him, breathing him in, feeling the sense of love that she'd been dreaming about the last few weeks.

"I can't believe it's really you." He pulled back. "Do you remember me?"

Sydria looked into his brown eyes. Sparks of memories shot through her mind. Him teaching her how to ride a horse. The way his large hand felt holding hers. His adoring smile. Him bending over a map of all seven kingdoms. His glowing gaze, that always let her know he was proud of her.

"A little bit."

He grinned, love radiating from his eyes. "That's all I need." His eyes glanced behind her, and the delight in them was replaced by coldness.

"She's coming with me," he said in a harsh tone he hadn't used with her.

Sydria followed her father's stare to Marx. His expression was somber.

"Do you want to go with him?" Marx asked.

"Of course Seran wants to go with me. I'm her father."

"Seran," she whispered. She'd heard that name before. Her eyes dropped as she tried to remember.

The artifact room.

Seran Alyssa Haslet.

The princess who had been killed at her own wedding.

Her chest hardened, and she stumbled back. Marx grabbed one elbow and her father the other.

"Sydria!" Marx said, slipping his hand around her waist for support.

"Don't touch her!" Her father yelled.

Marx glanced at her, then her father, nodding as he backed off.

Her father was the king of New Hope.

King Bryant.

And she was the princess.

Sydria didn't remember that, only knew it as common knowledge.

"I just…" Marx blew out a breath as his worried eyes looked over her. "I just want to make sure she's okay. Sydria?" he asked again.

"Her name is Seran," her father snapped, pulling her to him.

Seran Haslet.

It felt right but also very, very wrong.

"Seran?" Marx's eyes were soft. "Are you okay?"

"I…" Anxiousness rolled in like a storm, squeezing the breath out of her lungs. She closed her eyes, trying to find some solid ground. She knew who she was, but she still didn't recognize herself.

"No, she's not okay," her father said. "And you're to blame."

Her eyes opened, and she looked at Marx. Why was he to blame?

"Did you know?" she asked.

Guilt swirled through his hazel eyes, and his gaze dropped.

"You knew who I was, and you didn't tell me?"

"I guessed it about a week ago, but I didn't know for sure." Marx rubbed his forehead, meeting her cold stare. "I wanted to tell you. I was *going* to tell you."

Everything felt overwhelming, and she needed to protect

her heart against the intense pain pummeling through her. She stiffened, putting walls up as fast as she could. "I see," she said, taking a step back. "I'm glad we got answers. Thank you for your help in the matter."

Marx reached for her. "Don't do that," he said. "Don't close yourself off."

She shook her head, fighting the raw emotion inside of her that begged to come out. "I'm fine."

"You're not fine." Marx's eyes filled with tears. "I can see that you're not fine, and I'm so sorry."

He reached for her again, but she stepped back.

"I don't want your pity," she said, gathering all of her pretend strength.

Marx's face fell, and she hated it. She hated that she'd done that to him, but even more, she hated that she'd lost herself once again.

Her father put a possessive arm around her shoulder. "Come on, Seran. Let me take you home."

She glanced around.

This wasn't her home.

This wasn't her family.

This wasn't her life.

Even though it was the only home, family, and life that she knew. She stepped toward the transporter, lost in limbo.

"Seran, wait," Marx pleaded, reaching out to her.

The New Hope soldiers drew their guns again, prompting the Cristole soldiers to raise theirs.

"Wait!" Marx said, holding up his hands in peace. His eyes begged her. "Don't go like this. Come inside." He looked at King Bryant. "Let's talk about this."

"You said you would fully cooperate," her father said, pinning her to his side.

"I will." He shook his head. "I am." He glanced at her again. "Can't we just talk?"

She bit her lip. Maybe they shouldn't leave like this. Maybe they should talk.

Everything was so confusing, and her head pounded with so much pressure she couldn't even think straight. A thousand thoughts ran through her empty mind, making her head spin even faster.

"You consorted with murderers and kidnappers, *purchased* my daughter, married her, hid her true identity from her, all for your personal gain," King Bryant said. "I don't think there's anything else left to talk about."

Listed out like that, it sounded terrible.

But was it all true?

Had Marx done *all* those things?

"That wasn't me!" he defended. "I didn't do any of that. It was my father."

"Do you really expect me to believe you?" Bryant flared.

"Yes. Ask Seran. She'll tell you."

That didn't feel like her name.

Her head hurt, and she didn't know what was real anymore. Everything she knew the last four months had been a lie.

She shook her head, trying to pull her mind out of processing mode, but it wouldn't budge.

"The fact that she's not responding or defending you is my answer," her father said as he ushered her toward the vehicle.

"She's not responding because she's in shock," he called after them. "You're pushing her too hard, too fast."

Marx always did know her better than anyone else—better than she knew herself.

She turned over her shoulder, looking back at him one last time.

"Seran, I need to know if you're okay," he said, placing his hands on his hips. His hazel eyes watched her in agony, waiting to see what she'd do.

"She'll be fine. I'll take care of her now." Her father opened the transporter door, and she climbed inside.

She didn't know what else to do or how to behave.

She'd never felt more lost than she did at that moment.

She closed her eyes and leaned her head back against the bench seat, letting numbness take over.

Marx

Marx watched Sydria go. It hurt like the day Palmer had died —sharp, overwhelming, crushing. But the worst part was seeing her go back into her shell again. She'd retreated to the woman he'd met the first day on the beach one month ago.

Scared.

Guarded.

Insecure.

Unsure.

He didn't blame her, but he hated it all the same. And he hated his part in it.

The first transporter—with her inside—drove down the lane of the castle. Palm trees swayed as the breeze from the vehicle blew past.

The other transporter, PTs, and the soldiers stayed with the barrel of their guns pointed at Marx.

His men held their ground, responding with their own weapons drawn. The head guard, the one who had been next to King Bryant, stepped forward, and his men readied their weapons.

"Back away from the king," Commander Tindale yelled.

In turn, the New Hope soldiers prepared for battle.

If Marx didn't stop this, every young man in that courtyard would lose his life. It wasn't worth it. Someone had to answer for Princess Seran's presence in Cristole. His father wasn't there to take the blame, but that didn't matter to King Bryant or the Council.

Marx was the fall guy.

It was his own fault.

He should've stood up to his father, contacted King Bryant as soon as he found out, or told Sydria the truth. But Marx hadn't done any of those things, and now he would pay the price for it.

"It's okay," he said to his men. "Lower your guns."

Commander Tindale shook his head. "But Your Majesty?"

"Lower your guns," Marx repeated.

Tindale nodded at his men, and their arms dropped.

The New Hope guard gestured to his own men. Three guards rushed forward, restraining Marx.

"King Marx McKane, you are under arrest for assisting in a kidnapping, harboring a fugitive of the Council of Essentials, and treason against the Council of Essentials. You will be transported to New Hope, where you will be held until your trial before the Council."

The New Hope guards pushed him toward the waiting transporter. Marx turned over his shoulder, talking to Commander Tindale. "Tell my mother and sister that everything will be all right. Inform the High Rulers what has happened. They'll know what to do. When Officer Kendrick arrives home, send him to New Hope." He got his last words out before they lowered him into the transporter and shut the door.

Marx placed his head in his hands.

All that mattered now was that Sydria—no, *Seran*—was free.

39

Seran

The Border of Cristole and New Hope
Two Days Later

The sun slipped behind the alfalfa fields outside of Seran's window. Without the glowing light, everything dimmed around her.

"We crossed the Cristole border. Isn't it nice to be home?" her father asked.

Seran turned to him, lifting her lips into a half-smile. That's how things had been the last few days since they'd left Cristole Castle and driven toward New Hope. Her father had timidly tried to make conversation while she stared blankly out the transporter window. Occasionally she'd commented or asked a simple question, but mostly she'd just nodded.

"We're almost to the inn where we'll rest for the night," her father said. "In fact," he leaned his head closer to his window. "I think we're coming up on Wellenbreck Farm, where Mariele used to live."

Seran gazed absently out her window. "Mariele doesn't like Wellenbreck Farm."

"Did you remember that?" Her father's spirits lifted. "Of

course you did. No one could have told you something like that. See, your memory is already being triggered by the familiarity of your surroundings."

She kept her eyes trained on the farmland.

"When we get to the inn, I'll have the guards do a sweep, and then we'll see about getting a room with two beds again so that—"

"No," she said plainly. "I'm not staying in your room again." The last two nights, Seran had let her father force her into sleeping in the same room as him. He'd said he wanted to protect her, not let her out of his sight, but enough was enough.

"Darling, I don't feel comfortable with you sleeping alone. It's not safe."

She looked at him. "Not everyone is out to kill me."

"In my experience, that isn't true."

Seran felt sorry for her father. She really did. Watching his only daughter get shot and then living through her death and loss was probably very difficult for him, but she couldn't take his hovering anymore. He suffocated her with his love and concern.

She sucked in a deep breath. "I want my own room."

"But how will I protect you?"

"You have guards," she said. "Use them."

She turned her head back to the window, letting her thoughts drift back to Marx, the way they had done since the moment she'd left his side.

40

King Ezra Trevenna

The Kingdom of Albion
One Week Later

"How about Joely if it's a girl and Kimball if it's a boy?" Renna said. Her head was in Trev's lap, and her legs were stretched out on the couch in front of her.

"Renna," Trev paused reading the letter in his hands, and looked down, meeting her gaze. "You're going to name the baby whatever you want regardless of what I say."

She smiled sweetly. "That's true."

"So why do you keep asking me if I like the names?"

"I'm trying to let you feel involved."

He glanced at her round belly, then back at her. "I'm pretty sure I'm already involved in the process."

"Very funny." She puffed.

"Thank you. I *am* funny." Trev flipped through the rest of the letters on the table next to the couch as Renna went back to writing names down in a notebook then promptly crossing them out. "Here's a letter from Bryant," he said, picking the envelope up and tearing it open.

He scanned the paper, reading through the first part of the letter.

"I like Audri for a girl," Renna prattled on. "Or how about Luna?"

Trev soaked in Bryant's words reading as fast as he could. He sat up, causing Renna to move her head.

"What? You don't like that one?"

His breath turned shallow as he finished the last words of Bryant's letter. He couldn't believe what he'd read.

She sat up too. "Trev, is everything okay?"

He shook his head as he looked at his wife.

"Seran is alive."

King Davin

The Kingdom of Enderlin

Davin sighed, glancing at King Bryant's letter on the nightstand next to his bed. "I can't believe King Marx would do something like this, and I can't believe Bryant's daughter is still alive. Can you imagine the rollercoaster of emotions he's going through?"

Emree leaned her head against his chest, her brown hair spread over his arm and shoulder as she cuddled up to him. "Maybe there's more to the story than what everyone thinks. I mean, you were on trial with your High Rulers when you announced that you wanted to marry me."

"That wasn't a trial," Davin said. "It was a vote. And I loved you, so it didn't matter the outcome." He pulled her closer, rubbing her arm.

"All I'm saying is don't pass a judgment against Marx until you hear the full story."

Davin breathed out. "I'll hear the whole story in two weeks at the trial, and then, I'll *have* to pass a judgment."

"Has this ever been done before?" Emree asked. "Every ruler meeting together outside of the Council of Essentials?"

"I don't think so, but since Marx is a king, the rulers are the ones who need to decide his fate."

"Why aren't you meeting in Albion?" Emree asked.

"New Hope hosted the last Council of Essentials. King Bryant is the hosting king and kingdom for everything until the next meeting in nine years," Davin explained.

"So you're going to New Hope?" Emree asked.

Davin pulled her close. "I have to."

Queen Myka

The Kingdom of Tolsten

"PRINCESS SERAN IS GOING TO *HATE* ME," Myka said, throwing herself onto her bed next to Drake. "My father tried to have her killed, kidnapped her, and held her hostage."

"Seran's not like that," Drake said as he played with the ends of her hair that were scattered around him. "And you're not your father."

"I can't believe she was in a coma in the basement of Tolsten house all that time." Myka shook her head. "I should have known."

"There's no way you could have possibly known. Your father, Stoddard, and Von did this. It's not your fault."

She twisted her neck so she could see him. "I hate Stoddard."

"I know you do."

"He's going to get away with everything again."

"We'll keep searching for him."

Myka sighed. "At least we have Doctor Von in custody."

"And Marx," Drake added.

"Do you think Marx is guilty?"

"I didn't like the guy when I met him at the last Council of Essentials. He only cared about himself."

Myka shrugged. "That doesn't mean he's guilty."

Drake leaned down, pressing a kiss to her forehead. "That's for *you* to decide. Not me."

41

Seran

The Kingdom of New Hope

After a week and a half of travel, Seran was finally home. She stepped out of the transporter and surveyed the New Hope Government Center. The building felt plain compared to the glistening stone and unique design of Cristole Castle. Even the landscaping felt bland. There were no palm trees or exotic plants and flowers, no butterfly terrariums, just green cut grass with a few scattered trees. The building felt vaguely familiar. She'd thought seeing it would bring back her entire memory, but so far, that wasn't how things had worked. Remembering came in pieces. There was no rhyme or reason to the flashbacks. She had to be patient.

"Welcome home." Her father smiled. He radiated happiness all of the time. It was exhausting and annoying. He'd been chatting for days, telling her stories from her childhood, naming every servant and guard at the Government Center. She wanted to scream at him and tell him she didn't care. She shouldn't be so hard on him. He'd just gotten his daughter back. He was the happiest man in all seven kingdoms. The problem was, she was the saddest woman.

She didn't care about her past…not like she used to. In the beginning, when she'd woken up from her coma, getting her memories back had consumed her, but now, it didn't seem to matter. She knew who she was, and the realization overwhelmed her to the point that she wanted to escape and hide.

"Come say hello to Mariele," her father said, coaxing her toward the house.

Queen Mariele smiled cautiously back at her. Her eyes welled up with tears, and she shook her head, visibly overcome with emotion. The woman clearly loved her, but it was hard for Seran. She didn't remember their love or their relationship. She had more flashbacks of her real mother, Queen Isadora.

She stepped forward. "Hello," she said, being polite like the good girl she was supposed to be.

Mariele placed her hand over her heart. "You look amazing. Better than before."

Seran doubted that.

She'd been shot, put in a medically induced coma for over a year, and had been traveling for the last week. If this was better than before, then she was angry at her old self for looking so bad all of the time.

"Come," Mariele said. "I've got your room ready, and I'm sure you're anxious to see your friends. I've invited them to dinner tonight."

Seran dug her heels into the ground, shaking her head. "I don't want to see anyone."

Mariele's face fell. That was clearly the wrong answer. The old Seran would have probably agreed to meet and entertain the moment she got home from an overwhelming and stressful ordeal because that was what was expected of her. The new Seran didn't want to.

Mariele looked to Bryant for some help.

Seran gritted her teeth and pressed her lips into one of her hollow smiles. The one she used to give Von and Edmay.

"That is, I don't want to see anyone right now. Perhaps tomorrow."

"Of course." Mariele smiled, pleased with that answer. "We'll see how you feel then."

Her father and Mariele talked the entire way to her room, pointing at things in the Government Center, asking if she remembered this or that. She wanted to glue a piece of paper on her head that said, 'I don't remember anything, so stop asking,' but she thought that might cause everyone around her some discomfort, and she couldn't have that.

"And here's your room," Mariele said.

She stepped inside. The room was painted a light cream. Dark oak furniture was spread about, and the comforter and curtains were a light blue. It was nice enough, but it didn't feel like home. It didn't feel like the queen's suite back at Cristole Castle.

"Would you like to go through your wardrobe?" Mariele asked. "We took most of the dresses to Albion for the we—"

"That's enough, Mariele," her father said, stopping her. In the stories her father had told her over the last week, he'd skimmed over the fact that Ezra was now married to Mariele's daughter, Renna, but Seran had had enough flashbacks to fill in the blanks herself.

"You took most of my dresses to Albion for the wedding to King Ezra," she said, finishing Mariele's sentence.

"Yes," the queen said, dropping her eyes to the floor.

Seran glanced around her bedroom, walking over to look at the perfumes lining her dresser. "Are Ezra and Renna happy?" she asked.

Her father stepped forward. "We don't need to talk about that right now."

Seran didn't need to talk about it. She'd already fit the pieces together. Ezra had fallen in love with Renna when he was supposed to marry her. Renna was the color red, and Ezra was constantly chasing after her. She didn't feel sad about it. She hadn't wanted to marry the prince of Albion anyway. She hadn't loved him then. She certainly didn't love him now.

"Why don't you change for dinner, and we'll meet downstairs," her father said, watching her closely.

Seran shook her head. "Thank you, but I think I'll have dinner in my room tonight. I'm quite tired from the journey."

"Whatever you need." Her father escorted Mariele to the door, turning around once before closing it with a big smile. "It's so good to have you home."

Seran tried to match his smile, to be as happy as he was about the fact that she was back in New Hope. "It's good to be home."

The door clicked shut, and she let the mask fall. She exhaled, falling onto her bed. She missed the ceiling fan above her in Cristole and the king who stayed in the room next door. He was the only one in the last four months who hadn't treated her like she was broken.

She'd heard the story from her father of where she'd been for the last year and a half. How King Adler had taken her, put her in a coma, and how she'd fallen into Stoddard's hands when the commander had killed King Adler. Then Stoddard had sold her to Cristole—to Marx. Although he'd always said that it was his father who had forced him into the marriage.

Seran hoped that was true.

She hated thinking about the alternative—Marx having used her the entire time. He'd said it was all pretend, but maybe his reasons for the fake relationship were different than what he'd said. Maybe the pretend game they'd played had been so that he could increase his position and power in Cristole. The day her father had come for her, she hadn't been able to face the possibility that their time together might have been an even bigger sham than she'd thought. She'd walked away—hadn't even say goodbye to Malory, Dannyn, and Idella. Now she would never know the truth. Seran probably wouldn't see Marx again. Maybe at the Council of Essentials in nine years, but why would she be there? Without him, she wasn't a queen.

Regret mixed with sadness, creating a crushing blow that hit the center of her heart. She mourned the loss of her mother all over again and the ease with which her own father had moved on with Queen Mariele. She mourned the life taken from her when they'd thought she was dead and how easy it had been for Ezra to move on with Renna.

The world hadn't stopped.

Everyone had done what they were supposed to do.

They had forgotten about her.

Would Marx simply move on too, forget about her, marry another?

Seran had no real home, no safe harbor.

She curled into a ball on her foreign bed. The comforter felt rough against her cheeks. She closed her eyes as the tears streamed down her face. It was the first time that she'd cried since she'd woken up from her coma. There was no one there to witness her vulnerability or to judge her for it. She let the tears fall as her mind drifted back to every moment and every memory she'd shared with Marx.

Marx

Marx had never been a prisoner before. He'd been a lot of things, but not that. He sat on the stiff mattress of his bed and watched as a New Hope guard slammed his cell door shut, dimming the room. He looked up at the yellow light hanging on the ceiling, buzzing annoyingly. His eyes darted around his new home. The walls were made of concrete blocks stacked together. There was a tan door with a slot wide enough to fit a plate through, a hard bed, a pail of water, and a drain.

He groaned.

It was luxury at its finest.

He lay down on the lumpy mattress, letting his hands fall limp on his chest.

Sydria—no, Seran—was home. He'd gone back and forth in his mind the last week. Sometimes he called her Sydria. Sometimes he called her Seran. Now that they were in New Hope, Marx probably should train his mind to *always* call her Seran.

He'd heard some of the guards talking on the journey here. His trial would be held in two weeks. Two weeks with the buzzing yellow light wasn't that bad. He could handle that. Then he'd get the chance to tell his side of the story, be acquitted, and go home...*alone.*

Marx deserved to be alone. He'd known that before Seran. Making a mess of things and disappointing people was what he did best. This wasn't anything new. He closed his eyes, letting his worry over Seran take control.

42

Kase Kendrick

The Kingdom of Cristole

Kase was supposed to go to Tolsten. Marx had asked him to go to Tolsten, but Kase wouldn't be the best guard Cristole had if he didn't follow his own intuition.

Follow the money.

That's what he'd always been taught, and that's precisely what he'd done. The money led Kase right to Otis Sutton and his newly purchased beach house. It was relatively easy. Stoddard must not have thought anyone would connect Otis Sutton to Commander Stoddard. Even Kase had almost missed it.

It was lucky that he'd even seen him exiting Cristole Castle the day of the wedding. Kase was the one person in Cristole who knew what Stoddard looked like. The one person who could recognize him and connect all the dots.

Marx would be surprised he'd found him. He couldn't wait to gloat.

Why go to Tolsten for answers when he could get answers directly from the source?

Kase calmly knocked on the door of Stoddard's two-story home. He held his gun at his side.

Stoddard opened the door, and his face tensed. "Can I help you?"

That's when Kase lifted his gun, pointing right at Commander Stoddard's forehead.

43

Seran

Seran had managed to keep visitors away for a week after she arrived at the New Hope Government Center, but she'd run out of excuses and now found herself in the middle of one of her friend's stories about her rich fiancé.

"Lafferty's family comes from new money," Jenica explained, flipping her blonde hair away from her face with a jerk of her head. "Normally, I wouldn't stand for that, and neither would my father, but times are changing, and when someone has *that* much money, you make allowances."

Seran slowly nodded, wondering how this Jenica girl had become her friend in the first place. "Seems like you have it all figured out," she said with a tight smile.

Jenica huffed. "I really do."

"Lizanne got married," Sheridan said, looking over at the redhead. "You heard, of course, that King Ezra's commander, Drake Vestry, passed her over for Princess Mykaleen."

Lizanne's eyes cast downward.

"I hadn't heard that," Seran said, sipping her tea. "It's hard to hear the latest gossip when you're in a coma."

Sheridan's eyes widened. "Oh, my goodness. How insensitive of me. Of course, you wouldn't have heard that."

"So tell us about the king of Cristole," Jenica said.

Seran tensed. She dropped her arms, resting her teacup in her lap. "What about him?"

Jenica smiled. "Give us the juicy details. You married him, didn't you?"

"Jenica," Lizanne chided, "she was forced into marrying him."

"I know that." Jenica laughed. "I just wanted to know if he's as awful as everyone says he is."

Seran pinned her with her gaze. "Who says he's awful?"

"My father said he's a terrible king."

"Marx McKane is an excellent king. I found him to be a very generous ruler."

And kind, funny, handsome, athletic, charming, sweet, intuitive, thoughtful.

"I guess my father was misinformed."

"Yes. I suppose he was."

"How sad that you've had *two* arranged marriages, and neither one of them has worked out," Sheridan bemoaned.

Seran hadn't thought about that before.

That *was* kind of sad.

Would she ever find a man who would marry her because he *wanted* to? The problem was, she didn't want just any man. She had a very specific man in mind.

"At least the divorce to King Marx is almost finalized."

"I'm sorry. What was that?" Seran asked, focusing back on Sheridan.

She shrugged. "My father said that King Bryant has already taken the necessary steps in Cristole to end your marriage."

"It must be such a relief." Jenica placed her hand on Seran's arm. Her fake kindness reminded her of Cheney.

"Yes, such a relief."

"The worst part about it is that you're no longer a queen.

You've been demoted back down to a princess. You're running out of kings to marry." Jenica laughed.

Lizanne hit Jenica on the shoulder.

"What?" she said, glaring at Lizanne. "Seran knows I'm joking. I know she's been drugged and lost her memory, but surely she remembers us and the way we joke," she said, gesturing to the three of them. "We're her oldest friends."

Seran picked up her teacup. "It's strange. I find I only remember people that I really liked." She turned to Lizanne. "I remember Lizanne."

Sheridan and Jenica's mouths dropped in unison.

Seran took another sip of her tea, feigning innocence. She probably should be better behaved, more civilized, more of what these women wanted her to be, but lately, she'd been adopting Marx's motto.

Just be who you want to be. Like what you want to like.

The new Seran found that she didn't like her old friends.

Seran walked into dinner that night, hearing the last of the whispers between her father and Mariele.

"I don't want her to be bothered with the details," her father said in a hushed voice. "She's not strong enough for that."

"What am I not strong enough for?" she asked, assuming they were talking about her. Lately, everyone talked about her behind her back.

Her father stood, helping her into her chair. "Nothing. We were discussing the Council of Essentials."

She lifted her brows, not believing him. At this point, she didn't even care what they were talking about, but she pressed the issue anyway. "The next Council of Essentials is in nine years. You seem to be getting an early jump on it." She tilted her head. "Unless that isn't really what you were talking about."

"It wasn't." Her father sighed. "There is something we need to tell you."

"And what's that?" She smiled at the waiter, who had deposited a tray of food in front of her.

"The Council will be gathering together in the next few days to discuss…" he hesitated, searching for the right words.

"To discuss *me*?" she finished for him.

"Not you specifically, but the situation *against* you."

"What will happen to Doctor Von and Nurse Edmay?" Seran asked.

"Nurse Edmay was found in Appa. Instead of bringing her all the way to New Hope, she will be tried there for her involvement."

"And Doctor Von?"

Her father fidgeted with his napkin. "He'll most likely be executed. We need to see that justice is done."

"How can justice be done when Commander Stoddard is still out there?"

He shifted his eyes to Mariele. "Commander Stoddard has been found."

Seran remained composed though inside her heart raced. "Where?"

"Officer Kendrick found him close to the border of Cristole and Appa. He's bringing him to New Hope to be tried for his crimes in front of the Council."

Seran wasn't scared of Stoddard, but the thought of him on the loose had caused her some anxiety. The fact that Kase had found him and was bringing him to New Hope lightened the heaviness inside her.

"Will King Marx be attending?" she asked, keeping her tone even, though everything inside of her hoped she'd see him again.

Her father shifted in his chair. "No."

Her heart sank.

There was only one reason why he wouldn't come, and that was because he *didn't* want to see her. It was probably for the best. His presence would only confuse things more—things like her heart.

"When is the trial supposed to be?"

"All the rulers will arrive in the next few days," her father said.

All the rulers except Marx.

Her chest filled with heaviness again.

"We'll be one big happy family." Seran gave a terse smile. "You, Mariele, me, Ezra, Renna. It's a family reunion."

Her father and Mariele exchanged worried looks, the way Von and Edmay always had. Except Von and Edmay hadn't really loved her. They had been her captors.

"Seran," her father said, "don't be like that. Ezra and Renna were both very shaken up over your death."

"I'm sure they were." She took a sip of her drink. "And I'm thrilled to meet King Adler's daughter. I have so much to thank her for."

Mariele grabbed her chest. "I think…I think I might need my pills." She looked at one of the servants. "Can you tell Cypress to bring me my pills?"

"Yes, Your Majesty," the servant said, rushing out of the room.

Seran glanced away from her father's sad eyes. This wasn't who she was. She wasn't mean-spirited and catty, but she also couldn't sit here and pretend like she wasn't upset about everything that had happened to her over the last year and a half.

She was angry.

She hated King Adler.

She hated Commander Stoddard, Doctor Von, and Nurse Edmay, and King McKane.

They all had taken more pieces of her than she'd given them.

Most importantly, Seran hated that she loved Marx because loving him made it impossible for her to hate him too.

And she really wanted to hate him.

She took a deep breath. "I'm sorry. I shouldn't have said any of that. I didn't really mean it. I don't know who I am." She chuckled, though her eyes filled with emotion. "Literally, I don't know who I am or which mask I should put on each day. I'm just a ghost of who I once was."

Her father leaned over, hugging her to him. "It's okay. We'll figure this out together." He released his hug, wiping at his own eyes. "You need more time."

Seran nodded. "You're right." She reached for her cup as a sharp pain bolted through her head. Her hand missed the glass, knocking it over, sending champagne spilling over the table.

She grabbed her head, crying out.

"Seran!" Her father jumped up, bending over her. "Send for the doctor!" he barked at the servants.

She groaned as the searing ache inside of her head intensified.

Then everything went black.

44

Seran

A harsh smell penetrated Seran's nose, and she breathed quickly and deeply, slowly coming to her senses. Familiar voices whispered around her as she opened her eyes. Doctor Ames leaned over her bed. She hadn't remembered him until that moment. His reddish-brown hair and freckles made him stand out.

"I told you smelling salts would work," Doctor Ames said.

"Yes, but can you tell us what happened to her?" her father said, worry etched in his voice.

Seran gently sat up. Her head felt like someone had banged a hammer against it for the last hour.

Ames turned to her. "Princess Seran, it's good to see you again."

She squinted back at the doctor, trying to muster a smile.

"How's your pain?" he asked.

She looked at her father's worried expression. She could lie, but what good would that do? She didn't want to have a pounding headache for the rest of her life.

"It's pretty intense."

Her father's eyes filled with tears.

"When did the headaches start?"

That was an easy answer. "When I stopped taking the drug Doctor Von gave me."

"Are the headaches the only side effects you've had?" Doctor Ames asked.

"Yes," she nodded. "They aren't always this intense. I think I've only blacked out one or two other times. But there have been other times when the pain has been so significant that I've thrown up."

"Why didn't you say anything?" her father asked.

She shrugged. She didn't need another reason for people to think she was weak.

"Can you make her headaches stop?" her father asked the doctor.

Ames straightened. "I don't know. Von's drug is untested. She's the first person it's ever been used on. I'll have to monitor her. Track her progress. Run some tests. But I think the headaches will lessen and maybe even go away once the drug has fully worked its way out of her. Right now, her body is going through withdrawals, and that's probably what's causing the headaches."

"So you think they'll go away in a few weeks?" her father clarified.

Doctor Ames shrugged. "There's no telling what kind of neurological damage her brain has experienced from Doctor Von's drug, but I'm hopeful that after some time, she'll be back to normal."

Not normal.

Without Marx, Seran doubted she'd ever feel normal again.

45

Seran

Seran spent the next day in bed. She'd been overly tired since the intense headache, and she'd experienced several smaller ones, like aftershocks to an earthquake.

She lay with her eyes closed, trying to sleep, when a soft knock rattled her bedroom door.

"Come in," she said.

Her father peeked his head inside. "Are you up for some visitors?" he asked.

"Sure," she said, sitting up in bed. Her father wouldn't have disturbed her unless he thought it was important.

He smiled, opening the door a little wider.

Seran's eyes immediately went to Ezra's dark curly hair, and then she saw Renna. Her blonde hair was pinned up on the sides, the rest of it flowing down over her shoulders to her protruding belly.

She was pregnant.

The thought made Seran sad.

Not because Renna was married to Ezra and having his baby, but because it made her miss Marx and everything that she'd never be able to have with him.

They both hesitated by the door.

"You don't have to stand by the door. You can come in," she said.

Renna smiled with relief, walking into the room first. Her green eyes were filled with tears. "I'm so happy to see you."

"It's a little weird," Ezra said, with a giant smile, "but really good."

Seran remembered that mischievous smile—he was no longer faceless in her mind now that the gaps had filled in.

"Trev, we talked about how you weren't going to say anything awkward," Renna said, nudging him on the side.

Seran laughed. "It's good to see you guys too." She looked at Renna's warm smile, and it immediately reminded her of Dannyn, making her feel instantly at home in her presence. "Come in more," she said, waving them to her.

Renna sat down on the edge of the bed, and Ezra pulled over a chair, taking a seat.

Seran looked between the two of them. "You guys look so happy. Everything worked out exactly as it should have."

"Well, not exactly." Trev grimaced. "You got shot."

Renna's mouth dropped open in disbelief as she stared back at him.

"Was that too soon?" he asked. "Should I have waited five more minutes to bring up the obvious?"

Seran smiled. "It's actually kind of refreshing. Everyone around here walks on eggshells around me. It's getting really old."

Renna placed a hand on her arm. "I don't know how much you remember, but I want to apologize again." She looked at Ezra. "*We* want to apologize for everything that happened. It was never our intention to hurt you, but we did."

"Especially me," Ezra said. "I'm sorry for the many ways I hurt you. I'm so ashamed of how things ended." His eyes filled to the brim with moisture. "I was about to call off the wedding."

Seran bit her lip, trying to remain composed. "I know."

Her lips pulled into a soft smile. "I'm so glad that you were strong enough to do that…because I wasn't. You were setting me free, and I'll always be grateful to you for that. And," she said, placing her hand on top of his, "thank you for jumping in front of me when the gun was fired."

"You remember that?" he asked.

She nodded.

He shook his head. "It didn't help."

"But you did it."

They stared at each other for a long moment, closing the door of the past.

"I'll let you two catch up," Ezra said, standing. "It's so good to see you, Seran."

"You too."

He smiled, then turned and left.

Seran watched his retreating back. Seeing Ezra had healed a wound inside her. Forgiveness had been given, and a big piece of her heart felt like it had been mended back together.

She turned her gaze to Renna, smiling. "You're having a baby."

"Yes…soon." Renna patted her stomach.

"Was it a good idea for you to travel so late in your pregnancy?" Seran asked.

"When I heard you were alive, there was nothing that could have stop me from coming to see you."

"You look beautiful. Happier than I remember you."

"I am." Her eyes dropped. "But I feel like I'm happy at your expense."

Seran took her hand, prompting Renna to look up. "It's not at my expense. Ezra and I never would have been happy together. I knew it then, and I know it now." She smiled, thinking about Marx. "I need a man who balances my serious side. Who challenges me to do things I would never think of but lets me do them on my own. He must be strong but vulnerable. Give me confidence and let me build him up too."

She shrugged. "Ezra and I didn't have that kind of relationship."

"That is a very well-thought and *detailed* list." Renna gave her a knowing look. "Did you have that kind of relationship with someone else?"

Seran bit her lip. She hadn't talked about her feelings for Marx with anyone. Even Dannyn didn't have the whole story. She hadn't seen Renna in a year and a half, had only remembered her a few days ago, and even before her accident, they hadn't been close, but for some reason, she wanted to open up to her.

"I did," Seran said, fidgeting with her hands in her lap. "That's how things were with Marx."

Renna raised her brows. "Marx McKane? The man you were forced to marry?"

"Yes." Seran bit her lip harder. "I know it's crazy, but we fit together."

Renna smiled. "Love should be crazy."

She shook her head. "Oh, he doesn't love me. He was just pretending."

"Are you sure about that?"

There were times when Marx's feelings, looks, actions, caresses had felt real. She saw the tears in his eyes and the pain in his face when her father had taken her away from Cristole. His feelings seemed genuine. But she couldn't think that or hope for that now. He was back in Cristole, and she was there. He hadn't come for the trial. She had to take that as a sign he didn't feel the same way she did.

Seran nodded. "Yes, I'm sure."

"How are things going in New Hope?"

She was glad Renna didn't press the issue of Marx more. "I feel out of place, and it's not helping that my father is acting so strange. He hovers and smothers, all in the name of protecting me. He's so fixated on getting me justice."

"I noticed that," Renna said. "He's pretty intense right now."

"I don't even recognize him."

"I'm sure things will calm down with him after the trial. Let him get his justice and then maybe he'll loosen up a little bit."

Seran nodded. She hoped Renna was right. She didn't know how much longer she could deal with this new version of King Bryant.

46

Marx

The cell door swung open, and Dannyn rushed inside, with Kase on her heels. She jumped into Marx's arms, hugging him tightly.

"Oh my gosh," she said, pulling back. Tears teetered on the tips of her eyelids. "You smell so bad."

Marx wiped at his own fresh tears, laughing. "That's what happens when you've been in prison for two weeks."

Kase stepped forward, grabbing him into another hug. "We've missed you, buddy. But you do stink."

"Thanks," Marx said.

"I'm going to throw a fit to King Bryant and demand that you be moved to a better room with a bed and shower," Dannyn said.

Marx glanced over his shoulder. "I have a bed."

"That's not a bed. That's a..." She shook her head. "I don't even know what that is. You're a king, for heaven's sake! How can they treat you like this? Why not put you up in an inn on house arrest?"

"I doubt King Bryant wants to show me any leniency."

"King Bryant is not my favorite person right now." She

looked back at Marx with pity in her eyes. "I brought a suit for you to wear at the trial tomorrow."

"Thanks for coming." He glanced between the two of them.

"You think we'd miss this?" Kase said. "Besides, I had to come. I brought Commander Stoddard here to be tried for his crimes."

Marx looked at Kase. "You found Stoddard?"

"You bet I did. In a beach house on the border between Cristole and Appa."

He didn't even mind Kase's cocky smile.

"That's great. It changes everything."

Dannyn nodded. "They have to let you go now that they have Doctor Von and Stoddard."

"You know, Stoddard's the one that killed Dad. It wasn't a heart attack. He poisoned his blood with some kind of drug."

Dannyn pressed her hand to her chest. "What?"

"I'm sure Doctor Von helped with that too," Kase said. "Those two worked together on everything."

Dannyn shook her head, still reeling.

"How's Mom?" he asked.

"She's an absolute wreck. Thank goodness for those butterflies, or I don't think she'd get out of bed each day."

He frowned, hating the fact that he was adding to his mother's stress.

"Have you seen Sydria?" Dannyn asked.

"You mean Seran?" Marx sighed, walking over to his bed and sinking down into it.

"Did you know who she was?"

"I didn't figure it out until the night Dad died, and even then, I didn't know for sure. It was only a guess, a theory."

"They're saying you knew all along, that you're the one who made the arrangements with Stoddard, not your father," Kase said.

Marx dropped his head into his hands. "I know what the

charges are."

"Why are you letting them think that?" Dannyn asked.

He looked up. "I haven't really had a chance to change anyone's mind. I went from Cristole Castle to this jail cell."

Dannyn lifted her brows. "But you're going to tell them tomorrow that it's all a big misunderstanding, right?"

"Yeah. I'll tell the Council my side of the story and hope that some of the rulers believe me."

"Now that we have Stoddard," Dannyn said, "I'm sure you'll be fine. He's clearly the one to blame for all of this. Him and Adler."

"I asked if I could testify at the trial," Kase said.

"And are they going to let you?"

Kase shook his head.

"Why not?" Dannyn pouted.

Kase shrugged. "Since Bryant is the hosting king, he gets to decide how the proceedings go. Apparently, there will only be a few testimonies."

Dannyn gave a reassuring smile. "That's probably a good sign. They must already know you're innocent, and they don't need to hear anymore."

Marx nodded at his sister, trying to keep her optimism intact. But he knew the truth. These trials weren't like pre-Desolation trials. There wouldn't be a lawyer or anyone there to help represent him. A person wasn't innocent until proven guilty. Every testimony and piece of evidence wouldn't be exhausted. The hosting king decided the format. He had the final say.

Unfortunately for Marx, King Bryant was the hosting king.

"What about Seran?" Dannyn asked, pulling him away from his worries.

"What about her?"

"Are you going to talk to her tomorrow?"

"I want to, but I don't know if I'll get the chance. She

hates me."

Dannyn slugged him in the shoulder. "She should hate you, but she doesn't."

"Have you talked to her?" His hopes were raised.

"No, but I've seen the way she looks at you. She's completely in love with you."

"Ugh," Marx groaned, throwing his hands out. "She was *pretending*. I told her to fake like she fell in love with me so that Dad would be satisfied and get off my case about the marriage. She's just a really good actress."

Dannyn folded her arms across her chest. "If everything was fake, then why didn't you tell her who she was once you found out?"

Marx banged his head on the cement wall behind him. "I should have but—"

"You didn't want to lose her?" his sister guessed.

It was a good guess.

He kept his head against the wall, shifting his eyes so he could see Dannyn. "No, I didn't want to lose her."

"And you still love her?"

He nodded his head. "And I *still* love her."

It was another good guess.

"Then you'll be sad to know her father has already made the arrangements for a divorce," Dannyn said.

He was sad, but he pushed the feeling aside, sitting up. "It doesn't matter now. The plan was always that she'd go back home when we found out who she was, and now she's home. It's over. The only thing that matters is that we convince the Council that I'm innocent so I can go home too."

Dannyn blew out a deep breath. "Fine. Let's start with that, then we'll worry about getting you and *Seran*," she said her name dramatically, "back together again once you're free."

He admired his sister's confidence when it came to Seran.

Marx wished he felt the same way.

47

Commander Stoddard

Stoddard shuffled through the dim halls of the New Hope Government Center basement. The guard behind him pushed his lower back with the tip of a gun to keep him walking, but when a person's feet and hands were tied together, the simple act of walking was difficult.

He looked around at the pathetic excuse for a jail and shook his head. He couldn't believe he was there. He'd let his defenses down, had gotten too comfortable in his situation, and now he was paying the price for it.

"Does this hallway ever end?" Stoddard snapped at the guard behind him.

"We're taking you to the older part of the jail. King Bryant didn't think you or that doctor deserved any better than that."

Was Von there too?

Stoddard looked around. He'd already heard the other guards say that Marx McKane was here. His plan was already in action. Luckily, when the guard had shown up at his house, he'd had the foresight to grab the letter from the first time he'd met with King McKane. Stoddard just needed Von to do his part. He hoped the doctor would remember what they'd discussed and stick to it. If they worked together, they might be able to make some fireworks tomorrow at the trial.

Blame Marx.

That was the plan Stoddard had set forth.

Hopefully, Von would follow it.

Incriminating Marx wouldn't save Stoddard. He would be executed no matter what, but if he had to go out, he'd take another king down with him.

Stoddard would be known in history as the one man who had single-handedly killed three kings.

No one had ever done that before.

48

Seran

"I want to go to the trial," Seran said to her father.

King Bryant sat on the edge of her bed, holding her hand. "Doctor Ames said you had another bad migraine in the middle of the night last night."

She bit the side of her cheek, looking away. The headache in the middle of the night had been severe, and even now, a thick pain pierced the spot above her brows, causing blurry dots in the corners of her vision.

"Why do you even want to go to the trial?" her father asked.

"I don't know. Maybe I need it for closure. Maybe I should stand before Doctor Von and Commander Stoddard and show them that they didn't break me."

Her father squeezed her hand. "The closure will come when you know that the people who hurt you have all paid for their crimes. I don't think it's a good idea for you to sit there and relive everything again."

"I'm done with people deciding what's best for me." She sat up, ready to get out of bed, but the pressure in her forehead intensified, causing her to wince, sending a wave of nausea through her stomach.

Her father bent over her, gently pushing her back down. "Seran, stop this. You are in no condition to get out of bed and go to the trial today."

She closed her eyes as she melted back into her pillow. Moisture gathered behind her eyelids. She knew her father was right, but she was tired of being broken.

"I'm only trying to protect you." Her father's voice was so kind, so full of love. "Your headaches scare me, and I don't want to see you in pain anymore."

Her headaches scared her too. "I know."

"Give it a few more hours. Take a nap," her father said. "If you feel better after that, then you can come down to the trial."

She conceded, only because the pain in her head dulled her resolve to fight. "Okay. I can do that."

Her father bent over, kissing her head on the exact spot of the pressure. "This will all be over soon." He smiled back at her as he walked out of the room, leaving her all alone.

She closed her eyes, willing the ache to go away. It didn't take long until her thoughts drifted to a memory. The memories had been coming back at full speed the last couple of days. Her mind had opened up more as the drug worked its way out of her system. Seran leaned into the flashback, hoping it would lead her to a peaceful slumber.

"Your Highness, it's a pleasure to meet you. I'm Palmer McKane, the prince of Cristole." He had blonde hair that was cropped short and stylishly swept to the side. His smile was endearing, and his hazel eyes were big and friendly.

Seran smiled as the prince kissed the top of her hand. "Thank you for traveling the long distance to celebrate my wedding with Prince Ezra."

"I'm thrilled to be here. I haven't been outside of Cristole before, so this is a lot of fun."

"Cristole has an election coming up, around the same time as the election in Albion. Will your older brother be running for king?"

Prince Palmer smiled. "Marx? Nah, he doesn't want to be the king."

Her eyebrows lifted. "Why not?"

"He thinks he'd mess everything up, but he'd actually be great at it. In fact, everything that's good about me comes from Marx. He's taught me all I know."

Seran smiled. "It sounds like you look up to him a lot."

"I do," Prince Palmer leaned in like it was a secret, "but I don't want him to know that."

"Then who will be running for king in your upcoming election?"

"My father is set on me doing it."

"Well, I hope you win."

Prince Palmer nodded. "I hope that Prince Ezra wins too, then I can see you again at the 2260 Council of Essentials."

She smiled. "Yes, if all goes well, we both should be there."

49

Marx

Marx sat on a cushioned bench outside the Government Center's large meeting room, waiting for his time to testify…at *his* trial. Two New Hope guards stood on either side of him, not because he was the king of Cristole, but because he was a prisoner.

It was a new turn of events.

He rested his elbows on his knees, bending over. At least he smelled good and had on his new favorite blue suit—the one Seran had requested to be made for him. Dannyn had really pulled through with the shower. He tapped his toe on the ground, trying to find something to do with the restless energy inside of him.

Marx was nervous about the trial. When it came to the other six rulers, he didn't have a lot of allies. At the last Council of Essentials over a year ago, he hadn't cared much about building relationships with the other kings. Palmer had just died. Marx had only been king for a few weeks and hadn't even wanted to be at the Council of Essentials. And on top of all of that, the only policy he'd put forth had been something trivial. His enthusiasm for colorful clothing had probably made him seem vain.

He shouldn't have been there.

Palmer should have.

How different would everything have been if Palmer hadn't died? Marx had messed that up, and now he'd messed everything up with his reign and with Seran.

The door to the meeting room swung open, and a woman in a tight cream dress nodded at him. "Your Majesty, they're ready for you."

Marx stood, tugging his suit jacket down. He breathed in and exhaled, then followed the woman through the door. Commander Stoddard was being escorted out after his own testimony. As he passed, he gave Marx a look that set him on edge, a look like he'd won. Marx watched over his shoulder as the commander walked out. Then he turned his eyes to the rest of the room. Several rows of chairs had been set up with a long aisle down the middle. He glanced toward the front, seeing Dannyn and Kase. They both wore a solemn expression. What was going on? Why did they look so depressed?

He didn't know who the rest of the people that filled the chairs were, most likely newswriters, High Rulers, and other important political figures. Ahead of him, on the dais, was a long rectangular table with seven chairs. Five kings and one queen stared back at Marx. His eyes glanced to the seventh chair, the empty one where the king of Cristole was supposed to sit. Had the servant who'd set up the venue forgotten that it was the seventh ruler who was on trial, or had they purposely set a chair for him to draw attention to his guilt?

Marx walked down the aisle. He glanced to the sides, looking for Seran. He hoped she was there so she could hear his side of the story. It wouldn't be the whole story. He didn't plan on telling the Council that he'd fallen in love with his wife, but she'd hear everything else. His eyes quickly jumped from row to row, but he didn't see her.

She hadn't wanted to come.

It was another blow.

When she'd left Cristole, she hadn't looked back.

He stopped at the single table and chair that faced the Council.

King Bryant stood as hosting king. This was his show. "Marx McKane, as a Council, we commit you to honesty. Any untruths against the Council will result in execution for treason. Do you understand?"

He raised his chin. "Yes."

"You may sit," Bryant said, taking his own seat.

Marx sat, resting his elbows on the table.

King Bryant stared down at him. "You are charged with assisting in the kidnapping of Princess Seran Haslet, aiding fugitives of the Council of Essentials such as Commander Stoddard, Doctor Von O'Neil, and Edmay Darrow, as well as committing treason against the Council of Essentials and its members. How do you respond?"

"I'm innocent," he said, looking straight into Bryant's eyes.

Whispers funneled through the room.

"Speak your defense," Bryant said.

Marx swallowed. This was his chance. He'd gone over what he wanted to say in his mind fifty times in the last two weeks, but sitting there with condemnation slapping him in the face, the words escaped him.

"I, uh..." He looked down, sucking in a breath. He glanced back up, meeting King Ezra's gaze. The king's dark curly hair spilled over his forehead, reaching his eyes. He was the guy who had jumped in front of Seran when there was a gun pointed at her. He'd stanched the bleeding wound in her chest with his own hand. Marx looked at Bryant. He'd brought his entire army to Cristole to bring Seran home. These people before him weren't that much different from him. They all loved Seran and wanted what was best for her. He had nothing to fear.

"As cliché as it sounds, I *am* innocent," Marx said. "My

father, Meldrum McKane, was the one who set up the arranged marriage to the princess. He kept me in the dark about her identity, claiming she was from Northland and had suffered memory loss because of a carriage accident. It took me a long time to figure out who she was, and even then, I didn't know for sure until the day Bryant showed up at Cristole Castle."

"So you claim you had no part in this, and it was all your father?" King Bryant asked.

"Yes."

"If what you say is true, why would Meldrum McKane do something like this?"

Marx pulled in a deep breath. "I have no clue. He didn't tell me what he was doing, nor did he expound on his motive. I figured out who Seran was the night my father was killed, so I never got the chance to talk to him about it."

King Ezra raised his brows. "You said *killed* when talking about your father's death."

He nodded. "My father was killed by Commander Stoddard. He visited him earlier that day and poisoned him with something that impacted his brain and stopped his heart."

The Council all exchanged looks with each other as the room murmured behind him.

"I'm going to turn the time over to the Council for questions." King Bryant looked down the row at Queen Myka.

The queen sat up a little taller. She had dark hair and blue eyes. She was pretty, but beyond her dark hair, Marx didn't think she could've passed as Seran's sister. "I have two questions. When exactly did you find out who Princess Seran was, and how did you figure it out?"

"I found out about three weeks into our marriage. But it was only a guess. I didn't know for sure. I was suspicious about her identity from the start. I didn't know who Sydria was, but I knew my father would never marry me to someone insignificant. My guard, Kase Kendrick, recognized Commander

Stoddard coming out of Cristole Castle the day of the wedding. Which led me to believe that she was the mystery woman you'd seen Stoddard escape with." Marx gestured to Myka. "At first, I thought she was your long-lost sister." She raised her brow, intrigued. "But in the end, Seran was the one who told me who she was. She remembered small things. For example, she remembered marrying a man with dark curly hair." Marx's eyes jumped to King Ezra. "All I had to do was listen long enough and put the pieces together."

"King Davin?" Bryant said, motioning for him to ask his question.

"Once you knew Princess Seran's identity, why didn't you tell her or reach out to King Bryant?" King Davin asked.

"I was going to, but my father died that day. I spent the next week making arrangements for his funeral. I should have told her, but I was stalling because I didn't know for sure. You probably won't believe this, but I was working on a letter to King Bryant the day he came to Cristole Castle."

Bryant huffed, then looked down the line of rulers. "King Hilton, it's your turn to address King Marx."

King Hilton from Northland leaned forward. "Mine is more of a statement than a question. It doesn't take all day or an entire week to plan a funeral. Surely, there were times you could have sent a note off to King Bryant or had a conversation with Princess Seran, letting her know who she was."

"Yes, there probably were times during that week I could have brought it up. I deeply regret that I didn't."

"King Ezra?" Bryant prompted.

King Ezra met his gaze. "Doctor Von and Commander Stoddard tell a completely different story, a story that incriminates you."

Marx looked to the side where Dannyn and Kase sat, and he understood the gloomy look behind their eyes.

King Ezra continued. "They both said *you* were the one who made all the arrangements. *You* were the one Stoddard worked with. *You* were the one who paid them and that *you* were the one who killed your father."

Marx furrowed his brows, confused by what Ezra had said. "None of that's true. I made some mistakes, but I didn't assist in a kidnapping or aid a fugitive, and I certainly did not kill my father. I had no part in assassinating the princess, kidnapping her, drugging her. All I did was agree to an arranged marriage and try to figure out who she was. You can ask Princess Seran. We had our own agreement—something that was respectful to her."

"So you're saying Doctor Von and Commander Stoddard are lying?" Ezra asked.

"Yes." He let out a sharp laugh. "It wouldn't be the first time."

Bryant looked at the man next to him. "King Reddick, it's your question."

"Let's go back to your father's murder because I think that's an important thing to discuss. Doctor Von said you begged for a drug, something easy you could use against your father to kill him without people knowing."

Marx ground his teeth together, feeling his frustration intensify.

King Reddick stared him down. "So I'm asking again, did you kill your father?"

"No. I did not kill my father. Our relationship was strained, but I would never do something like that. Stoddard was the one who killed my father, not me. They're lying to you."

King Bryant turned to him. "You say that Stoddard and Von are lying, but I want to know why they would make all that up? Everyone already knows they're guilty. There's no point in them dragging you through the mud too."

Marx shrugged, feeling the weight of Bryant's accusations on his shoulders. "I don't know why. Maybe Stoddard has a plan. Maybe he's trying to get a lesser sentence. After everything they've done, are you really going to believe them over me? They've been deceiving the Council for nearly two years."

King Bryant folded his arms. "Von and Stoddard have nothing else to lose. They know it's over for them no matter what. They have no reason to lie to us. Whereas, *you* have everything to lose."

"I can't believe this," Marx muttered. "I'm not a criminal. Ask Princess Seran. She'll tell you that I never once treated her unkindly."

"The princess wants nothing more to do with you," Bryant said.

Marx's chest tightened uncomfortably, and his resolve shattered.

"I understand that Commander Stoddard and Doctor Von are liars, and I wouldn't put it past them to fabricate this entire story," Bryant said. "But the evidence doesn't lie."

Marx straightened. "What evidence do you have besides their testimony?"

King Bryant held up a cream-colored paper. "Stoddard gave us the letter you sent in reply, setting up your very first meeting with him. The date, time, and location."

"I've never seen that letter before."

Bryant raised a brow. "Really? Because it has your signature on it."

"It's not my signature. Stoddard or my father must have forged it." Marx leaned forward, trying to see the curves of the writing.

Bryant flipped the paper down. "You want me to believe that your own father would betray you like that?"

Marx closed his eyes. How could he explain to a room full of people that his father never loved him the way he loved Palmer?

But maybe this entire thing wasn't about his father.

Maybe it was about Marx.

He was a screwup. He'd always been a screwup. No matter how hard he tried, he always seemed to fail. That's how it had been with Palmer's death. He should have done more to save him. And now, that's how things were with Seran. Marx should have seen the signs earlier. He should've demanded answers from his father or worked harder to find the truth. He'd been lazy, coasting by because he loved her and didn't want to lose her.

It was his fault he was in this mess.

Everything was his fault, and it was time he faced it. There wasn't anything he could say that would change King Bryant's mind. He'd already decided that Marx was guilty. The trial was as good as rigged.

Marx looked up at King Bryant and the other rulers. "I don't want you to believe anything. I only want to say that I'm sorry for Princess Seran. I'm sorry for everything that happened to her. I'm sorry that I didn't do more to help her. I only want what's best for her."

"Justice is what's best for her," King Bryant barked.

"I agree."

Hushed whispers filed through the meeting room.

"Very well," King Bryant said. "The rulers will take a short pause for deliberation before casting our votes."

The six rulers stood and filed out of a side door.

Marx leaned his head down on the table. He couldn't face his sister. He couldn't face anyone.

Trev

"Stoddard and Von are liars, and we can't believe anything they say," Queen Myka said. Her fists pounded against the table where the rulers sat, her eyes blazing with passion. "Do not trust them."

Trev shook his head. "I know they're liars, but I don't trust King Marx either. At first, he defended himself, but then when

Bryant pulled out the letter, he crumbled. It was as if he knew he'd been caught, and there was no way out."

"I agree!" Bryant said. "He's definitely guilty. He had no rebuttal for the letter."

"Yes, but it's his word against Von's and Stoddard's," Myka said. "Maybe he felt defeat, not guilt."

"I think Queen Myka is right," Davin agreed. "Besides, Marx is a king. He's one of us. We need more than the testimony of two criminals to vote guilty against him."

"We have more," King Hilton chirped. "We have the letter with his signature on it."

King Reddick leaned forward. "And we completely forgot about the fact that he killed his own father."

"We don't know that he did that," Myka defended.

"Von's and Stoddard's testimonies about that were very similar. Marx asked for a drug to kill his father," Reddick said.

"Are you all crazy?" Myka asked. "Stoddard killed *my* father and my friend, Joett. Of course he killed King McKane too."

Bryant shook his head. "I think you are letting your own experience dictate your emotions. You are more concerned about revenge against Stoddard than the facts of Marx's trial."

Myka's jaw dropped. "And I think you are letting your love for your daughter dictate *your* emotions. You're more concerned about getting revenge on Marx than actually looking at all the evidence."

"Fighting between us isn't going to solve anything," Davin said.

Trev ran a hand through his hair. He hated being in this position. He hated deciding the fate of another man's life, but he wanted justice for Seran. She'd been wronged so many times, even by him. It was time he did the right thing for her.

"King Reddick brings up an interesting point," Trev said, looking around the table. "Doctor Von's and Commander

Stoddard's testimonies weren't exactly the same. There were a few mix-ups and things that each of them left out, but nothing super inconsistent. If they had been identical, I would've thought that they were rehearsed. But they were questioned separately, and they haven't seen each other in weeks. There is no way they could have corroborated all that information."

Bryant raised a brow. "Yes, because what they said was the truth, and they didn't need to corroborate."

Trev nodded.

Myka slapped the table with her hand, clearly frustrated. "You're all underestimating Stoddard. He could have planned something like this months ago."

"Maybe we should hear testimony from Seran," Trev said. "She lived through all of this. She could give us a better idea of who Marx is."

Bryant shook his head. "I don't trust my daughter's memories right now. She's not strong enough to give her testimony. But I've talked to her about Marx, and I know that she wants justice."

"Are you sure about that?" Myka asked.

Bryant bristled. "Positive. She wants nothing more to do with Marx and wants to see justice served when it comes to him and his involvement in her kidnapping."

That changed everything.

Trev trusted Bryant. He'd never known him to be a vengeful man. Bryant and Seran were close. At least they had been before. Bryant would know what Seran wanted. There wasn't any point in debating. Trev had failed at protecting her once before. He wouldn't fail again. He would put Seran's wishes before anything else. She deserved that much from him.

"I know how I'm going to vote," Bryant said, standing. "I don't need any more time to think about it." He looked at Trev. "Are you ready?"

He nodded.

Marx

After thirty minutes, the door to the large meeting room swung open, and the rulers filed back into their seats.

"It's time for the vote," King Bryant said, looking around the room.

Already?

That's it?

Most of the rulers had traveled at least a week to get to New Hope. It seemed premature to vote after only thirty minutes of deliberation. Didn't they want to make their journey worth their time? Shouldn't they ask more questions —poll the audience, hear more testimonies?

Their quick deliberation meant one of two things. Either Bryant had convinced them all to vote with him, or it was going to be a tie, resulting in a mistrial.

"Queen Myka, how do you find the accused?" Bryant asked.

Myka's cool blue eyes landed on Marx. "Not guilty."

He gave her a thankful nod.

"King Davin, what's your vote?"

Davin studied Marx as if he were undecided. "Not guilty," he finally said.

Maybe it would be a tie.

"King Ezra?"

Marx fidgeted with his fingers, unsure how King Ezra would vote. He'd married the woman Ezra was supposed to marry. There had to be some feelings. Heck, Marx had unresolved *feelings* toward the king of Albion, mostly the jealous kind.

Ezra clasped his hand together in front of him. "Guilty."

Dannyn gasped behind him and the room tensed.

Well, that answered the question of whether King Ezra had unresolved feelings toward Marx.

Bryant looked at the last two kings. "King Reddick?"

The king from Appa leaned forward in his chair. "I think he's lying. I vote guilty."

Murmurs expanded throughout the room as Marx swallowed.

Things weren't looking good.

"King Hilton?" Bryant said, looking at the man next to him.

Hilton narrowed his eyes on him, a look that couldn't be good. "Guilty."

The room seemed to still as all eyes set on King Bryant. He was the last one. If Bryant voted not guilty, forcing a tie, then Marx would be free.

Bryant swept his eyes over the spectators. "Both Doctor Von's and Commander Stoddard's testimonies were solid. I don't see how they could have corroborated their stories unless what they said was true. Therefore," his eyes bounced to him, "I find King Marx *guilty*."

His stomach fell.

The crowd erupted in noise.

"Quiet! Quiet!" Bryant said, standing.

Two New Hope guards pulled Marx up from his seat.

"Marx McKane, the Council of Essentials finds you guilty. You are to be taken immediately to the square for execution."

50

Princess Dannyn McKane

Dannyn and Kase stood outside the meeting room of the Government Center as the arrangements for the execution were being set up in the square. They needed to find somebody who could help them save Marx. Time was running out.

"Drake, you know they're making a mistake," Kase said, pleading with the king and queen of Tolsten. "Can't you guys do something?"

"We've done all we could do." Drake turned to his wife. "Myka voted *not guilty*."

"Then tell me who can do something!" Dannyn burst. She was sick of these rulers acting like her brother's life wasn't worth something.

Everyone looked at her, and Drake narrowed his eyes. "I'm sorry, who are you?"

Dannyn's mouth dropped in disbelief. "Who am I?" she said, getting in his face. "Who are *you*?" Her finger landed on the middle of the king of Tolsten's chest. "You can't even help me save my brother."

Kase grabbed her shoulders, pulling her back from Drake. "This is Dannyn McKane, the princess of Cristole."

"Ah, now I see why she's so passionate," Drake said as his lips turned into a frown.

Myka looked at Dannyn. "During deliberation, I tried to change everyone's opinions, but Stoddard's and Von's testimonies were compelling."

King Ezra walked up, joining the group. He combed a hand through his hair. "I hate executions."

"This is your fault!" Dannyn snapped at him.

Ezra was taken aback, and he looked at Drake.

"Trev, meet Dannyn McKane, King Marx's sister," Drake said.

"Oh." Ezra shifted nervously. "I'm sorry about your brother."

"You should be. My brother is innocent."

"The evidence proved otherwise."

"Stoddard is a liar and a murderer!" Dannyn's chest puffed up and down with anger as she spoke.

Myka folded her arms across her chest. "He killed my father by smothering him with a pillow."

"Because he's a murderer," Dannyn said, pleading her case to the queen. Right now, she was her only ally. "He's lying about that and everything else."

Kase glanced at Myka. "Stoddard wrote that letter about you, saying that you knew where the weapons were and that you were hiding them."

"I know," Myka agreed.

"He forged letters and signatures back then, and he could've easily done that same thing now to frame Marx," Kase said.

Drake nodded. "That's true. He's known for the lies he's told in the past."

Queen Renna walked up, grabbing Ezra's hand.

"There you are," Ezra said. "Are you feeling alright?"

"Yes." She let out a heavy breath, patting her pregnant

stomach. "Sorry. I couldn't get myself out of bed this morning for the trial."

Myka smiled. "That's understandable. You're due to have a baby in two weeks."

Dannyn grew impatient. "I'm sorry, but can we get back to my brother and what we're going to do about him?"

"What happened at the trial?" Renna looked at the group expectantly.

"Stoddard, Doctor Von, and King Marx were all found guilty."

Renna inhaled. "King Marx, too? Who found him guilty?"

"Your step-father and your husband," Dannyn sneered.

Renna's eyes widened, and she turned to Ezra. "You found Marx guilty?"

"I did what I thought was best."

"Trev, I think you're projecting your own guilt and regret about Seran onto this trial," Myka said. Drake raised an eyebrow at her as if he disapproved of what she'd said to his best friend. "What? King Bryant thinks I'm projecting my own issues onto the verdict. If I am, then surely Trev is too."

"None of that matters," Dannyn said. Time was running out. "If we don't do something, Marx will be executed in the square in a few minutes."

Renna gasped. "We have an emergency! We have to go."

"What? Are you having the baby right now?" Ezra asked, clutching her arm.

"No." She swatted him away. "Seran is in love with Marx!"

"I knew it." Dannyn huffed. "And Marx is in love with her."

"How do you know?" Ezra asked his wife.

"Because Seran told me."

"Why didn't you tell me?" he asked.

"Not everything involves you," Renna said. She looked

around the group. "Seran will be destroyed all over again if Marx is executed."

"Exactly!" Dannyn raised her voice. "Thank you for having a clue about the gravity of the situation."

Ezra threw his arm out. "But King Bryant said—"

"You can't trust anything King Bryant says right now," Myka interjected. "He's blinded by his anger."

"The vote's already been done," Drake said. "Justice has been served."

"If we want justice for Seran, then we can't let the man she loves die," Renna said.

"What are we waiting for?" Dannyn asked. "Let's go get Seran so she can plead with her father and stop the execution."

"She's in bed," Renna said. "But I can get her."

"How are you going to get past the guards?" Drake asked.

Renna shrugged. "I lived at The Government Center for four years. The guards aren't a problem."

"Drake and I can go can find King Bryant and tell him I want to change my vote," Ezra said. He looked at Renna. "This is one bullet I *can* stop."

Renna grabbed Myka and Dannyn's hands. "Let's go."

A rush of adrenaline swept through Dannyn. These women were exactly the team she needed.

51

Seran

The door to Seran's room flung open, waking her from her sleep.

"Dannyn?" she exclaimed, blinking her eyes. "What are you doing here?"

Princess Dannyn scrambled into the room with Renna and another woman with dark brown hair and blue eyes.

Dannyn scurried to the side of her bed, looking her over. "What are *you* doing here? You're in pajamas, for heaven's sake!"

Seran glanced at the blue nightgown she wore then her eyes skipped to Dannyn. "Is Marx here with you?"

Had Marx come for her? It wouldn't make sense for Dannyn to come all the way to New Hope without her brother. Or maybe her headache was so bad she was hallucinating.

"Is she trying to make me crazy?" Dannyn asked the woman that Seran didn't recognize.

The mystery woman shook her head. "No, I don't think she knows what's going on."

Seran looked between the two of them. "What *is* going on, and who are you?"

The woman smiled. "I'm Myka."

Her eyes raised. "Adler's daughter?"

"Yes. I'm so sorry about my father and all that he did to you. I didn't—"

"We don't have time for this forgiveness session," Dannyn interrupted. She grabbed Seran's arm, pulling her out of bed.

"What are you doing?" Seran asked. A sharp pain throbbed through her head.

"Marx is about to be executed," Dannyn said.

"What?" Her hand went to her chest, and she forgot all about the headache.

"Yeah, executed," Dannyn said again. "I know I can be a little dramatic, but this is not me being dramatic."

Renna put her hand on Seran's shoulder. "It's true, Seran. The Council held a trial accusing Marx of being involved with Stoddard in the planning of your kidnapping."

"But he wasn't involved," Dannyn said. She looked at Seran. "Do you think he's guilty?"

Seran had been hurt by Marx, hurt that he hadn't told her who she was as soon as he'd found out, but everything else that she knew about him made her think that he would never deliberately hurt her. He'd stood up for her when no one else had, noticed when she was in pain or sad, and was the first to comfort her and offer confidence.

Seran knew Marx.

The *real* Marx.

"No." She looked at them. "He wasn't involved. Who voted to have him executed?"

Myka shook her head, raising her palms up. "Not me."

"Trev," Renna grimaced.

"It was four to two," Dannyn explained. "Ezra, your father, King Reddick, and King Hilton all voted that Marx was guilty."

"Why?"

"Because Stoddard and Doctor Von lied on the stand.

They told everyone that Marx had been working with them. They even fabricated a letter with his signature on it." Dannyn shook her head in frustration.

"And everyone believed them?"

"Yes, and we need to do something to stop it." Dannyn ran to Seran's closet flipping through dresses. "No one's going to take you seriously in your pajamas."

Renna eyed her. "Are you strong enough for this?"

"I feel okay," she said as she stood.

"Hurry!" Dannyn said, bringing a dress over. "Help me get her dressed. We're running out of time."

"They wouldn't shoot him without us, would they?" Renna asked.

Seran's eyes went wide.

They were going to *shoot* Marx.

"I wouldn't put it past them," Myka said. "You know men. They always think they're the ones in charge."

Seran lifted her arms and a leg, wiggling out of her pajamas as fast as she could. Myka and Renna tugged her dress on, pulling it up her body. She looked down at the chartreuse fabric.

That seemed fitting.

Dannyn ran a comb through her hair.

"I thought you said we had no time?" Seran said.

"I can't send you out there looking like this." Dannyn huffed. "You can't look like you just rolled out of bed. We need everyone to listen to you."

"It's fine. It's fine." Renna swatted the comb away from her hair. "We need to go."

Myka helped her slip her shoes on, and the four women rushed out of her room. Seran didn't know what was happening. But she was used to it. Over the last few months, she'd grown accustomed to being in the dark. The only thing she did know was that even if he didn't love her back, she would not let Marx McKane die because of her.

52

Marx

Marx stood on the podium in the middle of the Government Center square, awaiting his execution.

On one side of him, Doctor Von wept. "Stoddard said to stick to the plan. He'd said he'd save me. Stoddard will save me. Save me."

Marx wanted to feel bad for the guy—he'd obviously been taken advantage of by Stoddard too—but since he was partly to blame for his own guilty verdict, he couldn't muster the compassion.

Commander Stoddard stood on the other side of him, chin up, expression detached. "Will Von ever stop whining?" he muttered under his breath. Marx turned his head to look at him. He wanted to strangle him for everything he'd done to Seran, but his bound hands and feet robbed him of the opportunity.

Marx cast his eyes around the crowd. Kase stood near the front, but no Dannyn. It was probably for the best. Marx didn't want the last memories his little sister had of him to be of him bleeding out.

Another makeshift podium had been erected to his right,

with seven chairs for the seven rulers. Three of the chairs were empty this time. His, Ezra's, and Myka's.

Ezra wasn't even man enough to face the execution he'd sentenced Marx to.

The crowd held their breath, nothing but eerie silence filling the air. He looked over at King Bryant, wondering if he would give some kind of speech or announcement. Marx had never been at an execution before. If he had, maybe then he could figure out a way out of this mess.

"What order will they go in?" Von asked. His voice trembled. "Left to right? Or right to left? Or maybe they will shoot Marx first?" Von looked over at both of them, expecting an answer, but neither of them said anything.

Ezra and his friend Drake entered the side of the square, skipping quickly up the steps of the podium to get to King Bryant. Harsh whispers went back and forth between the three of them, but Bryant shook his head, indignation crossing his brow. Whatever they were talking about, Bryant didn't like it. He nodded at the guard standing twenty feet in front of the three prisoners.

No speech.

This was it.

Marx watched as the guard lifted his gun. His heart pounded inside his chest as he cocked the weapon and fired. The bullet zipped through the air, hitting the doctor directly in the chest. Von let out a strangled cry and dropped to the ground. Marx jerked, his instinct directing him to somehow try to save the man, but he couldn't. His eyes closed, and he looked away from the doctor's wrenching body. The crowd erupted. Some cried. Some cheered. Some called out in anger.

Chaos.

This was organized chaos.

Von's execution was over before he'd even had the chance to think about it. Marx couldn't believe how abrupt everything was. Shouldn't there have been a dramatic pause? Shouldn't

Von have said some last words? The whole thing seemed premature.

Two guards grabbed the doctor under his arms and dragged his bloody body off the podium as Ezra and Drake continued to argue with Bryant.

Stoddard let out a rough laugh. "I guess that answers the doctor's question on who gets shot first."

Marx turned to look at Stoddard, astonished by how deranged he was.

The commander's gray eyes met his. "Next it will be you. I must say, you're handling it better than your father did. He whimpered like Von."

Marx's jaw hardened.

"If I had known how things would end, I would've killed Princess Seran too. Then I could have gone down in history as the man responsible for four royal deaths. Three will have to do." His thin lips quirked into an evil smirk. "And it was kind of fun drugging Princess Seran and erasing all her memories. Breaking her down was easy. She's such a fragile little wench."

Marx swung his bound hands through the air, sending his elbow into Stoddard's nose. The commander's head jarred back with the force of the blow, and he stumbled to the ground.

Marx leaned over him, a fresh wave of anger funneling through his chest. "You're wrong about Seran. Don't you see? She's the one everyone will remember, not you. Her strength erases everything you did. You are nothing."

Defeat fell over Stoddard's bloody face.

Then the next bullet was fired.

Marx flinched.

Blood spilled out of Stoddard's stomach, and he began wheezing and coughing. Marx wasn't sure if the guard had missed killing Stoddard with one shot on purpose or if it was because he was already lying on the ground.

Another shot was fired, hitting his leg, causing Stoddard to cry out.

The next shot hit his shoulder.

The misses were definitely on purpose. Any skilled guard wouldn't have missed that many times.

Two more guards came and dragged Stoddard's body off the podium even though he wasn't dead yet. Bryant probably wanted him to suffer a long and painful death. Was that what Bryant wanted for him too?

Marx glanced at the shooter. His eyes were pinned on him —brown, like the color of Seran's, but they lacked the sincerity that hers held.

He'd once told her that he would never regret kissing her or marrying her, and standing there in that moment, with a gun pointed at his chest, he still felt the same. He would never regret Seran or his time with her, even though it had cost him his life.

The guard readied his gun.

This was it.

Marx closed his eyes, holding his breath as the shot was fired.

Seran

SERAN FROZE.

They were too late.

She watched Marx, waiting for him to collapse to the ground or for bright red blood to spill across his chest, but nothing happened. The guard firing the gun cried out in pain, dropping the weapon to the ground. He pulled his bloody hand into his chest.

Her brows furrowed as she looked over her shoulder to Myka and the gun in her hand.

"You shot the guard!" Renna gasped.

Myka shrugged, lowering her gun. "It's just a flesh wound. A perfect shot, really."

"You should have shot him in the heart," Dannyn snarled; then realizing what she'd said, she placed a light hand on Seran's shoulder. "Sorry. That was insensitive."

"Where did you get a gun?" Renna asked, still baffled by Myka.

"From my dress."

"You keep a gun in your dress?"

Myka blinked back at her. "Don't you?"

"No!" Renna shook her head.

"He'll be fine." Myka motioned to the guard.

Seran felt the entire square looking at the four of them. She glanced at Marx, on her right, unsure of what she saw in his eyes. Relief, of course, but there was more than that. Tenderness, maybe? Astonishment?

"Seran, what's going on?" Her father stood at his spot across the square with Ezra and Drake behind him.

"Oh, boy," Myka said, tucking her gun back under the skirt of her dress. "I think we're in trouble."

Seran cleared her throat, walking forward until she was in the middle of the square between her father and Marx.

She gathered all the poise she could muster. "I'm here to speak on behalf of King Marx's innocence," she said to the Council.

"My darling," her father said. "Why don't you go back inside? You don't need to worry about any of this."

She shook her head. "No. I'm not going back inside."

"He's guilty as charged," King Hilton from Northland said.

"No, he's not." She squared her shoulders.

"Seran, your headaches make you confused." Her father reached his hand out for her to come to him. "King Marx *is* guilty. He's the bad guy here."

Slowly she faced Marx.

His hair seemed longer, and his face held more stubble than she was used to. His hazel eyes looked back at her, piercing her heart. He was the only one who truly saw *her*. He didn't try to make her something she wasn't or what he wanted. Instead, he patiently waited for her to discover who she was.

Who *she* wanted to be.

He made her feel strong, valued, beautiful, alive, and she loved him for it.

"You're wrong about him," she said, still staring into his eyes.

"Well, you are too late." Her father shrugged. "We've already voted, and he's been found guilty."

Ezra raised his hand. "I would actually like to change my vote to innocent." He gave Seran an apologetic look.

King Reddick from Appa scoffed. "You can't change your vote."

"Yes, he can," Seran said. "The law states that members of the Council can change their vote and render mercy at any point *before* the execution." She looked at her father. "You taught me that."

Tears filled her father's eyes. "You remember that?"

She nodded.

His voice was firm, counteracting the softness in his eyes. "Someone has to pay for everything that has happened to you. Marx McKane is at fault and should be punished for his involvement." He gestured to her. "Can't you see what he's done to you?"

"Yes, I can." She lifted her chin. "Marx McKane taught me how to speak up, to find my inner strength and that owning my inner strength is more than just doing what's expected. I nearly married a man I didn't love in a marriage arrangement I didn't want because I wasn't strong enough to speak my mind, but now I know better." Her eyes skipped to him. "I know better because of Marx."

Her father shook his head. "But if King Ezra changes his vote, then it will be a mistrial."

"It should be a mistrial. King Marx is innocent, and I will not let you shed the blood of an innocent man for me."

His shoulders dropped like a balloon that lost its air. "This is what you want?"

Seran looked at Marx. "This is what I want."

His eyes filled with emotion and the corner of his mouth lifted into an unsure smile. Had he read between the lines? Did he know that she loved him?

"Then I guess I'd like to change my vote too," her father said.

She skipped her eyes to her father. There was so much love behind everything he did, but lately his love had suffocated her.

"I think I've wrongly accused King Marx," he said to the crowd. "If Seran believes him innocent, then he is in my eyes too. I trust her judgment."

The crowd erupted in noise.

It was her turn to set Marx free.

53

Marx

Marx watched as New Hope guards worked to clear the spectators from the square. A team of servants disassembled the podium where the rulers had been seated while other servants scrubbed away Doctor Von's and Stoddard's scattered blood.

His eyes met King Ezra's. Both men stared at each other for a moment before Ezra nodded in his direction. It was his offering of peace. His apology for everything that had happened that day. In time, he'd forgive Ezra, just not right after he had nearly been executed. Marx needed a few days.

Dannyn pushed him from behind. "If it wasn't for me, you would have died today."

Marx puffed out a laugh, slinging his arm around his sister. "I can see you're going to be really humble about this."

She wrapped her arms around his waist, hugging him. "No, I don't want to think about this day ever again."

He looked at Kase. "Let's go home."

Dannyn shifted her head so she could see him. "To Cristole?"

"Yeah. Where else would we go?"

She released her hug. "I thought you'd want to stay around here for a little bit."

"Half of these people tried to kill me." Marx shook his head. "I don't feel like hanging out with them."

"That makes sense."

"We'll go get the transporter ready and meet you out front," Kase said, reaching for Dannyn's hand.

He looked over at Seran. She was talking to King Davin. Then her dark eyes found him. Marx gave a noncommittal wave, a signal letting her know that he was leaving. She nodded at King Davin and then walked toward Marx. He didn't know what to say to her. It had been three weeks since they'd last seen each other. So much had happened between them. Would they ever be able to get back to how things had been before? Did she even want to?

She offered a small smile as she closed the gap until she stood in front of him. They stared at each other for a moment.

"I like your suit," she finally said.

"I like your dress. I thought we outlawed chartreuse."

"That was Dannyn."

"Thank you for saving my life today," he said. It sounded stupid, but what else was he going to say?

"It was all Dannyn."

"It wasn't *all* Dannyn." Marx shook his head. "It's kind of crazy."

"What?"

"You and me." He shrugged. "How in the end, you're the one who set me free. It was supposed to be the other way around."

"Perhaps we both set each other free."

His lips pressed together. "I hope."

"Then our deal was successful." She forced a bright smile, but her eyes betrayed her.

"You must be happy you're home."

Seran glanced around. “I’m getting used to it.”

“And your memories? Have they been coming back?”

“Enough.” Her lips lifted. “I remembered meeting Palmer. He said that everything good about him came from you.”

His eyes filled with tears. “He said that?”

She nodded. “He looked up to you a lot.”

Marx smiled. “I guess we looked up to each other. And, what about your headaches? I’ve been worried about you.”

“You were the one in prison, and you were worried about me?”

He raised his shoulders. “I had a lot of time to think. So put me out of my misery. Tell me how the headaches are.”

“I’m taking them day by day, but the doctor believes they are caused by withdrawals from the drug and are hopeful they will stop soon.”

“I’m glad to hear it.” Marx rubbed the back of his neck. He’d stalled long enough. “Seran, I’m sorry I didn’t tell you who you were the moment I found out. I wanted to be sure, to talk to my father, but I was an idiot, and I made a huge mess of everything.”

“I was hurt,” she said, looking down. “I thought you were the one person on my side, and then it felt like you weren’t on my side anymore. Like I was all alone again.”

“I’ll always be on your side.” Marx wanted to reach for her hand, but he didn’t. He’d lost that privilege.

“Are you leaving now?” she asked.

“I have no reason to stay.”

No reason because Seran didn’t love him back.

“Besides,” he said, “if I stay too long, your father might try to kill me again.”

Her lips fell to a frown. “I’m sorry about that.”

“It’s no big deal. I’d always wanted to see what the New Hope Government Center prison cells were like.”

She laughed. “They’re actually really terrible.”

"Eh, they're not that bad. I'm thinking about making them my summer vacation spot."

Another puff of laughter escaped her lips.

He would miss her light laughter. He'd miss everything about her. She might as well know it.

"I'm going to miss you," he confessed.

She bit her lip. "I'm going to miss you too."

Part of him was happy that she would miss him, like he wasn't the only one who'd formed real feelings.

"You're welcome in Cristole anytime you want to visit," he said, though he doubted she ever would.

"Same in New Hope."

Marx hated leaving things like this. He didn't want to say goodbye. He'd almost died five minutes ago and because of that, his courage was at an all-time high. He wanted to tell her that he loved her and see if the reason she'd saved him was because *maybe* she had feelings for him too. But he couldn't say all that. She was finally home. From the day he'd met her, this was all she had wanted. He'd promised to set her free, and right now, that meant letting her go. She was where she was meant to be. She belonged in New Hope, and he belonged in Cristole. They'd go their separate ways and live out separate futures. That's all they could do. Their make-believe life was the happiest time Marx had ever had, but it was over now. He had to give her up.

He swallowed back the emotion rising up his throat, but it didn't help. Despite his efforts, his eyes filled with tears again. "Can I at least hug you?"

"Of course."

Marx slowly stepped forward, cautiously wrapping his arms around her body, afraid that any sudden movement would make her disappear sooner. Seran melted into him, closing her arms around his back and shoulders. He buried his head into her neck, breathing her in. She smelled different but the same. Her perfume was a new scent, but the smell of her skin would be with him forever. Her racing heart beat in rhythm with his as he held her close.

Fifty people were probably watching them, wondering why he clung to her so desperately, but Marx didn't care. He closed his eyes, hoping that he would somehow be able to remember the way her arms felt around him or the way her body fit with his.

He pressed his head deeper into her neck, whispering in her ear. "I meant what I said. I will never regret marrying you."

"Thank you," she whispered back.

"For what?"

"For helping me discover who I *really* am."

She wasn't talking about her real name or where she lived. She was talking about the woman deep inside of her.

"You did that yourself, and I'm grateful I got to be by your side to see it."

"You're a good man, Marx McKane." Her voice wobbled. "You'll make some woman very happy one day…when you let yourself love instead of just pretending, like we did."

Marx held her tighter, his lips brushing against her ear. "Maybe I wasn't pretending."

Her body trembled, but she didn't say anything. She didn't have to. Marx knew what they were up against.

He closed his eyes one last time, breathing her in as his tears fell.

He'd already let go of Sydria. Now it was time to let go of Seran.

54

Seran

Seran stood alone in the middle of the square, watching as Marx walked away. The heartache inside of her wasn't like any other pain she'd ever experienced before. People moved and worked around her, but she stood numb. A steady stream of tears dripped down her cheeks as Marx rounded the corner and vanished.

There went her life.

She pulled in a ragged breath and looked around the square, recognizing people and servants.

This was her home, but it wasn't where she belonged.

She wiped at her tears as she raced to find her father, pulling him away from a group of High Rulers.

"Seran, what's the matter?" He gently touched her head. "Are you not feeling well?"

"I don't belong here," she said.

Worry crossed over his face. "Don't be ridiculous. Of course, you belong here."

She shook her head, glancing around. "This isn't my home anymore or who I want to be."

Her father frowned. "I don't understand."

"Did you push through my divorce with Marx?" she asked.

"What does that have to do with anything?"

"Did you?"

He shook his head. "I began the paperwork. There are still a few signatures I need to make it final. But don't worry, I'll take care of it."

"I love him." She shrugged. "I love him."

"How could you possibly—"

"You said at the execution that you trust my judgment."

"I do, but you're very fragile right now, and I don't think—"

"I'm not fragile," she said, standing her ground. "I've actually never been stronger." She knew exactly who she wanted to be and who she wanted to spend her life with. She'd never had this much clarity, even before she'd been shot. "I'm going after him," she said, turning on her heels.

Her father followed behind her. "Now?"

"Yes."

"But you just got home. Why don't you wait a few months? See how you feel then."

She stopped walking, turning to face her father. "I know this is hard for you. You just got me back, but you aren't losing me again. You're setting me free."

Tears fell from his kind brown eyes. "Are you sure this is what you want?"

She nodded.

"Then I won't stand in your way."

Seran smiled, hugging her father close. "Thank you. Thank you for trusting me and letting me choose the life that I want."

He patted her back. "I always knew you were meant to be a queen. I just never knew it would be in Cristole."

55

Marx

Marx had only traveled a few hours before they decided to rest for the night. They stopped at the nearest inn, somewhere in the middle of New Hope. He didn't know the name of the province they were in, and he didn't even care. All he wanted to do was get back to Cristole as soon as he could and bury himself in his work as king.

That's all he had left.

"We've secured a bunch of rooms," Kase said, flipping him a key.

Marx smiled at his friend and sister. "You two had better be in separate ones."

Kase feigned like he was insulted. "Come on, man. Don't you know me?"

He gave his friend a smile. "I *do* know you. That's why I said something."

Dannyn rolled her eyes as she walked past them. "Don't worry. Everyone has their own room."

Kase playfully raised his eyebrows as he followed after Dannyn. "That doesn't mean I can't tuck her in."

Marx watched them. He was happy for his sister—glad

that she wasn't alone. His own loneliness was so intense, he felt like he couldn't breathe.

He reached down for his bag and followed after them. A guard held the door open for him, and he stepped inside the lobby. The room was full of people eating dinner and relaxing as they listened to live music.

The innkeeper bowed in front of him. "Your Majesty, it's an honor to have you stay here with us. I hope you find everything to your liking."

"We will," Kase said as he chased Dannyn up the stairs.

"Thank you," Marx said to the innkeeper. He looked down at his key, trying to see what his room number was. He took a step forward.

"Why did you leave?" a familiar voice behind him halted his steps. His heart stopped, and he pulled in a breath, preparing himself for the moment when he would turn around and realize that he'd imagined her because there was no way she could really be there.

Slowly he turned around.

Seran stood five feet away, wearing the same chartreuse dress she'd had on earlier that day. Her beauty took his breath away. He didn't smile. He didn't even move a muscle. He stood frozen.

"Am I dreaming?" he asked, not sure he trusted himself.

She shook her head. "I hope not."

His lips moved into a cautious smile as he stepped closer. "It feels like a dream."

She met his step with one of her own. "Why did you leave?"

He lowered his chin, confused by her question. "Because I need to go back to Cristole."

"Without me?"

Had Marx heard her correctly? It was loud inside the inn, and he needed to be sure he'd heard her right. He looked around. Groups of people had paused what they were doing, watching the two of them converse.

He held up his finger to the innkeeper. "Can you give us a moment?" He grabbed Seran by the hand and pulled her toward the closest door. "What's this?" he asked the innkeeper.

His brows bent inward. "A coat closet."

"Perfect," Marx said, swinging the door open. He tugged Seran inside the tiny room and flipped the light on before closing the door.

Her eyes danced as she looked up at him.

Marx pressed his lips together. "I'm sorry, but can you repeat the last thing you said?"

Her lips stretched into a cute smile. "I asked why you left for Cristole without me."

Everything inside of him lightened. "I didn't know you wanted to come."

"You said I was welcome there anytime."

"I meant it."

She shrugged. "Well, I really love the ocean. I think I'd miss it. I love the way it's so constant and steady. I love the way it makes me feel."

"I love the ocean too." He smiled. "If I was away from it, I'd miss it too. I'm my best self when I'm with it, and I don't want to live without it."

"I don't want to live without it either," Seran said.

He reached out, slowly skimming his fingers over hers. "Are we still talking about the ocean?"

"No." She lifted the corner of her mouth. "I'm talking about *you*."

He puffed out a small laugh, fully grabbing her hand, lacing his fingers through hers as a nervous thrill shot through his body. "I was talking about you too."

"Here's the deal—"

"No more deals." Marx shook his head. "I'm sick of deals and fake relationships and pretending."

"Okay," Seran said. "Here's the *thing*. I tried to stay in New Hope and build a life and a future there. But it only took me thirty seconds to realize that something was missing."

"Was it my mother's butterflies?"

She laughed. "No, it was you. You're my home."

Marx closed his eyes briefly, soaking in her words.

"I've been so lonely my entire life, trying to fit the mold of what I thought everyone else wanted me to be. Then I met you, and there was no mold, no expectations, just pure acceptance."

Marx could have said the exact same thing about her.

Seran bit the side of her cheek, the way she always did when she was nervous. "I was broken, but you didn't try to fix me—you gave me room to fix myself. You taught me to want more out of life, believe in myself, trust my instincts, and not settle for what everyone else said I had to be. You didn't set me free. You broke down the walls so I could free myself, and I love you for that."

Marx had definitely heard her say that. He stared back at her, a wave of affection pouring over him. In one motion, he threw his bag and gathered her in his arms. His mouth came down to hers, soft and hungry. Seran's body reacted. She wrapped her arms around him, pressing her chest into his, their two bodies becoming one. Her fingers skimmed across his shoulders and into his hair as their lips moved together. Seran tasted like freedom and happiness. He pulled her closer as the kiss turned more passionate—accelerating zero to sixty. He felt the curves of her body as his hands roamed across her back. With every breath, he fell deeper into her. They both wanted something from the other, and neither one of them held back.

His lips broke apart from hers, hovering close. "I must be a really good teacher," he breathed.

She cracked a smile. "Maybe I'm a really good student."

Marx pressed a few soft kisses against her mouth, then pulled his head back, meeting her eyes. "I love you so much. You're the only woman I will ever love. I knew the second I left New Hope today that if I couldn't be with you, there wasn't anyone else I wanted to be with. The last few weeks without you have been the worst days of my life. Being with you completed me, and I was worried I'd never feel that way again." He slipped his hands around her waist, keeping her close. "Your goodness has redeemed me, and I'm never letting you go again."

She smiled as Marx tilted his chin, kissing her forehead. "Come on," he said, breaking apart. "We'd better get out of the closet now."

He opened the door, and every head in the inn's lobby turned to them. "Thank you for letting us borrow your coat closet," Marx said to the innkeeper.

The man shot him a confused nod.

They walked hand in hand up the stairs and down the hall. It seemed surreal, having Seran there, like at any moment, he would wake up from his dream and be alone again.

"I guess you'll want to go say hi to Dannyn and Kase." Marx wanted Seran all to himself…at least for a little bit, but he knew they would be as happy to see her as he was.

Well, almost as happy.

"Can that wait until tomorrow?" She smiled, reaching up on her toes to kiss him.

Marx had no problem with that.

Their kiss heated, lighting a fire in his soul. He groaned and reluctantly pulled away. He motioned toward the door of his room. "You can have my room. I'll go talk to the innkeeper about getting something else for me."

"Why wouldn't we stay in the same room *together*?" she

asked, pressing both hands against his chest. There was a sultry undercurrent in her eyes that scared Marx.

Scared him to death.

He wasn't strong enough to withstand that look. He combed a hand through his hair. "We can't stay together. I want to do things right. When I thought I'd lost you, I spent a lot of time thinking about what I would do if I ever got the chance to be with you, and this is part of it."

"What else would you do?" she asked.

"Well, for starters, I would want to actually *ask* you to marry me. Give you a choice. And give your father a choice."

Her lips pursed together. "Give me an example of how you would do it?"

Marx raised his brows. "Now? In the hallway of an inn?"

Seran shrugged. "Why not?"

"Well, I'd probably use your full name—your *real* full name—and say something traditional like Seran Alyssa Haslet, will you marry me again?"

"Marry me again?" She raised her eyebrows.

He scrunched his nose. "You don't like it?"

Seran glowed with beauty. Her palms slid up his chest, and she pressed a soft kiss to his lips and then continued and *continued*.

Marx closed his eyes.

His defenses were weakening—he was putty in her hands.

His mind needed to focus on something else besides her kisses, and quick.

His thoughts switched to the first thing that popped into his head.

Butterflies.

His mother and butterflies.

That should do the trick.

He pushed her away from him as his jaw hardened. He *hated* pushing her away. He forced his thoughts to catalog every stupid color on a butterfly's wing.

"So I take it you'd marry me again if I asked?"

She smiled. "No, I wouldn't."

His brows bent.

She pulled him close again. This new version of her was a lot more aggressive than Marx remembered.

She kissed his cheek. "We're *already* married," she whispered.

Marx straightened. "But I thought—"

Seran shook her head. "Our divorce never went through. My father didn't get all the signatures he needed. I *asked* him not to get the signatures."

"So we're still married?"

She nodded, pulling him toward the door.

Marx laughed.

They were still married.

56

Seran

The Kingdom of Cristole
One Month Later

Seran walked along the beach, letting her toes sink into the sand. She smelled the salty air and felt the damp breeze brush up against her hair and face. The sun spilled its last rays of orange and pink across the dancing water, causing the skyline to glow.

She scanned the cresting waves in the distance, looking for Marx. She placed her hand above her eyes, shielding the sunset from her view. Marx's yellow and blue surfboard caught her eye. He floated on top of the water, turning and swaying with the wave.

She smiled.

He looked good surfing.

He rode the wave until the water lost its momentum and died down, then he twisted the board one last time, sending a spray of water into the air. He faced the beach, then his head jerked toward where she was. A giant smile spread across his lips, and he dove forward, swimming toward her. When it was too shallow for him to swim, he picked up his board and sloshed through the water. His bare chest glistened with drops of water, and his triceps stood out from holding the surfboard. He flipped his head to the side, trying to move the wet strands of hair away from his forehead. Seran lifted the hem of her yellow dress and stepped into the rippling waves to meet him halfway.

"Did you come to surf with me?" he asked as he scooped her into his arms.

She leaned her hip into him, gripping his muscled back. "I don't have a board."

"You don't need a board," he said, kissing the side of her cheek and down to her ear. "My surfer girl. We're going to ride together."

His lips traveled across her neck and cheek, eventually finding her mouth until Seran was lost in his arms. His kiss. His love. She felt wholly adored and complete. Her true self. Not the Seran she used to be before the shooting, and not the shadow of the woman she had been when she had woken up from her coma. This was a new version. Marx had helped her become better than she had been before.

She'd been through a lot, but her past didn't define her. She wasn't broken. She'd gotten stronger, learned how to fight for the life she wanted. Her story hadn't ended in Albion the day she'd been shot. The quicksand of life hadn't dragged her down. She could write her own ending, and she could do it with Marx.

He stepped back, pulling her farther into the water. Her dress darkened and felt heavier as the water crept up her legs to her torso.

"Hop on," he said, holding the board steady. "I'm going to take you for a ride."

Epilogue

SERAN

Fall 2261

Seran leaned over in the back of the transporter and unbuttoned the top three buttons of Marx's shirt.

"I thought you didn't like that," Marx said, eyeing her.

"I never said I didn't like it. I said I liked it *too* much."

His lips curved into a playful smile as his finger tapped on the middle of her chest. "Maybe we should get you a dress with buttons on the front. Then I could unbutton the top three buttons on you."

Seran shook her head. "Nice try, but I have a scar there."

"So?"

"So it's ugly, and I don't want anyone to see it."

He smirked. "You let me see it."

She rolled her eyes. "That's different. I don't feel self-conscious about anything in front of you."

Marx pressed a kiss to the back of her hand. "Seran, even your scar is beautiful. *Everything* about you is beautiful."

His unconditional love would never get old.

Never.

The vehicle rolled to a stop.

"It's time," he breathed between them.

The door opened, and she exited the vehicle, turning to him. "Marx, this is stupid. I don't know what we're doing."

"We're getting married."

"But we're *already* married."

He slid his hand down the side of her cheek, tucking a strand of her hair behind her ear. "You deserve the wedding you want."

Dannyn walked up beside them. "Yes, you do! I was at your last wedding, and it was so awkward."

"I was at your first wedding two years ago," her father said, standing behind their transporter, "and we don't need to talk about how terrible that was."

Seran smiled, looking back at Marx. "Okay, then. Let's get married."

He kissed her cheek softly, then let her go. "I'll see you down there."

She admired the back of Marx as he walked away. He had light blue shorts on and a white button-up shirt. The top three buttons were undone—thanks to her—and his sleeves were rolled up. He looked casual and handsome, the way she liked him best.

Dannyn handed her a bouquet of tropical flowers. "You look beautiful."

Seran dropped her eyes to her dress. The top half was made out of ivory lace with long sleeves. At her waist, the lace ended in an A-line of ivory chiffon fabric. The back of the dress was open, creating a deep V that ended inches above her tail bone. A few pieces of her dark hair were pulled back into a twisted braid, while the rest fell down her back in light waves. Her feet were bare, and the soft sand scrunched between her toes.

She felt beautiful.

Her father offered her his arm. "I hope this is the last time I give my daughter away."

"It will be."

They walked down the path, with Dannyn leading the way. Seran's eyes drifted across the beach. A few rows of benches had been set up with an aisle down the middle lined with greenery. She smiled at the guests who had been invited to the wedding. There was Queen Mariele. Renna and her baby girl. Drake, Myka, and Kase. Queen Malory, Idella, and Elsbeth.

Dannyn walked down the aisle before them. Then a soft violin played as her father escorted her toward Marx. Seran had never been so confident and sure of anything in her entire life. Such a contrast to the two other times she'd walked down the aisle.

Marx was her future.

The reason she'd found light outside of her dark broken road.

His smile stole her breath, and she couldn't wait to spend the rest of her life in Cristole with *him*.

Her father gave her to Marx, giving him a pat on his back. Seran was glad that the two of them had mended their relationship. They both had only wanted what was best for her.

She handed her flowers to Dannyn as Marx took her hand and led her to their spot in front of King Ezra. He seemed like a fitting choice to officiate their wedding. After the execution, Ezra had written a letter to Marx apologizing for everything. It didn't take long for the two of them to become friends. Seran's relationship with him had also evolved. She didn't see him as her ex-fiancé. She saw him as a friend and a brother.

Ezra smiled as he looked at them and the few special people in their lives who had come to witness this moment. "I'm glad to be here," he said, "and to be part of Seran's happy ending."

Seran's entire soul filled with happiness as Ezra continued.

"This is much better than the first time," Marx whispered in her ear, squeezing her hand lightly.

She kept her focus on Ezra, whispering back through her teeth as she tried to keep her lips still. "Are you really going to talk during this wedding too?"

"No." He leaned in. "But are you going to run away when it is time for the kiss?"

"If you keep talking, then I might run away."

He straightened for a moment, listening to the words Ezra said, but after a few seconds, Marx's lips were back by her ear.

"Can I kiss you, or do I have to wait for you to ask me to?"

Seran elbowed him.

"Okay, okay," he whispered. "Last thing, I promise. I just want to say that the third time's the charm."

Seran smiled, looking at him from the side.

The third time *was* the charm.

THE END

I hope you enjoyed Seran and Marx's story. I love hearing what readers liked most about a book, so don't forget to leave a review and tell me.

If you'd like to learn about future books and read sneak peeks, sign up for my newsletter at www.kortneykeisel.com and receive a copy of a deleted scene from The Promised Prince. Stay connected with me on Instagram, Facebook, or Pinterest

---

Did you know I also write contemporary romcoms?
Check out my Sweet Rom"Com" Series

a sweet romantic comedy
COMPARED
KORTNEY KEISEL

Also by Kortney Keisel

The Sweet Rom"Com" Series

Commit

Compared

Complex

The Desolation Series

The Rejected King

The Promised Prince

The Stolen Princess

The Forgotten Queen

Acknowledgments

I always say that I could never write a book alone. It's the truth. Take The Forgotten Queen as an example. So many of my friends spent a ton of time reading, commenting, thinking, and talking on the phone with me about this book.

Stacy and Anne, you both were with me from the beginning. You dreamed about these characters and where the story could go. Those early phone calls and conversations helped me shape this book and made the writing process so much easier. You read the first cheesy meet-cute—the one where Marx had to undergo a dolphin rescue (this is me shaking my head at myself for even writing that scene). You dealt with flat, unlikeable characters, but instead of just saying, "I don't like it," you both came with ideas to make things better, and I am so grateful for it all.

Working on a book with your sister is the best thing. My sister, Stacy, has been with me for every single book. She lives and breaths these storylines as much as I do. Stacy, I loved getting your 5 AM texts, letting me know all the plot holes you had thought about when you couldn't sleep. I also loved it when you asked for book recommendations from me, but then an hour later, you would text me something about The Forgotten Queen that you had just read...*again*, letting me know that you preferred to read my book for the hundredth time over reading something new. I appreciate all you do and love having you with me every step of the way. Please don't ever stop.

Anne, you've ruined me. I feel like I can't write a book without you there analyzing everything with me. I have PAGES of notes just from you. I love the way you think about the story's big picture and who the characters really are. You are something special, and I am so grateful that you chose to spend your time and talents on me and this book. Thanking you doesn't even seem good enough.

Thank you to my other beta readers:

Kaylen, I love how you are always so willing to beta read for me. You've been with me on every single book. You're a fast reader. You give me great comments and suggestions, and you hang with me even when I don't know where a story is going. And, you are my Instagram music extraordinaire...it's a thing.

Tasha, you read my book during your busy schedule and even offered to talk on the phone ON your birthday. That is true friendship, right there. Thanks for your never-ending support.

Michelle, we had two phone conversations about this book where I took notes on all your great suggestions. You know, I love your honesty. Thanks for being such a great friend.

Madi, the level of commitment that you had to this book and plot astonishes me. Very few other beta readers would facetime/talk about a book for almost three hours. I'm sure you had so many other things you could be doing, but you gave your time to me. You have serious skills when it comes to dissecting a book. I appreciated everything you said. I owe the ending to you.

Meredith, you crack me up. You left great notes on the document, but I loved talking about the book on the phone with you. That's where you really opened up. Your ideas came to life, and you added so much to the plot and characters. You are so well-read, and I drew so much knowledge from you.

Shelly, thanks for patiently waiting for my book and coming in clutch at the last second to proofread for me. I love how you call me out on my ridiculous sentences and poor word choice. Without you, Dannyn still would be saying "Boo!" One of these years, I'm going to convince you to become a real editor because you'd be fabulous at it.

Thank you to my editors, Jenny Proctor and Emily Poole. Jenny, I just love you. I loved the thoughtful notes, insights, and questions you had about this book that made it one thousand times better. And, I loved talking on the phone with you about all things bookish. I have a feeling we could talk for hours. Emily, your edits always help me breathe easier when I push "publish."

Thank you to my readers. Oh my gosh! I have readers. I can't even believe it sometimes. Your love of my books makes this difficult process so much easier. I love hearing from you and am encouraged by all your kind words and reviews. Without readers, I wouldn't be able to keep doing this. So thank you!

Thank you to Kurt and my kids. You are all the reason I am doing this. I love you all so much. And Kurt, if you read this, know that I think you are devastatingly handsome.

As always, I have to thank my Heavenly Father and Jesus Christ. I keep thinking that I will run out of ideas or have a nervous breakdown or something, but somehow I keep finding the strength to keep doing this author thing. I know that strength comes from Them. I'm grateful God has blessed me with this writing and publishing experience. I am truly so blessed.

About the Author

Kortney loves all things romance. Her devotion to romance was first apparent at three years old when her family caught her kissing the walls (she attributes this embarrassing part of her life to her mother's affinity for watching soap operas like Days of Our Lives). Luckily, Kortney has outgrown that phase and now only kisses her husband. Most days, Kortney is your typical stay-at-home mom. She has five kids that keep her busy cleaning, carpooling, and cooking.

Writing books was never part of Kortney's plan. She graduated from the University of Utah with an English degree and spent a few years before motherhood teaching 7th and 8th graders how to write a book report, among other things. But after a reading slump, where no plots seemed to satisfy, Kortney pulled out her laptop and started writing the "perfect" love story...or at least she tried. Her debut novel, The Promised Prince, took four years to write, mostly because she never worked on it and didn't plan on doing anything with it.

Kortney loves warm chocolate chip cookies, clever song lyrics, the perfect romance movie, analyzing and talking about the perfect romance movie, playing card games, traveling with her family, and laughing with her husband.

Printed in Great Britain
by Amazon